From the Pages of
the *Aeneid*

I sing of arms and of the man who first
Came from the coasts of Troy to Italy
And the Lavinian shores, exiled by fate.

(page 3)

Is there such anger in celestial minds?

(page 3)

She drove far from Latium
The Trojan remnant that escaped the Greeks
And fierce Achilles; and for many years
They wandered, driven by fate, round all the seas.
Such task it was to found the Roman state.

(page 4)

"Recall your courage; banish gloomy fears.
Some day perhaps the memory of these things
Shall yield delight."

(page 10)

"I am called the good Æneas, known to fame
Above the aether, who our household gods
Snatched from our enemies, and in my fleet
Convey. Italia, my ancestral land,
And the race sprung from Jove supreme, I seek." (pages 16–17)

While thus Æneas wondering views
These things, and stands with a bewildered gaze,
Dido the queen in all her loveliness
Has come into the temple, a great band
Of warrior youths attending on her steps.

(page 21)

"The city which I build is yours. Draw up
Your ships. Trojans and Tyrians from me
Shall no distinction know."

(page 24)

"Trojans, do not trust this horse.
Whatever it may be, I fear the Greeks,
Even when they bring us gifts."   (page 33)

"Cannot my love
For you, cannot this hand once given as yours,
Nor Dido ready here to die for you
A cruel death, detain you?"   (page 98)

"Son of Anchises, born of blood divine,"
The priestess thus began, "easy the way
Down to Avernus; night and day the gates
Of Dis stand open. But to retrace your steps
And reach the upper air—here lies the task,
The difficulty here."   (page 147)

"Others, I say,
Shall mold, more delicately, forms of bronze,
Lifelike, and shape the human face in stone;
Plead causes with more skill, describe the paths
Of heavenly orbs, and note the rising stars.
But you, O Roman, bend your mind to rule
Your people with strength. This shall be your art:
To impose both terms and rules of peace;
To spare the vanquished, and subdue the proud."   (page 172)

But if my power's not enough,
I shall not pause to seek what aid I may.
And if I cannot bend the gods above,
Then Acheron I'll move.   (page 186)

Relaxed, the limbs lay cold, and, with a groan,
Down to the Shades the soul, indignant, fled.   (page 354)

THE
AENEID

VERGIL

TRANSLATED INTO
ENGLISH BLANK VERSE BY
CHRISTOPHER PEARSE CRANCH

With an Introduction and Notes
by Sarah Spence

George Stade
Consulting Editorial Director

ℬ
BARNES & NOBLE CLASSICS
NEW YORK

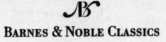

BARNES & NOBLE CLASSICS

NEW YORK

Published by Barnes & Noble Books
122 Fifth Avenue
New York, NY 10011

www.barnesandnoble.com/classics

The *Aeneid* was begun in 26 B.C. and remained unfinished at Vergil's death in 19 B.C. Christopher Pearse Cranch's translation was first published in 1872.

Published in 2007 by Barnes & Noble Classics with new Introduction, Note on the Translation, Notes, Biography, Chronology, Inspired By, Comments & Questions, and For Further Reading.

The Aeneid
ISBN 978-1-59308-237-6
LC Control Number 2006935995

Produced and published in conjunction with:
Fine Creative Media, Inc.
322 Eighth Avenue
New York, NY 10001

Michael J. Fine, President and Publisher

Printed in the United States of America

QM

5   7   9   11   13   15   14   12   10   8   6   4

Vergil

The author of one of Western literature's great epic poems, Vergil was born Publius Vergilius Maro on October 15, 70 B.C. in Andes, a village in Cisalpine Gaul, a fertile frontier region northwest of Rome. Legend has it that his father owned an estate on which he farmed, produced pottery, and kept bees. Vergil's father sent him to school in Cremona and Milan; his early instruction emphasized literature, philosophy, and history. His training in Rome, begun in 54 B.C., centered on rhetoric. Starting in 48, he pursued philosophy at Siro's academy in Naples.

Vergil completed his first major work, the *Eclogues* (or *Bucolics*), around 37 B.C. The ten poems in the *Eclogues*—modeled on the pastoral poetry of the third-century Greek poet Theocritus—were unusual both for their celebration of provincial life, not a popular topic for poets of the day, and for their innovative construction. The *Eclogues* secured Vergil the patronage of Gaius Maecenas, a friend and adviser to the emperor Octavian.

In a series of military and political victories in the late 30s B.C., Octavian emerged as the sole leader of what, under his statesmanship, was fast becoming the Roman Empire. The *Georgics*, which Maecenas suggested Vergil write and which he completed in 29 B.C., looks back on the chaos of the years following Julius Caesar's murder in 44 B.C. and the emergence of Octavian as Italy's savior. Superficially modeled on *Works and Days*, by the eighth-century Greek poet Hesiod, the *Georgics* was written as four books—"Crops," "Trees," "Beasts," and "Bees," each a moral testament to farming. Vergil viewed agriculture as essential to Italy's well-being and a source of its strength.

Starting in 29 B.C., Vergil dedicated himself to telling the story of Aeneas's adventure-filled journey from Troy to a new home on the Italian peninsula, a project he had had in mind for years and one that it is said Octavian pressed him to develop. Before Vergil finished the

Aeneid, he set out for Greece. In 19 B.C. he fell ill with a fever in Megara. He was taken back to Brundisium and died there, on September 21. It is said that he had instructed his executors to burn the unfinished manuscript of the *Aeneid,* but that Octavian, now emperor and known as Augustus Caesar, had the poem published. Vergil's twelve-book masterpiece offers a mythological summation of Roman history and articulates the aspirations of the Romans at a critical point in their history. Vergil is the best known and most influential writer in all of Latin literature.

Table of Contents

The World of Vergil and the *Aeneid*

70 B.C. Publius Vergilius Maro is born on October 15 in Andes, a Roman village near the city of Mantua in the province of Cisalpine Gaul (in the Po Valley in modern-day northern Italy). Forest clearing and drainage have made Cisalpine Gaul exceptionally fertile land and one of Rome's most valued provinces. Legend has it that, on his estate, Vergil's father produces pottery, keeps bees, and farms. He sends Vergil to school in Cremona, about 25 miles west of Andes. Vergil's impressions of farming life and the beauty of the Italian countryside will become central to his poetry.

c.69 Julius Caesar serves as quaestor (treasurer) of Rome, a position he holds while posted in Farther Spain (modern Andalusia and Portugal). Cleopatra, who will become queen of Egypt, is born.

MID-60s Julius Caesar returns to Rome; over the next several years, he will become a popular leader, though members of the Senate view him with suspicion.

63 Octavian is born; the grandnephew and adopted son of Julius Caesar, he will later be known as Augustus Caesar.

61 Julius Caesar serves as Roman proconsul (governor) in Farther Spain.

60 Caesar returns to Rome and forms, with the statesman and general Pompey (the Great) and the wealthy Marcus Licinius Crassus, a political alliance (sometimes called the First Triumvirate) that runs the government.

58 Caesar leaves Rome for Gaul, conquering it and most of central Europe over the next nine years.

55 Finishing his studies in Cremona, Vergil assumes the *toga virilis*, the white dress worn by men to signify their entry into adulthood.

54   Vergil studies rhetoric in Rome. Gaius Valerius Catullus, the
      great lyric poet and a major influence on Vergil, dies. Catullus'
      poetry was revolutionary for its irony, playfulness, and self-
      consciousness. Vergil will imitate him, even borrowing phrases
      and images for the *Aeneid.*

52   Vercingetorix, leader of the last of the Gallic tribes resisting
      Caesar, revolts against Caesar.

51   *The Gallic Wars,* Caesar's account of his conquest of Gaul,
      appears; it contains seven books, each covering a single year
      starting with 58 B.C., and is written in the third person.

50   Titus Lucretius Carus (Lucretius) publishes *On the Nature of
      Things,* a six-part poem expounding the scientific theories of
      the Greek philosopher Epicurus; the poem elevates science and
      rationality as sources of happiness for man.

49   Pompey sails with his legions to Greece. Caesar leaves Gaul,
      advances to Rome, and declares himself dictator.

48   Vergil concentrates on philosophy for the remainder of his
      education and moves to Naples to study philosophy at the
      Epicurean Siro's academy. Caesar defeats Pompey in Greece
      and follows him to Alexandria, where Pompey is murdered.
      Caesar spends some months in Alexandria while civil war rages
      in Egypt. Caesar and Cleopatra begin an affair, and he helps
      establish her firmly on the throne.

47   On his return home from Egypt, Caesar defeats King Phar-
      naces of Pontus in Asia Minor, noting *Veni, vidi, vici* ("I
      came, I saw, I conquered").

46   Vercingetorix is defeated by Caesar and is killed. Caesar has
      now added much land to the republic's holdings and attained
      great fame and popularity.

46   Caesar introduces a calendar of 365.25 days, designed by Sosi-
      genes of Alexandria; it will take effect in 45.

44   Caesar is assassinated in a meeting with the Senate. Marc
      Antony seizes Caesar's treasury and will, which promises a
      legacy to every Roman citizen. Octavian, age eighteen, chal-
      lenges Antony's claim on his inheritance and pays the prom-
      ised legacies out of his own pocket, thus ensuring the loyalty
      of the people. Marcus Tullius Cicero, the greatest Latin prose
      writer and orator and a Senate leader, delivers the first of his

Philippics, speeches against Antony that characterize him as an enemy of the state and that bolster Octavian's standing among the Senate and the people.

43 Octavian, Antony, and Marcus Lepidus form a triumvirate, (sometimes called the Second Triumvirate) and assume the ruling power in Italy; they issue a proscription, a list of enemies of the state condemned to death or banishment. Cicero is put on the proscription list and decapitated.

42 Sextus Pompey (the son of Pompey the Great) defeats Octavian at Rhegium. The Battle of Philippi in northern Greece ends with the rout of Brutus' army and the deaths of Brutus and Cassius, Caesar's chief assassins.

41 Vergil's father's farm is threatened with confiscation by the triumvirate, to be resettled by veterans of Antony's army (some sources say the farm was confiscated, others that it was spared through the influence of patrons of the young Vergil). Vergil's early writings have come to the attention of Gaius Maecenas, a statesman, literary patron, and adviser to Octavian.

40 Antony and Octavian reconcile via the Treaty of Brundisium and agree to divide the republic, Antony taking the east (including Egypt, which Rome does not rule but controls) and Octavian the west; Lepidus is given Africa. To strengthen their alliance, Antony marries Octavian's sister Octavia.

c.37 Vergil publishes the *Eclogues* (or *Bucolics*), ten poems closely modeled on the *Idylls*, pastoral poetry written in Greek by Theocritus two centuries earlier. Though still married to Octavia, Antony lives with Cleopatra; they have had two children, and will have another in 36, much to the dismay of the Romans.

36 Octavian defeats Sextus Pompey at Naulochus.

c.35 Quintus Horatius Flaccus (Horace) publishes his first book, *Satires*, commenting on war, conflict, and greed.

32 Antony divorces Octavia. Octavian responds by publicly reading Antony's will, which promises large inheritances to his children by Cleopatra and stipulates his burial with her in Egypt when he dies. Antony is now seen as disloyal to Rome. The Senate declares war against Cleopatra.

31 Octavian defeats Antony and Cleopatra's armies in western Greece at the Battle of Actium. In retrospect, this victory

marked the end of the Roman Republic and the birth of the
Roman Empire.

30   Antony and Cleopatra commit suicide. Octavian, now the
sole and undisputed master of the Roman world, stays away
from Rome in order to organize the territories in the east
that had been under Antony's governance. Horace publishes
the *Epodes*, short poems adapted from Greek lyrics, that explore political themes, lampoon the poet's enemies, and
ponder love.

c.29   Vergil publishes the *Georgics*; a poem conceived as four books
of farming instruction ("Crops," "Trees," "Beasts," and
"Bees") and based on *Works and Days*, by the eighth-century
Greek poet Hesiod; it considers man's relationship to nature
and highlights the importance of the land and man's work in
cultivating it. Vergil has gained the patronage of important
men, including those close to the emperor.

29   Octavian returns to Rome for the first time since the Battle of
Actium, to much fanfare. Sextus Propertius publishes his first
book, *Cynthia*, about his mistress.

27   Octavian surrenders his position, saying he'll retire to private
life, but the Senate insists he remain as head of state. After a
show of reluctance, he accepts a share in governance and is given
the title Augustus Caesar. He leaves Rome to tour Gaul and
Spain for the next three years. The Pantheon is first built under
Roman general Marcus Agrippa, a close friend of Octavian.

26   Vergil starts his final project, an epic about Aeneas' founding
of Rome. Titus Livius (Livy) begins his 142-book history of
Rome; it will become a classic in the author's lifetime because
of its vividness and the flexible style Livy develops for writing
history in Latin.

23   Horace publishes the first three books of his *Odes*—eighty-
eight short poems praising peace, love, wine, and the countryside that are considered his greatest accomplishment. Marcus
Vitruvius Pollio (Vitrivius) publishes *On Architecture*, which
is a treatise on architecture presented in the context of the liberal arts that covers mathematics, astronomy, meteorology, and
medicine.

20   Horace publishes the *Epistles*, verse letters that extol the

virtues of the simple life.

19   Vergil sets out for Greece to research places he describes in his poem. He meets Octavian in Athens and accompanies him to Megara. There Vergil contracts a fever, is transported back to Italy, and dies in Brundisium on September 21. The *Aeneid*, left uncompleted at his death, is published by order of the emperor. Publius Ovidius Naso (Ovid) publishes his first collection of poetry, *Loves*, whose opening line begins with *arma* ("weapons"), the word that begins the *Aeneid*.

Introduction

for Michael Putnam

As Aeneas departs from Troy the night it falls to the Greeks, he leaves his wife Creüsa behind. Carrying his father on his shoulders and leading his son by the hand, he heads for a shrine outside the city where he has arranged to meet other Trojans who will join him in exile. Arriving there, Aeneas sees that his wife is missing, and returning to the burning city made foreign by the Greek occupation, he encounters her ghost, which prophesies that

> Long exile
> Must be your lot, the vast expanse of sea
> Be ploughed; and you shall see the Hesperian land,
> Where Lydian Tiber flows with gentle course
> (2.1049–1052).

Aeneas tries to embrace his wife, but "her image from [his] hands escaped, / that sought, but all in vain, to grasp her form." The juxtaposition of the prophecy with the ghost is made all the more striking by the fact that the prediction of what will be grasped at the end of his journey is set against the image of Creüsa, who can no longer be held.

The *Aeneid* is a poem about promise and loss. Creüsa is the first character to escape the Trojans' grasp. She will be joined by others, including Anchises in the underworld and, strikingly, Italy itself, which throughout the odyssey from Troy to Rome persistently refuses to be attained. The Trojan women in book 5 are urged by one of their own to burn their ships in Sicily, since

> The seventh summer now is passing by,
> Since Troy was doomed, and still upon the seas
> We are borne away, and traverse every land,

> Over so many inhospitable rocks,
> Beneath so many stars, still rolling on
> The billows, following an Italy
> That flees before (5.738–744).

The same Italy that holds out promise in Creüsa's prophecy recedes like her ghost from the Trojans' grasp.

Named for its hero, Aeneas, the poem charts his progress from that last night of the Trojan War (when the Greeks, hidden inside the belly of a wooden horse, took Troy) to his victory in Latium, where he will be awarded an Italian bride, Lavinia, who ensures the start of the new race, the Romans. The poem opens off the coast of Sicily, where the Trojans who had survived the fall of Troy are preparing to cross over to Italy, the goal of their journey. They are, however, blown off course by the will of the goddess Juno and land at Carthage in North Africa. There they meet the beautiful Dido, an exile in her own right, who is caused to fall in love with Aeneas by the meddling of two gods: Venus, who knows the destructive power of love, and Juno, who wants Carthage to rule widely. While at Carthage, Aeneas recounts the events of the last night at Troy and the years wandering through the Mediterranean looking for the place where they are meant to land. Leaving Carthage, Aeneas travels first to Sicily, where he honors the memory of his father who had died there the year before, then to the underworld, where he encounters many ghosts, including those of both Dido and his father, and hears his father predict that Rome will excel in imperial leadership:

> "Others, I say,
> Shall mold, more delicately, forms of bronze,
> Lifelike, and shape the human face in stone;
> Plead causes with more skill, describe the paths
> Of heavenly orbs, and note the rising stars.
> But you, O Roman, bend your mind to rule
> Your people with strength. This shall be your art:
> To impose both terms and rules of peace;
> To spare the vanquished and subdue the proud"
> (6.1064–1072).

Aeneas is shown a parade of Roman heroes who bridge the gap between his own generation and that of Vergil and establish the genealogical link between Aeneas and the emperor Augustus, formerly Octavius (known to us as Octavian). Leaving the underworld, which he entered at Cumae, Aeneas travels up the coast to Latium, where he encounters its king, Latinus, and becomes involved in a struggle to claim the land as his. Latinus' daughter, promised to the Rutulian Turnus, becomes the Helen-like prize in this struggle, as the king decides that Aeneas is the foreigner prophesied to wed Lavinia. Each side seeks to enlist allies from the neighboring regions, and therefore Aeneas voyages up the Tiber to Pallanteum, where the Arcadian king, Evander, promises aid and sends his son, Pallas. It is Pallas' death during the ensuing struggles that causes Aeneas, in the end, to kill Turnus.

Written between 26 and 19 B.C., the *Aeneid* was virtually finished, if somewhat unpolished, at the time of Vergil's death. Unlike the poem's major precursors, the Greek epics of Homer, the *Aeneid* aims to illuminate the historical and cultural complexity of the world that surrounded its first audience. The poem looks back to the prehistory of Rome and forward to the Rome of Vergil's day, a perspective that has led some to characterize it as nostalgic. Yet the real beauty and strength of the work lies in its ability to provide a glimpse of the underpinnings of the very world its early audience inhabited—both its strengths and its weaknesses. It is, in short, a poem that in taking us back to the origins of the Roman people takes us forward to the world of Vergil and, to a large extent, to the world we live in today. The theme of the poem is not so much a lament over the necessity of sacrifice, as it is sometimes read, but an assertion that loss is embedded in the imperial vision—that the intertwined strands of promise and loss lie at the heart of the imperial enterprise, be it Augustan or contemporary.

Aeneas' importance derives from two sources. On the one hand, it is fated in the *Iliad* (20.302) that he will escape Troy and his offspring will rule over fellow Trojans. Vergil connects Aeneas' rule with Rome, and thus establishes a clear movement of the gods and so of culture from east to west, from Troy to Latium. Alongside this, we are told in the first book by Jupiter, the king of the gods, and in the sixth book by Anchises, Aeneas' father, that Aeneas is genealogically linked to Caesar, to whom Jupiter has granted an empire without end. Through

Aeneas' son Ascanius, also known as Iulus, the line of the Caesars will be founded; they will trace their family back to Venus, Aeneas' mother, and Jupiter, her father.

The poem is often approached through the opposition offered in the opening lines between *pietas* (the honor man pays god and son pays father) and *furor* (rage). Aeneas is first characterized as a man marked by piety, while his primary antagonist, the goddess Juno, is marked by her rage. Throughout the poem, the struggles to achieve the goal of reaching Rome play out between these opposing forces. Aeneas' honor of both his father and the gods—dominated by the figure of Jupiter—propels him out of Troy and through years on the ocean; it is the reason he leaves the beautiful Dido, whom he encounters in Carthage; it is the mark of his leadership during the games on Sicily and his battles in Italy. *Furor*, on thfffe other hand, accounts not only for the rage of Juno, Jupiter's wife and sister (angry because the victory of her Greeks at Troy has not destroyed the Trojans), but also for a series of characters who participate in that anger, including Dido, once spurned by Aeneas, and Turnus, whose land and betrothed are offered by his king to Aeneas. The progress of *pius* Aeneas from Troy to Latium is impeded by Juno and the characters in whom she inspires *furor*.

The interaction of *pietas* and *furor* plays out against the background of the imperial landscape. As Aeneas travels from Troy to Latium he sketches out the reach of the later empire, and in so doing, he lays his people's future claim to that path. Key landings that will later become part of the Roman imperial project are noted. Having Aeneas land at Buthrotum, for example, Vergil lays the groundwork for the later development of a Roman colony there. When, at the end of book 5, Aeneas decides to leave some of the older Trojans on Sicily, Vergil not only explains the presence of Trojan archeological finds there; he also justifies the development of Sicily as a Roman province. The stop at Actium, brief though it is, introduces Actium into the imperial language and projects Octavian's victory there. The lands Aeneas touches become marked for the imperial cause—they are lands that the emperor will later claim as his own. Aeneas will see them only as false Italys; they mean nothing to him except failure, both to obtain his goal and to return home. Yet that very failure offers proof that the imperial project is underway.

The literary past participates in this enterprise. Vergil's literary models are many. On the one hand, there are the Greek epics of Homer, whose *Iliad* and *Odyssey* took four times as many books to relay their story; on the other, there is the newer movement of Alexandrian poetry (including both Apollonius' *Argonautica* and the works of Callimachus), whose spare aesthetics argued that less is more, that recondite allusion and sharp delineation were the marks of cleaner, better poetry. Against these Greek traditions lies the Latin project: starting with Ennius, whose epic about the founding of Rome exists only in fragments, the tradition of telling Roman origins in Latin and highlighting the connection of the language to the Roman mission and identity was taken up by Lucretius and continued throughout the republic and into the empire, with the poetry of Catullus, Horace, Propertius, Tibullus, Vergil and Ovid. Every one of these poets aimed to grapple with the inherited Greek past in an effort not only to recast the works into a new language but, more, to show that that new literature was essential to the success and definition of the Roman mission.

The *Aeneid* was Vergil's third major work. His poetic career began with the publication of the ten *Eclogues*, also known as the *Bucolics*. These short works, many in dialogue, are largely based on Greek pastoral poems by Theocritus, but with the addition of a pointedly Italian setting and tone. In these poems we can see Vergil confronting issues of the late republic, including conflicts between city life and country life, and the importance of Greek poetry to Roman. In his second work, the didactic agricultural poem known as the *Georgics*, which is divided into four books, Vergil relied heavily on the Greek poet Hesiod and the Latin Lucretius, both of whom had written didactic works about nature. In the *Georgics* we find Vergil addressing issues of man's relationship to nature and the Roman state, and touching frequently on the importance of the Italian land.

Vergil's poetic mission in the *Aeneid* picks up where the *Georgics* leave off. At the start of the second half of the epic, when the Trojans have reached Italy and met the local inhabitants, the Latins, the poem explains that Saturn lived in Italy when he was exiled from Olympus and there created a golden age, a time when man was at one with the land and the world was at peace. By establishing this myth as the starting point of his epic, chronologically speaking, Vergil also establishes an unstated goal for his poem as it drives ever forward toward recovering that unity and peace: a new golden age in Italy, after all, is what the emperor Augustus promised through his empire.

Three years before Vergil started writing the *Aeneid*, Octavian celebrated his triple triumph for victories at Actium, Illyricum and Egypt, and thereby acknowledged his position as sole leader of the Roman Empire. Octavian's journey to this point had been many years in the making. Born into the struggles of the civil wars, in which his adoptive father, Julius Caesar, had both made his reputation and lost his life, Octavian grew up knowing only a world embroiled in civil war. The last years of Octavian's rise in power are indicative of this instability. This is the time of the triumvirate in which Octavian banded together with Mark Antony and Lepidus. Yet Lepidus remained a weak and unimportant figure compared to that of Sextus Pompey, the son of Pompey the Great and a powerful outsider in the later days of the republic. For all intents and purposes, the endgame of the Republic was a struggle between Octavian, Sextus, and Antony from which Octavian (defeating Sextus at Naulochus in 36 B.C. and Antony at Actium in 31 B.C.) emerged as sole leader of the Roman world.

In book 8 of the *Aeneid*, we see these events recounted on a shield. Given to Aeneas by his mother, the goddess Venus, before the epic's final battle, the shield is covered with images of Roman history, from the birth of Romulus and Remus to the future figure of the emperor Augustus surveying his vanquished peoples before the temple of Apollo on the Palatine. Through this, Vergil skillfully conflates the two reigning origin myths, one that grants the founding of Rome to Romulus and Remus, the other to Aeneas. By portraying Romulus and Remus on a shield that both represents Augustus and is carried by Aeneas, Vergil posits a continuity between these competing stories. A large part of the description of the shield focuses on Octavian's last battles: the defeat of Sextus at Naulochus is alluded to and the victory over Antony at Actium is described in detail, while the defeat of Egypt is portrayed through the retreat of Cleopatra to the Nile.

The view we get on the shield is, up to a point, like that found in the official imperial histories, both those contemporary with the *Aeneid*, such as the one written by Livy, and later. In Dio's account (late second to early third century A.D.), Octavian and Antony are paired through matched speeches, and within Octavian's speech, the opposition between the two is made clear through rhetorical structure.

Octavian first sets Antony against Cleopatra (he the citizen, she foreign) and then moves to argue that he is assimilated to her in all ways and so stands in direct opposition to himself (Octavian):

> Therefore let no one count him a Roman, but rather an Egyptian, nor call him Antony but rather Serapion; let no one think he was ever consul or imperator, but only gymnasiarch. . . . Again, let no one fear him . . . for even in the past he was of no account. . . . For it is impossible for one who leads a life of royal luxury, and coddles himself like a woman, to have a manly thought or do a manly deed. . . . His physical fitness? But he has passed his prime and become effeminate. His strength of mind? But he plays the woman and has worn himself out with unnatural lust. His piety toward our gods? But he is at war with them as well as with his country. His faithfulness to his allies? But who does not know how he deceived and imprisoned the Armenian? His kindness to his friends? But who has not seen the men who have miserably perished at his hands? His reputation with the soldiers? But who even of them has not condemned [him]? (*Dio's Roman History*, book 50, section 27, translated by Earnest Cary, Loeb Classical Library, Cambridge, MA: Harvard University Press, 1969).

Each rhetorical question serves to underscore what is positive about Octavian while reiterating what is negative about Antony. Antony's traits—his uxoriousness, lack of piety, faithfulness and kindness, his miserable reputation with his soldiers—are all derived out of opposition from Octavian's strengths; indeed they are drawn from what constituted the foundation of Octavian's moral program as described in the *Res gestae*, his own account of his achievements: masculinity, piety, clemency, justice. In Dio's depiction, Octavian's moral profile is justified through Antony's negative profile, which matches Vergil's depiction of Antony on the shield:

> There, with barbaric allies, and with arms
> Of fashion multiform, comes Antony,
> Victorious from the East and Indian shores;

> Egypt, and forces of the Orient lands
> He brings, and distant Bactra; and behind
> Follows his course—O shame!—the Egyptian wife
> (8.815–820).

Both the images on the shield and the writings of the historians suggest that Antony's foreignness stems from his alliance with Cleopatra. But the shield, unlike the histories, ties Cleopatra through verbal echoes to the character of Dido, whom Aeneas visits early in the epic and whom he leaves only after much prodding by the gods. Since the Dido of the poem differs from the Cleopatra of the histories, likening Cleopatra to Dido opens a window onto the complexity of character and offers an example of the ways in which the *Aeneid* makes poetry of history.

While Dido may end up like Cleopatra, a foreign enemy who threatens Rome and must be vanquished, like Antony, she did not begin as an enemy. Instead, Vergil goes to some lengths to show her first as an ally and leader similar to Aeneas in many ways. Also an exile, also building a city and establishing a rule that is arguably Roman in many ways, she is introduced as Aeneas' equal, as similar to him as Penelope is to Odysseus or Diana to Apollo. Through the course of book 4, however, the book that tells of Dido's affections for Aeneas, she is shown to become less and less like him, a route that ends in her leveling a curse against the future Rome (the posited cause of the Punic Wars) and, like Cleopatra, committing suicide.

Moreover, Vergil's account does not tell this story from Aeneas' point of view, but rather from Dido's. Using many of the same techniques as Apollonius in his depiction of Medea in the *Argonautica*, Vergil offers a privileged view of Dido's inner life. We watch Aeneas' affection turn into alienation, and we know little more than Dido does of the reasons why. We look down from her position in the lofty tower on the Trojans preparing to embark; we hear her curse the Trojans and their descendants; and, most strikingly, we stay with her as she commits suicide after Aeneas, unaware, has sailed away. Though clearly backed by the gods and victorious on some level, Aeneas is in this account the one who plays the foreigner; for the duration of Dido's book, it is he who is the enemy, while Dido appears steadfast. When we encounter Cleopatra, then, on the shield, we are brought up short: our understanding of Roman history will have been tempered, or at least complicated, by our reading of the story of Dido.

Vergil suggests the complexity of the imperial project through other female characters as well, a number of whom follow Dido's course, starting out successfully and ending in tragedy: so, for instance, Camilla, the Volscian who fights for the Latins, is first described at the end of book 7 as a woman admired by all; she is felled from a distance, having been distracted by the glittering armor of the enemy. Nevertheless, along the way we have been told the story of her life and led to admire her as both a daughter and a fighter. As with Dido, this sympathy complicates the picture as we realize that she opposes the Roman cause.

Indeed, whether the poem, Aeneas' story, supports or criticizes the emperor Augustus in his enterprise has been the subject of much debate. Referred to as optimistic or pessimistic readings, some interpretations of the poem have been advanced that support the emperor (especially in its efforts to establish the bloodline that runs from Aeneas to the emperor and aligns Aeneas with Jupiter) while others have suggested that the poem criticizes Augustus (in the attention it pays to the pain Aeneas causes as leader): we watch Dido die; we are encouraged to sympathize with Aeneas' enemies (including Turnus and Camilla). If Vergil seems to be making a case for empire, he also seems to be questioning the reach of that empire and the cost of its founding.

Aeneas himself displays the conflicts of the poem, especially in his relations to the models Vergil draws on in constructing him. Passingly described in Homer's *Iliad* as second only to the greatest Trojan, Hector, Aeneas (who is protected in the *Iliad* by his mother, Venus, and the god Apollo, and beloved of his people) is likened by Vergil to Hector and to Paris; at other points, he is allied with Jupiter, and the two are seen as a prototype for the emperor. However, Aeneas is also likened to Achilles and Odysseus and, when in Carthage, to Antony. That we are meant to read Aeneas against a complex backdrop of literary and political precursors is evident; equally evident is the fact that this is neither an allegory nor a historical tract, nor is it just a reworking of an earlier text. Vergil uses his poem to lay out the issues that led up to the complicated literary and political scene in which he found himself. While Aeneas may in fact be the precursor for the emperor, that same Aeneas is precursor to Antony (although in this case Aeneas as Antony leaves his Cleopatra). Aeneas is thus both winner and loser, even as he is also simultaneously in exile and at home. Troy becomes diminished through the progress of the poem, and Aeneas' homeland—the land where he lived and where his wife died—dissolves in the distance. He is to assume the new identity of a Roman at the end of the poem; he will marry a new wife and have a child; his line will culminate in the birth of Octavian. Yet the sense that he has returned home is true only on an abstract level: personally he remains in exile, and it is that exile that enables the founding of the Roman Empire. The myth of the golden age is tempered by a similar complexity: alongside the argument that Saturn created a golden age in Italy, Vergil reminds us that he did so while in exile.

Exile and homecoming are intertwined throughout the poem. While Aeneas is first introduced as "exiled by fate" he is also represented as coming home, in that the poem does not just recount the history of the Trojans from Troy to Rome, but rather tells the story from their origins *in Italy* to their return there with Aeneas. While the stated purpose of the poem is to describe the movement from Troy to Rome, the actual events of the poem serve to rewind history back before Troy and replay it in a new and different way. By the end of the poem, Troy has become a stop not unlike that at Delos—a way station along the path to the true home. In this, Aeneas is to a certain extent an Odyssean character, coming home: Dardanus, Aeneas' ancestor, came from northern Italy, and it is to the Tiber basin that Aeneas returns his people. This concept of homecoming is played out in many ways, most notably in the prophecy given by Apollo in book 3, in which the Trojans are told they are to seek out their ancient mother, advice that leads them, ultimately, to Italy. As the poem pushes forward from Troy to Rome, then, it also pushes us back in time to an even earlier era. Not unlike the other stops Aeneas makes during the first half of the poem, including Sicily and Carthage, Troy is a place that Aeneas' ancestor, Dardanus, and his followers inhabited after they left home and before they returned.

At the end of the epic we find that Troy has been brought to Latium, but perhaps not in the sense we might originally have thought. Through the course of the epic Vergil has shown again and again that he is laying out a strand that, like Ariadne's thread, will enable us to understand the labyrinthine twists and turns of empire. He has posited that if we go back far enough we will discover that Troy was not the great signal event of Western history; rather, it pales by comparison with events that both precede and follow it. What we have at the end of the poem is a new view of history that starts well before Troy and, as with the oldest gods—Terra and Saturn, in particular— we find that the future is rooted not in the more recent events, but in the events of the deepest past. The poem succeeds in refocusing our vision on the Roman west. Troy is redefined with reference to Rome, and Rome becomes identified as the once and future empire. The promise of that vision is defined by loss, and homecoming becomes a form of exile.

There is a passage in the third book that draws together the themes of alienation and reunion in a striking fashion. The prophet Helenus describes the origin of the island of Sicily:

> Those lands, it's said, by vast convulsions once
> Were torn asunder (such the changes wrought
> By time), when both united stood as one.
> Between them rushed the sea, and with its waves
> Cut off the Italian side from Sicily,
> And now between their fields and cities flows
> With narrow tide (3.527–533).

The lands of Italy and Sicily were once joined across the straits of Messina. According to Vergil (and many other Latin poets) these lands were wrenched apart by waves breaking through, thus creating the narrow channel that to this day remains unbridged. This is where Scylla and Charybdis, the rock and the whirlpool that caused such anxiety to Greek heroes like Odysseus and Jason, are located. Aeneas is told in a prophecy that he is not to follow the paths of these heroes and try to pass through these straits. Instead, he is to go around Sicily on his way to Italy—the long way around, the prophet Helenus says. In going around and not through, Aeneas figuratively draws the island back to the mainland; reuniting it, at least conceptually if not geo-graphically. In so doing, he returns the lands to something approximating their original state, much as his journey to Latium returns the Dardanians home to Italy.

The story of Sicily has a second chapter, as it were. In having Aeneas sail around the island Vergil looks forward as well as back. In 42 B.C., having been trounced by Sextus Pompey at Reggio, Octavian ordered his fleet to sail south to Brundisium (where they were to meet up with Antony) keeping, as Appian tells us, "Sicily on the left." Moses Hadas explains it this way:

> Antony was urging his colleague to hasten to join him in the campaign against the Liberators in Macedonia, but it was essential for Octavian to secure the good will of the cities of Vibo and Rhegium before leaving Italy; this he did by giving solemn promises that he would never distribute their fields and houses to the soldiers. Then he left to join Antony, sailing "with Sicily on his left," according to Appian, that is, he was forced by Sextus to circumnavigate Sicily in order to reach Brundisium (p. 77).

Octavian is camped in Reggio (Rhegium), on the south side of the straits. Yet rather than sailing just around the boot of Italy to Brundisium, he opts, we are told, to sail around Sicily. Aeneas' itinerary can be seen to pave the way for this later choice, and Octavian's ultimate victory over Sextus and Sicily can be traced back to the journey of Aeneas, which, in turn, can be seen to be rooted in the unification of Italy and Sicily in archaic times.

Vergil's poetry guides our reading of history throughout the poem. It does this in part by focusing our attention on a narrow geographic field. While the narrative arc of the epic moves from Troy to Rome, the text itself takes place in a much more limited space. The actual events within the poem—as distinguished from those related in flashback or prophecy—all unfold in a limited geographic scope, between Carthage on the west and Rome on the east. It is while Aeneas is in Carthage that he recounts the last hours of Troy and his journey across the seas. Many of the stories we associate with the *Aeneid* are reported, not enacted during the poem: the trick of the Trojan horse; the assault on that horse by Laocoön, and his death, with his sons, at the hands of the gods; the appearance of Hector in a dream to Aeneas, telling him to leave, leading a band of Trojans; the final skirmishes of Aeneas with the Greeks, including Helen; Aeneas' witnessing the death of Priam and one of Priam's sons, Polites; and Aeneas' own dealings with his father, who wants to die in Troy until two signs from the gods convince him to leave. Departing from Troy, he journeys for years across the Aegean, where he tries again and again to land and found Rome. Five false starts are recounted; at each a city is named and a foundation begun, and there are encounters with local inhabitants, including Polydorus, the man-turned-bush who bleeds when plucked, and the Harpies, whose dire prophecy turns out to be overblown. Italy keeps receding from Aeneas' grasp, and even when the Trojans see the peninsula and when they land on its southern coast they are urged not to stay because of the presence of Greeks. They move on, first to Sicily, where Aeneas' father dies, then to Carthage.

All of this is presented as flashback, recounted while Aeneas is Dido's guest. Once Aeneas has completed his tale leading up to the landing at Carthage, the fourth book pauses there, telling of Dido's love for Aeneas. Carthage is foregrounded, established as more important than the previous stops. Had things been different, the text suggests, Carthage might well have been the dominant city in the region and defeated Rome during the Punic Wars (264–146 B.C.). But Aeneas moves on, first to Sicily, then Italy, where he stops first at Cumae, to journey to the underworld, then up to the mouth of the Tiber, where much of the second half of the poem takes place. The effect of focusing the action of the poem on this limited geographic area is to draw our attention away from Troy. As important as Troy is to the political and mythic material that Vergil adapts to his purposes, it is nonetheless in the past. By turning our gaze west, Vergil subtly, yet effectively, makes this point. Troy is then; Italy is now.

So, too, with the literary past. Odysseus' journey is alluded to throughout the first six books—as Aeneas sails past Ithaca, or catches sight of the cyclops Polyphemus from a distance on Sicily, or sails by Circe's island. All the way to the mouth of the Tiber, Aeneas is shown to be tracing a journey similar to that of Odysseus, but, Vergil argues, he does it with a major difference: his journey ends up in Italy, rather than back on the coast of Greece. In a similar way, Homer's battle scenes are replayed in Italy in the second half of the poem, as if to say that the battle of Troy was just a warm-up, a practice run, for the battle that truly mattered in Italy.

Vergil leads us to read the poem this way by setting up numerous trial runs within the epic itself. In the fifth book, the Trojans, having landed on Sicily after leaving Dido in Carthage, celebrate the anniversary of the death of Aeneas' father, Anchises, with a series of funeral games. Each of the games—a boat race, a foot race, a bow-and-arrow contest, and a boxing match—include elements that point back to Homer, where similar games were played to commemorate the death of the Greek Patroclus, and forward to Roman times, as many participants are identified in relation to their later Roman families. Similar foreshadowing occurs within the poem itself: scenes from the games are replayed in the battles of the later books. So, for instance, Vergil makes it clear through a simile that the story of Nisus and Euryalus (who engage in a footrace on Sicily in which one slips and the other, to help his friend, trips up an opponent) is based on the chariot race in *Iliad* 23, in which a similar series of events occurs. Yet both of these series of events provide the basis for the battle scene in book 9 of the *Aeneid* when Nisus and Euryalus, once again, go together, this time on a nighttime raid, and find themselves in circumstances comparable to those of the race, except that this time Nisus and Euryalus both die.

It is perhaps most useful to approach the poem not as twelve books or two groupings of six but as three groupings of four: books 1–4 are united in that they take place on Carthage; books 5–8 are transitional, from the testing games on the in-between stop on Sicily through the trip to the liminal space of the underworld, the journey up the coast, the first skirmishes of war in book 7 and Aeneas' trip up the Tiber in search of allies in Pallanteum, the future site of Rome, in book 8. By the end of the second third, then, we have reached the goal of the journey, a fact Vergil underscores by ending book 8 with a description of the events of Roman history from Aeneas to Augustus as portrayed on the shield. Books 9–12 are the battle books, in which Aeneas fights for his right to the land of Rome. Each third includes a key encounter for Aeneas: Dido in the first, Evander in the second, and Turnus in the third. Vergil draws each of these characters with sympathy: Dido, above all, whose story in book 4 is told entirely from her point of view, rather than that of Aeneas; Evander, who as surrogate father shows him around the future site of Rome and offers up the figure of Hercules as the great Roman savior; and Turnus, who is drawn early on as an Achilles figure, yet who as the end approaches becomes more and more of a sympathetic Hector figure.

Aeneas links the stories of these characters together. Once he leaves

Carthage he is forced to land again at Sicily, where he rules over the funeral games in honor of his father with a fair and just hand and shows himself to be an emerging leader; he stops the fights that become too vicious and rewards even those heroes who win by supernatural means. Between Sicily and Italy he loses his helmsman Palinurus, and thereby becomes sole leader of the mission. In the underworld, which he enters only after proving himself by plucking—with his mother's help—the golden bough, he encounters characters from his past and future, including Palinurus, Dido, and Anchises, and Roman heroes leading up to a contemporary of Augustus, Marcellus. Aeneas' departure from the underworld through the gate of false dreams puts into question either the truth of what he has seen, or the truth of what is to come, neither of which, the text suggests, he is fully prepared for.

Once in Italy, he works first to meet the king of Latium, Latinus, then, once battle is imminent, to round up allies, whom he finds in Pallanteum (Rome) and farther up the coast. He is thus absent for the opening of the battle and in this is comparable to Achilles, who sits out of the action for much of the *Iliad*. His final battle with the Latin Turnus is provoked by the death of Evander's son, Pallas, who, as Patroclus with Achilles in the *Iliad*, had been under Aeneas' care. Not only does Turnus kill Pallas as Hector kills Patroclus, but he takes his swordbelt, as Hector takes the armor of Patroclus (who had, in turn, borrowed it from Achilles); it is the sight of Pallas' swordbelt, in the final confrontation at the end of the poem, that leads Aeneas to kill Turnus, much as Achilles is reminded of Patroclus through the armor Hector wears. But before Aeneas kills Turnus he kills Mezentius, who had terrorized the Arcadians, and so aligns himself with Hercules, who had freed Pallanteum from the monster Cacus.

Much recent discussion of the poem has focused on the final scene, for here the roles of *pietas* and *furor* are intertwined. The final confrontation of the epic, between Turnus and Aeneas, is so packed with intertextual references that it becomes difficult to read. Turnus, having been struck by Aeneas and fallen to the ground, is said to be *supplex* (suppliant), a description that is followed immediately by the request that Aeneas remember his father. Whose father? In addition to Daunus, Turnus' own father, there is Aeneas' father, Anchises, who warned Aeneas in the sixth book that what would set the Romans apart was their ability to spare the suppliant even as they warred down

the proud. There is also Evander, whose son Aeneas promised but
failed to protect; and Priam, Hector's father, who comes to Achilles in
the last book of the *Iliad* begging that his son's dead body be returned
and reminding him, at that point, of his own father, who grows old far
from the Trojan battlefield. There are other fathers as well: Daedalus,
who lost his son Icarus when he didn't heed his advice (the story is described on the doors of Apollo's temple at Cumae near the entrance to
the underworld); Saturn, who landed in Italy, like Daedalus, having
warred with his son, and finally Latinus, who can be said to have initiated the struggle between Aeneas and Turnus with his decision to give
Lavinia to Aeneas in marriage. Aeneas will kill Turnus, but by invoking images of supplication and fathers, Vergil fuses the warrior's *furor*
and the elder-respect of *pietas*.

Juno's role in the poem, too, can be approached as a means to understanding its dynamics. Alienated at the start, angry at being overlooked, she is affiliated with memory from her initial appearance. But
she is also associated with Troy, through the anecdotes explaining the
source of her anger and through her persistent association with memory. As Jupiter's plot moves forward, replacing Troy with Rome, Juno's
counterplot works to remind us constantly of the importance of the
Greeks. Her acceptance and involvement in the final scene speak to an
incorporation of the past in the future, of the *furor* in *pietas*. By the
end of the poem, the perspective has shifted, not only from East to
West but also from an understanding of victory as the opposite of defeat to one in which defeat, with the loss it entails, is incorporated into
the very idea of victory. It is Troy's defeat that Juno insists on: Rome
will not be Troy reborn; it will be a city that combines the loss of the
past with the promise of the future.

Shortly before Dido's death, Juno, for the first time in the poem, is
called *omnipotens*, all-powerful, thus matching, briefly, Jupiter's epi-
thet of *omnipotens* in the opening book. The opposing deities—
brother against sister, husband against wife—are initially matched in
strength as their battle begins in earnest; they are at war. But at the end
as they approach a compromise that foreshadows not only the treaty
between Trojans and Latins but also forges the outlines for later imperial relationships, it is Olympus that is *omnipotens*. Different as the
gods are, they have found a common ground, and it is the commonal-
ity that is all-powerful. War, which for Vergil was often cast as civil

war, provides an image, a discourse, a historic situation that enables the outlines of empire to evolve.

Speaking of the aftermath of the American Civil War, Ulysses S. Grant concluded that "wars are not always evils unmixed with some good. . . . The war [between the states]," he continues,

> begot a spirit of independence and enterprise. The feeling now is, that a youth must cut loose from his old surroundings to enable him to get up in the world. There is now such a commingling of the people that particular idioms and pronunciation are no longer localized to any great extent; the country has filled up "from the centre all around to the sea"; . . . The war has made us a nation of great power and intelligence" (*Memoirs and Selected Letters*, New York: Library of America, pp. 664–665).

For Grant, the promise of the future—the imperial strength of the United States that began in the wake of the Civil War—derives paradoxically from the war: it was the crisis of the war itself that led to the expansion of the nation. The *Aeneid*, too, speaks to a vision of empire that builds up from the rift of war even as it builds into its understanding of empire the memory of difference. The epic focuses at the last on the dying Turnus, whose soul fled, unavenged "down to the Shades." Exile and flight remain central to this poem; the loss introduced in its opening lines is never fully resolved by its end. Turnus' body, unlike Hector's, is not returned in the space of the text; like Creüsa, Turnus escapes the grasp of the poem. The final vision of empire the *Aeneid* offers is founded on the loss that pervades the epic from its start.

———

SARAH SPENCE is Professor of Classics at the University of Georgia. Founding editor of the journal *Literary Imagination*, she has published widely on Vergil and medieval vernacular poetry. She is author of two books, *Rhetorics of Reason and Desire: Vergil, Augustine, and the Troubadours* (Cornell University Press) and *Texts and the Self in the Twelfth Century* (Cambridge University Press), and has edited two volumes of essays on Vergil, *Poets and Critics Read Vergil*

(Yale University Press) and, with Glenn Most, *Re-Presenting Vergil*, a special issue of *Materiali e discussioni* (2005; vol. 52). She lives in Athens, Georgia, with her husband, comparatist James McGregor, and their teen-aged son and middle-aged Bouvier.

––––––––

I wish to acknowledge my debts, first to three students: Andrew Lemons, who labored through the notes with me; Mary Orwig, who read parts of the edited translation for flow; and Leslie Harkema, who helped transcribe the textual edits. My colleagues Keith Dix and Christine Perkell read the introduction and offered helpful suggestions. Most nobly of all, Nicholas Horsfall reviewed an early version of the endnotes and footnotes with his usual discerning eye and kept me from tripping over myself. To all, thank you deeply.

Major Characters and Places in the *Aeneid*

Humans

AENEAS: A Trojan prince; son of the goddess Venus and the Trojan Anchises; father of Ascanius; husband of Creüsa, and after the end of the poem, Lavinia; founder of Rome.

AMATA: Wife of Latinus and mother of Lavinia. Her name derives from the Latin for "beloved." In the quest for Lavinia's hand, she supports Turnus rather than Aeneas, and becomes an agent of Juno and the Fury Allecto.

ANCHISES: Aeneas' father, who accompanies Aeneas from Troy and dies on Sicily. He guides the journey—often misleading it—during the early travels. His presence is strongly felt until and after he dies. He appears to Aeneas in a dream in book 5, telling him he is to visit the underworld. When they meet there, in book 6, Anchises describes for Aeneas the parade of Roman heroes, from Aeneas' sons to figures from Vergil's day. Anchises is marked by his piety for the gods and his compassion—for example, when they encounter the Greek Achaemenides on Sicily. Aeneas is the product of Anchises' sexual liaison with Venus, for which he was made lame by a thunderbolt from Jupiter.

ASCANIUS: Aeneas' son by his first wife, Creüsa, who was left behind and died in Troy. Ascanius matures through the poem from a small boy, walking with uneven steps next to his father as they leave Troy, to a youth chasing down wild animals in Carthage, to a leader of the young Romans in Sicily, and finally to the general in charge in Italy while Aeneas is away. Ascanius, as the future of the Roman race, is carefully guarded by his grandmother, Venus, and is seen as the start of the future in discussions of Roman heroes.

CAMILLA: Volscian warrior who fights for Turnus. She is Diana's rather than Juno's protégé, yet her function is comparable to that of Turnus or Dido as she opposes Aeneas' victory at Rome.

DIDO: Queen of Carthage. A figure likened to Aeneas when she first appears, she is an exile, a powerful leader, and focused on building a city for her people. Dido and Aeneas are matched through description and simile: Dido is likened to Diana, while Aeneas is compared to Diana's brother, Apollo. Book 4, which is devoted to Dido, is structured as a tragedy; it is also told from her point of view, as the narrator sides with her and stays with her after Aeneas has left. Aeneas is portrayed as joining in with Dido's endeavors to build up her home, Carthage, until the gods Jupiter and Mercury tell him to stop. During his stay in Carthage, Aeneas is likened to a decadent easterner, which prompts a comparison between Dido and Cleopatra—a similarity reinforced by the fact that the depiction of Cleopatra on the shield at the end of the *Aeneid* recalls the character of Dido. As Aeneas prepares to leave Carthage, Dido becomes more and more desperate, and eventually builds a funeral pyre and commits suicide, but not before leveling a curse against the Romans—a literary explanation of the enmity between Carthage and Rome in the Punic Wars (264–241 B.C., 218–202 B.C., 149–146 B.C.). Dido sees Aeneas in the underworld but refuses to talk to him, thus echoing the character Ajax in the *Odyssey*, who refuses to talk to Odysseus because of the loss of Achilles' armor. Dido's curse is carried out thematically through other characters in the poem, most notably Turnus and Camilla.

EVANDER: An Arcadian who had known Aeneas' father and so was willing to help Aeneas' cause. Evander lives in Pallanteum, on the future Palatine Hill—Aeneas' visit to him there offers the reader a rare view of Rome. Evander is joined by his son Pallas, who accompanies Aeneas to battle and is killed by Turnus.

HERCULES: Also called Alcides and the Tirynthian hero; son of Jupiter and Alcmena, and hero of the twelve labors imposed by Eurystheus. In the *Aeneid* he is described as liberating the early inhabitants of the Palatine from the monster Cacus.

MEZENTIUS: Renegade Etruscan warrior who had terrorized Evander's community and taken refuge with Turnus. It is to stop him that Evander agrees to round up allies to help Aeneas. Mezentius is shown to be similar to the monster Cacus, who had terrorized the

Roman landscape before Hercules arrived and subdued him; he introduces a monstrous element into the mix, while suggesting that Aeneas be seen as a Hercules character who frees the land from monsters, using violence when necessary.

RUTULI: People of Latium, led by Turnus in a war against the Trojans when Latinus denies him the hand of Lavinia. An Italian tribe, they made their capital at Ardea.

TURNUS: Rutulian warrior engaged to Lavinia, the daughter of the Latin king Latinus. Turnus is Aeneas' major antagonist once he reaches Italy, since he stands between Aeneas and Italian rule. Turnus' character is informed strongly by Homeric counterparts Hector and Achilles; the final confrontation at the end of the *Aeneid* draws largely on the Homeric depiction of these two figures and their battle toward the end of the *Iliad*.

Gods

APOLLO: Also called Phoebus, and associated with the sun. He appears briefly, to aid Ascanius, in book 9, yet he is often invoked, both to help Aeneas and as a supporter of Octavian, especially in the victory at Actium.

DIANA: Apollo's sister and goddess of the hunt. She does not appear in the poem, yet she is alluded to in discussions of Dido and Camilla in particular.

JUNO: Sister and wife of Jupiter and daughter of Saturn. She is a blend of the Greek Hera and the Carthaginian Tanit, the goddess of marriage, but is also known for her wrath. Having sided with the Greeks in Troy, she is antagonistic to the Trojans and the project of refounding Troy in Rome. She works against Aeneas whenever and however she can. At the start of the second half of the poem she turns not to the Olympians for aid, but to the chthonic forces of the underworld.

JUPITER: King of the gods. He is shown mostly on Olympus, weighing in on the future of the Trojan race and ensuring Venus that Aeneas and his men will prevail and that the Roman Empire will rule without end. He bears few traces of the philandering king of the gods depicted by Homer. Rather, presented as a statesman, he rules with a near-legal authority.

MARS: The god of war. He appears only briefly in the *Aeneid* and serves both a martial and a protective role.

MERCURY: Also called Cyllenius, after his mother, and Hermes, his Greek name; messenger of the gods. In book 4 Jupiter sends him to Aeneas in Carthage to command the Trojan prince to abandon Dido and continue his journey.

MINERVA: Also called Pallas and Tritonia; daughter of Jupiter, goddess of wisdom and craft, both domestic and martial. She does not appear in the poem, except in one scene during the last night at Troy. She is a supporter of the Greeks, especially Odysseus, in the Trojan War and its aftermath.

PENATES: Guardians of the home; Aeneas carries them with him from Troy to Rome. They appear to him in a vision in book 3 and advise about the correct route to Rome.

VENUS: Aeneas' mother and goddess of erotic love; in Greek she is called Aphrodite. Closely tied with Jupiter in the mission of founding Rome, she watches over Aeneas and, more carefully, Ascanius, to ensure the future of the Roman race.

VULCAN: God of fire and metalworking; son of Jupiter and Juno; husband of Venus. Venus persuades Vulcan to create the shield of Aeneas, which she presents to Aeneas in book 8.

Places

CARTHAGE: City of North Africa and longtime rival of Rome; destroyed by Rome in 146 B.C. in the Third Punic War. A Phoenician settlement founded by Dido, also known as Elissa.

ETRURIA: Ancient region within what is now Italy, comprising modern Tuscany and part of Umbria; located to the west and north of the Tiber along the Tyrrhenian Sea.

HESPERIA: Literally, the western land; becomes synonymous with Italy.

ITALIA (Italy): Country of southern Europe. Also called Hesperia, Ausonia, Oenotria (originally used of one section only, then of the whole), and Saturnia tellus.

LATIUM: Region of what is now Italy that lies south of Etruria; the river Tiber marked its northern limit.

LIBYA: Used by Cranch poetically for Libya or Africa in general.

PHRYGIA: West-central Anatolia.

ROME: Chief city of Italy and capital of the Roman Empire; situated on the banks of the Tiber.

TROY: City also known poetically as Ilium or Pergama, famous for its part in the ten-year war between the Greeks and the Trojans. It is located, according to Vergil, at the eastern edge of the Aegean.

TYRE: Major city in Phoenicia, located 20 miles south of Sidon on the coast of modern Lebanon. Dido's home, from which she escapes and founds Carthage.

Note on the Translation

Christopher Pearse Cranch's 1872 translation of the *Aeneid* is little known today, but it has the virtue of being composed in a free verse that closely matches the dactylic hexameter of Vergil's line. Cranch's translation is, at the same time, remarkably accurate. Edgar Allan Poe wrote that Cranch's original verse "possess[es] unusual vivacity of fancy and dexterity of expression, while his versification is remarkable for its accuracy, vigor, and . . . originality of effect" (*Godey's Lady's Book*, 1846). His translation shares many of these virtues. Consider, for instance, the following passage from book 2, as Aeneas becomes aware of the Greek invasion in the last night at Troy:

> As when the flames are raging through the corn,
> Driven by the furious winds; or a mountain stream,
> Swollen to a rapid torrent, floods the fields,
> And desolates the smiling crops and all
> The labors of the oxen, and drags down
> The forests; and the unconscious shepherd stands
> Listening upon the peak of some high rock,
> Bewildered by the rushing noise below (lines 420–427).

Cranch uses an unrhymed iambic pentameter line to great effect, especially in scenes such as this one or those found in books 2, 5, and 9–11. "What I have aimed at," he wrote in his introduction, "has been to render [the epic] simply and concisely, without omission, addition, or periphrasis, at the same time fluently, keeping in mind the best ideals of blank verse." In two passages where oracles speak—in book 3 with Helenus' prophecy and in book 6 with Sibyl's prophecy—Cranch deliberately moves to a rhyming pentameter.

While the line flows smoothly and the translation is for the most part accurate, Cranch chose to use an archaizing (thee's and thou's) form of English. In an effort to make this translation as accessible as possible to today's reader, I have reworded the archaisms and clarified word choice where necessary. Occasionally I changed the word order to avoid what reads today like "Yoda-speak," though I refrained from altering either the sense or the meter of the original translation. Proper nouns posed a particular problem, since Cranch altered them often to fit the line or meter. I have opted to leave them as he had them in order to keep the meter, even though names are often misspelled as a result. Despite these weaknesses, the Cranch translation has strengths enough to warrant its being read alongside the better-known and often-reprinted translations of Conington and Dryden.

Cranch's Latin source was the Anthon text of the *Aeneid*, which is very close to the modern standard Oxford text edited by Mynors. There are discrepancies between the two source texts, but few affect meaning or sense, and all of the oddities of the Cranch translation can be traced to editorial choices made by Anthon, including most notably some misplaced lines.

—Sarah Spence

MAPS

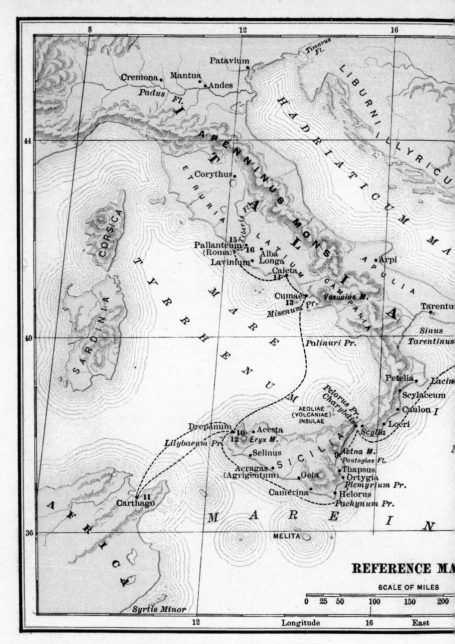

THE WANDERINGS OF AENEAS—The broken line shows Aeneas' journey. The figures indicate, in

1. MT. IDA, ANTANDROS: 2.1081; 3.7

2. AENOS: 3.26

3. DELOS: 3.92

4. PERGAMUM, IN CRETE: 3.169

5. STROPHADES: 3.271

6. ACTIUM: 3.357

7. BUTHROTUM: 3.375

8. CASTRUM MINERVAE: 3.674

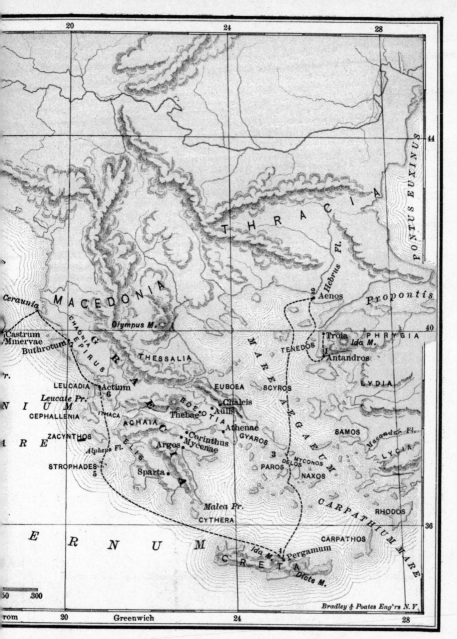

order, the places visited; corresponding references to the *Aeneid* are here given:

9. ORAE CYCLOPUM: 3.719

10. DREPANUM: 3.883

11. AFRICA: 1.200

12. DREPANUM: 5.42

13. CUMAE: 6.2

14. CAIETA: 6.1136

15. TIBER: 7.37

16. PALLANTEUM, LATER ROME: 8.125

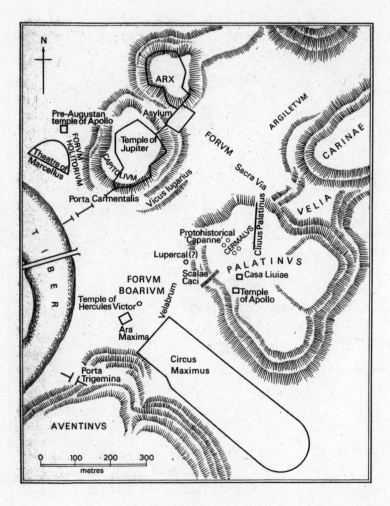

The Site of Rome.

THE
AENEID

BOOK 1

I SING of arms and of the man[1] who first
Came from the coasts of Troy to Italy
And the Lavinian shores, exiled by fate.[2]
Much was he tossed about upon the lands
And on the ocean by supernal powers,   5
Because of cruel Juno's sleepless wrath.[3]
Many things he also suffered in war,
Until he built a city, and brought his gods
Into Latium; from which came the Latin race,
The Alban sires, and walls of lofty Rome.[4]   10

O Muse,[5] tell the causes, for what affront,
And why incensed, the queen of gods compelled
A hero renowned for his piety
To undergo such sufferings and such toils.
Is there such anger in celestial minds?   15

There was an ancient city, Carthage,[6] held
By Tyrian settlers, facing from afar
Italia, and the distant Tiber's mouth;
Rich in resources, fierce in war's pursuits:
And this one city, Juno, it was said,   20
Esteemed far more than every other land,
Samos itself being less. Here were her arms,
Her chariot here; even then the goddess strives
With earnest hope to found a kingdom here
Of universal sway, should fate permit.   25
But of a race derived from Trojan blood
She had heard, who would overturn the Tyrian towers
One day, and that a people of wide rule
And proud in war descended from them, would come
For Libya's doom. So did the Fates decree.   30

3

Fearing this, mindful of the former war
She had led at Troy for her belovèd Greeks,
The causes of her ire and cruel griefs
Saturnia* had not forgot, but still
Remembered, hoarded in her deepest thought,   35
The judgment given by Paris, and the affront
Of beauty scorned—the hated Trojan race,
And honors granted to snatched Ganymede.[7]
Inflamed by these, she drove far from Latium
The Trojan remnant that escaped the Greeks   40
And fierce Achilles;† and for many years
They wandered, driven by fate, round all the seas.
Such task it was to found the Roman state.

Scarce out of sight of Sicily,[8] they spread
Their sails with joyous hearts, and over the sea   45
With brazen prows were plunging through the foam,
When Juno, the eternal wound still fresh
Within her breast, thus with herself communed:—
"Shall I who have begun, desist, overcome,[9]
Nor avert from Italy this Trojan king?   50
The Fates forbid, indeed! Shall Pallas‡ burn
The fleet of the Greeks, and drown them in the sea,
All for the crime and furious lust of one,
Ajax, Oïleus' son? She, from the clouds,
Snatched the swift fire of Jove, and hurling, smote   55
The ships, and scattered them, and upturned all
The sea with winds; and he, by whirlwinds seized,
And breathing flames from his transfixèd breast,
On a sharp rock impaled. But I, who move as
Queen of the gods, Jove's sister and his spouse,   60
So many years with one sole race wage war.
And who henceforth will worship Juno's power,
Or suppliant at her altars lay his gifts?"

---

*Daughter of Saturn—that is, Juno.

†Achilles, the hero of the *Iliad*, was the best of the Greek fighters.

‡The goddess Minerva.

Revolving such things in her flaming heart,
She came to Æolia, region of the clouds,   65
Places that teemed with furious south winds.
Here, in a vast cavern, King Æolus
Holds his empire over the struggling winds and
Sounding storms, and binds them fast in chains.
They, chafing, with great mountain murmurs roar   70
Around their cloisters. On his lofty seat
Sits Æolus, with scepter, both their wrath
Assuages and their fury moderates.
Else they would bear away, with rapid force,
Sea, earth, and heaven, and sweep them through the air.   75
But the omnipotent father, fearing this,
Hid them in gloomy caves, and over them set
The mass of lofty mountains; and gave them
A king, who, by a compact sure, might know
When to restrain and when to loose the reins.   80
To him then, suppliant, Juno spoke these words:—
"O Æolus, I know that unto you,
The father of the gods and king of men
Grants to assuage and lift the waves with winds.
A race now sails upon the Tyrrhene* Sea   85
Hostile to me,—transporting
Ilium to Italy and their conquered household gods.
Strike force into your winds, and sink their ships,
Or drive them wide asunder, and the waves
Strew with their corpses. Twice seven nymphs are mine;   90
The fairest, Deïopea, will I give
To you in wedlock firm, to be your own,
And, for such service, pass her years with you,
And make you father of a lovely race."

Æolus answered: "Yours, O queen, whatever   95
You choose me to require, it's mine to obey.
You give to me whatever sovereignty
I hold—my sceptre, and the favor of Jove,

*Etruscan; sea nearest Rome.

And to recline at banquets of the gods,
And all the power I hold over clouds and storms."   100

Having spoken, with his inverted spear
He smote the hollow mountain on the side.
Then forth the winds, like some great marching host,
Being given vent, rush turbulent, and blow
In whirling storm abroad upon the lands: 105
Pressing down on the sea from lowest depths
Upturned, Eurus and Notus all in one
Blowing, and Africus with rainy squalls,
Dense on the vast waves rolling to the shore.
Then follow clamoring shouts of men, and noise   110
Of whistling cordage. All of a sudden, clouds
Snatch from the Trojans all the light of day
And the great sky. Black night lies on the sea.
The thunder rolls, the incessant lightnings flash;
And to the crews all bodes a present death.   115
Æneas' limbs grow limp with sudden cold;
Groaning, he stretches his hands to the stars.
"O, three and four times happy they," he cries,
"To whom it fell beneath Troy's lofty walls
To encounter death before their fathers' eyes!   120
O Diomed,* you bravest of the Greeks,
Why could I not have fallen on Ilium's fields,
Pouring my warm life out beneath your hand?—
Where valiant Hector§ lies, slain by Achilles'
Spear, and where tall Sarpedon‡ was overthrown,—   125
Where Simoïs rolls along, bearing away
Beneath his waves so many shields and helmets,
So many corpses of brave heroes slain!"

---

*Diomedes; Aeneas' major antagonist in the war at Troy; son of Tydeus; wounded both Aeneas
and Venus; with Odysseus, carried off Palladium; moved to Italy and founded a city, Argyripa.
The Latins will appeal to him for advice in book 8 and he provides it in book 11.

§Trojan hero killed by Achilles in the climactic encounter in the *Iliad.* Aeneas will see Hector's
ghost in book 2, and Vergil will draw on the encounter between Hector and Achilles in his portrayal of the final battle of the *Aeneid.*

‡Son of Jupiter, killed by Patroclus.

Thus while he cried aloud, a roaring blast
From out the north strikes full against the sails,   130
And the waves touch the stars; the oars are snapped;
The ship swings round, and gives its side to the waves.
A steep and watery mountain rolls apace:
Some on its summit hang; and some beneath
Behold the earth between the yawning waves: 135
Mingled with sand the boiling waters hiss.
On hidden rocks three ships the south wind hurls,—
Rocks called "Altars" by the Italian sailors;
A vast ridge on a level with the sea.
Three others by the east wind from the deep   140
Are driven upon the quicksands and the shoals,
Dreadful to see, dashed upon the shallows,
And bound around by drifting heaps of sand.
One, that conveyed the Lycians, and that bore
Faithful Orontes, there, before his eyes,   145
A huge sea from above strikes on the stern,
Dashing the pilot headlong on the waves.
Three times the surges whirl the ship around,
Engulfed in the swift vortex of the sea;
Then scattered swimmers in the vast abyss   150
Are seen, and arms, and planks, and Trojan spoils.
Now the strong ship of Ilioneus, now
Of brave Achates,* and the boats that bore
Abas, and old Aletes, are overwhelmed,
And all their yawning sides with loosened joints   155
Drink in the bitter drench.
      Meanwhile, below,
Neptune was conscious of the sea disturbed
With loud uproar, and of the tempest sent,
And the calm deeps convulsed. Profoundly moved,
He gazes up, and lifts his placid head   160
Above the waves; over all the ocean sees
Æneas' scattered fleet; the Trojan hosts
Oppressed with waves and the down-rushing sky.

---

*Companion of Aeneas.

And not to Juno's brother were unknown
Her arts and anger. Then he calls to him   165
Eurus and Zephyrus, and thus he speaks:—
"Can such reliance on your birth be yours,
O Winds, that now, without authority
Of mine, you dare to mingle heaven and earth
In discord, and such mountain waves upraise?   170
Whom I— But best allay these angry seas.
Not thus shall you escape your next offence.
Away!—say this unto your king: Not his
The empire of the seas, the trident stern,
But given to me, by fate. The savage rocks   175
He holds, O Eurus, your abiding place.
Let Æolus boast his power within those halls,
And reign in the pent prison of the winds!"

So spoke the god: and swifter than his speech
He smooths the swelling waves, the gathered clouds   180
Disperses, and the sunshine brings again.
With him Cymothoë and Triton bend
With all their force, and from the jagged rocks
Push off the ships: with trident he himself
Upheaves them, and lays open the vast shoals,   185
And smoothes the deep, as with light wheels he glides
Along the surface of the waves. As when
Sedition rises[10] in a multitude,
And the base mob is raging with fierce minds,
And stones and firebrands fly, and fury lends   190
Arms to the populace—then should some man
Of reverence and of worth appear, they stand
Silent, and listen with attentive ears:
He rules their minds with words, and calms their breasts:
So all the clamor of the sea subsides,   195
When, looking forth, the father, borne along
Beneath the open sky, directs his steeds,
And flying, to his swift car gives the reins.

The weary Trojans aim to reach the shores
That lie nearest, and turn to the Libyan coasts. 200
Within a deep recess there is a place[11]
Where with its jutting sides an island forms
A port, by which the rolling ocean waves
Are broken, and divide in lesser curves.
On either side vast rocks and twin-like cliffs 205
Threaten the sky; beneath whose towering tops
The sea lies safe and tranquil all around.
Above, a wall, with trembling foliage stands,
Overshadowed by a dark and gloomy grove;
And underneath the opposing front, a cave 210
Is seen amid the hanging cliffs. Within
Are pleasant springs and seats of natural rock,
A dwelling for the nymphs. No cable here,
Nor any anchor holds with crooked fluke
The weary ships. To here Æneas brings 215
Seven of the ships collected from his fleet.
And here, with a great longing for the land,
The Trojans disembark, and gain the desired
Beach; and drenched and dripping with the brine,
They stretch their weary limbs upon the shore. 220
And first, with flint, Achates struck a spark,
And caught the fire in leaves; and round about
Piled dry fuel, and swiftly fanned the flame.
They bring forth then their corn, spoiled by water,
And implements of Ceres—exhausted 225
With their toils—and prepare to scorch with fire
Their rescued grain, and break it with a stone.

Meanwhile Æneas climbs upon a cliff,[12]
And far out on the ocean strains his eyes,
If any one like Antheus he may spot, 230
Tossed by the wind in any Phrygian boat;
Or Capys, or Caïcus, with his arms
Upon the stern. No sail in sight. He sees
Upon the shore, straying about, three stags;
And following these, the whole herd comes behind, 235

And browses all along the valleys. Here
He stopped and seized his bow and arrows swift,
Which arms the trusty Achates bore. And first
He strikes the leaders down, their lofty heads
With branching antlers crowned; and next he smites   240
The vulgar herd, and drives them with his darts,
Mixed in confusion through the leafy woods.
Nor does the victor stop till he has felled
Seven huge beasts, the number of his ships;
Then to the port returning, shares the prey   245
Among his comrades. And the wines with which
The good Acestes had filled full their casks,
On the Trinacrian shore, when leaving him,
These he divides among them; and with words
Of comfort thus consoles their sorrowing hearts: 250

"O friends, who greater sufferings still have borne,
(For not unknown to us are former griefs,)
The deity will also give an end
To these. You have approached the furious rage
Of Scylla* and her hoarse resounding cliffs.   255
You the Cyclopean rocks have known full well.
Recall your courage; banish gloomy fears.
Some day perhaps the memory of these things
Shall yield delight. Through various accidents,
Through many a strait of fortune, we are bound   260
For Latium, where our fates point out to us
A quiet resting place. There it's decreed
Troy's kingdom shall arise again. Be firm,
And keep your hearts in hope of brighter days."

Such were his words: yet sick with weighty cares,   265
He in his features still dissembled hope,
And pressed his heavy trouble down. But they
Busy themselves about their captured game

---

*The sea-monster who threatens on the eastern side of the straits of Messina: Mentioned in the *Odyssey* as living in a cavern and having six necks and heads, she destroyed men from ships that passed by.

And preparations for approaching feasts.
They strip the skin from off the ribs, lay bare   270
The carcasses, and cut the meat apart,
And fix the quivering limbs upon the spits.
Others set brazen cauldrons on the sand,
And tend the fires beneath; then they refresh
Their strength with food, and, stretched upon the grass,   275
Are filled with the old wine and juicy meat.
Hunger appeased, and dishes then removed,
In long discourse about their comrades lost
They make conjectures, between hope and fear,
Uncertain if they still may be alive,   280
Or have suffered death, nor hear when they are called.
Chiefly the good Æneas mourns the lot
And cruel fate, now of brave Orontes,
And now of Amycus, and Gyas strong,
And strong Cloanthus.

               Now there was an end   285
At length; when Jove from his ethereal heights
Looking down upon the sail-winged ocean,
And the wide lands, and shores, and nations spread
Beneath, stood on the pinnacle of heaven,
And on the realm of Libya fixed his eyes.   290
Venus, sadder than was her wont, addressed
Him, revolving in his mind such cares,
Her brilliant eyes suffused with tears: "O you
Who does rule over men and gods[13] with eternal
Sway,—terrible with lightning!—what   295
So great offence has my Æneas done
Against you, what have the Trojans done, that they,
Suffering so many deaths, the entire earth,
On Italy's account, is shut to them?
For surely you did promise that one day   300
In the revolving years, from these should spring
The Romans, leaders from the Teucrian blood
Restored, and hold the sea, and hold the land
In sovereign sway. What new resolve has changed
Your mind, O sire? For I am used to solace   305

Myself with this for Troy's overthrow,
And its sad ruin, weighing adverse fates
With fates. But now the same mischance pursues
These men long driven by calamities.
What end, great king, do you give to their toils?   310
Antenor, from the midst of Grecian hosts
Escaped, was able, safe, to penetrate
The Illyrian bay, and see the interior realms
Of the Liburni; and to pass beyond
The source of the Timavus, from where, issuing   315
With a vast mountain murmur from nine springs,
A bursting flood goes forth, and on the fields
Crowds with resounding waters. Yet he here
Founded the walls of Padua, and built
The Trojan seats, and to the people gave   320
A name, and there affixed the arms of Troy.
Now, laid at rest, he sleeps in placid peace.
But we, your offspring, to whom you do give
The promise of the palaces of heaven,
Our ships are lost—ah bitter woe!—and we   325
Betrayed, to satisfy the wrath of one,
And driven far from the Italian shores.
Is this the reward of filial piety?
And do you thus restore our sceptred sway?"

Then with that countenance with which he calms   330
The stormy skies, the Sire of men and gods,
Smiling, his daughter fondly kissed, and spoke:—
"Spare your fears, Cytherea,[14] for unmoved
Your people's fates remain for you; and you
Shall see Lavinium and its promised walls,   335
And to the stars of heaven shall bear sublime
The noble-souled Æneas; nor do I turn
From my intent. He (but to you alone
I tell it, since these cares oppress your mind;
The secrets of the Fates revolving far   340
In future eras, I will move for you—
On Italia a great war he shall wage,

And shall subdue the fierce and hostile tribes,
And give them laws, and manners, and walled towns,
Till the third summer shall have seen him king 345
In Latium, and three winters shall have passed
After the Rutuli have been subdued.
But the young boy Ascanius, unto whom
The name Iulus now is added (he
Ilus was called, while stood the Ilian realm), 350
Thirty great circles of revolving months
Shall in his reign complete, and shall transfer
The kingdom from Lavinium, and with strength
Fortify Alba Longa. Here shall reign
Kings of Hectorean race, three hundred years, 355
Till Ilia, a priestess and a queen,
Pregnant by Mars, has given birth to twins.
Then, in the tawny shelter of a wolf,
His nurse, exulting, Romulus shall take
The nation in his sway, and build the walls 360
Of the Mavortian city, and his name
Give to the Romans. Nor shall I set bounds
To them or seasons. Empire without end
I have given. Nay, harsh Juno, who disturbs
With fear the sea and land and sky, will change 365
Her counsels for the better, and with me
Cherish the Romans, masters of affairs,
The toga'd nation. Such is my decree.
An age is coming in the gliding years,
When the descendants of Assaracus* 370
Shall subdue Phthia and famed Mycenæ
And conquered Argos. Of illustrious birth
The Trojan Cæsar shall be born, whose sway
The ocean, and whose fame the stars alone
Shall limit; called Julius, a name derived 375
From great Iulus. Free from all your cares,
At length in heaven you shall receive him, rich
With Orient spoils, invoked with prayers and vows.
Then shall the barbarous centuries grow mild,

---

*Grandfather of Anchises.

Wars end, and gray-haired Faith and Vesta rule;   380
And Romulus with his brother Remus give
Laws to the land. The dreadful gates of war
Will then be shut with iron bolts and bars.
The wicked Furor on his cruel arms,
Bound with a hundred brazen knots behind,   385
Will sit within, and rage with bloody mouth."

He spoke; and from on high sends down the son
Of Maia, that the lands and new-built towers
Of Carthage might be opened to receive
As guests the Trojans; lest in ignorance   390
Of fate, Dido should drive them from her shores.
Through the vast air with rowing wings he flies,
And quickly alighted on the Libyan coasts.
And now he executes his high commands;
And at his will the Carthaginians lay   395
Aside their fierceness; and the queen in charge
Turns toward the Trojans with friendly thoughts.

But good Æneas, pondering many things
All through the night, soon as the cheering dawn
Of day should come, resolved to issue forth,   400
And to explore this country all unknown;
Upon what shores the wind had driven him;
By whom inhabited, or men or beasts,
For all seemed wild, and to his friends report
What he might find. Beneath a hollow rock   405
With overhanging woods he hid his fleet,
Shut in around by trees and gloomy shades.
Then forth he goes, accompanied alone
By Achates; in his hand two broad-tipped spears.
To him then, in the middle of a wood,   410
Appeared his mother,[15] with a virgin's face
And robe, and weapons of a virgin too;
Either of Spartan race, or like the fair
Thracian Harpalyce when she fatigues
Her steeds, more swift than Hebrus in his course.   415

For from the shoulders of the huntress hung
The ready bow, and to the winds she had given
Her loosened locks. Bare to the knee she stood.
Her flowing robe was gathered in a knot.
"Ho, warriors!" she cried; "tell me if you   420
Here have seen any one of my sisters
Wandering, with quiver girt, and spotted hide
Of lynx; or pressing on the foaming boar
With clamorous cries." So Venus spoke; and thus
Her son: "None of your sisters have I seen   425
Or heard; O Virgin! tell me by what name
Shall I address you; for your countenance,
Your voice, are not a mortal's; surely then
A goddess,—Phœbus' sister, or a nymph.
O, be propitious! and, whoever you are,   430
Relieve our sufferings; tell us in what clime,
On what shores, we are cast; for ignorant
Alike of men and places here we stray,
Driven here by the winds and by the waves;
And on your altars we'll offer you   435
Many victims slain!" Then Venus: "I indeed
Am all unworthy to receive such honor.
It is the custom of the Tyrian maids
To bear the quiver, and about the leg
To bind the purple buskin. Tyrians here   440
You see—Agenor's city, and the realm
Of Carthage, on the Libyan land—a race
Untamable in war. Dido from Tyre
Rules the kingdom, who from her brother fled.
Long is the story of her wrongs, and long   445
Its windings; but the chief events I'll tell.
Sychæus was her spouse, of all Phœnicians
The wealthiest in lands, and greatly loved
By her, unlucky. She was given to him
A virgin by her father, and was wed   450
With fairest omens. But Pygmalion,
Her brother, ruled in Tyre; a monster, he,
Of crime. A feud arose between the two.

Regardless of his sister's wedded love,
He, blind with lust of gold, in secrecy   455
Slayed the unguarded husband at the altar.
Long he concealed the crime, and wickedly
Inventing many a tale, the loving queen
Deceived with empty hope. But in her sleep
The ghost of her unburied husband came,   460
Lifting a visage marvelously pale;
And showed the cruel altars, and laid bare
The breast the dagger pierced, uncovering all
The hidden crimes of his detested house;
And counseled her to leave the land, and flee;   465
And, for her journey's aid, disclosed to her
Much ancient treasure hidden in the earth,
An unknown heap of silver and of gold.
Thus moved, Dido prepared for flight, and chose
Companions. All assembled who were led   470
By hatred of the tyrant or by fear.
They seized upon some ships, ready by chance,
And loaded them with treasure; and the wealth
Of covetous Pygmalion was conveyed
Away across the sea. A woman led   475
The enterprise. They reached the shores (where now
You soon shall see the mighty battlements
And citadel of our new Carthage rise),
And purchased ground, called Byrsa, from the fact,
As much as a bull's hide could compass round.[16]   480
      "But who are you? From what shores do you come?
And where then are you going?" With a sigh,
And voice dragged from his deepest breast, he spoke:—
"O goddess, if I should recount our woes
From their first origin, and you find time   485
To hear, the evening star would lead the day
To rest, and all the Olympian sky be shut!
      "From ancient Troy, if you perhaps have heard
The name of Troy, we have been driven by storms
Over various seas, upon these Libyan coasts.   490
I am called the good Æneas, known to fame
Above the aether, who our household gods

Snatched from our enemies, and in my fleet
Convey. Italia, my ancestral land,
And the race sprung from Jove supreme, I seek.   495
With twice ten ships upon the Phrygian Sea,
I, following my destinies, embarked,
My divine mother showing me the way.
Scarce seven of these, shattered by storms, are saved.
And I, unknown and needy, traverse here   500
The Libyan deserts, banished from the shores
Of Europe and of Asia—"

                              But no more
Did Venus endure of her son's complaint,
But in the middle of his grief, thus spoke:—
    "Whoever you are, not hated, I believe,   505
By the celestials, do you breathe this air,
Since to the Tyrian city you have come.
Continue now your course, and so proceed
Toward the royal palace of the queen.
For I announce to you your friends returned,   510
Your fleet brought back safe into a harbor,
The north winds having changed; unless to me
My parents taught false augury, self-deceived.
See there twelve swans rejoicing in a flock,
Which, but a moment since, Jove's eagle scared,   515
And gliding from on high, drove through the air.
Now in long line either they light on earth,
Or, looking down, see their companions land.
As they, returning, sport with whistling wings,
Clustered together with their joyful cries,   520
Just so your ships and your brave youths even now
Are either safe in port or sailing in.
Go then, and bend your steps where your path leads."

She spoke; and turning, gleamed with rosy neck,
And from her head, divinest odors breathed   525
In her ambrosial hair. Around her feet
Floated her flowing robe; and in her gait
All the true goddess was revealed. But he,
When now he knew his mother as she fled,

Thus followed with his voice: "Ah, why so often   530
Do you deceive your son, oh cruel one,
With airy images? Why not join hand
With hand, and hear and speak real language?"
    Thus he reproaches her, and onward moves
Toward the walls. But Venus with a mist   535
Obscured them, walking, and around their forms
Wove a thick veil, lest any should perceive
Or harm them, or delay, or seek to know
Why they had come. But she herself on high
Took her way to Paphos, and saw again   540
With joy her seats, and saw her temples, where
A hundred altars stand, and glow with sweet
Sabæan incense and with fresh-culled flowers.

Following their pathway then they hastened on
And now ascended a hill, which overlooked   545
The city and its towers.[17] Æneas there
Admires the mass of buildings, once mere huts;
Admires the gates, the bustle, and the streets.
The ardent Tyrians ply their busy tasks;
Some at the walls, some at the citadel   550
Toil, rolling up the stones. Some choose a spot
For building, and trace a furrow around.
And they make forms of law and magistrates,
And choose a reverend senate. Others here
Are scooping docks; and others still lay down   555
The large foundations of a theatre,
And cut huge columns from the quarried rocks,
The lofty ornaments for future scenes.
As in the early summer when the bees
Toil in the sunshine through the flowery fields,   560
And lead their full-grown offspring from their hives;
Or pack their liquid honey into cells,
Distending them with sweet nectar; or take
The loads of those that come; or forming lines,
Expel the lazy drones; the work grows warm,   565
And all the honey smells of fragrant thyme.

"O happy ones, whose walls are rising now!"
Æneas says, as on their towers he looks;
Then moving on, surrounded by the cloud,
And, wonderful to tell, amid the throng   570
Mingles, and passes through, unseen by all.

There stood a grove within the city's midst,
Delicious for its shade; where, when they came
First to this place, by waves and tempest tossed,
The Carthaginians dug up from the earth   575
An omen royal Juno had foretold
That they should find, a noble horse's head,
Thus intimating that this race would shine,
Famous in war, and furnished with supplies
For ages. Here the great Sidonian queen   580
Built a temple to Juno,[18] rich in gifts,
And blessed in the presence of the goddess.
A brazen threshold rose above the steps,
With brazen posts connecting, and the hinge
Creaked upon brazen doors. Within this grove   585
A new thing they beheld, which their first fear
Relieved; and here Æneas first began
To hope for safety, with a better trust
In his afflicted state. For while he waits
The coming of the queen, and looks around   590
At every object in the spacious temple,
And wondering about the city's fortune,
And skill and labor of the artisans,
He sees the Trojan battles painted there
In order, and the wars now known to fame   595
Through the whole earth. The Atridæ* there he sees,
And Priam,† and Achilles, foe to both.
Fixed to the spot he stood, and weeping, said:
"What place, Achates, and what land on earth
Is not replete with stories of our woes?   600
See, Priam!—Worthy deeds even here are praised,

---

*Atreidae: Agamemnon and Menelaus, the sons of Atreus.
†King of Troy.

And mortal sufferings move their thoughts and tears.
Banish all fear! This fame some safety brings."
So saying, he on the unreal picture fed
His mind, with heavy sighs, and streaming tears.   605
For now he saw how, battling around Troy,
Here fled the Greeks, and pressed the Trojan youths,
The Phrygians there, and crested Achilles urged
His chariot on. And next, with tears, he saw
The snow-white tents of Rhesus,* which, betrayed   610
By the first sleep, the cruel Diomed
Laid waste with carnage, and into his camp
The fiery coursers turned, before they taste
Of Trojan pasture, or drink the Xanthian wave.†
Here Troilus§ he sees, the unhappy youth   615
Fleeing, his shield lost, in unequal fight
Met by Achilles; now by his horses whirled,
Still to his empty chariot, thrown to earth,
Grasping his reins, he clings; his neck and hair
Are dragged along the earth, and through the dust   620
His pointed spear reversed makes idle tracks.
Meanwhile the Trojan women to the shrine
Of unpropitious Pallas go, with hair
Unbound, bearing the peplus, suppliant all
And sad, and beat their breasts. The goddess still   625
Averts her eyes fixed sternly on the ground.
Three times Achilles round the walls of Troy
Had dragged the lifeless Hector, and his corpse
Was bartering for gold. Æneas here
Groaned from his inmost breast, as he beheld   630
The chariot, spoils, and his friend's corpse itself;
And Priam stretching out his helpless arms.
Also he saw himself, mixed with the chiefs
Of Greece, and the Eastern forces, and the arms
Of swarthy Memnon. Penthesilea‡ next,   635

---

*Thracian ally of Priam, whose horses were carried off by Diomedes.

†Xanthus is a river near Troy; also called Scamander. Together the rivers Simois and Xanthus defined the borders of Troy.

§Son of Priam and Hecuba; defeated by Achilles.

‡An Amazon warrior; fighting on the Trojan side, killed by Achilles.

Raging, led on the Amazonian bands,
With crescent bucklers, eager in the fight;
A golden girdle beneath her naked breast;—
A maiden warrior, daring to contend
With men!

          While thus Æneas wondering views   640
These things, and stands with a bewildered gaze,
Dido the queen in all her loveliness[19]
Has come into the temple, a great band
Of warrior youths attending on her steps.
As on Eurota's banks, or on the tops   645
Of Cynthus, when Diana leads along
Her dancing choirs, a thousand mountain nymphs
Follow and cluster, right and left; but she,
Bearing the quiver on her shoulder, walks
Taller than all the goddesses around;   650
While rapture fills Latona's silent breast:
Such Dido was, as radiantly she stood
Amid the throng, her mind bent on affairs,
And busy with her future sovereignty.
Then in the temple's sacred gates, beneath   655
The vaulted roof, her armèd bands around,
And raised upon a lofty throne, she sat,
To administer the laws and rights to all,
And by division just to equalize
Their tasks, or else determine them by lot—   660
When suddenly Æneas sees approach,
With a great multitude surrounding them,
Antheus, Sergestus, and the strong Cloanthus,
And other Trojans, whom the frowning storm
Had scattered on the sea, or carried off   665
To other coasts. Astonished he stood there,
As did Achates, struck with joy and fear.
Eager, they burned to grasp their comrades' hands;
But the uncertain issue troubled them.
So they refrain, and from their hollow cloud   670
Observe what chance may have befallen their friends;
Upon what shore they left their fleet, and why

They came together; for from every ship
They came, as though selected, and approached
The temple, loudly begging to be heard.   675

When they had entered, and full leave was given
To speak, their eldest, Ilioneus, thus
With tranquil tones began: "O queen, to whom
Jove has given power to found a new city,
And with just rule to curb the haughty tribes,   680
We, miserable Trojans, tossed about
By storms upon the seas, appeal to you.
Defend our galleys from the dreadful flames;
Spare a devout and unoffending race,
And take a nearer view of our affairs.   685
We do not come with swords to desolate
The Libyan homes, or to the shores bear off
The plunder. No such hostile mind is ours;
Nor can we, vanquished, entertain such pride.
There is a place, by Greeks Hesperia called;   690
An ancient land it is, potent in arms,
And rich in fertile soil; by Œnotrian men
Once tilled. Now, their descendants, it is said,
Call it Italia, from their leader's name.
Our course was shaped to here, when suddenly,   695
Stormy Orion rising, on blind shoals
Swept us, the sport of insolent south winds,
And overpowered by the drenching brine,
Across the sea, and over pathless rocks;
We few have floated here now to your shores.   700
But what a race is this—what barbarous land,
Permitting such a custom—to refuse
Its sea-coast's barren hospitalities,
And stir up war on us, forbid to set
Our feet upon the first shore that we see!   705
If you despise the human race, and arms
Of mortal men, yet must you know the gods
Are mindful evermore of right and wrong.
Æneas was our king, than whom no man

More just in piety, or great in war   710
And arms ever lived; whom if the Fates preserve,—
If still he breathes the ethereal air, not yet
A dweller in the cruel shades of death,—
We have no fear that you will ever repent
To have surpassed him in a generous deed.   715
In the Sicilian lands there are fields for us,
And cities; and renowned Acestes* there
Derives his lineage from the Trojan blood.
Allow us just to draw our fleet on shore
Shattered by winds, and from the woods to choose   720
New timbers and new oars, if so we may,
Holding our course to Italy, our friends
And king restored, joyfully yet attain
That land and Latium. But if our chief hope
Is gone,—if you, best father of our race,   725
The Libyan sea engulfs, nor hope remains
Of young Iulus,—we may seek at least
The straits of Sicily, the seats prepared
In King Acestes' realm, from which we came."
Thus pleaded Ilioneus. With one voice   730
The other Trojans murmured their consent.

Then briefly Dido spoke, with downcast eyes:—
"Trojans, dismiss your fears, banish your cares.[20]
Hard experience and my new kingdom's needs
Force me to use such measures, and to guard   735
My boundaries far and wide. But who does not know
Æneas' race, and Troy—her valorous deeds,
Her men, and devastations of her war?
We Carthaginians bear not hearts so dull;
Nor does the Sun his coursers yoke so far   740
From this our Tyrian city. Whether you
Desire, the great Hesperia and Saturnian
Fields or land of Eryx† and the king
Acestes, I will send you safe away,

---

*King of Sicily; son of a river-god and a Trojan woman.

†Mountain in northwestern Sicily, sacred to Venus.

With help from my resources. Or if here   745
On equal terms with us you would remain,
The city which I build is yours. Draw up
Your ships. Trojans and Tyrians from me
Shall no distinction know. And would to heaven
Your king himself, Æneas, here be borne   750
By those same winds; may he come! I to the coasts
Will send sure messengers, and give commands
To search the farthest parts of Libya,
If, wrecked, he wanders in some wood or town."

Their minds excited by these words, long since   755
Æneas and Achates burned to break
Forth from the cloud. But first Achates urged
Æneas thus: "O you of birth divine,
What wish is this that rises in your mind?
All now is safe—our fleet, our friends restored—   760
One only absent, whom with our own eyes
We saw the sea engulf; but all the rest
Accords with what your mother's words foretold."
Scarce had he spoken, when the veiling cloud
Suddenly broke, dissolving into air.   765
There stood Æneas, shining in the light,
With countenance and shoulders like a god.
For she herself, his mother, on her son
Had breathed a glory in his locks, and light
Of radiant youth, and splendor in his eyes.   770
So skill adds beauty to the ivory,
Or gives the silver or the Parian stone
Setting of yellow gold. Then to the queen,
Sudden and unforeseen by all, he said:
"Behold me here before you—him you seek,   775
Trojan Æneas, snatched from Libyan waves!
O you who alone have pitied our woes—
The unutterable sufferings of our Troy!
Who to us, a remnant from the Greeks, long tossed
On sea and land, worn by much disaster,   780
And wanting everything, do give a share

Of city and home; it is not in our power,
O Dido! nor in that of any men
Of Trojan race, scattered about the world,
To give you worthy thanks. If anywhere   785
The gods regard the good; if anywhere
Be justice and a mind within itself
Conscious of rectitude, the gods shall give
Deserved reward to you. What times so blest
As those that bear you? Or what parents boast   790
Such offspring? While the rivers to the sea
Shall run, while mountain shadows move around
Their sides, and while the heavens shall feed the stars,
So long your honor, and your name and praise
Shall last, whatever lands may call me from here."   795
This said, with his right hand he grasps the hand
Of Ilioneus, Serestus with his left—
Then Gyas, and Cloanthus, and the rest.

Dumb with amazement at first sight of him
And his hard lot, Sidonian Dido stood,   800
And thus began: "O you of divine birth,
What destiny pursues you through a course
Of so much peril? On these savage coasts
What power has thrown you? Are you then indeed
Æneas, whom the lovely Venus bore*   805
To Anchises by the Phrygian Simois' wave?
And I indeed recall that Teucer† came
To Sidon, from his native land expelled,
Seeking out a new kingdom, with the help
Of Belus:‡ he, my father, at that time   810
Was devastating Cyprus, which, subdued,
He held; and from that day were known to me
The Trojan city's fortunes, and your name,
And the Pelasgian kings. Your enemy

---

*As told most clearly in the *Homeric Hymns*, Aeneas was the product of Venus' affair with the mortal Anchises.

†King of Troy, whose daughter married Dardanus.

‡King of Tyre; father of Dido.

Himself the Trojan nation loudly praised,   815
And deemed himself descended from their line.
Come then, O warriors, enter our abodes!
I also from calamities like yours
Have suffered much, till here I set my feet.
Not ignorant of trouble, I have learned   820
To care for the distressed."

                                As thus she spoke,
She leads Æneas to the royal courts;
And in the temples of the gods, commands
A sacrifice. Meanwhile, with no less care,
Down to the seashore twenty bulls she sends,   825
A hundred bristly backs of full-grown swine,
And of fat lambs a hundred, with their dams.
Such were her gifts, designed for joyous feasts.
But all the interior palace is arranged
With splendor and with regal luxury,   830
And banquets are prepared, and draperies
Of purple dye, elaborately wrought;
And on the tables massive silver shines,
And records of ancestral deeds, engraved
In gold, in a long series of events   835
Traced step by step from ancient lineage down.

Æneas—for a father's love forbade
His mind repose—the swift Achates sends
Back to the ships, to bear to Ascanius
The tidings, and to lead him to the city.   840
In his Ascanius centers all his care.
Gifts too, that from the wreck of Troy were snatched,
He orders him to bring; a mantle stiff
With figures and with gold; also a veil
With saffron-hued acanthus embroidered round;—   845
The Grecian Helen's* ornaments,[21] the rare
And wondrous gifts her mother Leda gave,
And which her daughter from Mycenæ brought

---

*Daughter of Leda and Zeus; wife of Menelaus; her abduction by the Trojan Paris initiated the war at Troy.

To Troy, seeking illicit marriage rites.
Also the scepter Ilione once had borne,   850
Eldest of Priam's daughters;—and with these
A beaded necklace, and a diadem
Double with gems and gold. Hastening for these,
Achates to the ships pursued his way.
But Cytherea in her breast revolves   855
New arts and new designs; that Cupid, changed
In face and form, may pass for Ascanius,
Enflame with gifts the ardent queen, and send
The fire of love through all her glowing limbs.
She fears the dubious faith and double tongues   860
Of Tyrians. Fierce Juno vexes her;
And with the night her troubled thoughts return.
Then to the wingèd god of love she speaks:
"O son, who are my strength, my mighty power;[22]
Son, who alone does despise the dread   865
Typhœan bolts of the great father; to you
I fly, and, suppliant, demand your aid.
How by fell Juno's hate, on every coast
Your brother Æneas is driven about the seas,
You know well, and often sorrow for our grief.   870
The Phœnician Dido with sweet words
Detains him; I have fears how it may fare
With these Junonian hospitalities.
At such a turning point in these affairs
She will not pause. Therefore I meditate   875
How I beforehand may possess this queen,
And gird her round with flames, lest she should change
By influence of any deity,
But side with me in the great love she bears
To Æneas. In what way you can do this,—   880
Now listen to my scheme. The princely boy
(This is my cherished plan) prepares to go
To Carthage, at the summons of his sire,
With gifts from seas and rescued from the flames
Of Troy. Him, having lulled in deepest sleep,   885
I shall conceal on high Cythera's top,

Or on Idalium,* my sacred seat,
Lest he should know our wiles, or thwart our schemes.
Do you with guileful art assume his face
Not longer than one night, and, boy yourself,   890
Put on the well-known features of the boy.
And when the joyous Dido takes you up
Upon her lap, amid the royal feast,
When the Lyæan wine is foaming high;
When she embraces you with kisses soft,—   895
Then breathe into her heart your hidden fire,
Beguiling her with poison." Love obeys
The charge of his dear mother, doffs his wings,
And, smiling, imitates Iulus' gait.
But Venus with a placid sleep enfolds   900
Ascanius' limbs, and fondly taking him
Upon her bosom, bears him far away
To the high Idalian groves, where breathing soft,
Sweet marjoram beds with perfume and with shade
Embrace him sleeping. And now Cupid went,   905
Obeying her request, the royal gifts
Conveying to the Tyrians, and led on,
Well pleased to have Achates for his guide.
When he arrived, upon a golden couch
With sumptuous tapestry, the queen reclined   910
In state within the middle of the hall.

And now Æneas, now the Trojan youths
Assemble, and lie on purple couches.
Then the servants bring water for their hands,
And bread from baskets, and around supply   915
Towels with nap well shorn. Within are seen
Fifty maid-servants, who in long array
Attend the hearths, and with burnt sacrifice
Enlarge the influence of the household gods;
A hundred others too, of equal age,   920
Who serve the dishes, and who fill the cups.

---

*Cythera (an island in the Peloponnese where Venus was born) and Idalium (a city on Cyprus)
were locations sacred to the goddess Venus.

And crowds of Tyrians also come, and throng
The festive rooms, invited to recline
Upon the embroidered couches. Much they admire
The gifts Æneas brought; Iulus too,   925
The glowing beauty of the godlike face,
And simulated speech; the cloak, the veil
With saffron-hued acanthus embroidered round.
But the Phœnician queen, dedicated
To passion fraught with coming misery,   930
With soul insatiate burns, and gazes long,
Moved by the boy and by his gifts alike.
He, having hung about Æneas' neck,
Locked in a fond embrace, and the deep love
Of his false father satisfied, then seeks   935
The queen; she with her eyes and all her heart
Clings to him, fondles him upon her lap;—
Nor knows, unhappy one, how great the god
Who presses on her breast. He, mindful of
His Acidalian mother, by degrees   940
Begins to abolish all the memory
Of her Sychæus,* and with living love
Preoccupy the mind long since unmoved,
And unaccustomed motions of her heart.

When in the feast there came a pause, the plates   945
Removed, large bowls are set, the wines are crowned;
The rooms are filled with noise; the spacious halls
Resound with voices. From the ceilings high
Overlaid with gold, hang lighted lamps, and night
Is vanquished by the torches' blaze. And now   950
The queen demands a bowl heavy with gems
And gold, and fills it high with unmixed wine,
As Belus did, and his descendants all.
Then silence hushed the rooms, while thus the queen:—
"O Jove,—for you, it's said, do give the laws   955
Of guests and hosts alike,—be it your will,

---

*Dido's first husband; killed by her brother, Pygmalion, to obtain his treasure.

That this may be a joyful day to all,
Tyrians and Trojans, in remembrance held
By our descendants. Bacchus, giver of joy,
Be present; and, propitious Juno, smile!   960
And you, O Tyrians, favoring, celebrate
The meeting!" With these words she poured upon
The table a libation of the wine;
And what was left touched lightly to her lips,
And, with a bantering tone, to Bitias gave.   965
He, not unwilling, drained the foaming bowl,
And from the full gold drenched himself with wine.
Then followed other guests of lordly rank.
Long-haired Iopas with his golden lyre
Pours out with ringing voice what Atlas taught.   970
He sings the wandering moon, and of the sun
The laboring eclipses; and of men,
And cattle, and of showers, and fires of heaven;
Arcturus, and the rainy Hyades;
And the two constellations of the Bears;   975
And why the winter suns make haste to dip
In ocean, and what causes the delay
Of slowly moving nights. The Tyrians shout,
Redoubling their applause; the Trojans join.

Thus did the unlucky queen prolong the night[23]   980
With varied converse, drinking in the while
Long draughts of love: and asked much of Priam
And much of Hector; how equipped in arms
Aurora's son had come; how looked the steeds
Of Diomed; how large Achilles stood.   985
"Come now, my guest," she said; "and from the first
Relate to us the Grecian stratagems,
And all your people's sad mishaps, and all
Your voyages; for now the seventh year
Bears you still wandering over land and sea."   990

BOOK 2

ALL sat silent, with looks intent; when thus
Æneas from his lofty couch began.[1]

O queen, you do command me to renew
A grief unutterable;[2] how the Greeks
Overturned the power and lamentable realm   5
Of Troy: the afflicting scenes that I myself
Beheld, and a great part of which I was.
Who of the Myrmidons or Dolopes,*
Or of the hard Ulysses'† soldiery,
Can, speaking of such things, refrain from tears?   10
Now too the humid night from heaven descends,
And all the sinking stars persuade to sleep.
Still, if there be such earnest wish to hear
Our sad disasters, and in brief to know
The last expiring sufferings of Troy,   15
Though my soul shudders at the memory,
And in its grief shrinks back, I will begin.
Broken by war, and baffled by the fates
Through such a lapse of years, the Grecian chiefs
Construct a horse,[3] by Pallas' art divine,   20
Huge as a mountain, and enlaced and ribbed
With beams of fir. This they pretend to be
A votive offering for their safe return.
So went the rumor. But they secretly,
To its blind sides conveyed a chosen band,   25
Of warriors, and so filled the vast caverns
Of the dark womb with armèd soldiery.

---

*The Myrmidons were followers of Achilles; the Dolopes, or Dolopians, were people of Thessaly, allied with the Greeks during the war.

†Odysseus: Greek hero of Homer's epic *Odyssey*; son of Laertes and husband of Penelope.

The isle of Tenedos lies full in sight,
Well known to fame and in resources rich
While Priam's empire stood; but now it holds   30
Merely a bay, a faithless port for ships.
And here our foes upon the desert coast
Conceal themselves, while we suppose them gone,
Returning to Mycenæ with the wind.
Therefore all Troy her long grief throws aside;   35
The gates stand open; and we go to see
With joy the Doric camps, the abandoned posts,
And the deserted shore. The Dolopes
Were here, and here the fierce Achilles camped;
Here lay their fleet; and here were battles fought.   40
Some at the virgin Pallas' fatal gift
Stare astonished, and the huge horse's size
Admire. And first Thymœtes gives advice
To carry it within the city's walls,
And place it in the citadel, thus moved   45
By treacherous design; or else the fates
Of Troy so ordered it. But Capys urged
(With those who stood in wisest opinion)
That we should either throw into the sea
The Greeks' insidious snare and suspect gift,   50
And burn it, setting fire beneath; or else
Bore through it, and explore its secret caves.
So the uncertain crowd divided stood
With conflicting views.[4]
                            First, in front of all,
Attended by a numerous throng of men,   55
Laocoön* from the citadel runs down,
Impetuously, and from a distance cries:
"O wretched men! What madness, citizens,
Is this? Do you believe then that our foes are gone?
Do you suppose that any Grecian gifts   60
Are lacking in deceit? Or is it thus
Ulysses has been known? Either the Greeks
Within this wooden fabric are concealed,

---

*Trojan priest of Neptune.

Or it is framed to bear against our walls,
And overlook our houses, and descend   65
Upon our city; or some other guile
Is lurking. Trojans, do not trust this horse.
Whatever it may be, I fear the Greeks,
Even when they bring us gifts." As thus he spoke,
With all his strength he hurled a mighty spear   70
Against its side and belly rounded firm
With jointed timbers. Quivering beneath the blow
It stood, and all the caverns of its womb
Resounded with a roar. And if the divine
Fates had favored, and a serious mind been ours,   75
He would have then impelled us to destroy
The hiding-places of the Greeks with arms;
And Troy would now be standing, and you saved,
O lofty citadel of Priam!
                    Lo,
Meanwhile the Trojan shepherds with loud cries   80
Dragged to the king a young man tightly bound[5]
With hands behind his back, who, quite unknown
To them, surrendered of his own accord;
(With the design to open to the Greeks
The gates of Troy, and, resolute of will,   85
Either to use deceit, or encounter death.)
Eager to see, the Trojan youths then rush,
In a tumultuous throng, from every quarter
And vie in insults on the captive. Now
Hear what the treachery of the Grecians was,   90
And from one crime learn all. For while he stood,
Troubled, defenseless, in the sight of all,
And gazed around upon the Trojan bands;
He said, "Alas, what land now, or what sea
Can harbor me? Or what remains for me,   95
Unhappy wretch, for whom there is no place
Among the Greeks, and upon whom besides
The vengeful Trojans seek a bloody death!"
At this lamenting groan our minds are changed,
And every violent impulse checked at once.   100

We ask him then to tell us of what race
He comes, and what he has to say; how far
We may put faith in him, a captive. He,
Fear at length laid aside, addressed us thus:—

"To you, O king, whatever the result   105
May be, I will confess the entire truth;
Nor shall I deny that I'm by birth a Greek.
This first. For if Sinon has been made wretched
By fortune hard, not therefore was he made
Faithless and false. In conversation you   110
Perhaps have heard the name and famous deeds
Of Palamedes, of the line of Belus;
Whom, innocent, accused of treachery,
And by false witnesses, the Greeks condemned
To death, because he had opposed the war.   115
But now they mourn for him, his life being gone.
My father, who was poor, and near of kin,
Sent me as his companion to the war
To attend him, from the earliest years of youth.
As long as he stood firm in princely power,   120
And flourished in the councils of the kings,
I, too, somewhat of name and honor bore.
But afterwards—I speak of things well known—
When by the plausible Ulysses' hate,
He from these upper realms of earth went down,   125
In gloom and grief I dragged my life along,
Afflicted and indignant at the fate
Of him, my guiltless friend. Nor did I hold
My peace, fool that I was, but vowed revenge,
If chance in any way should favor me,   130
And to my native Argos I should ever
Return victorious; and with words I stirred
Fierce hatred. Here came ruin's first plague-spot.
For from this time, with new accusations
Ulysses ever sought to frighten me,   135
And spread ambiguous rumors through the crowd;
And, conscious of his guilt, sought armed defense.

Nor did he rest, until by Calchas' means—
But why should I recall these painful themes
In vain? Or why detain you, if you deem   140
That all the Greeks are fashioned in one mold,
And to hear this is proof enough for you?
Now then at once inflict your punishment.
Ulysses wishes this, and Atreus' sons*
Will well reward it."

                    We then eagerly,   145
With many questions, seek to know the grounds
Of his assertions, unaware of all
His villainy and Grecian artifice.
He went on tremblingly, with words of guile:—
"The Greeks sought often to contrive their flight,   150
And, weary of long war, abandon Troy.
Would that they had! Often did the tempest rough
Upon the sea prevent, and southern winds
Deter them going; and especially
When now this horse stood there, with wooden beams   155
Constructed—then through all the sky the clouds
Pealed with their thunder. In suspense, we sent
Eurypylus to consult the oracle
Of Phœbus; he brought from its recesses
These sad words for answer: 'O Greeks, when first   160
You came unto these shores, you pacified
The winds with blood and with a virgin slain.
Even so through blood must your return be sought,
Propitiating heaven with Grecian life.'
When to the people's ears this answer came,   165
All were struck dumb, and through our limbs there ran
A cold tremor, thinking to whom this thing
Might come, and who Apollo might demand.
Ulysses then drags forth into the midst,
With loud uproar, Calchas the priest, and asks   170
What in such case the deities might want.
And many persons now presaged to me

---

*The Greeks Agamemnon and Menelaus.

This artful schemer's cruel wickedness,
And quietly foresaw the event to come.
The priest for ten days held his peace, and still   175
Refused, dissembling, to name any one
As doomed to death. At length reluctantly
Driven by the clamors of the Ithacan,
He breaks his silence, and, as was agreed,
He destines me to the altar. All assent.   180
And what each one was fearing for himself,
Turned to the ruin of one wretched man,
They patiently endure. And now had come
The dreadful day, the sacred rites prepared,
The salted meal, the fillets round my brows—   185
I broke away from death; I snapped my chains;
And in a miry swamp I lay all night
Hidden, and screened from view by long marsh grass,
Till they should spread (if so perhaps they should)
Their sails unto the wind. But now for me   190
There is no hope to see my native land,
Not my sweet children, nor my father dear,
Whom they will yet, perhaps, for my escape,
Demand for punishment, and this offence
Of mine will expiate by the death of those   195
Unhappy ones. Therefore I do entreat you,
By the supernal powers, and deities
Conscious of truth,—by unviolated faith,—
If there be such still remaining with man—
Pity these woes of mine—pity a soul   200
Deserving not such sufferings as these."

Moved by his tears, we granted him his life,
And freely pitied him. Priam himself
First of all gave commands to take away
His fetters, and remove the knotted cords,   205
And said in friendly tones: "Whoever you are,
Henceforth forget the Greeks whom you have lost;
Be one of us; and truly tell the things
That I shall ask of you. With what design

Have they constructed this gigantic horse?   210
Who's its inventor? What do they intend?
Is it religious in its aim, or is it
An engine framed for war?" He spoke. The man,
Skilled in deceit and Grecian artifice,
Raised his unfettered hands toward the stars,   215
"Witness," he cried, "eternal fires of heaven,
In your inviolable divinity!
And you, oh altars, and oh dreadful knives,—
You sacred fillets I, a victim, wore—
Be it right for me to break the hallowed ties   220
That bound me to the Greeks!—Be it right for me
To hate these men, and bring their crimes to light,
If any they conceal! Nor am I now
Bound by my country's laws. Only do you
Remain true to your promise, and, Troy saved   225
Keep faith with me, if I disclose the truth,
And largely pay you back what you have done.
The whole hope of the Greeks, and confidence
In the war commenced, stood always with the aid
Of Pallas. From the time when Diomed   230
With impious hand, and the author of these crimes,
Ulysses,—for it was they who did the deed,—
Having determined to remove by force
Her fatal image, the Palladium,*
Out from the hallowed temple—having slain   235
The guardians of the lofty citadel,
They snatched away the sacred effigy,
And with their bloody hands presumed to touch
The virgin fillets of the goddess—then,
Even from that time, the Greeks began to lose   240
Their hopes, which, slipping backward, flowed away,—
Their strength all broken, and the deity
Averse. Nor did Tritonia† indicate
These things by doubtful prodigies; for scarce
Had they deposited within their camp   245

---

*Sacred image of Pallas Minerva, stolen by Ulysses and Diomedes.

†Another name for Minerva.

The image, when from her wide-open eyes
Flashed gleaming flames, and through her limbs salt sweat
Exuded; and three times from off the ground—
Wonderful to relate!—she leapt, with shield
And quivering spear. Calchas* forthwith announced   250
That we should seek the sea in flight; nor could
The Grecian forces conquer Troy, unless
At Argos they renewed the auspices,
And brought the goddess back, now borne away
By them, in their curved ships, across the sea.   255
And now that to Mycenæ they are bound,
Arms they prepare to bring and guardian gods;
And, the sea crossed again, will soon be here.
Thus Calchas read the omens; and so warned,
They built in place of the Palladium   260
And of the violated deity,
This image, to atone for their foul crime.
It was Calchas who commanded them to raise
This enormous mass, with strong timbers laced,
And build it of a towering height, too large   265
To be received into your city's gates,
And so protect you with the ancient faith.
For if your hands should ever violate
Minerva's offering, immense ruin would come
(Which omen may the gods first turn upon   270
The seer himself!) to Priam's realm, and all
The Phrygians; but if by your hands this horse
Should mount into your city, Asia then,
Unchallenged, would advance to Pelops' walls
In mighty war, and our posterity   275
Experience these fates."

                    With treachery
Like this, and artful perjury, the tale
Of the false Sinon was believed by us—
Caught by his wiles, and by the tears he forced—
Whom neither Diomed, nor Larissa's chief,   280

---

*Seer who accompanied the Greeks to Troy.

Achilles, nor ten years, nor a thousand ships
Could conquer.
         Here another dire event[6]
More dreadful far befalls, disturbing us,
Wretched and unprepared, with gloomy thoughts.
Laocoön, chosen Neptune's priest by lot,   285
Was sacrificing at the solemn altars there
A huge bull, when behold, two snakes—
I shudder as I tell—from Tenedos
Come gliding on the deep, with rings immense,
Pressing upon the sea, and side by side   290
Toward the shore they move with necks erect
And bloody crests that tower above the waves;
Their other parts sweeping the sea behind,
With huge backs winding on in sinuous folds.
A noise of foaming brine is heard. And now   295
They reach the shores, their burning eyes suffused
With blood and fire, and lick their hissing mouths
With quivering tongues. We, pale with terror, fly.
But they seek Laocoön with steady pace.
First the two bodies of his little sons   300
Each serpent twines about, with tightening folds,
And bites into their miserable limbs.
Then him, as he with help and weapons comes,
They seize, and bind him in their mighty spires;
Twice round the middle, twice around his neck,   305
Twisting, with scaly backs, they raise on high
Their heads and lofty necks. He with his hands
Strains to untwine the knots, his fillets wet
With gore and poison black. His dreadful shrieks
Rise to the stars—such groans as when a bull   310
Flies from the altar wounded, and shakes free
His forehead from the ill-aimed axe. But they,
The dragons, slip away to the lofty shrine
And citadel of cruel Pallas. There,
Beneath the goddess' feet and orbèd shield,   315
They hide. Then indeed a new fear creeps
Into the trembling hearts of all. They said

Laocoön paid the penalty deserved
Of crime for having with his steel profaned
The sacred wood, when he had hurled his spear   320
Against the horse. And now all cry aloud
To take the image to its rightful seat,
And supplicate the goddess. We divide
The walls, and lay the battlements open.
All prepare for the work. Beneath the feet   325
We lay smooth rollers, and around the neck
Strain hempen ropes. The terrible machine
Passes the walls, filled full with armèd men.
Around, the youths and the unwedded maids
Sing sacred songs, rejoicing when they touch   330
Their hands against the ropes. Onward it moves,
And threatening glides into the city's midst.
Alas, my country! Ilium, home of gods!
Dardanian battlements renowned in war!
Four times, even at the threshold of the gate,   335
It stopped: four times we heard the noise of arms
Ring from the depths within. Yet on we press,
Thoughtless of omens, blind with furious zeal,
And in the sacred citadel we lodge
The fatal monster. And now Cassandra* parts   340
Her lips—that by the deity's command
Should never be believed by Trojan ears—
And prophesies to us our future fates.
We, miserable, for whom this day
Was doomed to be our last, hang on our shrines,   345
Throughout the city, wreaths of festive leaves.
Meanwhile, with changing sky night comes apace
Upon the ocean, wrapping with wide shade
Earth, sky, and crafty wiles of Myrmidons.
The Trojans, scattered through the town, are still,   350
For sleep embraces every weary frame.

---

*Daughter of Priam. Apollo loved Cassandra; when she refused him, his curse kept the truth she told from being believed.

And now the Grecian hosts were moving on
From Tenedos, their ships in order ranged,
Beneath the friendly silence of the moon,
Toward the well-known shores, soon as appeared 355
The blazing signal from the royal ship.
Defended by the adverse deities,
Sinon unbars the wooden prison doors,
And secretly lets loose the hidden Greeks.
The horse stands open wide, and to the air 360
Restores them. They leap from the hollow wood
Joyful—Tisandrus, Sthenelus, their chiefs,
And fierce Ulysses, sliding down a rope.
And with them Acamas and Thoas come,
And Peleus' offspring, Neoptolemus,* 365
Machaon leading; Menelaus too,
And even Epeus, inventor of the fraud.
They invade the city sunk in sleep and wine.
The guards are slain; they receive their comrades
With opened gates, and join the expectant bands. 370

It was the hour when first their sleep begins[7]
For wretched mortals, and most gratefully
Creeps over them, by bounty of the gods.
Then in my dreams, behold, Hector appeared,
Distinctly present; he was very sad, 375
And weeping floods of tears. So once he looked,
Dragged by the chariot wheels, and black with dust
And blood, his swollen feet pierced through with thongs.
Ah me, that face! How changed he was from him,
The Hector who returned clothed in the spoils 380
Won from Achilles, or when he had hurled
The Phrygian fires against the Grecian ships!
But now he wore a squalid beard, and hair
Matted with blood, and the wounds he took when dragged
Around the city's walls. Weeping myself, 385
I seemed to address him of my own accord,

---

*Achilles' son, also known as Pyrrhus.

And to draw out these melancholy words:—
"O light of Troy! the Trojans' surest hope!
Why have you stayed so long? And from what shores,
O long-expected Hector, do you come?   390
That now again, after so many deaths
Borne among your countrymen, and sufferings
So varied, we, exhausted with the war,
Behold you here? What undeservèd cause
Distorts your serene face? And why these wounds?"   395
But he made no reply, and took no heed
Of idle questions, but with a heavy groan
Fetched from the bottom of his breast:—"Ah, fly,
Oh goddess-born," he said, "fly from these flames!
The enemy holds the walls. Troy rushes down   400
From her high pinnacle. Enough is done
For Priam and our country. If right hand
Could have defended Troy, mine it would have been
That so defended. Troy to you commends
Her sacred rites and household gods. These take,   405
Companions of your fates. With these go seek
The mighty city you one day shall found
At last, after your wanderings over the sea."
He spoke; and from their secret inner crypts
Brought great Vesta's* fillets and her statue,   410
And the undying fire from out her shrines.

Meanwhile, with many a lamentable cry
The city is confused. And more and more,
Although my sire Anchises' house stood far
Away, hid and secluded amid the trees,   415
The noise grew loud, and all the horrible clang
Of arms increased. Starting from sleep, I gain
With swift ascent the house-top's loftiest verge,
And stand and listen with erected ears.
As when the flames are raging through the corn,   420
Driven by the furious winds; or a mountain stream,

---

*Vesta is the goddess of the hearth.

Swollen to a rapid torrent, floods the fields,
And desolates the smiling crops and all
The labors of the oxen, and drags down
The forests; and the unconscious shepherd stands   425
Listening upon the peak of some high rock,
Bewildered by the rushing noise below.
Then in truth the false faith of the Greeks
Is manifest, their treacherous arts revealed.
Down falls the palace of Deiphobus   430
Amid the conquering flames; Ucalegon
Next burns. The broad Sigean waves reflect
The fiery glow. And shouts of men are heard,
And blare of trumpets. Wildly I seize my arms—
Although for arms there seemed but little use.   435
But still I burned to gather a small band,
And with my comrades to the citadel
Rush on; for rage and fury hurried me.
A glorious thing it seemed to me to die
In arms.

       But now, behold, Panthus, escaped   440
From Grecian spears,—Panthus Othryades,
Priest of Apollo in the citadel,
Comes hurrying by, and bearing in his hands
The sacred vessels and the vanquished gods;
He leads his little grandson by the hand,   445
And wildly to my threshold bends his steps.
"What fortune, Panthus? On what citadel
Do we now seize?" I scarce had said the words,
When, groaning deeply, he this answer made:—
"Our last day comes,—the inevitable hour   450
Of Troy. We are Trojans no more. Gone now
Is Troy, and all our glory! Cruel Jove
Now transfers the imperial rule to Argos.
Over all the burning town the Greeks hold sway.
The towering horse stands in the city's midst,   455
And pours out armèd men. Sinon himself,
Exulting, spreads the flames. And others throng
The open gates; as many thousands come

As ever from mighty Greece. Others oppose
Our ranks, and barricade the narrow streets.   460
The gleaming swords are drawn, for death's dread work
Prepared. The foremost wardens of the gates
Scarce risk a contest, with blind resistance."
Fired by his words and by a power divine,
Through flames and arms I am borne along, wherever   465
The sad Erinyes* points, wherever the din
Of battle and the ascending clamor calls.
Rhipeus then, and Epytus, in arms
Excelling, join us, by the moonlight seen;
And Hypanis and Dymas on our side   470
Gather, and young Corœbus, Mygdon's son.
He in those latter days had come to Troy,
Wooing Cassandra with delirious love,
Hoping to bring a future son-in-law
To Priam, and bear assistance to him   475
And to the Trojans; but who, luckless youth,
Did not regard the warnings of his bride
Inspired. When I saw them in order ranged,
Ready for battle, thus I spoke to them:—
"O warriors, gallant hearts, who dare in vain!   480
If yours the strong desire to follow me
Venturing extremest things,—you see how stands
The fortune of affairs; for all the gods
Have gone from us, by whom our empire stood,
Their secret places and their altars left.   485
You help a burning city. Let us die,
And plunge into the middle of the fight.
The only safety of the vanquished is
To hope for none." Thus were the warriors' hearts
Kindled with added rage. As ravenous wolves   490
In cloudy darkness driven by fierce hunger,
Leaving their whelps behind, with dry throats seek
Their prey; so through the javelins and the foes
We rush to no uncertain death, and hold

---

*A name for any of the Furies.

Our way into the city's midst. Black night   495
Hovers around us with her hollow shade.
Who can describe the carnage of that night?
Down falls the ancient city, having ruled
So many years; and everywhere struck down
Lay many an unresisting corpse along   500
The streets, and through the houses, and beside
The sacred thresholds of the deities.
Not only do the Trojans suffer death.
Courage returns even to our vanquished hearts,
And in their turn the conquering Greeks are slain.   505
And everywhere are sounds of bitter grief,
And terror everywhere, and shapes of death.

And first, attended by a numerous band
Of Greeks, Androgeus meets us,[8] thinking we
Are on his side, and thus with friendly words   510
Salutes us: "Hasten, men! What sluggishness
Is this? While others plunder blazing Troy,
Are you just coming from our ships?" He spoke;
And all at once—for we made no answer
Which he could trust—he saw that he had fallen   515
Among his foes. Dumb with astonishment,
His footsteps and his voice he alike repressed.
As when a man who walks through tangled paths
Treads on a hidden snake, and trembling flies
Back from the reptile lifting up its head   520
In anger and its blue and swelling neck;
Even so Androgeus, starting, backward shrinks.
Forward we rush, and pour around, and charge
In dense array upon them, ignorant
Of all the ground, and overcome by fear,   525
And strike them down. At this first work achieved,
The breath of fortune favors us. But here
Corœbus, all exultant with success
And courage, cries: "O comrades, where so soon
Fortune the way of safety points, and where   530
She shows herself propitious, let us follow.

Let us change shields, and wear upon ourselves
The Grecian badges. Whether we make use
Of stratagem or valor, who inquires,
In dealing with an enemy? They themselves   535
Supply these arms." And having said these words,
He donned the long-haired helmet and the shield
Wondrous for beauty that Androgeus wore;
And at his side he hung the Grecian sword.
So likewise did Rhipeus, Dymas too,   540
And all the youths, quite smartly; every one
Arming himself with recent spoils. And so,
Mixed with the Greeks we go, under auspices
Not ours; and meeting with the foe, we engage
In many battles through the dark blind night,   545
And to the lower world send many a Greek.
Some to their ships escape, and trusty shores;
And others scale again the lofty horse,
Smitten with base fear. Alas, one ought
To trust in nothing, when the gods oppose.   550
But Priam's virgin daughter, borne along,
Cassandra, with her hair unbound, and dragged
From Pallas' temple, and her inmost shrines,
Raises her burning eyes in vain to heaven:
Her eyes, for they have bound her tender hands.   555
This sight Corœbus could not bear, but, wild
And maddened, throws himself, resolved to die,
Into the middle of the hostile band.
We all follow, and charge in close array.
Here from the temple's lofty roof at first   560
We are overpowered by weapons of our men;
And dreadful slaughter follows the mistake
Caused by our armor and our Grecian crests.
Also the Greeks, groaning with rage to see
The virgin snatched away, from all sides throng   565
To attack us—terrible Ajax, the two sons
Of Atreus, and the Dolopes with all
Their army. As when opposing winds conflict
In rushing hurricane, Zephyrus, Notus rush,

And Eurus, jubilant with his Eastern steeds,— 570
The forests groan, and foaming Nereus raves,
And with his trident lashes all the sea
From lowest depths; so they—whom in the dark
We by our stratagems had put to flight,
And driven through all the town—appear. They first 575
Our shields and our false weapons recognize;
And next they note our difference of speech.
At once we are overwhelmed—Corœbus first,
By Peneleus' hand laid low, before
The altar of the warrior goddess; next 580
Rhipeus, of all Trojans most upright
And just—such was the pleasure of the gods!
And Hypanis and Dymas die, pierced through
By their own friends; nor thee, O Panthus, did
Your piety nor sacred mitre shield 585
From death. O Trojan ashes, and you last
Expiring flames of my own countrymen!
Witness that when you fell, I neither shunned
The weapons of the Greeks, nor any risks
Of conflict; and if fate had so decreed 590
That I had fallen, I should have merited
My doom, for what I did! From there we are forced
Away and scattered. Iphitus with me
And Pelias remain; but Iphitus
Enfeebled by his age, and Pelias 595
Retarded by a wound Ulysses dealt.
Far off, we are summoned by the clamorous cries
To Priam's palace. Here a battle raged
So fierce, it seemed as if no other war
Were waged, nor through the city any deaths 600
Were known elsewhere; so furious a fight
We see—the Greeks rushing against the palace—
The threshold besieged by a roof of shields,
The scaling ladders clinging to the walls.
Beneath the very portals they ascend 605
Upon the steps; with their left hands oppose
Their shields against the missiles from above,

While with their right they grasp the battlements.
On the other hand the Trojans, tearing up
The turrets and the roofs, with these prepare   610
A last defense, since now they see that death
Is imminent. The gilded rafters down
They roll, and all the lofty ornaments
Of ancient sires; while others with drawn swords
Block up and guard the doors, in close phalanx.   615
Courage restored, we hasten to defend
The palace of the king, and by our aid
Relieve with added strength our men overpowered.

There was an entrance and a private door
Giving free passage between Priam's walls,[9]—   620
A postern gate, that stood neglected there,
Through which often the sad Andromache*
Was used to go, when she her husband's sire
And mother visited, and led along
With her her boy Astyanax.† Through this   625
I gain the summit of the roof, from which
The wretched Trojans hurled their useless shafts.
Here a steep turret rising from the roof,
And towering in the starlight, from which all Troy
Was seen, and all the well-known Grecian ships   630
And the Achaian camps,—around its walls
We work with iron implements, just where
The highest flooring offers loosening joints,
And wrench it from its ancient base, and push,
Till, slipping suddenly, with thundering crash   635
And ruin dragged downward, upon the bands
Of Greeks it falls, with desolation wide.
But others come beneath. Nor do we cease
To hurl down stones and missiles of all sorts.
And now before the vestibule itself,   640
And at the outer door, Pyrrhus exults,
Flashing with weapons and the brazen light

---

*Hector's wife.

†Hector's son.

Of armor. So in the sun a serpent gleams,
Which having fed on noxious herbs, and lain
Swollen in the earth, protected by the frost,   645
Now casting off its slough and bright with youth
Lifts up its head, and rolls with slippery back
Toward the sun, with quivering three-forked tongue.
With him huge Periphas, and Automedon
His armor-bearer, of Achilles' steeds   650
Once charioteer; and all the Scyran youth
Throng to the palace, hurling their brands
To the roof. Pyrrhus himself, among the first,
Seizing an axe, breaks through the stubborn door,
And tears the brazen pillars from the hinge;   655
And cutting through the panels and the beams,
Hollows an opening like a large window;
And all the inner house is seen, and all
The extended halls laid bare, and inmost rooms
Of Priam and the ancient kings; and there   660
Armed men are standing at the very door.

But all the interior rooms with sounds confused
Of groans and dreadful tumult rang. Within,
The hollow halls resounded with the shrieks
Of women; and the wailing seemed to strike   665
The golden stars. Then through the wide palace
Went wandering trembling matrons, while they clasped
And kissed the door-posts. With his father's strength
Pyrrhus comes pressing on. No bars avail,
Nor guards, against him. With his battering-ram   670
The trembling doors give way by frequent blows,
And from the hinges jarred, down fall the posts.
A breach is made. In rush the Greeks, and slay
The first they meet; and all the halls are filled
With soldiery. So a foaming river bursts   675
Away from its embankments, sweeping down
With turbulent vortex the opposing mounds,
And raging through the fields, drags down the herds
With all their stalls. With my own eyes I saw,

Furious for slaughter, Neoptolemus   680
And the two Atridæ before the gate.
And Hecuba I saw, and the hundred wives
Wed to her sons; and Priam, soiled with blood,
Before the altars he himself had blessed.
Also those fifty nuptial chambers, hope   685
Of future offspring; and the pillars rich
With spoils and with barbaric gold, overthrown.
And the Greeks held whatever the flames had spared.

Perhaps you will inquire of Priam's fate.
Soon as he saw the captured city's doom,   690
His palace gates torn down, the enemy
Within his inmost rooms, the aged king
Puts on his armor long disused, in vain
Casing his trembling limbs; his useless sword
Bound at his side; and goes to meet his foes,   695
Resolved to die. Within the palace court,
Beneath the bare sky stood a large altar,
Near which an ancient laurel overhung
And sheltered the Penates with its shade.
Here, round about the altars, Hecuba*   700
Sat with her daughters, like a flock of doves
Driven swift to earth by a dark tempest—
Crowding together, all in vain—and held
In their embrace the statues of their gods.
But when she saw Priam himself arrayed   705
In youthful arms, "What dire intent," she said,
"Unhappy husband, bids you take these arms?
And where now do you rush? No help like this,
Nor such defenders does the time require.
Even were my Hector here, he'd do no good.   710
Yield now to me; come here; for here,
This altar will protect us all, or else
We all will die together!" Saying this,
She drew the aged monarch to herself,
And placed him there upon the sacred seat.   715

---

*Wife of Priam.

But lo! escaped from Pyrrhus' murderous hand,
Polites, one of Priam's sons, has fled
Through the long galleries, past the spears and foes,
And, wounded, traverses the empty halls.
Pyrrhus pressing him, in hot haste pursues   720
With deadly weapon; now, even now his hand
Holds him within his grasp, and with his spear
Presses upon him, till he comes before
His parents' eyes, then falls, and bleeding fast,
Pours out his life. But Priam now, although   725
An instant death impends, did not refrain,
Nor did he spare his voice or anger. "May the gods,"
He cries, "if there be justice in the heavens
That cares for such things, make you fit return
And deal you your deserts, for this your foul   730
And daring crime,—you who have made me see
The slaughter of my son before my face,
And have defiled a father's sight with death!
But not the Achilles, from whom you do claim
Falsely that you are sprung, though Priam's foe,   735
Was such as you are; for he blushed to think
Of violating faith and common rights,
At my petition, but the lifeless corpse
Of Hector did restore for burial,
And sent me safely back to my kingdom."   740
Saying this, the old king hurled a feeble spear
That made no wound, but from the sounding brass
Repelled, hung harmless from the buckler's boss.
But Pyrrhus cried: "Be you the messenger,
And deliver this to Peleus' son. Tell   745
Him of degenerate Neoptolemus,
And all the cruel deeds he did. Now die!"
Saying this, he dragged him to the altar's foot,
Staggering and slipping amid the blood his son
Had shed. Twisting his left hand in his hair,   750
He raised his sword in his right, and to the hilt
Buried it in his side. Such was the end
Of Priam's destinies; such was his death

Ordained by fate, while he saw Troy in flames
And desolation, who to many a land   755
And people, once, Asia's proud ruler stood.
Now on the shore his mighty corpse is thrown,
And lies a headless trunk without a name.

Then, for the first time, a dread horror fell,
And compassed me around. I stood aghast;   760
And my dear father's image came to me,
When I beheld the king, as old as he,
Breathing his life out beneath a cruel wound;
Creüsa too deserted, and my home
Ravaged, and young Iulus' luckless lot,   765
Came to my mind. I looked around to note
What forces might remain; and saw that all
Had left, exhausted—either having thrown
Their wretched bodies, leaping, down to earth,
Or given them to the flames.
　　　　　　　　　　So I alone   770
Remained[10]—when, keeping close within the door
Of Vesta's temple, in a secret place
Close hiding, Tyndarus' daughter I discern.
The bright flames light my wandering steps, as round
I glance at all things. She, the common scourge   775
Of Troy, and her own country, fearing now
The Trojans' vengeance at Troy's overthrow,
And punishment the Greeks might deal, and all
The anger her deserted husband bore,
Had hid herself, and at the altars sat,   780
A hated object. Fire raged in my heart,
And through me ran an impulse to avenge
My falling country, and inflict on her
The penalty deserved. Shall she, indeed,
In safety see her Sparta, and the lands   785
Of Greece, and move like a triumphant queen?
Shall she behold her husband, parents, home
And sons, attended by a Trojan troop
And Phrygian slaves? Shall Priam fall by the sword?

Shall Troy be burned, and all her shores distill   790
Dardanian blood? Not so. For though there be
No glory in a woman's punishment,
Nor any praise in such a victory,
Yet shall I be commended to have quenched
Such crime; and it will please me to have wreaked   795
My vengeance, and the ashes thus appease
Of slaughtered countrymen. Such were the thoughts
My mind turned over, transported by my rage.
When to my sight, never before so clear,
My gracious mother appeared, and, in the dark,   800
A goddess all confessed, with such light shone,
As when to the celestials she is used
To show herself. She held my hand, and spoke
These words with roseate lips: "O son, what grief
Arouses in your breast such untamed wrath?   805
What rage is this? Where has your reverence gone
For us? Look rather where you may have left
Your sire Anchises, encumbered with old age;
Whether your wife Creüsa* be alive;
Ascanius too, your son, whom on all sides   810
The Grecian troops surround; and whom, unless
My care of them oppose, the flames will now
Have swept away, and hostile swords have slain.
It's not the Spartan Helen's hated face,
Nor faulty Paris, but the inclement gods—   815
The gods, I say—who overthrow this power,
And from its lofty summit lay Troy low.
See: I will break the cloud which, now overdrawn,
Obscures your mortal vision with dark mists.
Do not fear to obey your parent's will,   820
Nor slight her precepts. Here, where ruined piles,
And stones from stones uptorn you do behold,
And waving clouds of mingled smoke and dust,
It's Neptune jars the walls, and with the might
Of his great trident shakes the foundations   825

---

*Aeneas' first wife, who died at Troy.

So the whole city topples from its base.
Here fiercely cruel Juno, first of all,
The Scaean gate does hold, and girt with steel,
Summons, in wrath, her allies from the ships.
Now look, where the Tritonian Pallas sits   830
Above the highest citadels, and gleams
With cruel Gorgon's head, amid the cloud.
The Sire himself supplies the Greeks with strength
And conquering courage; he himself stirs up
The deities against the Trojan arms.   835
Fly, O my son, and end your woes and toils!
I will never be absent, but will set
You on the threshold of your father, safe."
She spoke, and in the thickest shades of night
Concealed herself. The appalling Forms appear,   840
And the great deities who hated Troy.

Then indeed all Ilium seemed to sink
In flames, and from her base Neptunian Troy
To be overturned. As when an ancient ash
Upon the mountaintop, by axes hewed   845
With frequent blows, the peasants all contend,
Eager to overthrow it; all the while
With each concussion of its top, it nods,
Threatening, and trembling through its leafy hair,
Till vanquished by degrees, with many a wound,   850
It groans its last, and crashing down the cliff,
Drags ruin in its fall. Descending now,
Led by the goddess, through the enemies
And through the flames I am borne, while all around
The weapons yield a place, the fires recede.   855

But when I reached my old paternal home,[11]
My father, whom I wished to bear away
To the high mountains, and whom first of all
I sought, refused to lengthen out his life,
And suffer exile, now that Troy was lost.   860
"O you," he said, "whose blood is full of life,

Whose solid strength in youthful vigor stands,—
Plan out your flight! But if the heavenly powers
Had destined me to live, they would have kept
These seats for me. Enough, more than enough,   865
That one destruction I have seen, and I
Survive the captured city. Go forth then,
Bidding my body farewell; thus, O thus
Extended on the earth!—I shall find death
From some hand. The foe will be merciful,   870
And seek for spoils. The loss of burial will be
Slight. Long have I lingered out my years,
Useless, and hated by the deities,
Since the great sire of gods and king of men
Breathed on me with his storms and thunderbolts."   875
Thus saying, he remained with purpose fixed.
Then we, Creüsa and Ascanius,
And all the household, weeping, begged that he
Would not thus ruin all our hopes, and urge
The impending doom. But he refused, and kept   880
Unmoved and firm in what he had resolved.
Back to my arms I fly—so sick at heart,
I long for death. For what expedient now,
What chance remains? "O father, do you think
That I can go and leave you here alone?   885
Does such bad counsel come from my father's lips?
If it's the pleasure of the gods that nothing
From the whole city should be left, and this
Is your determined thought and wish, to add
To perishing Troy yourself and all your kin,—   890
The gate lies open for that desired death.
Pyrrhus will soon be here, fresh from the blood
Of Priam—he who before a father's face
Butchers his son, and stabs the father next
Before the altars. Was it then for this,   895
Mother benign, that you did snatch me forth
From weapons and from flames, that I should see
The enemy within our inmost home?—
And see Ascanius, and my agèd sire,

And, by their side, Creüsa, sacrificed   900
All, in each other's blood? My armor then,
Give me my arms! It is the last hour that calls
Upon the vanquished! Give me to the Greeks;—
Let me renew the battles I began.
Today we shall not all die unavenged!"   905

Forthwith I gird myself anew in steel,
And, inserting my left hand in my shield,
Began to put it on, and was going forth.
But lo! upon the threshold stood my wife,
And hung upon me, and embraced my feet,   910
And held the young Iulus to his sire.
"If you go forth, resolved to die," she said,
"Take us along with you, to share all fates.
But if, from trial, you have hope in arms,
Protect this household first. To whom do you   915
Abandon little Iulus, and your sire,
Or her whom once you called your wife?"
                                        So she
Complaining filled the house; when suddenly
A prodigy most wonderful appeared.
For in the midst of our embracing arms,   920
And faces of his sorrowing parents, lo!
Upon Iulus' head a luminous flame
With lambent flashes shone, and played about
His soft hair with a harmless touch, and round
His temples hovered. We with trembling fear   925
Sought to brush off the blaze, and ran to quench
The sacred fire with water from the fount.
But father Anchises lifted his eyes with joy
To the stars, and raised his hands to heaven,
Exclaiming, "Jupiter omnipotent!   930
If you will yield to any prayers of ours,
Look upon us, this once; and if we deserve
Anything by any piety, give help,
O Father, and these omens now confirm!"

Scarce had my agèd father said these words,   935
When, with a sudden peal, upon the left
It thundered, and down gliding from the skies,
A star, that drew a fiery train behind,
Streamed through the darkness with resplendent light.
We saw it glide above the highest roofs,   940
And plunge into the Idæan woods, and mark
Our course. The shining furrow gave light
All along its track, and sulphurous fumes around.
And now, convinced, my father lifts himself;
Speaks to the gods, adores the sacred star.   945
"Now, now," he cries, "for us no more delay!
I follow; and wherever you may lead,
Gods of my country, I will go! Guard then
My family, my little grandson guard.
This augury is yours; and yours the power   950
That watches Troy. And now, my son, I yield,
Nor will refuse to go along with you."
And now through all the city we can hear
The roaring flames, which nearer roll their heat.
"Come then, dear father! On my shoulders I   955
Will bear you, nor will think the task severe.
Whatever lot awaits us, there shall be
One danger and one safety for us both.
Little Iulus be my companion;
And at a distance let my wife observe   960
Our footsteps. You, my servants, take good heed
Of what I say. Beyond the city stands
Upon a rising ground an old temple
Of the deserted Ceres,* and near by
An ancient cypress tree, for many years   965
By the religion of our sires preserved.
To this, by different ways, we all will come
Together. And do you, my father, here
Take in your hands our country's guardian gods,
And our Penates. I, who have just come forth   970

---

*Goddess of grain and fruits; mother of Proserpina, who is queen of the underworld.

From war and recent slaughter, may not touch
Such sacred things till in some flowing stream
I wash." This said, a tawny lion's skin
On my broad shoulders and my stooping neck
I throw, and take my burden. At my side   975
Little Iulus links his hand in mine,
Following his father with unequal steps.
Behind us walks my wife. Through paths obscure
We go; and I, who but a moment since
Dreaded no flying weapons of the Greeks,   980
Nor dense battalions of the adverse hosts,
Now start in terror at each rustling breeze,
And every common sound, held in suspense
With equal fears for those attending me,
And for the burden that I bore along.   985

And now I approached the city gates, and seemed
Thus far to have accomplished all our course;
When suddenly we heard a trampling sound
Of footsteps, and my father, peering through
The darkness, cries: "Fly, fly, my son! they come!   990
I see their blazing shields and brazen arms!"

Here I know not what malign influence
Bewildered me. For while along my way
I traced my course through unfrequented paths,
And shunned the beaten track—ah, woe is me!   995
Whether, delayed by some unhappy fate,
Creüsa stopped, or wandered from the road,
Or sat down weary, is unknown to me.

I saw her not again;[12] nor did I note
That she was lost, nor fix my mind on her,   1000
Until we had come unto the mound
And sacred shrine of Ceres. Together met
At last, here, she alone was absent:—she
Escaped the sight of husband, son, and friends.
Distracted, whom did I not then accuse,   1005

Of men and gods? or what more cruel loss
Had I met through all the city's overthrow?
To my companions I commend my son
Ascanius, and my father, and the gods
Of Troy, and in a winding valley hide them safe;   1010
Back to the city I go, and gird myself
With shining armor, firmly bent to renew
All risks, and through all Troy retrace my steps,
Exposed to every peril. First the walls,
And the dark gateway from which I'd issued forth,   1015
I seek; and every track seen through the night
I follow backward, and observe with care.
Everywhere horror fills my soul, and even
The silence terrifies. Then to my home
I go, if she—ah, if she should, perhaps,   1020
Have headed there! The Greeks had broken in,
And they held the whole house. Devouring fire
Rolled in the wind, and reached the lofty roof.
Onward I move, and see again the house
Of Priam and the citadel. And now   1025
In the deserted porticos, within
Juno's asylum, stood the chosen guards,
Phœnix and fierce Ulysses, keeping watch
Over their spoils. Here from all sides heaped up
Lay Trojan treasure, snatched from burning crypts;   1030
And tables of the gods, and robes, and cups
Of solid gold. And in a long array
Stood youths, and trembling matrons round about.
And yet I dared to raise my voice across
The shades, and filled the streets with fruitless cries, 1035
And called upon Creüsa, in my grief,
Again and yet again. Then as I went
Searching from house to house, distraught and wild,
I saw, before my eyes, the sad specter,
The shadowy image, of Creüsa stand,   1040
Larger than life. Aghast I stood, with hair
Erect: my voice clung to my throat. But she
Thus spoke, and with these words allayed my pain:—

"Sweet husband, what avails it to indulge
This insane grief? These things do not occur   1045
Without divine consent. It was not ordained
That you should bear away Creüsa hence
As your companion, nor does the arbiter
Of high Olympus will it. Long exile
Must be your lot, the vast expanse of sea   1050
Be ploughed; and you shall see the Hesperian land,
Where Lydian Tiber flows with gentle course
Between the fertile fields where heroes dwell.
Prosperity, a kingdom, and a spouse
Of royal rank are there obtained for you.   1055
For your beloved Creüsa cease your tears.
The Myrmidons' and Dolopes' proud seats
I shall not see: nor shall I go away
A slave to Grecian matrons—I who come
From Dardanus, and am the daughter-in-law   1060
Of divine Venus. But upon these shores
The mighty mother of the gods* detains me.
And now farewell, and cherish with your love
Your son and mine!" Saying this, she left me there
Weeping, and wishing to say many things;   1065
And, fading in the thin air, left my sight.
Three times round her neck I tried to throw my arms;
And three times her image from my hands escaped,
That sought, but all in vain, to grasp her form,
Borne like a wingèd dream along the winds.   1070
Thus finally, the night being worn away,
I saw my friends again. But here, surprised,
I found a multitude of new-arrived
Companions, who had flocked into this place,—
Matrons, and men, and youths, doomed to exile: 1075
A wretched crowd: they collect from all sides,
Prepared, with courage and resource, to go
To whatsoever lands across the seas
I might desire to carry them. And now

---

* Cybele, identified with Rhea, mother of Jupiter.

The star of morning,[13] over the mountaintops   1080
Of lofty Ida rising, led the day.
The Greeks still held the closely guarded gates;
Nor was there any further hope of aid.
I yielded to my fate, and, bearing still
My sire, toward the mountains took my way.   1085

BOOK 3

When by the mandate of the gods the power[1]
Of Asia and Priam's race was overthrown,
Deserving better fate; when Ilium fell,
And all Neptunian Troy upon the ground
Lay smoking; we by divine auguries   5
In distant and deserted lands were driven
To seek our exile. Beneath Antandros' walls,
And Phrygian Ida's slopes, we built a fleet,
Uncertain where our fate should carry us,
And where our course should end. We summon all   10
Our men. The early summer scarce begun,
My sire Anchises bids us give our sails
Unto the fates. Weeping, I leave behind
My native shores, the harbors, and the fields
Where Troy once stood—an exile borne away   15
Upon the deep: with me my friends, my son,
And household gods, and those of mightier power.

Not far away there lies a peopled land,[2]
Sacred to Mars, with spreading fields, and tilled
By Thracians (stern Lycurgus ruled it once);   20
Of old in hospitable league with Troy,
And with our household gods, while fortune smiled.
Here, landing, on the winding shore I laid
The first foundations of a town—the fates
Against me—and from my own name I called   25
The spot Æneades.
                          A sacrifice
To my Dionean mother, and the gods
Favoring my works commenced, I here began
To offer, and to Heaven's supernal king

Was slaughtering on the shore a snow-white bull. 30
It chanced there was a mound hard by, on which
Some twigs of cornel grew and myrtles thick,
With spear-like shoots. Approaching, I essayed
To pull a leafy sapling from the ground,
That I might deck the altars with the leaves, 35
When, dreadful to relate, a marvelous thing
I witnessed. For the first plant that I plucked,
Dark oozing blood dripped from its broken roots,
And specked the ground with gore. A shudder cold
Shook all my limbs, and froze my blood with fear. 40
Seeking to penetrate the mystery,
I pulled again another pliant shoot;
Again the black blood oozes from the bark.
Disturbed in mind, I prayed to woodland nymphs,
And Father Mars, who over the fields of Thrace 45
Presides, that they would bless this vision strange,
And make the omen light. But when again,
The third time, with a tighter clutch I seized
A twig, and, with my knees against the ground,
Pulled—shall I say it, or be mute?—a groan, 50
Grievous to hear, came from beneath the mound,
And a voice spoke: "Æneas, why do you
Thus tear my wretched limbs? Spare now my tomb!
Keep from polluting your pure hands; for I
Am Trojan, and not alien to your race; 55
Nor flows this blood from wood. Ah, leave, and flee
These cruel lands, these avaricious shores:
For I am Polydore; and these were spears
That pierced me, now sprung up, an iron crop
Of javelins." Then aghast and all perplexed 60
I stood, with hair erect and palsied tongue.
This Polydore with a great sum of gold
By the unhappy Priam had been sent
In secret to the Thracian monarch's care,
When first he doubted the success of Troy 65
Beleaguered by the Greeks. But he, when now
The Trojan power and fortune had declined,

Followed the conquering arms of Agamemnon,—
Broke through all faith, and murdered Polydore,
And seized his treasure. Cursèd thirst for gold,   70
What crimes do you not prompt in mortal breasts!
 Soon as this fear had left me, I announced
These portents of the gods to our chosen chiefs,
And to my father first, and asked of them
Their counsel. All with one accord advise   75
To leave this land, by violated laws
Of hospitality accursed, and sail
Away. Then funeral rites for Polydore
We celebrate, and heap a mound of earth;
And altars to his shade are built, and hung   80
With fillets blue, and sombre cypress boughs.
And round about the Trojan women go,
As they are wont, with loosely flowing hair.
And bowls of warm frothed milk are placed around,
And cups of sacred blood; while in the tomb   85
We lay his ghost, with invocations loud.

Then, when the sea first smiled, and when the breeze
Played lightly on the waves, and south winds called
With gentle murmuring to the deep, our crews
Draw down the ships, and occupy the shores.   90
From port we sail, and towns and lands recede.

Amid the sea there lies a lovely isle,[3]
Sacred to Doris, mother of the nymphs
Of ocean, and Ægean Neptune. This,
Once floating round the shores, Apollo bound   95
Fast to Gyaros and to Myconos,
And bade it stay unmoved, and scorn the winds.
Here now I sail. This pleasant isle receives
Within its port the weary voyagers.
Landing, we hail with praise Apollo's seat.   100
King Anius, Phœbus'* priest and king in one,

---

*That is, Apollo's.

His temples bound with fillets and with bays,
Meets us, and knows Anchises his old friend.
Then hands are grasped, with hospitable cheer,
Under his roof. And honors due I paid   105
The ancient temple stones. "Grant us," I cried,
"Thymbræan Apollo, grant these weary ones
A home to call our own, with families,
And walls; a city where we may remain.
Preserve this newer Pergamus of Troy,   110
Saved from the fierce Achilles and the Greeks.
Whom shall we follow? How far do you want
Us all to go? And where abide? Grant now,
Father, some sign, and glide into our souls!"

Scarce had I spoken, when everything around   115
Suddenly trembled, all the sacred doors,
And laurels of the god. The mountain heaved,
And from the deep recess the tripod moaned.
With reverent submission on the earth
We fall; and thus a voice strikes on our ears: 120
"Brave Dardan men, that land from which you trace
Your birth and first beginnings of your race
Shall take you back unto its joyful breast.
Go seek your ancient mother, and there rest.
There shall all shores Æneas' rule obey,   125
And a long line of sons hold sovereign sway."

So Phœbus spoke. A great tumultuous joy
Arose among us. All, inquiring, ask
What city this may be: where does this voice
Direct us, and command us to return?   130
My father then, revolving in his mind
The legends of the olden time, thus spoke:—
"Hear me, O chiefs, and learn what you may hope.
The isle of Crete,* the land of mighty Jove
Lies in mid-ocean: an Idæan mount   135

---

*Island in the eastern Mediterranean where Jupiter is believed to have been born.

Is there, and there the cradle of our race.
There stand a hundred peopled cities,—realms
Most fertile—from where our great progenitor,
Teucer, if I remember well the things
I've heard, passed over to the Rhœtean shores,   140
And for a kingdom chose a place. Not yet
Had Ilium and its citadels arisen:
The inhabitants in lowly valleys dwelt.
From there the mother goddess, Cybele,
The Corybantian cymbals, and the Idæan   145
Grove; from there the faithful secrecy
Of sacred rites; and there the lions yoked
Beneath the chariot of the queen divine.
Come then, and follow where the gods direct.
Let us propitiate the winds, and seek   150
The Gnossian shores. Nor are they all too far.
If Jupiter but aid us, the third day
Shall land our ships upon the Cretan coast."
So saying, he sacrificed the victims due:
A bull to Neptune, and a bull to you,   155
O bright Apollo; a black sheep to the Storm;
A white one to the favoring western winds.
A rumor ran that King Idomeneus,*
Expelled from his paternal realms, had ceased
To reign, and that the shores of Crete were left   160
Deserted—houses void, and settlements
Abandoned. Passing by the Ortygian port,
By Naxos' Bacchanalian heights we sail;
By green Donysa and Olearos;
By snow-white Paros, and the Cyclades   165
Scattered along the sea, and channels thick
With islands; and the shouting mariners
Pull at the oars with spirits emulous,
And upon Crete and our forefathers call.⁴
A rising wind comes blowing on our stern,   170

---

*King from Crete, who distinguished himself at the Trojan War. Having vowed to Neptune to
sacrifice the first living thing he encountered upon returning home, he was forced to kill his son,
causing a pestilence that forced him into exile.

And follows, till at length we glide along
The ancient shores of the Curetan race.

Here I eagerly choose the site, and raise
Walls of a wished-for city, which I call
Pergamia, and exhort my people, proud   175
Of such a name, to watch with loving care
Their hearths, and guard them with a citadel.

Now hauled upon the dry shore stand the ships.
Our youths employ their time in choosing wives,
And tilling the new fields; laws I began   180
To give, and dwellings; when the air is filled
With sudden blight, a slow-consuming plague
Dreadful and dire, that falls upon the limbs
Of men, and on the trees, and on the crops.
It proved a fatal year. Either they left   185
Their pleasant lives, or their sick bodies dragged
About; the dog-star parched the sterile fields;
And all the grass was dry; the sickly crops
Refused their grain. Once more across the sea
To the Ortygian oracle, my sire   190
Advises us to send, and supplicate
Apollo, and implore his grace, and ask
What end may be to our distressed affairs;
Where turn for help, and whither bend our course.

It was night; and all the living things of earth   195
Were sleeping; when the sacred images,
The Phrygian household gods that I had brought
From Troy, borne through the city's flames, I saw
Standing before me as I slept, distinct
In the broad moonlight pouring full and clear   200
Through the inserted windows. Then they spoke,
And with their words relieved my anxious fears:
"That which Apollo would announce to you
Going to Ortygia, here, unsought, through us
He brings to your own doors. We, who, since Troy   205
Was burned, have followed you, and helped your arms,

And in your ships have crossed the swelling seas,—
We your descendants also will exalt
Unto the stars, and to your city give
Imperial power. Do then build your walls   210
Of ample size, fitting a noble race,
Nor grow disheartened in your wanderings.
Change your abiding place. Not on these shores
Of Crete did Delian Apollo bid
The Trojans fix their seats. There is a place,   215
An ancient country, called among the Greeks
Hesperia, of a fertile soil, and strong
In arms, once settled by Œnotrian men;
Now, from their leader's name, called Italy.
That is our destined home. There Dardanus*   220
Was born—Iasius too—and from this chief
Our race. Rise then, and to your aged sire
Rejoicing bear this news, which none may doubt.
Seek for Cortona and the Ausonian lands,
For Jove denies to you these Cretan fields."   225
Astonished at the vision, and the divine
Voice (for it was not deep sleep; I seemed
To know their countenances and veiled locks,
And distinct forms), a cold sweat bathed my limbs;
Leaping from bed, I raised my hands and voice   230
To heaven, and on the altar fires of home,
With fitting rites, poured offerings undefiled.
This sacrifice completed, I with joy
Inform Anchises of the whole event.
At once he saw the double ancestry   235
And line, and how by error of new names
He was deceived about the ancient spots.
"My son," he said, "by Trojan fates still held!
Cassandra alone foretold such things to me.
Now I remember how she prophesied   240
This destiny for us; and often she spoke
About Hesperia and the Italian realms.

---

*Son of Jupiter and Electra, founder of the Trojan line.

But who believed the Trojans ever should come
To the Hesperian shores? or who did ever
To prophetess Cassandra give belief?   245
To Phœbus let us yield, and, warned by him,
Seek better fortune." Thus he spoke; we all
Obey with joy. This place we also quit,
Leaving a few behind; and setting sail
In our hollow boats we skim along the sea.   250

    Our ships kept to the open main. No more
We saw the land; on all sides sky and sea.
Then overhead there stood a cloud that scowled
With night and storm, and in the gathering gloom
The waves grew rough, and all at once the wind   255
Swept over them, and surging billows rose.
On the vast roaring deep dispersed, we are thrown.
The day is wrapped in clouds, and the wet night
Snatches away the heavens. From bursting clouds
Redoubling thunders crash. Driven from our course,   260
We wander through the blind and misty waves.
Even Palinurus owns he cannot now
Distinguish night from day, nor recollect
His course. For three uncertain days we grope
In the thick fog and as many starless nights.   265
On the fourth day at length the land appears,
And distant mountains rise and curling smoke.
Our sails are lowered. We bend upon our oars,
And dash the spray and sweep the waters blue.

    Safe from the waves, I landed on the shores   270
And islands of the Strophades[5] (so called
In Greece); amid the great Ionian sea
They lie. And here the fell Celæno dwelt,
And the other Harpies, after Phineus' house
Was closed upon them, forced by fear to quit   275
The tables where they once had banqueted.
So dire a monster and so foul a pest
And scourge, sent by the gods, never arose
From Stygian waters; wingèd like the birds,
And with a virgin's face; a foul discharge   280

Comes from their bodies; crooked claws for hands;
And faces pale with perpetual hunger.
    Here, entering the port, behold, we see
Fair herds of cattle grazing in the fields,
And flocks of goats, without a keeper, browse   285
Amid the grass. We with our weapons rush
Upon them; and invoke the gods and Jove
Himself to share our booty. Next we spread
Our couches on the winding shore, and fall
To feasting; when with swift terrific flight   290
The Harpies from the mountains flock, and shake
Their clanging wings, and snatch away our food,
Defiling everything with contact foul;
And, amid the hideous stench, a dreadful voice
Is heard. Again, in a remote retreat,   295
Under a hollow rock, shut in by shade
Of arching trees, we set our tables forth,
And on the altars we replace the fire.
Again, from a different quarter of the sky,
And secret hiding-places, hovering round,   300
The noisy troop with crooked claws alight,
And with their mouths defile our food. I then
Bid my companions take their arms, and fight
Against this cursèd race. So charged, they hide
Their swords and shining shields beneath the grass.   305
So, when we heard again their clattering wings
Flying along the shore, Misenus gives
A signal from his brazen trumpet, perched
Upon a height. My comrades rush to try
This novel war, and maim these fell sea-birds;   310
But neither in their feathers nor their flesh
Do they receive a wound. Swiftly they cleave
The air, and leave their filthy tracks behind
On the half-eaten banquet. All but one,
Celæno. She, the gloomy prophetess,   315
On a high rock alighting, thus broke forth
In words: "Is it war you wage on us—yea, war,
Sons of Laomedon,* for these cattle you've slain,

---

*King of Troy, son of Ilus; known for treachery.

Our slaughtered steers—from our own land to drive
The unoffending Harpies? Hear ye then   320
My words, and fix this presage in your minds,
Which Jove foretold to Phœbus, he to me,—
And I, the eldest of the Furies, tell
To you. You hold your course to Italy;
Your Italy you shall find, with winds invoked,   325
And sail into her ports. But ere you gird
Your city with its walls, by famine dire,
For this your outrage, you shall be compelled
To gnaw the very boards on which you eat."

    She spoke; and, borne upon her wings, she fled   330
Into the wood. But sudden fear congealed
My comrades' blood; their courage fell; no more
By arms, but with our vows and prayers, they wish
To ask for peace; whether these creatures be
Of rank divine, or birds obscene and dire.   335
And father Anchises from the shore spreads forth
His hands, invoking the great deities;
And offerings due commands: "O gods, forfend
Those threats! O gods, avert such hard mishap!
And kindly save your pious votaries."   340
Then he commands to tear our ships from shore,
And to uncoil the ropes, and cast them loose.
The south winds stretch our sails: through foaming waves
We are borne, wherever the winds and pilot point.
Now looms in sight Zacynthus, crowned with woods;   345
Dulichium, Same, and steep Neritus;
And past the rocks of Ithaca we fly,
Laertes' kingdom, while we curse the land
That reared the cruel Ulysses. Soon appear
The cloud-capped mountaintops of Leucate,   350
And Phœbus' temple, feared by mariners.
Weary, we make for this, and now approach
The little city. From the prow we cast
The anchor, and draw up our ships on shore.

    Thus having gained the unexpected coast,[6]   355
We sacrifice to Jove, and light the fires

Of votive offerings; then make Actium famed
With Trojan games. My comrades, naked, smear
Their limbs with slippery oil, for wrestling bouts,
As in their native land. And much delight   360
It gave to have passed so many Grecian towns
Unharmed, and held our passage through our foes.
    Meanwhile, the great sun rolls around the year,
And icy winter with his northern winds
Roughens the waves. A shield of hollow brass   365
Once worn by mighty Abas I affix
Upon the door-posts, and this verse inscribe
Thereon, commemorative of the event:
THESE ARMS ÆNEAS TOOK FROM CONQUERING GREEKS.
Then I command to quit these ports, and take   370
Our oars. So, rowing, over the waves we sweep.
Phæacia's summits of aerial hue
Are hid behind us, and we coast along
Epirus, entering the Chaonian ports,
And toward Buthrotum's lofty city sail.   375

Here an incredible report we hear:[7]
How Helenus, the son of Priam, reigns
Over Grecian cities; of the spouse and throne
Of Pyrrhus now possessed; and thus again
Andromache was given as the wife   380
Of one from her own native land. Amazed
I heard it, and my heart was all aflame
With marvelous desire to meet the man
And hear his story. From the port I go,
Leaving my ships upon the shore. It chanced   385
Andromache that day, outside the walls,
Within a grove by a mimic Simois stream,
Was making solemn feast, and offering there
Her sad libations on a mound she called
Her Hector's, green with turf, where she invoked   390
His shade; also two altars she with tears
Had consecrated. As she saw me approach,
And knew our Trojan arms, in wild amaze
And terror at this wondrous prodigy,

She stiffened as she gazed; her color fled; 395
Fainting she falls; and after a long pause
Can scarcely speak. "And are you real?" she said;
"A real and living messenger to me,
O goddess-born! Or, if the light of life
Has left you, tell me, where is Hector then!" 400
Saying this, her tears fell fast; her cries of grief
Filled all the place. To her wild words I scarce
Can frame a brief reply; but deeply moved,
With parted lips and interrupted speech,
I cry: "I am indeed alive: through all 405
Extremes I drag my days. Doubt not; it is real
All that you now see. But ah, what fate is yours,
Deprived of such a husband? Or what lot
Worthy of you has fallen to you again?
Hector's Andromache, are you the wife 410
Of Pyrrhus?"* She with downcast looks, and voice
Lowered, replied: "O, happier than all others
Was Priam's virgin daughter,† when condemned
To die upon a hostile mound, beneath
The walls of Troy; no casting of lots she bore, 415
Nor was led captive to a conqueror's bed!
While we—our country burned, over many seas
Conveyed, having in servitude brought forth
Our children—we were forced to bear the pride
And insult of the Achillean race, 420
And of a haughty youth, who seeking then
Hermione‡ in Spartan nuptial bonds,
Transferred me, slave to him, to be possessed
By Helenus, who also was his slave.
But, fired with love excessive for his bride 425
Snatched from him, and by Furies goaded on,
Orestes§ takes this Pyrrhus in an hour
Unguarded, and beside his altar fires

---

*Alternate name for Achilles' son Neoptolemus.

†Polyxena; sacrificed on the tomb of Achilles.

‡Daughter of Menelaus and Helen; betrothed at different times to Orestes and Neoptolemus.

§He avenged the death of his father, Agamemnon, by killing his mother, Clytemnestra, and her partner in crime, Aegisthus.

Slays him. At Pyrrhus' death, to Helenus
A portion of his kingdom fell, which he   430
Called the Chaonian land, from Chaon's name,
Of Troy; and on these hills a citadel
Has built—a second Pergamus. But you—
What winds, what fates have so far shaped your course?
Or what divinity has driven you here   435
Upon our shores, unknowing of what has passed?
What of your boy Ascanius? Lives he still?
And does he miss the mother he has lost?
And does his sire Æneas—Hector too,
His uncle—kindle somewhat in his breast   440
The olden virtues and the manly glow
Of courage?" So she poured her feelings out,
Weeping, with long and fruitless floods of tears:
When from the city, with a numerous train,
Brave Helenus the son of Priam comes,   445
And knows his friends, and gladly conducts them
Into his palace; and between each word
Weeps many a tear. Then moving on, I see
A little Troy, a mimic Pergamus,
A scanty stream of Xanthus, and embrace   450
The threshold of another Scæan gate
My Trojans too the hospitality
Enjoy, the king receiving them within
His ample galleries. In the palace halls
They pour the wine. The feast is served in gold.   455

And now a day and yet another day
Had passed. The breezes call; the south wind swells
Our sails. Then thus to our prophet host I spoke:—
"O you of true Trojan birth, interpreter
Of things divine, who know Apollo's will,   460
The tripods, and the laurels of the god;—
Who know the stars, the language of the birds,
And omens of their flight; tell me, I pray,—
Since favoring religious auguries
Have pointed my whole course, and all the gods   465

Urge us toward Italy, and lands remote
(Celæno the fell Harpy, she alone
Foretells a strange and dreadful prodigy,
And threatens vengeful wrath and famine dire),
Tell me what dangers I must chiefly avoid,   470
Or by what guidance I may overtop
My many trials." Then with sacrifice
Of oxen duly offered, Helenus
Entreats the favor of the gods, unbinds
The fillets from his consecrated head,   475
And leads us to Apollo's temple, awed
To reverence by the presence of the god;
Then from his sacred lips thus prophesies:

"Son of a goddess, certain is my faith
That you with auspices of highest mark   480
Are sailing on the deep; (the king of gods
Distributes thus the fates, and rolls around
The order of events, even now going on.)
Of many things a few I will declare,
How you may safelier cross the friendly seas,   485
And reach the Ausonian port. For other things
The destinies forbid that you should know,
Or Juno wills not that I utter them.
And first, you do not know that Italy,
That seems so near, within an easy sail,   490
With neighboring ports, is distant far, by sea,
And by untrodden paths and tracts of land.
And first in the Trinacrian* waves your oars
Must bend, and you must cross the Ausonian sea,
The infernal lake, and Ææan Circe's isle,†   495
Before in safe lands your city will be built.
The signs I'll give you; bear them well in mind.
When, as you ponder anxiously beside
A hidden river, on the shores you'll see

---

*Sicilian; so called because of the island's triangular shape.

†Circe, daughter of the sun, was a sorceress who Vergil portrays as living on an island west of Italy.

A huge sow lying beneath the ilex trees,   500
White, on the ground, with thirty sucking young
Of the same color clustered round her teats,—
There shall your city be, there rest be found
From toil. Nor fear that prophecy that you
Shall eat your tables. Fate shall find a way;   505
Apollo, when invoked, will be your aid.
But for those nearer lands of Italy
Washed by our tides, avoid them; all their towns
Are inhabited by evil-minded Greeks.
Here the Narycian Locri built their walls;   510
And here Idomeneus of Crete has filled
With soldiery the Sallentinian plains.
And Philoctetes,* Melibœan chief,
Defends the small Petilia with his walls.
Moreover, when your fleet has crossed the seas,   515
And, building altars on the shore, you pay
Your vows, shroud with a purple veil† your head,
Lest amid the sacred fires and rites divine
Some hostile presence should present itself,
And so disturb the omens. Keep this rule   520
Of worship, you and all your companions,
And your descendants. But when near the coasts
Of Sicily, Pelorus' § narrow straits
Open to view, then take the land to the left,
And the left sea, with a wide circuit round,   525
And shun the shore and sea upon the right.
Those lands, it's said, by vast convulsions once
Were torn asunder (such the changes wrought
By time), when both united stood as one.
Between them rushed the sea, and with its waves   530
Cut off the Italian side from Sicily,

---

*Greek exiled for his noxious wound, then sought for the weapons of Hercules he possessed, which were needed to take Troy.

†The practice described in this prophecy of shrouding the head while sacrificing became a Roman custom—depicted, for example, on the Ara Pacis Augustae (a shrine in Rome's Campus Martius dedicated by Octavian in 9 B.C.).

§Northeastern corner of Sicily.

And now between their fields and cities flows
With narrow tide. There Scylla guards the right,
Charybdis* the implacable the left;
And three times its whirlpool sucks the vast waves down   535
Into the lowest depths of its abyss,
And spouts them forth into the air again,
Lashing the stars with waves. But Scylla lurks
Within the blind recesses of a cave,
Stretching her open jaws and dragging down   540
The ships upon the rocks. Foremost, a face,
Human, with comely virgin's breast, she seems,
Even to the middle; but her lower parts
A hideous monster of the sea, the tails
Of dolphins mingling with the womb of wolves.   545
Better to voyage, though delaying long,
Around Pachynus' cape, with circuit wide,
Than once the shapeless Scylla to behold
Under her caverns vast, and hear those rocks
Resounding with her dark blue ocean hounds.   550
And now besides, if there be any wisdom
In Helenus, or credit as a seer,—
If with true lore Apollo fills his mind,
One thing before all others I enjoin,
One admonition urge and urge again.   555
First of all, supplicate great Juno's power;
To Juno pay your vows with willing mind;
Overpower the mighty queen with gifts and prayers.
So, finally, Trinacria left behind,
Victorious you shall reach the Italian lands.   560
From there, when Cumæa's city† you have found,
And sounding forests of the Avernian lake,
Here the mad Sibyl you will see, who sits
Beneath a rock, announcing human fates,
And to her leaves commits her oracles.   565
What mystic lines the virgin writes, she lays

---

*Whirlpool on the Sicilian side of the straits, roughly opposite the monster Scylla.

†City near modern Naples where there was thought to be an entrance to the underworld.

Arranged, and leaves them shut within her cave;
Unmoved they lie, nor is their order changed.
But should the door upon its hinges turn,
And some light breeze disturb the delicate leaves,　　　570
And scatter them about the hollow cave,
She never cares to arrest them, or renew
Their order, and connect her oracles;
And they who came to her, uncounseled go,
Hating the Sibyl's seat. Here, do not grudge　　　575
Delay and loss of time too much, although
Your comrades chide you, and the voyage tempts
Your sails, with prospect of auspicious winds;
But to the Sibyl go, entreating her
That she herself will tell her oracles,　　　580
And open willingly her voice and lips.
She will unfold to you the Italian tribes,
Your coming wars, and how you may avoid,
How bear your sufferings. Reverently approached,
She will direct you on a prosperous course.　　　585
So far it is permitted I may speak
To you admonitory words. Now go,
And with your deeds bear Troy to heights divine."

When thus the prophet had with friendly speech
Addressed me, to our ships he sends rich gifts　　　590
Of gold, of ivory, and of silver plate,
And Dodonæan cauldrons; and with these
A corselet woven of triple links of gold,
And a proud helmet with a flowing crest
Of hair, the arms of Neoptolemus;　　　595
Gifts for my father also; horses too,
And guides, and bands of rowers he supplies;
And furnishes, withal, our crews with arms.

Meanwhile, Anchises bids us hoist our sails,
Lest by delay we miss the rising wind.　　　600
Then him Apollo's priest addresses thus,
With reverent face: "O you, who were deemed worthy

Of Venus' proud espousals—by heaven's care
Twice rescued from Troy's ruins—the Ausonian
Land is before you! With your ships   605
Go take it. Yet you must first pass it by
Upon this sea. Far distant is that part
Of Italy Apollo opens to you.
Go, happy in the filial piety
Of this your son! Why further speech from me?   610
Or why with words delay the rising winds?"
     Grieved, too, at taking leave, Andromache
Brings for Ascanius embroidered garments wrought
With golden thread; also a Phrygian cloak,
An offering not unworthy,—loading him   615
With gifts of woven stuffs; while thus she speaks:—
"Accept these too, my boy, and let them be
Memorials of my handiwork, and show
The unfading love of Andromache,
Once Hector's wife; your kindred's parting gifts;—   620
O sole surviving image of my boy
Astyanax! Such eyes, such hands had he,
Such features; and his budding youth would just
Have equalled yours in years." Departing now,
With gushing tears I said: "Happy be all   625
Whose fortune is achieved. For us, we are called
From one fate to another; but for you
Rest is secure: no ploughing of the deep,
No fields of distant Italy to seek,
Forever vanishing before your eyes.   630
An image of the Xanthus and of Troy
You have before you, by your own hands made,
With better auspices, I hope, and less
Exposed to hostile Greeks. If I should ever
Enter the Tiber, and the adjacent fields   635
Of Tiber, and behold the cities given
Unto my people,—then, our kindred towns
And neighboring populations shall one day—
Epirus and Hesperia (having both
One founder, Dardanus, one fortune too)—   640

Make a united Troy in our regard.
Be this the care of our posterity."

Close to the neighboring Ceraunia now
We sail, where lies our way to Italy,[8]
The shortest course by sea. Meanwhile the sun   645
Goes down; the shadowy mountains hide in night.
On the earth's welcome lap we throw ourselves,
Beside the waves, the watch being set on board,
And here and there along the sandy beach
Refresh ourselves with food. Our weary limbs   650
Are bathed in sleep. Not yet the night had reached
Her middle course, when Palinurus leaves
His bed, no sluggard he, and all the winds
Essays, listening to catch their sounds; and notes
In the still sky the softly gliding stars,   655
Arcturus, and the rainy Hyades,
And the two Bears, and armed Orion bright
With gold. And when he sees that all is still
Amid the heavens serene, he from the stern
Gives the clear signal. Then we strike our tents,   660
And try the voyage, with our wingèd sails
And now Aurora reddens in the east;
The stars had vanished; when, far off, we see
The dusky mountains and the long low shore
Of Italy. And ITALY rings first   665
Achates' voice, and Italy with shouts
Of joy my comrades greet. My father then
Wreathes a great cup, and fills it up with wine,
And, standing in the stern, invokes the gods:—
"Ye potent deities of sea and land,   670
And of the storms, grant us a safe passage,
And favoring breezes." Soon the wished-for winds
Freshen, and wider grows the harbor now;
Minerva's temple on a height appears;
We furl the sails, and turn our prows to land.   675
Hollowed by eastern tides the harbor lies,
And hidden by the jutting rocks on which

The salt waves dash. The cliffs, high-turreted,
Stretch out with double walls; the temple stands
Back from the shore. Here, our first augury,   680
We see four snow-white horses grazing free
Amid the grass. "Ah, hospitable land,"
My father cries, "for us you threaten war!
For war these steeds portend. Yet since they have known
The chariot, and the peaceful yoke and reins,   685
They also promise peace." The sacred power
Of Pallas with the ringing armor then
We supplicate, who first received us, glad
To gain the shore; and at the altars throw
The Phrygian veil about our heads; and then,   690
As Helenus prescribed, due offerings burn
To Argive Juno.
           Now, without delay,
Our vows performed, we turn our sails, and leave
The dwellings and suspected lands of men
Of Grecian race. And next Tarentum's bay,   695
Named, if report be true, from Hercules,
Is seen; and opposite lifts up her head
The goddess of Lacinia; and the heights
Appear of Caulon, and the dangerous rocks
Of Sylaceum. Then far off we see   700
Trinacrian Ætna rising from the waves;
And now we hear the ocean's awful roar,
The breakers dashing on the rocks, the moan
Of broken voices on the shore. The deep
Leaps up, and sand is mixed with boiling foam.   705
"Charybdis!" cries Anchises; "lo, the cliffs,
The dreadful rocks that Helenus foretold!
Save us—bear off, my men! With equal stroke
Bend on your oars!" No sooner said than done.
With groaning rudder Palinurus turns   710
The prow to the left, and the whole cohort strain
With oar and sail, and seek a southern course.
The curving wave one moment lifts us up
Skyward, then sinks us down as in the shades

Of death. Three times amid their hollow caves   715
The cliffs resound; three times we saw the foam
Dashed—that the stars hung dripping wet with dew.
Meanwhile, abandoned by the wind and sun,
Weary, and ignorant of our course, we are thrown
Upon the Cyclops' shore.
                              The port is large,   720
And sheltered from the winds. But Ætna near,
With frightful desolation roars, at times
Sending up bursts of black clouds in the air,
With rolling smoke of pitch, and flashing sparks,
And globes of flame that lick the very stars.   725
Then, from the bowels of the mountain torn,
Huge stones are hurled, and melted rocks heaped up,
A roaring flood of fire. It's said that here
Enceladus,* half blasted by the bolts
Of heaven, was thrust beneath the mountainous mass;   730
And mighty Ætna, piled above, sends forth
His fiery breathings from the broken flues;
And every time he turns his weary sides,
All Sicily groans and trembles, and the sky
Is wreathed in smoke. In the woods that night,   735
Strange sounds affright us, nor can we detect
Their cause; for in the sky no stars appeared,
And all the heavens were black with murky clouds,
And the moon shrouded by the untimely night.

At length the early dawn arose.[9] The day   740
Had drawn away the damp shades from the sky;
When suddenly a figure from the woods,
An unknown man with pale and wasted looks
And miserably clad, appeared, and stretched
His hands in supplication toward the shore.   745
Closely we scan him, filthy, with long beard,
And garment pinned with thorns; in all besides,
A Greek, as once he had been sent to fight
With Grecian arms against Troy. He, when he saw

---

*One of the giants who fought against the gods, now imprisoned under Aetna by Jupiter;
Enceladus' cries and shifting body were said to cause the mountain's volcanic eruptions.

From far our Trojan garments, and our arms,   750
Awhile in terror paused, and then went on;
Then rushing headlong to the shore he ran,
With tears and supplications: "By the stars,
The gods, the respirable air and light,—
Take me away, O Trojans,—wheresoever   755
You go! It'll be enough for me. I own
That I am one of those who from the fleets
Of Greece made war upon your household gods.
For which, if my offence be deemed too great,
Tear me in pieces, throw me in the sea;   760
At least I then shall die by human hands!"
So saying, he embraced our knees and rolled
Upon the ground, still clinging. Urgently
We ask his name, his family, and what
Hard lot pursues him. And my sire himself   765
At once presents his right hand to the youth,
And reassures his courage with that pledge.
Then, laying by his fears, he thus began:—

      "From Ithaca I came, my native land;
My name is Achaemenides; I was   770
Companion of Ulysses, hapless chief!
My father, Adamastus, being poor,
I went to Troy. (Would that my state remained
As once it was!) My comrades left me here,
Unmindful, in the Cyclops' cavern vast,—   775
When from this cruel shore they fled in fear,—
A huge and gloomy den defiled with gore
And bloody feasts. He, towering, strikes the stars.
(Ye gods, remove such scourges from the earth!)
Not to be seen or heard without a thrill   780
Of horror—on the entrails and the blood
Of miserable men he feeds. I myself saw,
When, with his huge hand seizing two of us,
Back bending in the middle of his cave,
He broke their bones upon a rock, and all   785
The threshold, spattered, swam with human blood.
I saw him when he chewed their limbs, that dripped
Dark blood, the warm flesh quivering in his teeth—

Not unrevenged—nor did Ulysses bear
Such things; nor was the chief of Ithaca   790
Forgetful of himself in such an hour.
For when, full of his food, and sunk in wine,
He threw his length immense upon the floor,
Belching the gore and gobbets in his sleep,
Mingled with wine, we, praying to the gods,   795
And casting lots, surround him on all sides,
And with a weapon sharp the eyeball pierced,
That huge and single beneath his scowling brow
Glared, like a Grecian shield, or Phœbus' lamp.*
And so at last we joyfully avenged   800
The shades of our companions. But fly, fly,
Unhappy men! Loose from the shore your ropes.
For vast as stands this Polyphemus there,
Penning his woolly sheep, or milking them
In his dark cave, a hundred more there are   805
Who haunt these winding shores, or wander high
Among the mountains. Now three moons have filled
Their horns since I have dragged my life along
In forests, and in desert haunts of beasts;
And the huge Cyclops from the rocks I see,   810
And tremble at their voices and their steps.
A wretched food the branches have supplied;
Berries and stony cornels and the roots
Of plants torn from the earth have fed me long.
Looking around on all sides, I at length   815
Descried your fleet, as it approached these shores.
Whatever it might be, I resolved to yield
Myself to it. Enough that I've escaped
That dreadful race; rather take my life,
By whatsoever death you choose to ordain."   820

Scarce had he spoken, when on a mountaintop
We saw the shepherd Polypheme† himself,

---

*The sun.

†Polyphemus: son of Neptune; leader of the cyclops; blinded by Odysseus.

With his vast bulk, stalking among his sheep,—
An awful monster, huge, misshapen, and blind.
Down to his well-known shores he came. His hand   825
A pine trunk held, and steadied thus his feet.
His woolly sheep accompanied his steps,
His sole delight and solace in his woes.
When to the deep sea he had come, he bathed
The gory socket where his eye had been,   830
Gnashing his teeth with groans. Then through the waves
He wades; the billows scarcely reach his sides.
Trembling, we haste to fly; and take away
With us the stranger, as he well deserved;
Silently cut the ropes, and bending, row,   835
And sweep the sea with our contending oars.
He hears a voice, and toward the sound he turns.
But when he cannot reach us with his hands,
Nor dare the depths of the Ionian seas
In his pursuit, with outcry terrible   840
He clamors, that the ocean and its waves
Tremble with fear; affrighted Italy
Shudders; and Ætna with its hollow caves
Reverberates the roar. But from the woods
And mountains rush the uproused Cyclop tribe,   845
Swarming upon the shore. We see them stand,
The Ætnean brothers, each with glaring eye,
Powerless for harm, their lofty heads high raised,
A dread assembly; as on some high hill
Stand windy oaks, or cone-clad cypress trees,   850
Jove's lofty forests, or Diana's groves.
Sharp fear impels us to unreef our sails
With speed, and take whatever winds may blow
To favor us. Still, Helenus' commands
We bear in mind, that warned us not to steer   855
Between Scylla and Charybdis, each the way
Of death, with little choice. Backward we tend;
When lo, a north wind from Pelorus sent
Came blowing; and we passed Pantagia's mouth
Of rock, the bay of Megara, and coast   860

Of Thapsa, lying low; so all these shores
Did Achaemenides, Ulysses' mate,
Point out, retracing his own wandering course.
Stretching in front of the Sicanian bay,
And opposite wave-washed Plemmyrium, lies   865
An isle, to which the ancients gave the name
Ortygia. To here, so the legends say,
Alpheus, Elis' river, underneath
The ocean found a secret way, and now
Mingles with Arethusa's stream,[10] and flows   870
With the Sicilian waves. Here, as prescribed,
We worship the deities who rule the place.
From there, passing the fat soil and stagnant stream
Of the Helorus, by Pachynus' crags
Of tall and jagged rock, we coast along;   875
And Camarina, which the fates forbade
That they should ever drain, is seen afar;
And Gela, with its city, fields, and stream.
Steep Agrigentum shows her stately walls,
Once famed for mettled steeds. We leave behind   880
Palmy Selinus, and the dangerous shoals
And rocks of Lilybeum. Then the port
Of Drepanum receives me[11]—joyless shore!—
For here, so long by tempests driven, at last,
Alas, I lose Anchises, honored sire,   885
Who was the solace of my cares and griefs.
Here, best of fathers, you did leave me, sad
And worn; you, from so many perils snatched,
Alas, now all in vain! Nor had the seer
Helenus, when so many dread events   890
In vision he foretold, predicted grief
Like this to me; nor warned Celæno at all.
This was my latest suffering, this the close
My long, long wanderings found. Thence borne away,
I am brought by some deity to your shores.   895

Thus while they all listened, Æneas told
His tale of divine fates and all his course;
At length he rested, having made an end.

BOOK 4

$\mathcal{B}$ UT pierced with grievous pangs long since, the queen[1]
Feeds in her veins the wound, by secret fire
Consumed. The hero's many virtues often
Recur to her mind and glories of his race.
Within her heart his looks, his words are fixed;   5
Her troubled soul allows her limbs no rest.

Now Morn with Phœbus' torch lit up the earth,
Driving the dewy shadows from the sky;
When with mind ill at ease, she thus addressed
Her loving sister: "Anna, sister dear,   10
What dreams affright and fill me with suspense!
What wondrous guest into our courts has come?
What bearing in his face! How brave he seems
In spirit and in arms! I do believe
(No groundless faith) his lineage is divine.   15
Fear shows degenerate souls. Ah, by what fates
Has he been buffeted—what weary wars!
If in my mind the purpose were not fixed,
To all myself with none in nuptial chains,
Since my first love was baffled by false death;   20
If marriage bed and bridal torch were not
A weary thought, perhaps I might succumb
To this one fault. For I confess to you,
Anna, that since Sychæus' wretched fate,
When by a brother's crime our household gods   25
Were stained with blood, this one alone has stirred
My feelings, and impressed my wavering mind.
I see the traces of my earlier flame.[2]
But I would rather that the steadfast earth
Should yawn beneath me, from its lowest depths,   30

87

Or the Omnipotent Father hurl me down
With thunder to the shades, the pallid shades
Of Erebus,* and night profound, before you,
O sacred shame, I violate, or break
Your laws. He who first joined me to himself   35
Took away all my love. Let him still hold
And guard it in his sepulchre." She spoke;
And bathed her breast with tears she could not check.

Anna replied: "O, dearer than the light
Unto your sister! Will you waste away,   40
Lonely and sad, your bloom of youth, nor know
Of children sweet, nor the rewards of love?
Or do you think the ashes of the dead,
Or that the buried ghosts will care for this?
Grant that, while grief was fresh, no suitor gained   45
Your heart, of Libya, or before, of Tyre;
Iarbas slighted, and the leaders all
Whom Africa, replete with triumphs, bore;
Yet will you fight against congenial love?
Do you recall who owns the fields whereon   50
You are seated? Here Gætulian cities stand,
And gird you round—the unconquerable race,
Unreined Numidian bands—and they who haunt
The inhospitable Syrtes; there a tract
Of thirsty desert, and the raging tribes   55
Of Barca. Why of wars that loom in Tyre
Should I speak, or of your brother's threats?
By auspices divine, I must believe,
And Juno's favor it was, the Trojan ships
Were driven to here. What a city yours   60
Will be! What kingdoms from such union spring!
With Teucrian forces joined to ours, to what
A height of power will Punic glory rise!
Only do you ask favor of the gods,
With all due rites, and hospitality   65

---

*The underworld.

Accord, devising reasons for delay,
While on the sea the stormy winter raves,
And watery Orion, and his ships
Are shattered, and the inclement sky still frowns."
With words like these she fanned the flame of love   70
Within her soul; gave hope to her doubting mind,
And freed her from the scruples for her fame.

    First to the shrines they go, and pray for peace
Before the altars. Choice sheep two years old,
As rule prescribed, to Ceres, giver of laws,   75
Phœbus, and Bacchus, there they sacrifice;
And above all, to Juno, who has care
Of marriage ties. Herself fair Dido holds
And pours the cup between the white cow's horns;
Or, at the unctuous altars, to and fro   80
She moves, before the presence of the gods;
Renews the gifts all day; and bending over
The victims' opened breasts, with parted lips
Of eager hope, consults the entrails still
Breathing with life. Alas, the ignorance   85
Of all prophetic lore! What vows, what shrines
Can help her raging love? The soft flame burns,
Meanwhile, the marrow of her life; the wound
Lives silently, and rankles beneath her breast.
The unhappy Dido through the city roams   90
With burning bosom; as a heedless deer[3]
Wandering far off amid the Cretan woods,
Struck by the random arrow of some swain,
Who sends his flying dart, nor knows the while
Where it has sped: but she through woods and wilds   95
Roams, the fell shaft still sticking in her side.

    Now she conducts Æneas through the midst
Of walls and battlements, and shows her wealth
Sidonian, as if all were built for him:
Begins to speak, and half-way checks her voice;   100
At night, impatient waits the banquet hour,
She asks again to hear his Trojan tale
Of sorrows, and infatuated hangs

Upon the speaker's lips. And now when all
Have gone, and the dim moon withdraws her light,   105
And the declining stars invite to rest,
Alone through all the empty house she sighs,
And on the banquet couch he left, reclines;
And hears and sees him though he is not near.
Or in her lap Ascanius she detains,   110
Snared by the father's image in the son,
If perhaps thus she may but cheat her love
Unutterable. Towers that were begun[4]
Now cease to rise. The warrior youths no more
Engage in martial exercise; not ports   115
Nor bulwarks are prepared for war. All works
Hang interrupted, both the ramparts huge,
And scaffoldings that climbed toward the sky.

When Juno saw that such a subtle pest
Possessed the queen,[5] regardless of her fame   120
In her mad passion, she thus to Venus
Addressed her speech: "Rare praise, and ample spoils
You bring indeed,—you, and that son of yours.
A great and memorable act of power,
When by the guile of two divinities   125
One woman is overcome! Nor have I failed
To see that you have feared our city's walls,
Suspicious of our Carthaginian rule.
What limit will there be to this? Or why
Such contests? Why not rather bring about   130
Eternal peace, and binding marriage rites?
What you did seek with all your mind, you have.
Ardently Dido loves; through all her limbs
Her passion beats. Then let us henceforth rule
With equal auspices this people: she   135
To serve a Phrygian husband, he to accept
From you her Tyrians as a marriage dowry."

Then Venus answered[6] (for she saw her deep
Dissembling mind, whose scheming would avert

Italia's kingdom to the Libyan shores):— 140
"Who is so void of sense he can refuse
Such terms, or who would strive with you in war?
If only what you say might prove success
When done. But I am uncertain what the fates
Decree, whether it be the will of Jove 145
That Tyrians and Trojans here should dwell
In the same city, mixing race with race,
And joining hands as allies. You are his spouse.
For you it is lawful with your prayers to sound
His deep intent. Go on. I follow you." 150

Then thus the royal Juno: "Be it mine
That task. And now my reasons, and the affair
Most urgent, can be briefly said. Attend,
And I will tell you. When tomorrow's sun
Shall light the world, the unhappy Dido goes, 155
Attended by Æneas, to the woods,
Prepared for hunting. While the plumage bright
Is fluttering in the wind, and they surround
The thicket with their nets, I from above
Will thunder through the heavens, and on them pour 160
A dark storm mixed with hail. The attendants all
By different ways will fly, covered by clouds
And darkness. Dido and the Trojan prince
To the same cave for shelter will repair.
I will be there, and, if your will be mine, 165
Will join them in firm wedlock, and declare
Their union. There the nuptial rites shall be."
    Not adverse, Cytherea nods assent
To her request, and smiles at the open fraud.

Meanwhile Aurora from the ocean wakes;[7] 170
And with the risen morning star come bands
Of chosen youths forth from the city gates,
With nets and snares, and broad-tipped hunting-spears,
Massylian riders and keen-scented hounds.
At the palace doors the Punic lords await 175

The queen within her chamber tarrying long.
Splendid in gold and purple stands her steed,
And fiercely champs upon his foaming bit.
At length she issues forth, with all her train.
A rich Sidonian scarf with embroidered hem   180
She wears; her quiver is of gold; her hair
In golden knots is bound; a golden clasp
Confines her robe of purple at the waist.
Also the Phrygian knights come moving on;
Joyous Iulus too. Most handsome   185
Among them all, Æneas comes, and joins
The troop. As when Apollo leaves behind
The wintry Lycia, and the Xanthian waves,
And to his native Delos turns again;
There he renews the dances, and around   190
The altars Cretans, mixed with Dryops, shout,
And painted Agathyrsi; he himself
Moves on the top of Cynthus, and adjusts
His flowing hair, binding it round with leaves
Fastened with gold; upon his shoulders ring   195
His arrows. So, no slower in his pace,
Æneas moves. So in his countenance
The radiant beauty shines.
                              Now they had gained
The mountains steep, and pathless haunts of beasts.[8]
Lo, here the wild goats, from the topmost rocks   200
Dislodged, run down the ridges; there the deer
Huddle in dusty squadrons. But the boy
Ascanius through the valleys bounds along
Rejoicing, on his mettled steed; and now
This way pursues, now that,—and much desires   205
That amid the timid herds he might pursue
A foaming boar, or see a lion come,
With tawny skin, down from the mountainsides.

Meanwhile the sky begins to be disturbed
With muttering thunder; and a storm ensues   210
Of mingled rain and hail. The Tyrian knights,

The Trojan youths, and young Ascanius, all
In fear seek different shelter here and there
About the fields. The swollen streams rush down
The mountains. Dido and the Trojan prince   215
Find refuge in the same cave.⁹ Tellus* then,
And Juno, goddess of the nuptial ties,
Give signal. Lightnings flash around. The sky
Is witness of the hymeneal rites;
And from the mountain summits shriek the nymphs.   220
That day first proved the source of death; that first
The origin of woes. For neither now
By seeming or good fame is Dido moved;
Nor does she meditate clandestine love.
She calls it marriage; and beneath this name   225
Conceals her fault.

       Then through the cities wide
Of Libya, all at once flies Rumor forth,—¹⁰
Rumor: no evil is more swift than her.
She grows by motion, gathers strength by flight.
Small at the first, through fear, soon to the skies   230
She lifts herself. She walks upon the ground,
And hides her head in clouds. Her parent Earth,
In ire, so they say, at the anger of the gods,
Gave birth to her, her latest progeny,
Sister to Cœus and Enceladus;†   235
With nimble feet, and swift persistent wings,
A monster huge and terrible is she.
As many feathers as her body bears,
So many watchful eyes beneath them lurk,
So many tongues and mouths, and ears erect.   240
By night between heaven and earth she flies, through shades,
With rushing wings, nor shuts her eyes in sleep.
By day she watches from the roofs or towers;
And the great cities fills with haunting fears;
As prone to crime and falsehood as to truth,   245

---

*Ancient goddess of the earth.

†Two of the giants, or sons of the earth.

She with her gossip multifold now filled
The people's ears, rejoicing—fiction and fact
Alike proclaiming; now that Æneas, born
Of Trojan blood, had come, whom Dido thought
Worthy her hand in marriage; now that they   250
Were passing the long winter in delight
Of luxury, unmindful of their realms,
Captive to low desires. The base goddess
Pours here and there into the mouths of men
Such things; then far off turns her course, and flies   255
To King Iarbas,* and inflames his mind
With sayings, and his anger aggravates.

He, sprung from Ammon, and the forced embrace
Of a Garamantian nymph, to Jove had built
A hundred altars and a hundred shrines   260
In his broad realms, and consecrated there
The eternal watch and vigil fires divine;
And all the ground was fat with blood of flocks:
And the doors decked with wreaths of various hue.
He, furious, it is said, and in his soul   265
Inflamed by bitter Rumor, prayed to Jove
Before the altars and the sacred shrines,
Suppliant, with earnest words and lifted hands:—
"O Jove Omnipotent, to whom the race
Maurusian, feasting on embroidered couches,   270
Lenæan honors pours, do you see these things?
When you do hurl your flaming bolts on us,
O Father, shall we feel no fear of you?
And is your lightning blind, that in the clouds
Affrights us, and its thunder empty noise?   275
A wandering woman, who in our domains
Has built a paltry city for a price,
To whom we gave a piece of land to till
And rule with laws, now spurns our suit, and takes
Æneas to her kingdom for her lord.   280

---

*Son of Jupiter Hammon; suitor of Dido.

And now this Paris,* with effeminate crew,
Tying his Lydian cap beneath his chin,
His hair all moist with perfume, can possess
The prize he snatches, while to thy temples we
Indeed bring gifts, and nurse an empty fame."   285

So praying, holding fast the altar's horns,
The omnipotent father heard, and turned his eyes
Toward the royal city, and the pair,
Forgetting in their love their better fame.
To Mercury then he spoke and gave commands: 290
"Go hasten now, my son, and call to you
The Zephyrs, and upon their pinions glide;
And to the Trojan leader speak, who now
Lingers in Tyrian Carthage, not regarding
The future cities given him by the fates;   295
And swiftly bear this message through the skies;
Not such a one his fairest mother gave
To us in promise, and so shielded twice
From Grecian swords: but that he should be one
To rule Italia, freighted with the weight   300
Of empire, fierce in war, and prove his race
To be of Teucer's lofty lineage,
And make the whole world subject to his laws.
If of such deeds no glory kindles him,
And for his own renown he meditates   305
No great trial, yet does the father grudge
Ascanius the Roman citadels?
What plan does he pursue? Or with what hope
Does he delay among a hostile race,
Nor think of his Ausonian progeny,   310
And the Lavinian fields? No, let him sail!
Such our decree. Our messenger, be gone!"

The mighty father's great command the god
Prepares to obey. And first upon his feet

---

*Trojan who abducted Helen, here a symbol of Eastern decadence.

He binds his golden sandals, with their wings   315
That bear him high aloft over sea and land,
Rapidly as the blast. His wand he takes;
With this he calls the pale ghosts from the shades,
And others sends to gloomy Tartarus;
Gives sleep, and takes, and opens once again   320
The eyes of the dead. With this he drives the winds,
And swims across the murky clouds. And now,
Flying, he sees the summit and steep sides
Of rugged Atlas,* bearing up the sky;
Atlas, whose piny head is bound about   325
Forever with black clouds, by winds and rains
Beaten, his shoulders veiled in drifted snow;
And down his aged chin dash waterfalls,
And all his bristly beard is stiff with ice.
Here first Cyllenius† lit with balanced wings;   330
And hence he plunges headlong toward the waves,
Like to a bird which round about the shores
And fishy rocks flies low, close to the sea;
So between earth and sky he flew, and skimmed
The sandy beach and cut the Libyan winds.[11]   335
When with his wingèd feet, among the huts
Of the new city he alights, he sees
Æneas founding towers and houses new,—
His sword-hilt starred with yellow jasper stones;
And from his shoulders hung a Tyrian cloak   340
Of brilliant hues, the sumptuous Dido's gift,
And wrought by her with slender threads of gold.
Forthwith he addresses him: "Is this a time
To lay the stones of Carthage, and build up,
Obedient to your dame, the lofty walls   345
Of her fair city? Alas, forgetting all
Your own affairs and kingdom! From the clear
Olympian heights, the Ruler of the gods,
By whose great will the heavens and earth revolve,

---

*Mountain at the western edge of the ocean.
†Mercury.

Has sent me down to you, and this command　　　350
I bring. What plan are you pursuing here?
Or with what hope do you consume your time
In Libyan lands? If glory of great deeds
Does not kindle you, if for your own renown
You meditate on no greater effort, at least　　　355
Regard Ascanius' hopes, your rising heir,
To whom are due the realms of Italy
And Rome." This having said, Cyllenius left,
Even as he spoke, the sphere of mortal sight,
And in the thin air vanished far away.　　　360

Dumb and bewildered at the vision then
Æneas stood, with hair erect with fear,
And gasping voice. He burned to fly and leave
These pleasant regions, stunned by such command
And warning of the gods. And yet, alas!　　　365
What shall he do? With what speech shall he now
Dare to appease the raging queen? How first
Begin to speak? And now his rapid thoughts
Fly this way and now that, in various ways
Impelled, but wide of all decision still;　　　370
Till to his dubious mind one course seems best.
Mnestheus and Sergestus then he calls,
And strong Serestus, bidding them equip
The fleet with silent speed; and to the shore
Urge their companions, and prepare their arms,　　　375
Dissembling the design of this new change.
Meanwhile, since generous Dido, ignorant
Of all, dreams not of broken ties of love,
He will attempt means of approach, and find
The hour most soft, the time most fit, for speech.　　　380
Then all prepare to obey with joyful speed,
And execute his orders.
　　　　　　　　　But the queen
(Who can deceive a lover?) soon foreknew
His wiles, and saw at once his future plans,
Fearing even what was safe. Her excited ears　　　385

Heard that same wicked Rumor bring report
Of the fleet arming, and the voyage planned.
Distracted, through the city then she raves,
As when a Bacchante by the opening rites
Is roused, that celebrate the festival,   390
When the triennial orgies fire her soul,
And all around the name of Bacchus rings,
Echoed from Mount Cithæron* through the night.

At length Æneas she addresses thus:—[12]
"And did you hope, perfidious one, to hide,   395
Dissembling, your base deed, and steal away
Secretly from my land? Cannot my love
For you, cannot this hand once given as yours,
Nor Dido ready here to die for you
A cruel death, detain you? Ay, in haste   400
To equip your fleet beneath a wintry star,
And sail the deep by bitter north winds driven?
Cruel! Why even if ancient Troy still stood,
And you were bound there—not to strange lands
And unknown homes—you would not trust your ships   405
On such a stormy sea! Do you flee from me?
Ah, by these tears, and by this hand of yours
(Since to me, wretched, nothing else is left),
By our marriage tie, our nuptial rites begun,
If any favor I deserved of you,   410
Or if in anything I have been sweet
And dear to you, pity this falling house!
I do beseech you, if there yet be room
For entreaty, change, ah, change that fixed intent!
For you I braved the Libyan people's hate;   415
For you, the tyrants of Numidia spurned;
The Tyrians I have angered. For your sake
My honor has been lost, and that fair name
I held in earlier days, by which alone
I was ascending to the very stars.   420

---

*Location in Thebes of a biennial bacchic festival.

To whom do you relinquish me, who soon
Must perish—O my guest?—since this sole name
Remains instead of husband. Why do I wait?
To see Pygmalion my brother lay
My walls in dust, or the Gætulian chief   425
Iarbas lead me captive? If at least,
Before you leave from me, I might have had
Some offspring of our love, some little Æneas
Playing about my halls, who would recall
Only your features, then I would not seem   430
So utterly deserted and deceived."

She paused. But he by Jove's monitions held
Immovable his eyes, and, struggling hard,
Suppressed the anguish rising in his heart.
At length he briefly spoke: "Never will I   435
Deny, my queen, that you have heaped on me
Abundant favors, which you can recount
In speaking. Never while my memory lasts,
And while the breath of life directs these limbs,
Shall I forget my Elissa.* Let me now   440
Speak briefly of this matter. Don't think I
Expected to conceal this departure
By secret plans. Nor did I ever pretend
A marriage bond, or compact such as this.
Had fate permitted I should lead my life   445
Under my own direction, and put off
My burdens at my will, I should have first
Had care for Troy, and for the dear remains
Of my own people. Priam's lofty roofs
Would have remained, and Pergamus again,   450
Rebuilt by me, take back our conquered race.
But now Grynæan Apollo points the way
To Italy. To Italy commands
The word of the Lycæan oracle.
This is my love, my country this. If you,   455

*Another name for Dido.

Phœnician born, the Libyan lands detain,
Why envy that we Trojans seek to fix
Upon Ausonian ground? It is but just
We look for foreign kingdoms. Many a time
When night lies on the earth with shadows moist,   460
And fiery stars are rising in the east,
My sire Anchises' troubled ghost affrights
My dreams, and warns me. And then too my boy
Ascanius, and the injury I've done
To his dear head, defrauding him of that   465
Hesperian kingdom and those destined lands.
Now too the messenger of the gods, sent down
By Jove himself (I swear it by your life
And mine), has brought his mandate through the air.
I myself saw the god in open light   470
Enter the walls, and with these ears I heard
His voice. Cease then with your complaints to inflame
Myself and you. Not of my own accord
Do I seek Italia."
        While he spoke these words,
For a long time she looked at him askance,   475
With eyes that darted here and there, and scanned
His form with silent gaze; then, flaming, spoke:—
"No goddess ever bore you, traitor; no,
Nor Dardanus was founder of your race!
Rough Caucasus on flinty rocks gave birth   480
To you;—Hyrcanian tigers gave you suck!
For why should I dissemble? Or what greater
Wrongs can I await?—Did he once sigh
When I was weeping?—Once bend eyes on me?
Give way to tears, or pity show for her   485
Who loved him? What first shall I say, what last?
Now, yes, even now, the mighty Juno turns
Away, nor does Saturnian Jove regard
These things with equal and impartial eyes.
Faith lives no more. Cast on my shores, in need,   490
He I took in, and, fool, gave him a part
Of my own kingdom, and his scattered fleet

Restored, and brought his comrades back from death.
Ah, I am whirled by maddening furies! Now
Prophet Apollo, now the Lycian fates, 495
And now, sent from above by Jove himself,
The messenger divine bears through the skies
His terrible commands. A labor this,
Indeed, for those supernal ones! Such care
Ruffles their calm repose! I keep you not 500
From going, nor shall I refute your words.
Go! find your Italy, and with the winds
Seek for your kingdoms. Truly I do hope,
If the just gods have any power, that you
Will drain your punishment even to the dregs 505
Amid the rocks of ocean, calling often
Upon the name of Dido! Though far off,
With gloomy fires I shall pursue your steps.
And when cold death shall separate my limbs
From breath of life, my ghost shall follow you 510
Wherever you go. Wretch! you shall render full
Atonement, and the fame of it shall come
To me, amid the lowest shades of death!"

So saying, abruptly she breaks off her speech,
And sick at heart, flees from the light, and shuns 515
His eyes, and leaves him hesitating much
In fear, with many things he wished to say.
Her maids receive and bear her fainting form
Back to her marble chamber and her bed.

But good Æneas, though he much desires 520
To calm and to console her in her grief
With soothing words, groans bitterly, his heart
Shaken by love for her;—but nonetheless
Prepares to execute the god's command,
And to his fleet returns. The Trojans now 525
Bend to their work, and all along the shore
Draw their tall vessels down, till the tarred keels
Are floating. Then they bring their leafy oars,

And unwrought timber fresh cut from the woods,
Eager for flight. You might have seen them move,   530
Hastening from every quarter; as the ants,
When, mindful of the winter, a great heap
Of corn they plunder, piling it away.
Across the fields the long black phalanx moves,
And through a narrow pathway in the grass   535
They bear their spoils: some of them pushing hard,
Thrust on the ponderous grain; and some drive on
The stragglers, and the loiterers chastise:
And all the pathway glows with fervent toil.

What were your thoughts, O Dido, seeing this?[13]   540
What groans were yours, when from a tower's high top,
You saw the shores alive with bustling crowds,
And the whole sea confused with clamorous cries!
Accursèd power of love, what mortal hearts
Do you not force to obey you! Once again   545
In tears the queen must go, and once again
Try him with prayers, and, suppliant, submit
Her anger to her love, lest dying in vain,
She leave anything untried.
                                      "Anna," she said,
"You see how they are hastening on the shore,   550
Crowding from all sides! Now their canvas woos
The breeze; the joyful sailors hang the sterns
With garlands. Since I could foresee this grief,
O sister, I can bear it. Yet for me
Do this one thing: for this perfidious man   555
Was in your confidence, his inmost thoughts
Disclosed to you; and you alone do know of
The soft approaches and the seasons best
For touching him. Go, sister, speak to him,
This haughty enemy, with suppliant words.[14]   560
I took no oath at Aulis with the Greeks,
To ruin the Trojans; sent no fleet to Troy;
Nor did I desecrate Anchises' tomb,
Or vex his ghost. Why does he turn deaf ears

To all my words? But where now does he go?   565
To his unhappy lover let him grant
Only this one last favor: that he wait
Till flight be easy and the winds propitious.
Not for the former marriage bond, which he
Forswore, do I entreat him now, nor yet   570
That he forgo fair Latium and his realm.
I only ask a little empty time
Of respite and of space, that I may calm
This wild delirium, and may teach my heart,
Conquered and crushed, the lesson how to grieve.   575
For this last boon I beg, which, granted me,
I will pay back, requited by my death."

So she entreats. Her message fraught with tears,
Again and yet again her sister takes.
No weeping moves him, nor can he be turned   580
Aside by any prayers. The fates oppose;
And by the gods the man's compliant ears
Are shut. As when the Alpine winds contend
Against an oak,[15] strong with the strength of years,
They strive to uproot it, now this side, now that,   585
With furious blasts; with roaring noise on high,
The scattered leaves from off the boughs are stripped;
But to the rocks it clings, and to the skies
Reaches its top, as with its roots it tends
Toward Tartarus:* so by their ceaseless prayers   590
The hero is assailed on every side.
Pain wrings his mighty breast; his mind remains
Unmoved, and all in vain their tears are shed.
Then, terrified by her fates, the unhappy queen
Prays for death, weary of the overarching skies.   595
Then, as she seeks how best she may pursue
That purpose, and may quit this light of life,—
When on the incense-burning altars laid
Her offerings she would give, she sees a sight

---

*Region of the underworld originally supposed to be a place of punishment for the Titans;
later, it became another name for the entire underworld.

Of horror: for the sacred liquors change   600
To black, and the poured out wine is turned to blood
Impure. This by no other eye was seen,
Nor told even to her sister. Then, besides,
There was a marble chapel in her house,
In memory of her former spouse: by her   605
Cherished with great reverence, and hung around
With snow-white fleeces and with festal wreaths.
Here were distinctly heard the voice, the words
Of her dead husband, in the shadowy night.
And from the roof the lonely owl prolonged   610
The sad complainings of her funeral notes.
Many things also prophesied of old
By pious seers, with dreadful warnings fright
Her soul. The cruel Æneas himself pursues
Her footsteps in the ravings of her dreams.   615
And ever unattended and alone
She seems, travelling along some lengthening road,
Seeking her Tyrians in a desert land.
As the crazed Pentheus* sees the Eumenides,
And two twin solar orbs display themselves,   620
And double images of Thebes; or as when
Orestes, son of Agamemnon, runs
Excited on the stage, and maddened, flees
His mother armed with torches and with snakes;
And at the door the avenging Scourges sit.   625

So, when she took the Furies to her breast,
Overmastered by her grief, resolved on death,
The time and mode within her mind she weighs;
And thus her sorrowing sister she addressed,
Veiling her purpose with her countenance,   630
Smoothing her brow with semblance of a hope:—
"I have found a way, my sister, (give me joy,)
Which will restore him to me or dissolve

---

*Son of Agave and Echion. His refusal to acknowledge Bacchus' divinity led to his being destroyed by frenzied bacchic worshipers, including his mother.

My love for him. There is a place hard by
The ocean's boundary and the setting sun, 635
It is the farthest spot of Ethiopia;
Where mighty Atlas on his shoulder turns
The axis of the sky with burning stars
Adorned. A priestess of Massylian race
Coming from there is known to me, who kept 640
The temple of the Hesperides, and gave
The dragon's meals, and guarded on the tree
The sacred branches, sprinkling them with dew
Of honey moist, and soporiferous juice
Of poppies. She with weird incantations 645
Can free what minds she wills, and cruel cares
Send on others; can stop the rivers' flow,
And backward turn the stars, and call pale ghosts
By night; and you shall hear the earth beneath
Your feet mutter and moan, and see the trees 650
Descend the mountainsides. I call the gods
To witness, and you too, my sister dear,
And your belovèd life, not willingly
Do I employ these arts of sorcery.
Will you erect beneath the open sky, 655
In the interior court, with secret care,
A lofty pile, and on it place the arms
The traitor in my chamber hung, and all
The garments he has left, and the bridal bed
That was my doom. The priestess gives commands 660
That all memorials of this treacherous man
Shall be destroyed." This said, she paused. Her face
Was deadly pale. Nor yet does Anna dream
Her sister hid the obsequies of death
Beneath these novel rites; nor understands 665
The frenzy of her soul; nor apprehends
A deeper woe than when Sychæus died.
Therefore her bidding she prepares to do.

But in the inner court, beneath the sky,
A lofty pile being built, of tarry pine 670

And ilex split, the queen hangs garlands round,
And crowns the pyre with funeral leaves, and lays
The robes and sword thereon; and on the couch
His effigy,—well knowing what should come.
Around, the altars stand. Then, with her hair   675
Unbound, the priestess thrice a hundred gods
Invokes, and Erebus, and Chaos old,
And triple Hecate, Dian's threefold face;
Then sprinkles the feigned waters of the fount
Avernian;* and they search for full-grown plants   680
With brazen sickles in the moonlight cut,
Swollen with the milk of poison black. Also
The mother's-love† is sought and snatched away,
Torn from the forehead of a new-born colt.
Then she herself, before the altars bent,   685
Holding with reverent hands the sacred meal—
One foot bare of its sandal, and her robe
Unbound—ere dying, calls upon the gods,
And the stars shining conscious of her fate.
Then—if there be a deity both just   690
And provident, who cares for those who love
Unequally—to him she lifts her prayer.

It was night; when every weary frame was sunk
In placid sleep; when woods and seas were still;
When in their middle courses rolled the stars;   695
When every field was hushed, and all the flocks,
And all the gay-winged birds, whether they fly
Abroad over liquid lakes, or haunt the fields
With bushes rough, in night and sleep reposed.
Cares were smoothed down, and hearts forgot their woes.   700
But not the unhappy queen. She finds no rest;
Nor with her eyes or heart receives the night.
With double weight her cares increase. Love wakes
Again, and rages on the swelling tide

---

*Avernus; lake near Baiae believed to provide access to the underworld; sometimes used poetically of the lower world.

†The forelock of a newborn colt, believed to possess magical powers.

Of anger fluctuating; and her thoughts   705
Thus roll within: "Behold, what shall I do!
Try once again my former suitors, scorned
By them? Or, suppliant, seek a marriage bond
With the Numidian, whom I often spurned?
Or shall I follow the Dardanian fleet,   710
Subjected to the Trojans' strict commands,—
Because it pleases them to have been relieved
By me, and gratitude must last with those
Remembering former favors? And yet who,
Though I might so desire, on their proud ships   715
Would take me, whom they hate? Ah, don't you know,
Lost one, the treachery of Laomedon's
False race? What then! Shall I accompany,
Alone, this crew, triumphant in their flight?
Or with my Tyrians be borne along,   720
Surrounded by my subjects, and compel
Those whom from Tyre I scarce could tear away,
To hoist their sails and try the sea again?
Die rather, as you so well deserved,—and end
Your anguish with the sword! You, sister, you,   725
Moved by my tears, you were the first to bring
These woes on me, and throw me to the foe.
Ah, had I been allowed to pass a life
Blameless, unfettered by the marriage tie,
Like the wild beasts, avoiding cares like these!   730
Or that the promise had been kept I made
To the ashes of Sychæus!" Such the plaint
That burst from Dido's heart.
                              Æneas now,
Resolved on his departure, in his ship,
All preparations made, lay wrapped in sleep.   735
When in his dreams the god's returning form,
With the same features, seemed again to warn him,—
In every aspect like to Mercury,
In voice, in color, and the golden hair,
And in the youthful beauty of his limbs.   740
"O goddess-born, can you here waste your hours

In sleep, at such a crisis—foolish man!
Nor see the perils that encompass you?
Do you not hear the favoring Zephyrs blow?
She in her breast is plotting wiles and crime,   745
Resolved on death, and on the varying tide
Of passions fluctuates; and will you not,
While there is time, precipitate your flight?
Soon you shall see the waves disturbed with ships,
And the fierce torches blaze, and all the shore   750
Grow hot with flames, if morning sees you still
A loiterer on these lands. Away! Pause not!
A woman is a fickle, changeful thing!"
He spoke, and mingled with the shades of night.

Then, frightened by the sudden gloom that fell,   755
Æneas leaps from sleep, and stirs his crew:—
"Awake, my men, and quickly! Take your oars!
Unfurl your sails! A god was sent to me
From the high heaven to hasten our flight,
And cut our twisted ropes. Behold, again   760
He urges us! We follow you, O most
Divine and holy one, whoever you are,
And your commands rejoicing will obey.
Be with us, kindly aid, and with you bring
Propitious stars!" So saying, from its sheath   765
He draws his flaming sword, and cuts the lines.
The same zeal fires them all, while round they fly
With busy hands and feet. The shores are left.
Beneath their keels the sea is hid. Their oars
Turn the white foam, as over the waves they sweep.   770

And now Aurora, from the saffron couch
Of Tithon* rising, shed her early rays
Upon the earth. At the first dawn of day
The queen looks from her palace towers, and sees
The fleet, with sails all spread, move on its way;   775

---

*Loved by Aurora (the dawn) and granted immortality (but not eternal youth) by Jupiter.

And not a boat upon the empty shore,
Or in the port. Three and four times she beats
Her lovely breast, and tears her golden hair.
"O Jupiter!" she cries, "and shall he go,
This stranger—shall he mock our queenly power?   780
Will not someone bring arms, and give him chase?
And others tear my vessels from their docks?
Quick, bring your torches, hoist your sails, ply oars!—
What am I saying? Where am I? What mad
Delirium is this? Ah, wretched Dido, now   785
His base deeds touch you! Thus they should have done,
When you did yield your scepter to his hands.
Behold the right hand and the faith of him
Who takes with him, they say, his household gods;
Who bore his aged sire on his shoulders!   790
And could I not have torn him limb from limb,*
And thrown him to the waves? And could I not
Have killed his comrades, and Ascanius
Himself, and on the tables of his sire
Served for a banquet?† Doubtful, say, the chance   795
Of war had been—grant that it had been so!
Whom should I fear, who am about to die?
I might have burned their camps, or filled their ships
With flames, destroying sire and son, with all
Their race; then sacrificed myself with them.   800
O sun, who shines on all the works of earth!
And you, O Juno, the interpreter
And witness of these woes! You, Hecate, howled
At night through cities where three cross-ways meet!
And you, you avenging Furies, and you gods   805
Of dying Elissa, hear me! Toward my wrongs
Turn your deservèd aid, and hear our prayers!
If it must be this wretch shall reach the port
And lands he seeks, and thus the fates of Jove
Demand that there his wanderings shall end,   810

---

*An allusion to the story of Medea, who threw the dismembered limbs of her brother in the wake of her ship to slow down the pursuit of her father.

†An allusion to the story of Thyestes, who was fed his sons by his brother Atreus.

Then, vexed by wars of an audacious people,
Exiled, and torn away from his son's embrace,
Let him implore for aid, and see his friends
Slain shamefully; nor, when he shall submit
To the conditions of unworthy peace,   815
May he enjoy his kingdom or his life,
But fall before his time, and in the sands
Unburied lie! These things I pray—and this
My dying voice, I pour out with my blood!
And you, O Tyrians, follow with your hate   820
His seed, and all his future race! Be this
Your offering on my tomb! No love, no league
Between you! O, may some avenger rise[16]
From out my ashes, who with fire and sword
Shall chase these Dardan settlers, now, and in   825
The coming time, wherever strength is given;
Shores with shores fighting, waves with waves, and arms
With arms—they and their last posterity!"

    So saying, on all sides her thoughts were turned,
How soonest from the hated light to break.   830
To Barce then she spoke, Sychæus' nurse
(Her own long since had died in ancient Tyre):—
"Dear nurse, my sister Anna bring to me.
Bid her make haste to sprinkle all her limbs
With running water, and to bring with her   835
The victims, and the offerings required.
You, too, bind a fillet around your brows.
My purpose is to make a sacrifice,
Which duly I've prepared, to Stygian Jove;
And end my griefs by giving to the flames   840
This Trojan's image, on his funeral pile."

The aged nurse quickens her feeble steps.
But Dido, trembling, wild with brooding over
Her dread design, rolling her blood-shot eyes,
Her quivering cheeks suffused with spots, bursts through   845
The inner threshold of the house, and mounts
With frantic look the lofty funeral pile,

Unsheathes the Trojan's sword—a gift not sought
For use like this—then, having gazed upon
The Ilian garments and the well-known bed,   850
She paused a little, full of tears and thoughts,—
Threw herself on the couch, and these last words
Escaped: "Sweet relics, dear to me when fate
And heaven were kind! Receive this life-blood now,
And free me from these sorrows! I have lived,   855
And have achieved the course that fortune gave.
And now of me the queenly shade shall pass
Beneath the earth. A city of high renown
I have founded and have seen my walls ascend;
Avenged my husband; for my brother's crime   860
Requital seen—happy, too happy alas,
Had the Dardanian fleet never touched my shores!"
With that she pressed her face upon the couch;
"I shall die unavenged—yet, let me die!
Thus, thus it is joy to seek the shades below.   865
These flames the cruel Trojan on the sea
Shall drink in with his eyes, and bear away
Along with him the omens of my death!"

While thus she spoke, the attendants saw her fall
Upon the steel, and the sword frothed with blood   870
That spurted on her hands. Loud clamor fills
The lofty halls. The rumor of the deed
Raves through the shaken city. Every house
Resounds with grief, and groans, and women's shrieks;
And all the air is filled with wailing tones;   875
As though all Carthage or the ancient Tyre
Were toppling down before their invading foes,
And over roofs and temples of the gods
The flames were rolling.[17]
                            Breathless, terrified,
With trembling steps, her sister hears, and through   880
The crowd she rushes; with her nails she rends
Her face, and with her hands she beats her breast,
And calls upon the dying queen by name:—

"Was this your meaning, sister? Have you thus
Deceived me? Was it this, that funeral pile,   885
And this, those altar fires prepared for me?
Deserted now, what shall I first deplore?
Did you spurn a sister near you in your death?
Had you but summoned me to share this fate,
One grief, one hour should here have stabbed us both!   890
Yea, with these hands I built this pile, and called
Upon our country's gods, that you might lie
Thereon—and I, ah cruel, not be there!
Myself and you, O sister, you have slain,
Your people, and the Tyrian fathers all,   895
And your proud city. Give me—let me bathe
Her wounds with water, and if any breath
Yet flickers, I will catch it with my lips!"

So saying, she ascended the high steps,
And clasped her dying sister in her arms,   900
And moaning, held her close upon her breast,
And sought to stanch the black blood with her robe.
The queen her heavy eyelids tried to raise,
And backward fell. The wound beneath her breast
Gurgled with blood. Three times she raised herself,   905
Leaning upon her elbow; and three times
She sank upon the couch—her wandering eyes
Turned to the blue sky, seeking for the light,—
And when she found it, groaned.
                              Great Juno, then,
Pitying her lingering agony and death,   910
Sent Iris* from Olympus† down to free
The struggling soul, and loose its mortal tie.
For since by fate she perished not, nor death
Deserved, but was made wretched before her time,
And by a sudden madness fired, not yet   915
Proserpina‡ had shorn the golden lock

---

*The rainbow.

†Mountain where the gods reside, located in Thessaly.

‡Daughter of Ceres, wife of Pluto.

From off her head, nor to the Stygian gloom
Condemned her. Therefore Iris, dewy soft,
Upon her saffron-colored pinions borne,
And flashing with a thousand varied hues   920
Caught from the opposing sun, flew down, and stood
Above her head, and said: "This lock I bear
Away, sacred to Dis;* such my command,—
And free you from that body." Saying this,
She cuts the lock. And the vital heat   925
Exhales, and in the winds life floats away.

---

*Hades.

BOOK 5

Æneas with his fleet was sailing on[1]
Meanwhile, in direct course, and with the wind
Cutting the darkened waves; and looking back,
He saw the city glaring with the flames
Of the unhappy Dido. What had lit   5
This fire, they knew not; but the cruel pangs
From outraged love, and what a woman's rage
Could do, they know; and through the Trojans' thoughts
Pass sad forebodings of the truth.
                                    The ships
Sailed on. The land no longer now was seen;   10
But on all sides the ocean and the sky;
When overhead there stood a dark gray cloud[2]
Fraught with night and tempest. The waves grew rough
Amid the gloom; and from his lofty stern,
Even Palinurus, helmsman of the ship,   15
Exclaimed: "Why have such clouds filled up the skies?
O father Neptune, what do you have in store?"
So saying, he bids them make all fast, and bend
Upon their sturdy oars; and to the wind
He slants the sail. "Noble Æneas," he said,   20
"Though Jupiter himself should pledge his word,
I could not hope beneath a sky like this
To touch the Italian shores. The winds are changed,
And from the black west blowing, roar athwart
Our course. The air is thickened into mist;   25
Nor can we strive against it, nor proceed.
Since Fortune conquers, let us follow her;
And where she calls, then there we bend our way.
Not far the faithful and fraternal shores,
I judge, of Eryx, the Sicanian ports,   30
If stars observed have not deceived my eyes."

Then good Æneas: "Long since I have seen
The winds' demand, and that in vain you strive.
Then turn your course. What shores more sweet to me,
Or where then would I bring my weary ships   35
More gladly, than to the land where I shall greet
Trojan Acestes, and the earth that holds
Within its lap my sire Anchises' bones?"
This said, the favoring west winds fill their sails
And they seek the harbor. Swiftly across   40
The gulf the fleet is borne, until at length
With joy they touch upon the well-known sands.

    But from a mountain-top Acestes sees,
With wonder from afar, the friendly ships
Approach, and comes to meet them, bristling over   45
With javelins, and in Libyan bear-skin dressed.
A Trojan he, upon his mother's side;
His sire the stream Crimisus. He had not
Been forgetful of ancient parentage;
And now he greets the voyagers returned,   50
And with his rustic riches entertains them
Gladly, and with his friendly aid consoles
Their weary frames.
                Then when the brightening dawn
Had chased away the stars, Æneas called
His comrades all together from the shores,   55
And from a rising ground addressed them thus:—
    "Brave Dardans, race of lineage divine,[3]
A year with its revolving months has passed
Since in the earth we laid my noble sire's
Remains, and consecrated to his name   60
Our mournful altars. Now that day has come
Which I shall ever hold to be a day
Of sorrow, yet of honored memory.
So the gods willed it. Were I exiled far
Amid the Gætulian sands, or Grecian sea,   65
Or in Mycenæ, still would I perform
My annual vows, and celebrate this day
With solemn pomp, and heap the altars high

With gifts. Now, of our own accord, we are here,
Near to my father's ashes and his bones;   70
Not, I believe, without divine intent,
And presence of the gods, to friendly ports
Conducted. Come then, let us render now
A joyous celebration to his name,
Praying for prosperous winds, and that he may   75
Accept such offerings annually given,
When I have built my city, in temples reared
And dedicated to his name. Two cattle
Trojan Acestes gives to every ship.
Invite to our feasts our home-and-country's gods,   80
And those our host Acestes venerates.
Moreover, if the morning sun shall bring,
Nine days from this, a fair and radiant day,
First, for the Trojan fleet I will appoint
A naval race; and see who best prevails   85
In speed of foot, and who in manly strength,
Either to throw the spear, or wing the shaft,
Or with the raw-hide gauntlet try the fight.
Let all be present, and expect the prize
Deserved. Keep a religious silence all,   90
And bind your brows with wreaths." Thus having said,
He with his mother's myrtle crowns his brows;
And so did Helymus, old Acestes too,
And young Ascanius, and the other youths.
He went then from the assembly toward the tomb,   95
Surrounded by a mighty multitude
Attending him. Here, offered in due form,
He pours upon the ground two cups of wine,
Two of new milk, and two of sacred blood,
And scatters purple flowers, while thus he speaks:—   100
    "Hail, sacred parent—hail, ye ashes snatched
From Troy in vain—paternal soul and shade!
It was not permitted me to see the shores,
The fated fields of Italy, with you;
Nor seek the Ausonian Tiber, wheresoever   105
It be." Then from the bottom of the shrine

A serpent huge with seven voluminous coils
Peacefully glided round the tomb, and slipped
Between the altars; azure blue its back,
And spotty splendor lit its scales with gold; 110
As when the rainbow with a thousand tints
Gleams in the opposing sun. Æneas stood
Astonished at the vision; while the snake
Wound its long trail between the bowls and cups,
And sipped the food, and harmlessly retired 115
Into the bottom of the tomb. He then
More zealously renews the rites commenced.
Whether this be the Genius of the place,
Or some attendant spirit of his sire,
Æneas knows not. Two young sheep, two swine, 120
And two black steers, he sacrifices then,
Pours out the sacred wine, and calls upon
The soul of great Anchises and the shade
Released from Acheron. His companions too,
Their offerings bring, according to their means, 125
With willing minds, the altars load with gifts,
And slay their steers; others in order place
Cauldrons of brass, and, stretched upon the turf,
Lay coals beneath the spits, and roast the flesh.

At length the expected time had come. The steeds 130
Of morning brought the ninth day clear and bright.
Acestes' fame and great renown had called
The neighboring people. Joyous groups filled all
The shores, coming to view the Trojan men,
And some expecting to contend. And first 135
The gifts were placed within the middle ring:
The sacred tripods, and the crowns of green,
And palms, the victors' prize, and arms, and robes
Of purple, gold and silver talents too.
And from a mound a trumpet rings, announce 140
The games commenced.
               And first, four well-matched ships
Chosen from all the fleet, with sturdy oars,

Enter the lists.[4] The rapid Sea-wolf first
Comes, urged by Mnestheus, with his rowers strong;
Mnestheus, Italian soon in his renown;   145
From whom the line of Memmius is derived.
The huge Chimæra with its stately bulk
Next comes, a floating city, Gyas' charge,
By Dardan youths impelled, with triple banks
Of oars ascending. Then Sergestus, he   150
From whom the Sergian family is named,
Borne in the mighty Centaur. Last, the chief
Cloanthus, in the dark blue Scylla comes;
From him, O Rome's Cluentius, your descent.

Far in the sea there is a rock that fronts   155
The foaming coast, at times by swelling waves
Submerged and buffeted, when winter winds
Obscure the stars. When skies are calm, it lifts
A level plain above the tranquil waves,
A pleasant haunt where sea birds love to bask.   160
And here Æneas plants an ilex tree,
A goal and signal green, to tell the crews
When to turn back upon their winding course.
Their places then are given to each by lot,
And the commanders, standing in the sterns,   165
Shine in proud robes of crimson and of gold.
The rest with leafy poplar wreathe their brows,
Their naked shoulders smeared with shining oil.
Upon their rowing-benches, side by side,
They sit, their arms extended to their oars;   170
Intent they wait the signal, and with hearts
Beating with mingled fear and love of praise.
    Then, when the trumpet sounds, they bound away
Swift from their barriers, all; the sailors' shouts
Resound; the frothy waves are turned beneath   175
Their sinewy arms; and keeping time, they cleave
The furrows of the yawning ocean deeps
Surging before their oars and trident-beaks.
Less swiftly start the chariots and their steeds

In the contesting race, across the field;   180
Less eagerly the charioteers shake loose
The waving reins upon the coursers' necks,
And bending forward, hang upon the lash.
Then, with the shouts and plaudits of the crowd,
And urging cries of friends, the woods resound.   185
The shores, shut in, roll on the loud acclaim,
Re-echoed from the hills. First, before all,
Amid the crowd and noise, flies Gyas past
Upon the waves. Cloanthus follows next,
With better oars, but lags from heavier weight.   190
Behind, at equal distance, in close strife
The Sea-wolf and the Centaur come; and now
The Sea-wolf gains, and now the Centaur huge
Passes her; now together both join fronts,
Ploughing long briny furrows with their keels.   195

And now they neared the rock, and almost touched
The goal, when Gyas, foremost on the waves,
Calls to Menœtes, helmsman of his ship:—
"Why so far to the right? Here lies your course!
Keep close to shore, and let the oar-blades graze   200
The rocks upon the left. Let others keep
The open main." But, fearing the blind rocks,
Toward the sea Menœtes turns his prow.
"Why steer so wide? Make for the rocks again,
Menœtes!" Gyas shouted; and behold,   205
He looks, and sees Cloanthus close behind
And gaining on him. He, between the ship
Of Gyas and the rocks, glides grazing by
Upon the left, and suddenly outstrips
Him who was first, and passes by the goal;   210
And, turning, holds his safe course over the deep.
Then grief and rage burned in the warrior's breast,
Nor did his cheeks lack tears. Forgetting then
His pride, reckless of safety for his crew,
He hurled the slow Menœtes from the stern   215
Into the sea, and takes the helm himself,

Pilot and master both, and cheers his men,
While to the shore he turns. But heavily built
And old, with difficulty struggling up,
Menœtes, dripping wet, climbs up the rock,   220
And sits on its dry top. The Trojans laughed
To see him fall, and laughed to see him swim,
And laugh again to see him spewing forth
The salt sea-brine. A joyful hope now flames
In Mnestheus and Sergestus, the two last,   225
To pass the lagging Gyas. First to gain
The space between, Sergestus nears the rock,
Not with his ship's whole length, for close behind
The Sea-wolf presses on him with her beak.
But pacing through his galley, Mnestheus cheers   230
His comrades: "Now, now bend upon your oars,
You friends of Hector, whom in Troy's last hours
I chose for my companions! Now put forth
Your strength, your courage, on Gætulian shoals
Once tried, and on the Ionian sea, and through   235
The close-pursuing waves of Malea.
It's not that Mnestheus hopes to gain the prize;—
Though, let those conquer, Neptune, who you will.
But shame if we are last! Be this your thought,
And win at least by shunning a disgrace!"   240
     They ply their oars with utmost rivalry;—
The brazen galley trembles as they pull
With long-drawn strokes. Beneath them flies the sea;
With panting breasts, parched mouths, and sweating limbs
They row. And now mere chance gives to the crew   245
The honor and success so hotly sought.
For while Sergestus, wild with furious haste,
Urges his vessel on the inner track
Toward the shore, far too narrow a space,
On the projecting crags he luckless struck.   250
Loud crash the struggling oars, and on a rock
The prow hangs fixed. Up rise the mariners,
And, shouting, strive to force the vessel back,
And ply their stakes with iron shod and poles

With sharpened points, and from the flood collect   255
Their broken oars. But Mnestheus, full of joy,
And animated more by this success,
With rapid march of oars, and winds to aid,
Runs on the smooth waves and the open sea.
As when a dove, whose home and cherished nest   260
Are in some secret rock, from out her cave
Suddenly startled, toward the fields she flies
Frightened, with loud flapping of her wings;
Then, gliding through the quiet air, she skims
Along her liquid path, nor moves her wings;—   265
So Mnestheus; so his ship the outer seas
Cuts in her flight, by her own impulse borne.
And first he leaves behind upon the rock
Sergestus, struggling in the shallow flats,
Calling for help in vain, and striving hard   270
To row with shattered oars. Then Gyas next,
In the huge Chimæra, he overtakes
And passes, he his helmsman having lost.
Cloanthus now alone has nearly won,
Whom he pursues, straining with all his strength.   275
The clamor then redoubles; with their shouts
All cheer him on. And thus they might have shared,
Perhaps, with equal prows, the expected prize;
When to the sea Cloanthus stretched his hands
In prayer, and called upon the deities:—   280
"You gods, whose empire is the watery main,
Whose waves I stem, to you I joyfully
Will place upon your altars, on the shore,
A snow-white bull, bound to fulfill my vow,
And throw the entrails in the sea, and pour   285
An offering of wine." He spoke; and all
The band of Nereids and of Phorcus heard,
And virgin Panopea, from the depths
Of ocean; and Portunus himself pushed
The ship with his great hands, which flew swifter   290
Than wind or flying dart, and reached the land,

And hid itself within the ample port.

Then, all being summoned, as the custom was,
Æneas by a herald's voice proclaims
Cloanthus victor, and with laurel green   295
He wreathes his brows. And to the ships he gives
Three steers for each, by choice, and also wines,
And a great silver talent. On the chiefs
He confers distinguished honors; a cloak
He gives the victor, wrought with work of gold   300
And Melibœan purple running round
In double windings. Woven through the cloth
The tale of Ganymede, as when he chased,
Eager, with panting breath, the flying stag
With javelins, on the leafy Ida's top;—   305
Or by the thunder-bearing eagle snatched,
While the old guardians stretch their hands in vain
To heaven, amid furious barking of the dogs.
Then next, to him who held the second place
In honor, a coat of mail with polished rings   310
In golden tissue triple-wrought, he gives,—
Which from Demoleos he himself had won
In battle by the Simois, under Troy.
For ornament and for defense alike
He gives it. The two servants Sagaris   315
And Phegeus scarcely can sustain its weight
Upon their shoulders; and yet, clothed in this,
Demoleos chased the scattered Trojans once.
The third gifts were two cauldrons made of brass,
And silver bowls embossed with rich chasings.   320

The honors now conferred, the rivals all,
Proud of their sumptuous gifts, were moving on,
With scarlet ribbons bound about their brows,
When, with his ship saved from the cruel rock
With difficulty and great skill, his oars   325
Lost, and disabled by one tier entire,
Sergestus slowly brought his vessel in,
Jeered and unhonored. As when on a road

A serpent by a wheel is crushed, or blow
Dealt by some traveler with a heavy stone, 330
And left half dead and wounded, all in vain
Seeking escape, it writhes, its foremost part
With flaming eyes defiant, and its head
Raised, hissing; but the other portion, maimed
By its wound, retards it, twisting into knots, 335
And doubling on itself—so moved the ship
With slow and crippled oars, yet set its sails,
And so steered into port. But nonetheless
Æneas to Sergestus gives a gift
As promised, glad to know his ship is saved, 340
And crew brought back. To him a female slave
Of Cretan race, called Pholoe, he gives,
Expert at weaving, with twins upon her breast.

The contest ended, to a grassy field
Æneas then repairs, by winding hills 345
Enclosed with woods: in the middle of a vale
Shaped like a theatre, a race-course ran;[5]
To which the chief with many thousands went,
And sat amid them on a lofty seat.
Here, all who would contend in speed of foot 350
He invites, with offered prizes and rewards.
From all sides Trojans and Sicanians mixed
Assemble; Nisus and Euryalus
First among these—Euryalus, for youth
And beauty eminent; Nisus, for love of him. 355
Royal Diores next, of Priam's race;
And Salius, and Patron, one of whom
Was Acarnanian, and the other born
In Arcady, and of Tegæan blood.
Then Helymus and Panopes, two youths 360
Trinacrian by birth, to sylvan sports
Well trained, attendants of Acestes old;
With many more hid by obscurer fame.
To whom Æneas, in the midst, thus spoke:
"Hear now my words, and yield me willing minds; 365
None shall go from here without a gift from me.

Two Cretan darts of polished steel I give,
Also a battle-axe in silver chased.
For all alike these presents. The first three
Who win, due prizes shall receive, and wreaths   370
Of olive deck their brows. A steed adorned
With trappings shall be given to the first;
An Amazonian quiver to the next,
With Thracian arrows filled, and broad gold belt
Fastened with jewelled clasp; and to the third   375
This Grecian helmet."
              Having said these words,
They take their places, and, the signal given,
Dash from the starting-point upon their course,
As when a storm-cloud pours. Their eyes are fixed
Upon the goal. First, before all the rest,   380
Flies Nisus, darting swifter than the wind,
Or wingèd thunderbolt. Then Salius next
Follows, but far behind; Euryalus
The third in speed. Helymus follows him.
Now close behind, behold, Diores flies,   385
Toe touching heel, and hangs upon his rear;
And had more space remained, he would have passed,
Or left the contest doubtful. Almost now
The last stage was completed, and they neared
The goal with weary feet, when Nisus slides   390
Unhappily amid some slippery blood
Of heifers slain, that, poured upon the ground,
Had wet the grass. Pressing exultant on,
The youth his foothold lost, and prone he falls
Amid the sacred blood and impure filth.   395
Yet not forgetful of Euryalus,
And of their love, he in the slippery place
Rising, obstructs the way of Salius,
Who, falling over him, sprawls upon the ground.
On flies Euryalus, and, through his friend,   400
Holds the first place, as amid the applauding shouts
He runs. Then Helymus comes in, and next
Diores, for the third. Here Salius fills

All the wide hollow of the assembled crowd,
And front seats of the fathers, with his cries,   405
Demanding that the prize should be restored,
Snatched from him by a trick. But favor smiles
For Euryalus, and his becoming tears;
And worth seems worthier in a lovely form.
Diores seconds him, and with loud voice   410
Declares that he in vain had striven to win
The last prize, if to Salius falls the first.
Then spoke Æneas: "Youths, your prizes all
Remain to you assured. No one may change
The order of the palm. But let me still   415
Pity a friend whose ill-luck merits not
Misfortune." Saying this, to Salius then
He gives a huge Gætulian lion's skin
Heavy with rough hair and with gilded claws.
Here Nisus spoke: "If such the prizes given   420
To those who lose, and falls win pity thus,
What boon worthy of Nisus will you give?
I who deserved the first crown, had not chance
To me, as well as Salius, proved unkind."
And as he spoke, he showed his face and limbs   425
Smeared with the mud and filth. The good sire smiled,
And bade a shield be brought, the skilful work
Of Didymaon, taken by the Greeks
From Neptune's sacred door; this signal gift
Presents Æneas to the worthy youth.   430

The race being ended, and the prizes given:—
"Now whosoever has courage and a mind
Cool and collected, let him show himself,
And raise his arms, his hands with gauntlets bound."[6]
So spoke the chief; and for the combat then   435
Proposed a double prize; a bullock decked
With gold and ribbons, for the one who wins;
And, to console the vanquished one, a sword
And splendid helmet. Then without delay,
Dares displays his mighty limbs and strength,   440

And lifts his head amid the murmuring crowd;—
He who alone with Paris could contend;
The same who at the tomb where Hector lies
Struck down the champion Butes, vast of bulk
(Boasting to have come of the Bebrycian race   445
Of Amycus), and stretched him on the sand,
Dying. So Dares rears his head aloft,
First in the lists, and shows his shoulders broad,
Throwing his arms out, with alternate blows
Beating the air. A rival then is sought;   450
But no one ventures from the crowd to approach
The champion, and to bind on the glove.
He therefore, overbold, supposing all
Declined the prize, before Æneas' feet
His station takes; and without more delay   455
On the bull's horn his left hand lays, and speaks:—
"Hero of divine birth, if none dare trust
Himself in combat, why do I stand here?
And how long must I wait? Command that I
Shall lead away the prize." The Trojans all   460
Shout their assent, and wish the promised gift
Bestowed.
          Then grave Acestes thus rebukes
Entellus, lying by him on the grass:—
"Entellus, once the bravest of the brave,
But to what end, if patiently you see   465
Such prizes without contest borne away?
Where is he now, Eryx, that god of ours
Whom you did call your master, yet in vain?
Where is your fame through all Trinacria?
And where those spoils that deck your house's walls?"   470
Then he: "Not love of praise or fame departs
From me, driven out by fear, but the cold blood
Of age moves slowly, and the limbs lack strength.
Had I but that which once I had,—the youth
That braggart boasts with such exulting taunt,—   475
Not for rewards, not for a comely steer
Would I then come here, nor expect a gift."

So saying, a pair of gauntlets in the midst
He threw, of enormous weight, with which once
The impetuous Eryx clothed his hands in combat,   480
And with the tough thongs bound his wrists about.
All were amazed; for seven great hides of bulls
Stiffened their bulk, with iron and with lead
Sewed in. Dares himself astonished stands,
And drawing back, declines to try the fight.   485
Æneas tests the gauntlets' weight and size,
And to and fro he turns their ponderous folds.
Then said the veteran: "What if you had seen
The gloves and the arms of Hercules
Himself, and watched the battle as it raged   490
Upon this very shore? These gloves were once
Worn by your brother Eryx (even now
The soil of brains and blood you may perceive).
With these he against the great Alcides stood;
With these I once was wont to fight, when youth   495
And strength were mine, nor envious age
Had bleached my brows. But if these arms of ours
The Trojan Dares here declines to test;
And if Æneas gives consent, and he
Who prompts the fight, Acestes, let us make   500
The battle even. I withdraw the hides
Of Eryx, fear not; and your Trojan gloves
Do now put off." So saying, he threw aside
His robe, and showed his mighty limbs, and stood
In the arena's midst with towering form.   505

Æneas then provides two equal pairs
Of gauntlets, and so both alike are armed.
Each stands on tiptoe; fearless, they extend
Their arms, with heads thrown back, to avoid the blows;
Hands crossing hands, provoking to the fight: 510
The one, of more elastic foot, and full
Of confidence in youth; the other strong
In weight and heavy limbs, but tottering
And feeble in his knees, with panting breath

That shakes his mighty joints. And many a blow   515
Is aimed in vain, upon their hollow sides
And chests resounding; round their ears and brows
The strokes fly thick and fast; beneath the shocks
Their jawbones seem to crack. But firmly stands
Entellus, from his posture still unmoved;   520
And with his body and his watchful eyes
Alone avoids the blows. Dares, as one
Who with his engines against a lofty town
Leads the attack, or lays his siege around
A mountain citadel, now here, now there   525
Seeks entrance, trying with his art each place,
Urging his various assaults in vain.
Entellus, rising, his right hand thrusts out;
The other, swift, foresees the coming blow,
Adroitly steps aside, and all the strength   530
Of the huge veteran spends itself in air;
And heavily down with his vast weight he falls:
As when, uprooted, falls a hollow pine
On Erymanthus, or Mount Ida's side.
Then rise the Trojan and Trinacrian youths   535
With eager impulse and a mighty shout.
And first Acestes runs and raises up
His friend of equal years, with pitying aid.
But the old hero, by his sudden fall
Neither intimidated nor delayed,   540
Fiercer returns, while anger lends him strength,
And shame and conscious valor stimulate
His spirit. And impetuous now he drives
Dares across the lists, redoubling blow
On blow, now with his right hand, now his left;   545
No respite or delay. As when the clouds
Pour rattling hailstones thick upon the roofs,
So with his frequent blows the hero beats
And drives his adversary with both hands.
But here Æneas suffered not their wrath   550
To go further, or rage with fiercer heat,
But to the combat put an end, and saved

The exhausted Dares, speaking soothing words:—
"Unhappy man," he said, "what folly so
Possessed your mind? Do you not here perceive   555
An alien strength, the gods turned against you?
Yield now to heaven." So saying, he stayed the fight.
Dragging his feeble knees, with head that drooped
This way and that, blood issuing from his mouth,
Mingled with loosened teeth, Dares is led   560
Away by his trusty comrades to the ships.
Then summoned, they receive the promised sword
And helmet; while the palm and bull are left
To Entellus. Proud and elated with his prize,
"Now know, O goddess-born," he said, "and you,   565
O Trojans, what my youthful strength once was,
And from what death your Dares has been saved."
He said; and standing opposite the bull,
The victor's prize, drew back his arm, and aimed
Between the horns the gauntlet's blow, and dashed   570
The bones sheer through the shattered skull. Down fell
The bull with quivering limbs upon the ground.
"Eryx," he said, "this better sacrifice
I make to you, instead of Dares' death.
Victorious, I here renounce the gauntlet."   575

Then all who would contend in archery[7]
Æneas next invites, with prizes fixed.
And with his strong hand he erects a mast
Brought from Serestus' ship. Upon its top
A dove is fastened as a mark. The men   580
Assemble, and a brazen helmet holds
The lots thrown in. And first Hippocöon's name
Comes forth, the son of Hyrtacus; and next
Mnestheus, crowned victor in the naval race.
Third came Eurytion's name, brother of you   585
O famous Pandarus, who, commanded, hurled
Among the Greeks the spear that broke the truce.
Last in the helmet came Acestes' name;

He, too, would try the task of younger hands.

Then, taking arrows from their quivers, each   590
Bends his lithe bow with all his strength and skill.
And first Hippocöon's shaft with twanging string
Cleaves the light air, and strikes the mast, and sticks.
The tall pole trembles, and the frightened bird
Flutters her wings. Around the plaudits ring.   595
Then boldly Mnestheus, with his bow full drawn,
Stands, aiming high, with eye and weapon fixed
He, luckless, fails to strike the bird, yet cuts
The knotted cord by which she hung. Aloft
Toward the clouds, and through the air she speeds.   600
Then, swift, with shaft already on the string,
Eurytion with his vows invoked his brother.
Fixing his eye upon the joyful dove,
As through the empty air she flapped her wings,
He pierced her underneath the shadowing cloud.   605
She dropped down dead, and left amid the stars
Her life, and fallen, brings the arrow back,
Fixed in her side. The prize thus lost to him,
Acestes was the only archer left.
But still, his arrow shooting in the air,   610
The sire displays his skill and sounding bow.
But here a sudden prodigy is shown,
An omen of the future, by events
Made manifest thereafter; too late the sign
By awe-inspiring prophets was revealed.   615
For, flying through the humid clouds, the shaft
Signaled its flight by flames, and disappeared,
Consumed amid thin air; as when from heaven
Unfixed, glide shooting stars with trailing light.
Trinacrians and Trojans stood amazed,   620
Calling upon the gods. Æneas sees
The omen, and the glad Acestes greets
With an embrace, and loads him with large gifts.
"Take, sire," he said; "the mighty Olympian king,
From auspices like these, for you intends   625
Distinguished honors. This gift you shall have,

A bowl Anchises once himself possessed,
Embossed with figures, which my father once
Received from Thracian Cisseus, to be kept,
A pledge and a memorial of his love." 630
This said, he wreathes his brows with laurel green,
And names Acestes victor over all.
Nor does the good Eurytion grudge the praise
That stood before his own, though he alone
Had brought the bird down from the upper air. 635
His gift came next, whose arrow cut the cords;
His last, whose wingèd shaft had pierced the mast.

Before the contest closed, Æneas calls
To him Epytides—he the guardian
Of young Iulus, and companion— 640
And thus addressed his trusty ear: "Go now,
And tell Ascanius,[8] if his band of boys
Be ready, and the movements of their steeds
Arranged in order, to bring up his troop
Of cavalry, to show themselves in arms, 645
In honor of his grandsire, and his day."
He then commands the crowd to leave the course,
And clear the open field. The boys advance;
With glittering arms and well-reined steeds they shine
In equal ranks before their parents' eyes; 650
And as they move, the admiring hosts of Troy
And of Trinacria shout in loud applause.
All have their hair confined by crowns of leaves;
Each bears two cornel spears with heads of steel.
Some on their shoulders carry quivers light; 655
And round their necks and falling on their breasts
Circles of soft and twisted gold are worn.
Three bands of riders, with three leaders, go
Coursing upon the plain, twelve boys in each;
And each division has a guide: one band 660
Led by a little Priam, named from him,
His famous grandsire, and Polites' son,
Destined one day to increase the Italian race.
On a white-dappled Thracian steed he rode,

His forefeet white, and white his forehead held   665
Aloft in pride. Atys came next, from whom
The house of Latin Atii is derived;
The little Atys, by Iulus loved.
And last, more beautiful than all the rest,
Iulus, borne on a Sidonian horse,   670
Fair Dido's gift, memorial of her love.
The rest rode on the king's Trinacrian steeds.

The Trojans greet them thrilling with the applause,
And gaze with pleasure, noting on each face
Their parents' features. When the joyous train   675
Had passed upon their steeds before the throng,
And their proud fathers' eyes, Epytides
Gave a signal by a shout from afar,
And cracked his whip. They equally divide
By threes, in separate bands. Then at command   680
They wheel, and charge each other with fixed spears,
With many a forward movement and retreat
Opposing, circles within circles mixed,
Through all the mimic battle's changes borne.
And now they turn and fly, now aim their darts   685
Each at the other; and now, peace restored,
They ride abreast; as once the labyrinth
In lofty Crete is said to have had a path
With blind walls through a thousand ways inwoven
Of doubt and artifice, which whosoever   690
By guiding marks endeavored to explore,
Unconscious error, irretraceable
Deceived his steps. Even so the Trojan youths
Interweave their courses, of sportive flight
And battle; as when dolphins swimming cleave   695
The Libyan and Carpathian seas, and sport
Amid the waves. These movements and these jousts
Ascanius afterwards revived, when he
The walls of Alba Longa built, and taught
The ancient Latin race to celebrate   700
The sports which he and Trojan youths with him

Had learned; the Albans taught them to their sons;
And mighty Rome adopted and preserved
Her fathers' honored custom, now called "Troy";
The youths performing it, "the Trojan band." 705

Thus far, in memory of a sacred sire,
His day was kept, with contests and with games.

Here, changing Fortune showed an altered face.[9]
For while about the tomb a holiday
They kept, with various games and solemn rites, 710
Saturnian Juno from the skies sent down
Iris her messenger to the Trojan fleet,
And breathed the winds upon her as she went.
Revolving many a scheme, the goddess kept
Her ancient enmity still unappeased. 715
The virgin down her bow of thousand tints
Glides softly on her way, unseen by all.
She notes the mighty concourse, and surveys
The shores, and sees the harbor and the ships
Deserted. On a lonely shore, afar, 720
The Trojan women mourned Anchises dead,
And sat weeping and gazed upon the deep.
"Alas, how many shoals, how many seas,"
They cried, "our weary hearts must still endure!"
Such was the complaint they uttered, one and all. 725
They pray for a city and a resting place,
And hate the thought of further sufferings
Upon the sea. Then in the midst of them,
Iris, her face and robes divine laid by,
Not inexpert in mischief, throws herself 730
In Beroës form, Doryclus' aged wife,
Who rank and name and family once had;
And thus the Trojan matrons she addressed:—
"Unhappy women, by no Grecian hands
Dragged to your death beneath your city's walls! 735
O ill-starred race! To what disastrous end
Does Fortune now reserve you, one and all?

The seventh summer now is passing by,
Since Troy was doomed, and still upon the seas
We are borne away, and traverse every land,   740
Over so many inhospitable rocks,
Beneath so many stars, still rolling on
The billows, following an Italy
That flees before. Here the fraternal shores
Of Eryx stand; Acestes is our host.   745
Who hinders us from building here our walls,
A city and a home? O fatherland,
And household gods snatched from the foe in vain!
Shall never walls again be named from Troy?
And shall I never the Hectorian streams,   750
Xanthus and Simois, again behold?
Come then, and burn with me these luckless ships.
For as I slept, I thought Cassandra's ghost
Brought to me burning torches, crying aloud,
'Here seek your Troy! Here find your house and home!'   755
The time now prompts the deed. No more delay,
With omens such as these. Four altars, see,
To Neptune. He himself, the god, supplies
The torches, and the courage for the attempt."

Saying this, she snatched a brand, and drawing back   760
Her arm, hurled it afar, with all her strength.
Excited and bewildered stood the dames
Of Troy. Then from the throng, eldest in years,
Pyrgo, the nurse of Priam's many sons,
Exclaimed: "Matrons, no Beroë is this,   765
No matron of Rhoeteum, nor the wife
Of our Doryclus. Do you not discern
The glorious signs of deity, how flame
Her sparkling eyes? What majesty is hers?
And what a countenance, and voice, and gait?   770
Beroë I myself just now have left,
Sick, and in grief that she alone must miss
The sacred rites, and honors that we pay
To Anchises."

But the matrons, doubtful first,
Began to scan the ships with eyes of hate,   775
Uncertain, between their yearning for this land
And that which called them with the voice of fate.
When upon balanced wings the goddess rose,
And flying tracked her pathway with an arc
Immense, a gleaming rainbow on the clouds.   780
Then they, astonished at this strange portent,
And maddened, shout; and from the inmost hearths
They snatch the burning coals; and some despoil
The altars, and throw branches, leaves, and brands.
Unchecked the fire now rages all across   785
The benches, oars, and sterns of painted fir.

Eumelus to the tomb and theatre
Brings news of the blazing ships. They all look back
And see the sparks and see the rolling smoke.
And first Ascanius, leading joyously   790
The equestrian band, even as he was, breaks off,
And to the excited camp in hot haste rides;
Nor can his breathless guardians stay his flight.
"What strange fury is this! What is it you do,
O wretched countrywomen?" he exclaims;   795
"What means this deed? No enemy, or camp
Of hostile Greeks, but your own hopes you burn.
Lo, I am your Ascanius!" At their feet
He casts the empty helmet he had worn
In mimic battle. Here came hurrying on   800
Æneas and the Trojan bands. But now,
The women, struck with fear, fly here and there
About the shores, and seek the woods and caves
With stealthy steps, ruing the deed commenced,
And loathing the bright day. Changed now, they see   805
And recognize their friends, and Juno's power
Is shaken from their breasts. But nonetheless
The flames rage on still fierce and unsubdued.
Beneath the wet planks still the smoldering torch
Burns with dull smoke; the lingering heat devours   810

The ships, and down through all their framework creeps;
No human strength avails, nor streaming floods.
    Then good Æneas rends his robes, and calls
Upon the gods for aid, with outstretched hands:—
"O Jove Omnipotent, if you do not   815
Altogether hate our race; if now
Your pity, shown of old, on human woes
Still looks with tenderness, then save our fleet
From the devouring flames! Now, father, snatch
The Trojans' slender fortunes from this death.   820
Or, if I so deserve, with your right hand
Blast with your thunder all that yet remains."
Scarce had he spoken, when a storm of rain
Darkened the sky, and poured down with fury,
With thunder peals that shook the hills and plains.   825
From the whole heavens, black gusts and windy floods
Down-rushing, drenched the ships. The half-charred beams
Are soaked; the flames are quenched; the vessels all,
Save four, are rescued from the fiery pest.

Æneas, by this grave disaster shocked,   830
Turned over and over his heavy cares, in doubt
Whether on these Sicilian fields to stay,
Forgetful of the fates, or try once more
To reach the Italian shores. Then Nautes, old
And wise, by Pallas taught, a sage renowned   835
For wisdom, thus gave his counsel, and showed
Both what the anger of the gods portends,
And what the order of the fates demands;
And with these words he cheers Æneas' thoughts:—
"Wherever Fate may lead us, whether on   840
Or backward, let us follow. Whatsoever
Occurs, all fortune must be overcome
By endurance. Here you have Acestes, born
Of race divine, and Trojan. Take then him
Into your counsels, ready to assist.   845
All those who, now these ships are lost, may prove
Superfluous, and all those who have grown tired

Of your great enterprise and plan—whoever
Is unavailable, or shrinks from fear
Of danger—these select, and leave with him.   850
Here let them settle, in a city built
For them, with his consent, called by his name."

Roused by such counsels from his aged friend,
He ponders still, his mind distraught with cares.
And now black Night, upon her chariot borne,   855
Held all the sky: when, gliding down, he sees
A vision of Anchises' face,[10] and hears
These words: "My son, more dear to me than life,
While life remained!—son, still by Trojan fates
Long tried—I come to you by Jove's command,   860
Who saved your ships from fire, and from on high
Looked with compassion. Follow then the advice
So excellent, the aged Nautes gives.
The chosen youths, the bravest hearts, take now
To Italy. A rough and hardy race   865
Must be subdued in Latium. But seek first
The lower realms of Dis, and through the deep
Avernus, O my son, go meet your sire.
For not in wicked Tartarus I dwell,
With sorrowing ghosts, but amid the companies   870
Of upright souls, in blest Elysium.
Hither, with offered blood of black sheep slain,
The virgin Sibyl will conduct your steps.
And what your future race shall be, and what
The cities to be given you, you shall learn.   875
And now farewell: the dewy Night has passed
Her high meridian, and the cruel Dawn
Is breathing on me with her panting steeds."
He said; and faded into air, like smoke.
"Ah, where then do you go?" Æneas cried;   880
"Why do you hasten away? Whom do you flee?
Or who constrains you from your son's embrace?"
With that, the slumbering embers he revives;
Suppliant, adores his Trojan household god,

And venerable Vesta, with the meal   885
Of sacrifice and with the censer full.

Forthwith he calls Acestes, and his friends;
And the commands of Jove and of his sire
Declares, and how his own intent now stands.
His plans are not opposed. Acestes yields   890
Assent to his demands. The matrons first
For the new city they enroll; then all
Who are willing, set apart—the souls who need
No loud applause of fame. The rowers' seats
They then replace, repair the timbers burned,   895
And fit the oars and ropes. A little band
They are, but valorous, and fresh for war.

Meanwhile Æneas with a plough marks out
The city's boundaries, and by lot assigns
The dwelling places,—Ilium here, here Troy,   900
As he determines. Pleased, Acestes views
The place he is to rule, declares the forum's
Code, and gives the assembled fathers laws.
Then, near the stars, upon Mount Eryx' top,
To Venus of Idalium they erect   905
A temple: and to Anchises' tomb they give
A ministering priest and sacred grove.

Now all had held their nine days' festival,
With offerings due upon the altars laid.
The waves are smoothed: the south-wind freshening blows   910
With breezy invitation to the deep.
Then all along the shore rise tones of grief;
And last embraces night and day delay.
Nay, even the mothers—they for whom before
The face of Ocean was a bitter thing   915
And an intolerable name—would now
Depart, and dare all hardships of the deep.
With friendly words Æneas comforts them;
And to his countryman Acestes he

With tears commends them. Three young heifers then   920
To Eryx he commands that they shall slay;
And to the Storms a lamb. The cables loosed,
He stands upon the prow, his temples wreathed
With olive-leaves, and holds a cup, and throws
The entrails on the waves, and pours the wine.   925
A wind arising, follows as they sail;
And rival crews ply oars, and sweep the sea.

But Venus, full of cares and fears,[11] meanwhile
Pours out her plaints to Neptune: "Juno's wrath
And insatiable hate compel me now,   930
O Neptune, to abase myself in prayers.
Nor lapse of time, nor any piety
Can mitigate her rage; nor doth she rest,
Baffled by Jove's decree, and by the fates.
It's not enough for her to have devoured   935
The Phrygian city with her wicked hate;
Nor to have dragged through every penal pain
The wretched remnants of the Trojan race:
The very ashes and the ruined bones
Of Troy she still pursues. What causes prompt   940
Such rage, she best can tell. You saw yourself
What storms she raised, of late, amid the waves
Of Libya; mingling all the sea and sky,
Vainly enforced with her Æolian blasts,
She dared to invade your realms. And now, behold!   945
Maddening the Trojan mothers, she basely burns
Their ships, and drives the crews to lands unknown.
For what remains, I do entreat that you
Will grant a voyage safe across the seas,
That soon they may reach Laurentian Tiber;   950
If what I ask be so allowed by Jove,
And fate may grant the cities which they seek."

To whom the Saturnian ruler of the deep:—
"It is right, O Cytherea, you should trust
My realms, from where your life was born. I too   955

Deserve this confidence, often having curbed
The rage of seas and skies. Nor less on land
(Let Simois and Xanthus testify)
Has your Æneas been my charge. What time
Achilles chased the breathless troops of Troy,   960
And pressed them hard against the city's walls,
When thousands fell, and the choked rivers groaned
With corpses, nor could Xanthus find a way,
Or roll his waters to the ocean; then
Æneas, having met Achilles there,   965
Ill-matched in strength, and aid from powers divine,
I snatched away, and hid him in a cloud:
Though I desired to overthrow the work
Of own hands, the walls of perjured Troy.
Now still my friendly purpose holds. Dismiss   970
Your fears. He, safe, will reach the Ausonian ports
Desired by you. One only shall he miss,
Lost in the waves—one life for many given."

Thus having soothed and filled her heart with joy,
The father harnesses his steeds in gold,   975
With foaming bits, and all his reins shakes loose
And in his sea-blue car glides over the waves.
The waves subside, the swelling plain is smooth
Beneath his thundering wheels; the clouds are driven
From the vast sky. Then thronging come the forms   980
Of his attendants, monsters of the deep:—
The train of Glaucus, and Palæmon, son
Of Ino, and the Tritons swift; the bands
Of Phorcus; with them Thetis, Melite,
Nesæe, and the virgin Panope,   985
Spio, Thalia, and Cymodoce.

Now joy in turn pervades Æneas' soul,
Late in suspense. He orders all the masts
To be erected, and the canvas spread.
The ships all move as one. Now to the left,   990
Now to the right they tack, and loose the sails,

Or turn and turn again their peakèd tops
Together. Favoring winds bear on the fleet;
And Palinurus leads the squadron on.
The rest all follow as the pilot bids.   995

And now moist Night had touched her goal midway
In heaven. Beneath their oars the sailors lie,
Amid their hard benches, lapped in sweet repose.
When, dropping from the stars, the god of sleep
Glides down the darkness and dispels the shades   1000
Bringing sad dreams into your guileless soul,
O Palinurus![12] On the lofty stern
He lights in Phorbas' shape, and pours these words
Into his ear: "The waves themselves bear on
Our fleet: the full breeze blows astern: this hour   1005
For sleep is meet. O Palinurus, rest
Your head, and close your eyes overtasked with toil.
I myself for a while will take your place."
But Palinurus scarcely raised his eyes,
And answered: "Do you ask me to forget   1010
The Ocean's placid face, these quiet waves?
And to confide in such a wondrous calm?
How to the treacherous south winds can I trust
Æneas, often by such skies serene
Deceived?" He spoke; and, clinging to the helm,   1015
Held fast, and fixed his eyes upon the stars.
But lo! the god shakes over his brows a branch
Dripping with Lethean dew and drowsy spells
Of Stygian strength, and seals his swimming eyes,
That strive to lift their lids. The untimely rest   1020
Had scarce relaxed his limbs, when, pressing hard
Upon his frame, the demon hurls him down
Prone on the waves, a fragment of the stern
And the whole rudder in his clutch, torn off;
And leaves him calling to his friends in vain: 1025
Then spreads his wings, and vanishes in air.
Yet onward sails the fleet, in safety borne
Unterrified, by Neptune's promised aid.

And now they near the Sirens' rocks, of old
A perilous shore, and white with many bones;   1030
Where the perpetual dashing of the waves
Hoarsely resounds from far. Æneas now
Perceives the unsteady wavering of his ship,
Its pilot being lost. Then he himself
Steers through the billows dark, with many a groan,   1035
Grieved to the heart to know his friend is lost.
"O Palinurus, who did trust too far
The skies and seas serene, a naked corpse
You now will lie, upon some unknown sands!"

BOOK 6

WEEPING he spoke, then gave his fleet the reins,[1]
Until at length they reach Eubœan Cumæ's
Shores. Seaward the prows are turned; the ships
Fast anchored, and the curved sterns fringe the beach.
On the Hesperian shore the warriors leap   5
With eager haste. Some seek the seminal flame
Hidden in veins of flint; some rob the woods,
The dense abode of beasts, and rivulets
Discover. But the good Æneas seeks
The heights over which the great Apollo rules,   10
And the dread cavern where the Sibyl dwells,
Revered afar, whose soul the Delian god*
Inspires with thought and passion, and to her
Reveals the future. And now Dian's groves
They enter, and the temple roofed with gold.   15

The story goes, that Dædalus, who fled
From Minos, dared to trust himself with wings
Upon the air, and sailed in untried flight
Toward the frigid Arctic, till at length
He hovered over the Cumæan towers.   20
Here first restored to earth, he gave to you,
Phœbus, his oar-like wings, a sacred gift,
And built a spacious temple to your name.
Upon the doors Androgeos'† death was carved:
Then Cecrops'‡ wretched sons, who year by year   25
Were doomed to yield their children up by sevens,
To atone for their misdeed. There stands the urn,

---

*Apollo.

†Androgeos was the son of Minos and Pasiphaë.

‡Cecrops was the earliest king of Athens.

The lots drawn out. Opposite, raised above
The sea, the isle of Crete; the base love
Of Pasiphaë, and the Minotaur,   30
The biformed offspring of unhallowed lust.
Here stands the labor of the labyrinth
And its inextricable winding maze.
But Dædalus, who pitied the great love
Of Ariadne, the blind, tortuous ways   35
Himself unriddled, guiding with a thread
The steps of Theseus. You too, Icarus,
Had grief permitted, would have had great part
In such a work. Twice he essayed to mold
Your fate in gold: twice dropped the father's hands.   40
And further they would have perused each work,
Had not Achates, sent before, appeared;
With him Deiphobe, the priestess there
Of Phœbus and Diana, who thus spoke:—
"This is no time to gaze at idle shows.   45
Best now, from out an untouched herd, to take
Seven steers, and offer as a sacrifice;
Also as many chosen two-year ewes."

This to Æneas. Then, without delay
They hasten to execute her high commands.   50
The priestess summons then the Trojan chiefs
To her high temple, a vast cavern hewn
From the Eubœan rock. A hundred doors
And avenues are there, from which come rushing
As many voices of prophetic power,   55
The Sibyl's answers.[2] At the threshold now,
"It's time," the virgin said, "to ask your fate
With prayers: the god! behold, the god!"
As thus before the gates she speaks, her face
And color suddenly change; her hair unkempt;   60
Her panting breast and wild heart madly heaves;
Larger she seems: unearthly rings her voice,
As nearer breathed the presence of the god.
"What, are you then so sluggish in your vows,

Trojan Æneas, and so slow to pray? 65
Haste, for not else will these awe-struck doors be opened!"
She ceased. A shudder ran through the Trojans;
And from his inmost soul the chief thus prays:
"Apollo, who the sufferings of Troy
Has ever pitied: you who did direct 70
The hand and shaft of Paris when it struck
Achilles,—led by you, so many seas
Circling so many realms, I have explored,
And distant dwellings of Massylian tribes,
And lands beyond the Syrtes. Now at length 75
We grasp the Italy that seemed so long
A fleeting vision. Though thus far we have come,
Pursued by a Trojan fortune, yet for you,
O gods and goddesses, to whom the name
And fame of Troy have proved an obstacle, 80
It is just that you should spare our nation now.
And you, most sacred prophetess, whose eye
Foresees the future, grant (I do not ask
A kingdom which my fates have never owed)
That I in Latium may establish all 85
My Trojans, and Troy's outcast household gods
Long tossed upon the seas. Then I will build
A marble temple sacred to the praise
Of Phœbus and Diana, and ordain
Great festal days called by Apollo's name. 90
A spacious sanctuary, too, for you
Shall stand. There will I place your oracles,
And secret fates delivered to my race,
And consecrate, O benign seer, to you
A chosen priesthood! Only do not write 95
Your prophecies on leaves, lest blown about
They fly, the sport of fitful winds. You now
Utter your oracles."
                    The prophetess,
Impatient of the overpowering god,
Here raves in a wild frenzy through her cave, 100
And strives from off her breast to shake the spell

Divine. But all the more the deity
Fatigues her foaming lips, and, pressing down,
Subdues her fiery heart. But now, behold,
The hundred doors fly open of their own   105
Accord, and bear this answer through the air:

"O you who hast passed the perils of the sea!
A heavier lot on land remains for thee.
Thy Trojans the Lavinian realm shall find.
Dismiss this doubt and trouble from thy mind.   110
Yet will they rue their coming. Dreadful war,
And Tiber frothed with blood, I see from far.
No Simois there nor Xanthus shalt thou lack,
Nor Grecian camps to threaten and attack.
Another Achilles there shall cross thy path,   115
Born of a goddess, and dire Juno's wrath
Never be absent. Desolate and poor,
What cities shalt thou not for aid implore!
Again a Trojan guest, a foreign wife
In Latium shall renew the bloody strife.   120
Yet yield not thou, but go more boldly on,
Where Fortune leads, till victory be won.
Thy safety first shall come when thou, cast down,
Shall least expect it, from a Grecian town."

Thus from her cave the Cumæan Sibyl pours   125
Her dread and mystic utterance, moaning low,
Enfolding in obscurity her truths.
And while she raves, Apollo seems to shake
His reins above her, and still turns his goad
Beneath her breast. Soon as the fury ceased,   130
And the wild lips were still, Æneas spoke:—
"None of these trials comes, O virgin seer,
With new and unexpected face to me.
All was foreseen and pondered in my mind.
One thing I ask of you,—since here, it's said   135
The gateway opens to the lower world,
And that dim shadowy lake, the overflowing tide

Of Acheron,—that I may, face to face,
Meet my dear father. Show me then the way;
Open the sacred portals. Him, through flames 140
And through a thousand flying javelins,
I bore upon these shoulders, from our foes
So rescued. He through all the dreary seas
Was my companion, and bore all threatenings
Of ocean and of sky, feeble and old, 145
Yet with a strength beyond the lot of age.
For, he it was whose prayer and whose command
Sent me a suppliant to your doors. I pray,
O virgin blest, that you will pity us,
Father and son; for all things you can do; 150
Nor was it in vain that Hecate set you over
The Avernian groves. If Orpheus could call back
His wife, confiding in his Thracian lyre
And ringing chords; if Pollux could redeem
His brother by alternate death, and goes 155
And comes so often this way (why need I speak
Of Theseus, or of mighty Hercules?),
I too, like them, derive my birth from Jove."
Thus he besought, and on the altar held.
"Son of Anchises, born of blood divine," 160
The priestess thus began, "easy the way
Down to Avernus; night and day the gates
Of Dis stand open. But to retrace your steps
And reach the upper air—here lies the task,
The difficulty here. A few by Jove 165
Beloved, or to ethereal heights upborne
By virtue's glowing force, sons of the gods,
The labor have achieved. Midway thick woods
The passage bar, and, winding all about,
Cocytus' black and sinuous river glides. 170
But if such strong desire be yours, to float
Twice over the Stygian lake; if the mad task
Delights you, twice to see the gloomy realms
Of Tartarus;—learn what must first be done.
Hidden in the leafy darkness of a tree, 175

There is a golden bough,[3] the leaves and stem
Also of gold, and sacred to the queen
Of the infernal realm. The grove around
Hides it from view; the shades of valleys dim
Close in and darken all the place. But none   180
At all can venture down the deep recesses
Of the underworld, till he has plucked that spray
With golden tresses. Fair Proserpina
Demands this gift as hers alone. When plucked,
Another shoot fails not, but buds again   185
With the same golden foliage and stalk.
Therefore look high among the leaves, and seize
The branch, when found. It will give itself to you
With ready will, if fate shall favor you.
If otherwise, no strength nor sharpened steel   190
Can sever it. But now—you know it not,
Alas!—a friend of yours lies dead: his corpse
Pollutes the entire fleet, while here you stay
Seeking our counsel, lingering at our doors.
First, bear him to his fitting burial-place,   195
Offering black cattle, your first sacrifice
Of expiation. So shall you at last
Behold the Stygian groves, by living souls
Untrod." She ceased to speak, with lips compressed.

Sad, and with downcast eyes, Æneas leaves   200
The Sibyl's cave, revolving in his mind
These mysteries. Trusty Achates too
Attending him, the same deep cares oppress.
Of many things they talked upon the way,
And wondered who the friend might be whose death   205
The prophetess announced,—what lifeless form
Demanding burial rites. But when they arrived,
Behold, they see Misenus* stretched upon
The shore, snatched by unworthy death away;

---

*Trumpeter of Aeneas punished by Triton. In order to enter the underworld, Aeneas must first bury Misenus.

Misenus, son of Æolus, than whom   210
None blew the trumpet with more skill, to call
The warriors and inflame to martial deeds.
He had been the mighty Hector's comrade,
With clarion and with spear alike renowned.
By Hector's side he had often fought; but when   215
Victorious Achilles slew this chief,
He joined Æneas, no inferior choice.
But now, when thoughtlessly with hollow shell
He made the seas resound—as though he called
The gods to match his strains—Triton,* if so   220
The tale may be believed, with jealous rage
Seized him among the rocks, and plunged him deep
Within the foaming waves. So, round his corpse,
With loud lamenting cries all gathered there,
Æneas grieving most. With tearful eyes   225
They hasten then, as by the Sibyl bid,
To build a funeral pile, and heap it high
With wood. Into the ancient forest then,
The lair of savage beasts, they go. Down fall
The pitch trees, and the ilex trunks resound   230
Beneath their axes; rowan and oak are split,
And from the mountain, ash trees huge are rolled.
Æneas, chief amid these labors, cheers
His comrades at their work, and wields the axe
With them. But gazing at the forest depths   235
Immense, from his sad heart escapes this prayer:—
"Ah, if within this wood that golden bough
Would now but show itself! For all comes true
The prophetess has told—too true of you,
Misenus!" Scarcely had he said these words,   240
When from the sky two doves before him flew,
And lit upon the grass. The hero knows
His mother's birds, and joyfully he prays:
"Be then my guides! O, if there be a way,

---

*Sea deity; son of Neptune.

Show me where that rich bough amid the trees 245
Shadows the fertile soil! And fail me not,
Mother divine, in this my doubtful quest."
So saying, he checked his steps, observing all
Their motions and their course. They, here and there
Feeding along their track, no farther flew 250
Than could be followed by the eye. At length
They reached the place where dark Avernus breathes
Its noisome fumes; then upward took their flight,
And, gliding through the yielding air, they perch
Upon the tree, their place of rest desired, 255
Where, with contrasted hue, the golden bough
Gleamed through the leaves. As in the frosty woods
The mistletoe, which springs not from the tree
On which it grows, puts forth a foliage new,
And rings the smooth round trunks with saffron tufts, 260
So on the dark tree shone the leafy gold
And rustled in the breeze. With eager hand
Æneas grasps and breaks the lingering branch,
And to the Sibyl's dwelling bears it off.

Meanwhile upon the shore the Trojans mourned 265
Misenus dead, and the last funeral rites
Paid to his unresponsive ashes. First
A lofty pile, split oak and unctuous pine,
They build, and twine the sides with somber boughs,
And place the funeral cypresses in front, 270
And deck the pyre with shining armor. Some
The bubbling cauldrons heat, bathe and anoint
The frigid corpse, with groans: upon a couch
Lay the lamented limbs, and over them throw
The well-known garments and the purple robes; 275
Some on their shoulders lift the bier—sad task!—
And, as the custom was, apply the torch
With heads averted. Offerings are burned
Of incense, sacrificial flesh, and oil.
The ashes having fallen, and the flame 280
Burned out, the smoldering remains are steeped

In wine; and Corynæus then collects
The bones, and stores them in a brazen urn.
Thrice round the friends, with fertile olive-branch,
He sprinkles water in a dewy shower   285
Of purifying drops; the last farewell
Then speaks. But good Æneas heaps a tomb
Of spacious size, and lays the implements
His friend was wont to use on top: the oar
And trumpet, under the aerial mount   290
Which now from him the name Misenus bears
And evermore will bear.

                  These things being done,
He hastens to perform the Sibyl's charge.
There was a cavern deep with yawning jaws
Enormous, stony, screened by a gloomy lake   295
And shadowy woods: no wingèd thing could fly
Unscathed above it, so baleful was the breath
That from the opening rose to the upper air:
(The place so called Aornos* by the Greeks.)
Here first the priestess placing four black steers,   300
Upon their foreheads pours the sacred wine,
And plucks the topmost hairs between the horns,
And lays them, the first offerings, on the flames,
Invoking Hecate, strong in heaven and hell.
The knives perform their work: the tepid blood   305
Is caught in bowls. Himself Æneas slays
To Night, the mother of the Eumenides,
And to her mighty sister, a black lamb;
Also a barren cow, Proserpina,
To you. Next to the Stygian king he builds   310
Nocturnal altars, and whole carcasses
Of bulls he burns, and on the burning pyre
Pours out the unctuous oil amid the flames.
When lo, as the first sunbeams lit the place,
The earth beneath began to rumble, and tops   315
Of wooded hills to move; and through the shades

---

*"Without birds" (Greek).

They seemed to hear the yelling of the hounds
Of hell, that told the goddess coming near.
"Away, unhallowed ones!" the Sibyl cries;
"And leave the whole grove clear. But do press on,   320
And draw your sword: for now, Æneas, now,
Firm and undaunted you must prove." She spoke,
And madly plunged into the open cave.
He with no timid step keeps pace with her.

Ye deities, whose empire is of souls!   325
Ye silent Shades,—Chaos and Phlegethon!
Ye wide mute spaces stretching through the night!
Be it lawful that I speak what I have heard,
And by your will divine unfold the things
Buried in gloomy depths of deepest earth!   330

Through shadows, through the lonely night they went,
Through the blank halls and empty realms of Dis:
As when by the uncertain moon one walks
Beneath a light malign, amid the woods,
When all the sky is overcast, and night   335
Robs all things of their color. In the throat
Of Hell, before the very vestibule
Of opening Orcus,[4] sit Remorse and Grief,
And pale Disease, and sad Old Age, and Fear,
And Hunger that persuades to crime, and Want:—   340
Forms terrible to see. Suffering and Death
Inhabit here, and Death's own brother, Sleep;
And the mind's evil Lusts, and deadly War
Lie at the threshold, and the iron beds
Of the Eumenides; and Discord wild,   345
Her viper-locks with bloody fillets bound.

Here in the midst, a huge and shadowy elm
Spreads out its aged boughs,—the seat, it's said,
Of empty dreams, that cling beneath the leaves.
And here besides are many savage shapes   350
Of monstrous phantoms—Centaurs, in their stalls;

Scylla of double form; and Briareus
The hundred-handed; and the hissing snake
Of Lerna; the Chimæra armed with flames;
And Gorgons, Harpies, and the triple shade   355
Of Geryon. Here with sudden tremor seized,
Æneas draws his sword, the keen bare edge
Opposing as they come. And had not then
His wise companion warned him that these forms
Were but a flitting swarm of bodiless   360
And unsubstantial ghosts, he would have rushed
Among them, cleaving but the empty air.

Hence downward leads the way to Tartarus
And Acheron. A gulf of turbid mire
Here foams with vortex vast, and belches forth   365
Into Cocytus all its floods of sand.
By these dread rivers waits the ferryman[5]
Squalid and grim, Charon, his grisly beard
Uncombed and thick; his eyes are flaming lamps;
A filthy garment from his shoulders hangs.   370
He tends his sails, and with his pole propels
His barge of dusky iron hue, that bears
The dead across the river. Old he seems,
But with a green old age. Down to the banks
Comes rushing the whole crowd, matrons and men,   375
Great heroes, boys, unwedded girls, and youths
Their parents saw stretched on their funeral pile;
Thick as the clustering leaves that fall amid
The forests in the first autumnal chill,
Or as the flocks of birds that from the sea   380
Fly landward, by the frigid season sent
Across the main, to seek a sunnier clime.
They, praying to be first to cross the stream,
Were standing, longing for the farther shore,
With outstretched arms. But the stern ferryman   385
Now these, now those, receives into his boat,
But drives afar the others from the beach.

Moved by the tumult, and with wonder filled,
Æneas cries: "O virgin, tell me what
This crowd may mean that to the river moves.   390
What do these spirits seek? What difference
Of fate leaves these behind, while those are rowed
Across the livid waves?" Then answered thus
The aged Sibyl: "Great Anchises' son,
You see here Cocytus, and the Stygian lake,   395
By which the gods do fear falsely to swear;
This crowd, the needy and unburied dead;
That ferryman is Charon. Those he bears
Across had burial rites. No one may pass
Those dreadful waves, until his bones repose   400
Within a quiet grave. A hundred years
They wander, flitting all around these shores,
Until at last they cross the wished-for lake."

Absorbed in thought, Æneas paused and stood,
Pitying their cruel lot. And now he sees,   405
Sad, and without their needed burial rites,
Leucaspis and Orontes who had led
The Lycian fleet, and both of whom, from Troy
Together driven across the stormy deeps,
The south wind struck, and ship and crew overwhelmed.   410
Lo, Palinurus too, his pilot, comes;
Who, while upon his Libyan course he watched
The stars, of late, down from the stern had fallen
Into the sea. His sad face in the gloom
Æneas scarcely knew. "Which of the gods,"   415
He said, "O Palinurus, snatched your form
Away from us, and plunged you in the waves?
Tell me, I pray; for great Apollo never
Deceived me, till this one response he gave,
That you should safely pass the sea, and reach   420
The Ausonian shores. This is how he keeps his word!"
Then he: "Neither did Phœbus' oracle
Deceive, nor me did any god immerse
In the deep sea: for falling headlong down,

I dragged the helm with me, by chance torn off,   425
To which I clung, being set to guard it there,
And guide our course. By the rough seas I swear,
That for myself I had no fear so great,
As that your ship, her rudder torn away,
Her pilot lost, might sink amid such waves.   430
Three wintry nights across the ocean wastes
The stormy south wind drifted me along,
Till on the fourth day, from the billow's top,
Italia I descried; and by degrees
Swam to the shore, where safe I should have been,   435
Had not a barbarous horde attacked me there
With swords (my heavy garments dripping wet,
And clinging to the rocks with claw-like clutch),
Hoping for plunder in their ignorance.
The waves and winds now toss me about the shore.   440
Therefore I pray you, by the precious light
And air of heaven, the memory of your sire,
And by the hopes your young Iulus brings,
O you unconquered, snatch me from these woes!
And either heap the earth upon my bones,—   445
For you can do it, seeking Velia's port,—
Or, if there be some way—some way made known
By your great goddess-mother unto you
(For I must think that not without divine
Consent, you are prepared to float across   450
The Stygian lake),—then give your hand to me
Wretched, and take me with you through the waves;
So I at least in death may find a place
Of rest." To whom the prophetess replied:—
"O Palinurus, whence this wild desire?   455
Can you cross the Stygian waves unburied,
And see the Eumenides' forbidding stream,
And reach that bank unsummoned? Cease to hope
By prayers to bend the destinies divine.
Yet take these words to mind, to cheer your lot.   460
For be assured, the people of that coast,
And through their cities far and wide, impelled

By omens from on high, shall expiate
Your death with fitting rites, and build a tomb
With annual offerings given; and by the name   465
Of Palinurus shall the place be called
Forevermore." These words a little while
Dispelled his grief, while he rejoiced to know
There was a land destined to bear his name.

So on their way they go, and near the stream: 470
When now the boatman from the Stygian wave
Spotted them moving through the silent woods,
And drawing near the bank, with chiding words
He thus accosts them: "Whosoever you are
That draws on near our river thus, all armed,   475
Say why you've come. Stop there where you are!
This is the realm of Shadows and of Sleep,
And drowsy Night. None living are allowed
To cross the river in the Stygian boat.
In truth I was not pleased to have received   480
Alcides, Theseus, nor Pirithoüs,*
Albeit divine and of unconquered strength.
The first of these with his own hand bound fast
The sentinel of Tartarus in chains,
And dragged him trembling from our king's own throne.   485
The others strove to bear away our queen
From Pluto's bridal-chamber." Briefly then
The Amphrysian prophetess replied: "No plots
Like those are here. Be not alarmed. This sword
Intends no violence. Let Cerberus,†   490
Forever barking in his cave, affright
These bloodless ghosts; let chaste Proserpina
Still keep within her uncle's doors, unharmed.
Trojan Æneas, well renowned for arms
And filial reverence, to these lower shades   495
Of Erebus descends to meet his sire.

---

*Pirithoüs was the son of Ixion's wife and a legendary friend of Theseus.

†Three-headed dog that guards the entrance to the underworld.

If by such piety you are not moved,
At least this branch you will acknowledge." Here
She showed the branch concealed within her robe.
At once his anger fell, he spoke no more;   500
But gazed, admiring, at the fated bough,
The offering revered, so long a time
Unseen; and toward them turns around his barge
Of dusky hue, and brings it to the shore.
The ghosts that all along its benches sat,   505
He hurries out, and clears the boat; then place
To great Æneas gives. Beneath his weight
The hide-patched vessel groans; its leaky sides
Drink in the marshy water; till at length
The priestess and the hero, safe across   510
The river, land upon the slimy mud
And weeds of dingy green. Here Cerberus,
Whose triple-throated barking echoes through
These realms, lies stretched immense across his den,
Confronting their approach. The prophetess,   515
Seeing his neck now bristling thick with snakes,
Throws him a cake of medicated seeds
With soporiferous honey moistened. He
With rabid hunger, opening his three throats,
Snaps up the offered sop; and on the ground   520
His hideous limbs relaxing, sprawls, and lies
Huge, and extended all along the cave.
The sentinel thus sunk in lethargy,
Æneas gains the entrance, hastening on
Beyond the stream from which there is no return.   525

Then as they entered, voices wild were heard,
Shrieking and wailing—souls of infants robbed
Of all their share of life, snatched from the breast,
And sunk by gloomy fate in cruel death.
Then next were those by accusations false   530
Condemned to suffer death. Nor were their lots
Assigned without a trial and a judge.
Minos presiding, shakes the urn: he calls

The silent multitude, and learns from each
The story of his life and crimes. Next come   535
The places where the sad and guiltless souls
Were seen, who, hating the warm light of day,
Wrought their own death and threw away their lives.
How willingly they now in the upper air
Their poverty and sufferings would endure!   540
But this Heaven's law forbids: the hateful lake
With its sad waves imprisons them, and Styx
Flowing between, nine times encircling, binds.

Not far from this the Fields of Mourning[6] lie
Extended wide: by this name they are called.   545
Here those whom tyrannous love with cruel blight
Has wasted, in secluded paths are hid,
And sheltered round about by myrtle groves.
Not even in death their cares are left behind.
Here Phædra and here Procris he now sees,[7]   550
And sad Eriphyle, who shows the wounds
Made by her cruel son; Evadne too,
And Pasiphaë; and along with these
Laodamia goes, and Cænis, once
A man, now woman, to her former sex   555
Returned by fate. Phœnician Dido here,
Her wound still fresh, was wandering in the woods;
Whom, as the Trojan hero nearer came,
And knew amid the shadows dim, as one
Who sees, or thinks he sees, amid the clouds,   560
The young moon rising,—tears fell from his eyes,
And thus with tones of tender love he spoke:
"Ah, Dido, was it true then, the report
That told of your death: slain by your own hands?
Alas! was I the cause? Now by the stars   565
I swear, and by the gods above, and all
There is of faith and truth below the earth,
Not willingly, O queen, I left your shore.
It was the gods, whose mandate sends me now
To journey here through gloom and shade profound,   570

And places rank with hideous mold, who then
Forced me by their decree. Nor did I know
That my departure would bring such a grief.
To you. Stay then your steps, nor turn away
From me. Ah, wherefore do you shun me thus?   575
It's the last word fate allows me to speak!"
So did Æneas strive to soothe her soul
Inflamed and aspect stern, while still he wept.
She turned away, her eyes fixed on the ground;
Nor, as he pleaded, was her face more moved   580
Than if she stood there, a hard block of flint,
Or cold Marpesian marble. Then away
She hurried, with defiance in her look,
And hid amid the shadows of the woods.
There, with Sychæus, her first spouse, she finds   585
Responsive sympathy and equal love.
But nonetheless, wrung by this cruel chance,
Æneas follows her with tearful eyes
And pitying heart.
     Then on his way he toils;
And now they reached the farthest fields, a place   590
Apart, by those frequented who in war
Were famous.[8] Tydeus here he meets, and here
Parthenopæus, well renowned in arms;
And the pale specter of Adrastus: there,
Trojans in battle slain, lamented much   595
In upper earth, whom with a sigh he sees
In long array. Glaucus and Medon there
Appear; Thersilochus; Antenor's sons;
And Polyphœtes, consecrated priest
To Ceres; and Idæus, holding still   600
His chariot and his arms. To right and left
The spirits crowd about him, not content
Merely to see him, but they indeed must wait
And hover round his steps, and know what cause
Has brought him here. But the Grecian chiefs   605
And hosts of Agamemnon, when they see
The hero and his glittering arms that flash

Across the shadows, tremble with great fear.
Some turn and flee, as to their ships of old
They fled; some raise thin voices, and their shouts   610
Die without sound within their gasping throats.

Here Priam's son Deiphobus* he sees,
Mangled, with lacerated face and hands,
Ears severed from his head, and nostrils gashed
With shameful wounds. Scarce does the hero know   615
His form, as cowering he essays to hide
His cruel punishment. Him then with voice
Well known he addressed: "Valiant Deiphobus,
Of Teucer's noble race, what enemy
Has wrought on you this cruel chastisement?   620
To whom was this permitted? I was told
That you on Troy's last night, worn out, and tired
Of Grecian slaughter, had sunk down amid heaps
Of confused carnage. Then an empty mound
I raised to you upon the Rhœtean shore,   625
Thrice calling on your shade. Your name and arms
Still keep the place. But you, O friend, I sought
In vain; nor could, departing, lay your limbs
Within our country's earth." To whom replied
The son of Priam: "Nothing, O my friend,   630
Was left undone by you: you did fulfill
All rites of burial for Deiphobus.
My fate it was, and her pernicious crime—
That Spartan—that immersed me in these woes.
It was she who left these traces of herself.   635
For how in illusive pleasures that last night
Of Troy was passed too well you can recall,
When over the steep walls leapt the fatal horse,
Filled with armed men. Feigning a sacred dance,
She led the Phrygian women round about,   640
With Bacchic cries and orgies, and herself
Held a great torch, and from the citadel

---

*Son of Priam who married Helen after the death of Paris.

Summoned the Greeks. Me, wearied out with cares,
And sunk in sleep, my unhappy chamber held.
Rest, sweet and deep, pressed on me as I lay,— 645
Deep as the calm of death. But she meanwhile,
My incomparable spouse, from out the house
Removed all weapons, and my faithful sword
Took from beneath my head, and summons in
Her Menelaus, and opens wide the doors; 650
Hoping, indeed, to give her amorous lord
A prize of value, and to cancel out
The infamy of all her old misdeeds.
Why need I linger?—Through my chamber door
They burst; with them they bring Æolides, 655
The inciter of the crime.—Ye gods, pay back
Unto the Greeks such deeds, if I demand
With pious lips the punishment! But you,—
Tell me what fortune brings you here, alive?
Do you come driven by wanderings over the seas, 660
Or by the mandate of the gods? What chance
Pursues you, that to these sad sunless realms
Of turbid gloom you come?" While thus they talked,
Aurora's car had passed the middle arch
Of heaven; and they perhaps had lingered out 665
The allotted time. But with brief warning spoke
The Sibyl: "Night, Æneas, rushes on,
While we in lamentation spend the hours.
Here is the place at which our path divides
In two: one leading to the right, beneath 670
The walls of mighty Dis—the way for us
Into Elysium; while the left way sends
The wicked to their punishment, and leads
To Tartarus." Then said Deiphobus:
"Great priestess, be not angry: I depart, 675
And will complete the number of the shades,
Returning to the darkness. You, our pride
And glory, pass, pass on—to destinies
More bright than mine!" Saying this, he turned and fled.

Then suddenly Æneas looking back,   680
Beneath a cliff upon the left beholds
A prison vast with triple ramparts girt,
Round which Tartarean Phlegethon, with surge
Of foaming torrents, raves, and thundering whirl
Of rocks. A huge gateway in front is seen,   685
With columns of the solid adamant.
No strength of man, or even of gods, avails
Against it.[9] Rising in the air a tower
Of iron appears: there sits Tisiphone,
Tucked in her blood-stained robes, and night and day   690
Guarding the entrance with her sleepless eyes.
Groans from within were heard; the cruel lash,
Then clank of iron, and of dragging chains.
Æneas stopped, and listened to the din,
Struck with dismay. "What forms of crime," he said,   695
"What punishments are these, O virgin, say?
What wailings that assail the skies?"
                                        Then she:
"O Trojan chief, pure souls can never pass
Those gates accursèd. Yet when Hecate gave
To me the keeping of the Avernian groves,   700
Herself she showed me all these penalties
Divine, and led me through them all. Here it is
That Rhadamanthus holds his severe sway;
He hears and punishes each secret fraud,
Forcing confession from the souls who once   705
Rejoicing in their self-deceiving guilt
Put off the atonement to the hour of death.
Armed with her whip, the avenging Fury comes
Scourging the guilty, with insulting taunts;
In her left hand she holds her angry snakes,   710
And calls her cruel sisters. Then at last
The accursèd portals open wide, with noise
Of grating horror, on their hinges turned.
Do you see what guard is seated at the gates?
Within, a Hydra sits, more terrible,   715
With fifty yawning mouths immense and black.

Then Tartarus itself sheer downward parts,
And stretches through the darkness twice as far
As upward heaven's Olympian heights are seen.
It's there Earth's ancient race, the Titan brood,   720
Hurled down and blasted by the thunderbolts,
Roll in the lowest gulf. There have I seen
The twin sons of Aloeus, with their limbs
Immense, who strove the mighty heavens to spoil,
And from his realms supernal tear Jove down.   725
Salmoneus, too, I saw in cruel pains,
For having dared to imitate the fires
Of Jove, and the Olympian thunder: him
Who, drawn by four steeds, brandishing a torch,
Drove through the streets of Elis, amid the crowd   730
Of Greeks, exulting, claiming for himself
The honors of the gods. Madman! to dream
That din of brass and trampling hoofs of steeds
Could counterfeit the inimitable crash
Of storms and thunder. But the Omnipotent   735
Amid the dense clouds hurled a blazing bolt
(No torches his, nor smoky fires of pitch),
And in the tempest smote him down headlong.
Here too was Tityos seen, the foster-child
Of the all-nurturing Earth; his body stretched   740
Across nine acres lies; a vulture huge
With crooked beak upon his liver gnaws,
Which never dies, and entrails still alive
With pain, and feeds and dwells forever there
Beneath his heart; nor finds he any rest,   745
The fibres still renewed. Why need I name
Pirithoüs, Ixion, or the race
Of Lapithæ? Or those above whose heads
A threatening rock seems ever about to fall,
Or falling? Sumptuous couches near them shine   750
With feet of gold, and banquets rich are spread
In royal luxury. But beside them sits
The queen of Furies, and forbids them touch
The food, and, shrieking, waves aloft her torch.

Here those who cherished hatred, during life,   755
Toward their brothers; or who lifted hands
Of violence against their parents; those
Who against their clients schemed and practised fraud;
Or those who brooded over their hoarded wealth,
Selfish and solitary, nor dispensed   760
A portion to their kin—the largest crowd
These formed; or those who for adulterous crimes
Were slain; or fought in wars unjust, nor feared
To violate allegiance to their lords:
These all await their doom. Seek not to know   765
What doom, or what the form of punishment
Allotted, into which they sink. Some roll
Enormous rocks, or on the spokes of wheels
Hang stretched and bound. Unhappy Theseus there
Sits, and will sit forever. Phlegyas too,   770
Most wretched, speaks to all with warning words,
And with a loud voice calls amid the gloom:—
'Take heed, learn justice, don't despise the gods!'
Here one is seen, who for a golden bribe
His country sold, and fixed a despot's throne;   775
And for a price made laws, and then unmade:
There one who invaded his own daughter's bed
In a forbidden marriage. All had dared
Some dreadful crime, succeeding where they dared.
Not if I had a hundred tongues, a voice   780
Of iron, could I tell thee all the forms
Of guilt, or number all their penalties."

So spoke the aged priestess. "But come now,"
She cries, "let us resume our way with speed,
And finish the great task we have begun.   785
I see the walls by Cyclops' forges built;
The gateway with its arch confronts our view,
Where by command we place our offering."
She spoke; and through the obscure paths they stepped
Together, passed the midway space, and neared   790
The gate. Æneas at the entrance stands,

Fresh lustral water sprinkles over his limbs,
And hangs upon the door the golden bough.

These rites performed, the gift the goddess asks
Being duly made, they reach the pleasant realms   795
Of verdant green, the blessed groves of peace.[10]
A larger sky here robes with rosy light
The fields, lit by a sun and stars, their own.
Some on the grassy plots pursue their games
Of manly strength, and wrestle on the sand.   800
Some in the dance beat time, and chant their hymns.
The Thracian priest with loosely flowing robes
Responds in numbers to his seven-toned lyre,
And now with fingers, now with ivory quill,
He strikes the chords. Here dwells the ancient race   805
Of Teucer's line, a noble progeny,
The great-souled heroes born in better years,
Ilus, Assaracus, and Dardanus,
Who founded Troy. Æneas wondering sees
Their arms and shadowy chariots from afar,   810
The spears fixed in the ground, the horses loose
Feeding about the fields. Whatever love
The living had for chariots or for arms,
Or care of pasturing their shining steeds,
Goes with them, though their bodies lie entombed.   815
Others he sees upon the right and left
Feasting about the field, while glad anthems
They sing in choral bands, amid a grove
Of fragrant laurel; whence Eridanus,
The abundant river, flowing from above,   820
Rolls through the woodlands. Here the bands are seen,
Of those who for their country fought and bled;
The chaste and holy priests; the reverent bards
Whose words were worthy of Apollo; those
Who enriched life with fine inventive arts;   825
And all who by deserving deeds had made
Their names remembered. These wore garlands all
Of snowy white upon their brows. To them,

Scattered about in groups, the Sibyl spoke;
And chiefly to Musæus; in the midst   830
He stood, and with his lofty shoulders towered
Above them all, admiring. "Happy souls,"
She said, "and you, O best of poets, say
What region and what spot Anchises makes
His home. For him we have come to seek, and crossed   835
The rivers wide of Erebus." Then answered
Briefly the noble bard: "No fixed abode
Is ours; we dwell amid the shady groves;
The river-banks our couches;—and we haunt
The meadows fresh with running rivulets.   840
But you, if such be your desire, pass over
This hill. I will point out an easy path."
He spoke; and leading on, he from above
Showed them the shining fields. They from the top
Move downward on their way.

                             Anchises there,   845
Down in a green valley, was noting all
The souls shut in, destined one day to pass
Into the upper light, and rapt in thought
He mused thereon. It chanced his future race
He was reviewing there, descendants dear,   850
And all their line—their fates and fortunes all—
Their characters, their future deeds, unborn.
He, when he saw Æneas over the grass
Coming to meet him, stretched his eager hands,
His cheeks all wet with tears, and from his lips   855
These accents fell: "And are you come at last?
That filial love I counted on so long,
Has it now overcome the arduous road?
My son, is it granted me to see your face,
And hear your well-known voice, and answer you?   860
Thus in my mind I hoped and guessed, indeed,
And numbered over the intervening times.
Nor have my anxious wishes been deceived.
What lands, what seas you have traversed, O my son!

Amid what dangers you were tossed about!   865
What harm from Libyan realms I feared for you!"
Æneas then: "O father, many a time
Your shade, your sad-eyed shade, has met my gaze,
And urged me to this place to bend my steps.
Within the Tyrrhene sea my fleet is moored.   870
Grasp now my hand, my father, grasp my hand
In yours; withdraw not from your son's embrace!"
So speaking, down his face the great tears streamed.
Three times round his neck he tried to throw his arms;
Three times the shadow flitted from his grasp,   875
And vanished like a wingèd dream away.

Meanwhile Æneas in a valley deep
Sees a secluded grove, with rustling leaves
And branches; there the river Lethe glides
Past many a tranquil home; and round about   880
Innumerable tribes and nations flit.
As in the meadows in the summer-time
The bees besiege the various flowers, and swarm
About the snow-white lilies, and the field
Is filled with soft murmurings. The sudden view   885
Startles him, and he asks what this may mean;
What rivers those may be that flow beyond;
And who this multitude that crowds the banks.
Anchises then replies: "These souls, by fate
Destined for other bodies, drink safe draughts   890
At Lethe's waters and oblivion deep
And lasting. Long since have I wished, in truth,
To speak of them to you, and show you all
This line of my descendants, so you may
Rejoice with me, now Italy is reached."   895
"O father, can we think that from this place
Any exalted souls return to upper
Skies to enter sluggish frames again?
Why so intensely do these luckless ones
Long for the light?" "My son," Anchises said,   900

"No further will I hold you in suspense,
But tell you all." Then thus in due order
He unfolds each mystery to his mind:

"Know first, the heavens, the earth, the flowing sea,[11]
The moon's bright globe, and the Titanian stars   905
Are sustained by one interior spirit:
Through all their members interfused, a mind
Quickens the entire mass, and mingling stirs
The mighty frame. From there springs the life of men,
And grazing flocks, and flying birds, and all   910
The strange shapes in the deep and shining sea.
A fiery vigor animates these germs,
And a celestial origin, so far
As our gross bodies clog them not, nor weight
Of perishable limbs impedes the soul.   915
Hence they desire and fear, rejoice and grieve;
And, shut in prisons dark, they look not back
Upon the skies. Not even when life's last ray
Has fled does every ill depart, nor all
Corporeal taints quite leave their unhappy frames.   920
And needs must be that many a hardened fault
Inheres in wondrous ways. Therefore the pains
Of punishment they undergo, for sins
Of former times. Some in the winds are hung
Suspended and exposed. Others beneath   925
A waste of waters from their guilt are cleansed,
Or purified by fire. We all endure
Our ghostly retribution. From there, a few
Attain the free Elysium's happy fields,
Till Time's great cycle of long years complete,   930
Clears the fixed taint, and leaves the ethereal sense
Pure, a bright flame of unmixed heavenly air.
All these, when for a thousand years the wheel
Of fate has turned, the Deity calls forth
To Lethe's stream, a mighty multitude;   935
That they, forgetful of the past, may see
Once more the vaulted sky, and may begin

To wish return into corporeal frames."
Thus spoke Anchises; and leads on his son,
Together with the Sibyl, through the throng   940
Of murmuring spirits. On a rising ground
He stands, from where opposite, in long array,
He may discern each face as it approached.

"Hear now what fame henceforward shall attend
The Dardan race,[12] and what posterity   945
From Italy shall come, illustrious souls,
And who they are succeeding to our name;
This will I show you, and your own fates foretell.
Do you see that youth who on a headless spear
Is leaning? Nearest to the light he stands,   950
By fate; the first to ascend to upper air,
Born of Italian blood commixed with ours,
Your last-born child, Silvius, an Alban name,
Whom to you late in life Lavinia
Your spouse shall bear, amid the sylvan shades;   955
A king, and parent too of kings,—from whom
Our race shall rule in Alba Longa. Next
Comes Procas, glory of the Trojan race;
And Capys next, and Numitor, and he,
Silvius Æneas, who restores your name,   960
In piety and arms alike renowned,
If ever he reigns over Alba. See, what youths!
What strength they show! But they whose brows are shaded
With civic oak, those shall for you build up
Nomentum, Gabii, and Fidena's walls;   965
These found Collatia's mountain citadels,
Pometia, and the camp of Inuus,
Bela, and Cora; so they shall be called,
Now lands without a name. Then next appears
Mavortian Romulus, who joins the cause   970
Of his grandsire,—the son of Ilia, born
Of Trojan blood. Do you see the double crest
Upon his head, the sign his father gives
Of his celestial destiny? Behold,

My son, beneath his auspices shall Rome   975
Match her great empire with the expanse of earth,
Her genius with Olympian heights. Alone
She will engird her seven hills with a wall,
Blest with a progeny of valiant men.
So does the Berecynthian Mother ride   980
Upon her car through Phrygian cities, crowned
With turrets, joyful in the birth of gods,
Circling a hundred grandsons with her arms,
All gods, all tenants of the upper realms.

"Now turn your eyes, and look upon this race,   985
Your Romans. This is Cæsar, this the line
Born of Iulus, destined to appear
Beneath the arch of heaven. This, this is he,
Whom you have heard foretold and promisèd,
Augustus Cæsar, of a race divine.   990
The golden age in Latium he shall bring
Again, to fields where Saturn reigned of old.
Over Garamantian climes and realms of India
His empire shall extend. Beyond the stars
His land shall reach, beyond the solar ways,   995
Where heaven-bearing Atlas on his shoulder turns
The constellated axis of the sky.
Even now, before his coming, the far realms
Of Caspia and Mæotia shuddering hear
The oracles divine, and Nile's seven mouths   1000
Are troubled. Nor indeed did Hercules
Traverse such lengths of land, although he chased
And pierced the brazen-footed hind, and calmed
The Erymanthian woods, and Lerna quailed
Before his deadly bow. Nor farther rode   1005
Bacchus in victory, who from the top
Of Nysa urged his tigers and his car,
His reins with vine-leaves wreathed. And shall we doubt
To extend our glory by our deeds? or fear
To plant ourselves upon the Ausonian land?   1010

"But who is he, far off, with olive crown
Distinguished, bearing in his hands the signs
Of priesthood? Now I can discern the locks
And hoary beard of him, the Roman king
Who first shall give the city established laws,   1015
From Cures' petty state and humble land
Sent to a mighty empire. Next comes he,—
Disturber of his country's long repose,
Tullus, who shall arouse to warlike deeds
His slothful subjects and the troops unused   1020
To triumphs. Following him, comes boastful Ancus,
Even now too glad to court the crowd's applause.
And would you look upon the Tarquin kings,
And the avenger Brutus' haughty soul,
And the recovered fasces? He the first,   1025
The rights of consular command shall take,
And the relentless axe and rods assume;
And his own sons conspiring in fresh wars,
He, for their treason to fair liberty,
Shall summon to their death; unhappy sire!   1030
However after times shall view these deeds,
His love of country and his large desire
Of praise shall conquer. At a distance now
The Decii come, and Drusus and his line;
And stern Torquatus with his axe, behold;   1035
Camillus too, the standards bearing back.
But those who shining now in equal arms
You see, accordant souls, while in these shades
They dwell—alas, what wars between the two,
Should they attain to life—what carnage dire!   1040
The father-in-law descending from the Alps
And from Monœcus' tower; the son-in-law
Furnished with forces from the Eastern lands,
Opposing comes. O sons, indulge not minds
For wars like these, nor against your country's life   1045
Direct such valor; and your first forebear,—
You who from Olympus claims your line—
My own blood—cast the weapons from your hand!

One up the lofty Capitol shall drive
His car in triumph from Corinthian wars   1050
And Grecians slain; the other shall overthrow
Mycenæ, pride of Agamemnon's race,
And even Æacides himself, a son
Of great Achilles' line, avenging thus
His Trojan sires, and Pallas' shrines profaned.   1055
    "Who, mighty Cato, leaves your name unsaid;
Or you, O Cossus? Who the Gracchi slights?
Or the two Scipios, thunderbolts of war,
And Libya's scourge? Fabricius, powerful
With slender means? Serranus, bending over   1060
His furrow? And you Fabii, say how far
You will transport my weary feet? You are
Our Maximus, who alone restores to us
Our fortunes by delay. Others, I say,
Shall mold, more delicately, forms of bronze,   1065
Lifelike, and shape the human face in stone;
Plead causes with more skill, describe the paths
Of heavenly orbs, and note the rising stars.
But you, O Roman, bend your mind to rule
Your people with strength. This shall be your art: 1070
To impose both terms and rules of peace;
To spare the vanquished, and subdue the proud."

So spoke Anchises, while they stood wondering;
And then resumes: "See where Marcellus moves,
Glorious with his triumphal spoils, and towers   1075
Over all, a victor. He the Roman state
Shall keep from tottering, in tumultuous days.
He, armed and horsed, shall overthrow the power
Of Carthaginia and rebellious Gaul;
And shall hang up the third captured trophy,   1080
An offering to his father Romulus."

But here Æneas spoke: for now he saw
Beside the hero, clad in glittering arms,
A youth in form and face exceeding fair;

But sad his brow, with joyless eyes cast down;—   1085
"O father, who is he who there attends
The hero's steps? His son, or someone else
Of his illustrious line descended? Hark,
What murmuring sounds surround him as he moves!
How noble is his glance! But gloomy Night   1090
With shadows sad is hovering round his head."
    To whom Anchises, weeping floods of tears,
Responded: "O my son, don't try to know
The heavy sorrows of your race! This youth
The Fates will only show a little while   1095
On earth, nor will permit a longer stay.
Too potent would the Roman race have seemed
To you, ye gods, had such gifts been our own.
What groans of heroes from that field shall rise,
Near Mars, his mighty city! or what gloom   1100
Of funeral pomp shall you, O Tiber, see,
When gliding by his new-raised mound of death!
No youth of Ilian race shall ever lift
To such great heights of hope the Latian sires;
Nor Rome shall boast henceforth so dear a child.   1105
Alas for virtue and the ancient faith!
Alas, the strong hands unsubdued in war!
No enemy could ever have opposed
His sword unscathed, whether on foot he charged,
Or spurred his foaming steed against the foe.   1110
Ah, dear lamented boy, could you but break
The stern decrees of fate, then you would be
Our own Marcellus! Give me lilies, brought
In heaping handfuls. Let me scatter here
Dark purple flowers; these offerings at least   1115
To my descendant's shade I would gladly pay,
Though now, alas, an unavailing rite."

Through the whole region thus they roam along
Amid wide fields of unsubstantial air,
Surveying all. And when Anchises thus   1120
Had led his son through each, and had inflamed

His mind with strong desire of future fame,
He tells him of the wars that would be waged;
The city of Latinus, and the lands
Of the Laurentian tribes; and how to bear,   1125
How shun, the hardships of his future lot.

Sleep has two gates:[13] one, said to be of horn,
To real visions easy exit gives;
The other, of white polished ivory,
Through which the Manes* send false dreams to earth.   1130
Anchises, having thus addressed his son,
Together with the Sibyl, leads them on,
And through the ivory gate dismisses them.
Back to his ships the chief pursues his way;
Again beholds his comrades; then sets sail   1135
Toward Caieta's port. The anchors now
Hang from the prows: the sterns stand on the beach.

*Spirits of the dead.

BOOK 7

You also to our shores, Æneas' nurse,[1]
Caieta, dying, gave eternal fame;
And still even now your honored memory keeps
Its fixed abode; your name still marks the spot
Where great Hesperia wraps your bones, if any   5
Glory that may be. Æneas now,
All obsequies performed, the funeral mound
Heaped up, when seas grew calm, sets sail and leaves
The port. As night comes on, the breeze blows fresh,
Nor does the clear white Moon oppose his course,   10
Flashing with tremulous splendor on the sea.

They skirt the nearest shores to Circe's land,[2]
Where she, the sumptuous daughter of the Sun,
Fills her secluded forests with the sounds
Of her assiduous singing, while within   15
Her proud palace the fragrant cedar burns,
Her nightly torch; and through her gauzy web
The whistling shuttle runs. Here, late at night,
The roar of angry lions in the dark,
Chafing against their prison bars, was heard;   20
And bristly boars and raging bears, pent up,
And howling wolves of size immense. All these,
From human shapes, by means of potent herbs,
The cruel goddess Circe had transformed
To faces and to bodies of wild beasts.   25
Then, lest the pious Trojans should endure
Such monstrous fate when brought into the port,
Nor touch a coast so dreadful, Neptune filled
Their sails with favoring winds, to aid their flight,
And wafted them beyond the boiling shoals.   30

175

The sea was blushing in the morning's rays,[3]
And from the ethereal heights Aurora's car
With rose and saffron gleamed; when suddenly
The winds were stilled, and every breath of air,
And the oars struggled through the sluggish sea.   35
And here Æneas from the deep descries
A spacious grove. Through this the Tiber pours
Its smiling waves along, with rapid whirls
And yellow sand, and bursts into the sea.
And all around and overhead were birds   40
Of various hues, accustomed to the banks
And riverbed; from tree to tree they flew,
Soothing the air with songs. Then to the land
He bids the crews direct the vessels' prows,
And joyfully the shadowy river gains.   45

Come now, O Erato,[4] while I relate
Who were the kings, what posture of affairs,
And what the state of ancient Latium was,
When first the stranger army brought the fleet
To the Ausonian shores; and the first feuds   50
Recall. You, goddess, now instruct your bard.
Of direful wars and battles I shall sing;
Of kings by anger spurred to bloody deaths;
And of the Tuscan warriors, and of all
Hesperia roused to arms. A loftier range   55
Of great events, a weightier task is mine.

Latinus, now an aged king, was reigning[5]
With long and peaceful sway, over fields and towns;
Said to be born of Faunus and Marica,
The Laurentian nymph. Faunus' sire   60
Was Picus, who from Saturn* traced his birth,
Remotest author of his race. No son
Was his, so fate decreed. In early youth,
Just budding into life, this progeny

---

*Son of Coelus and Terra, father of Jupiter.

Was snatched away. One daughter only kept 65
His line alive, heir to his ample realms;
Mature for marriage now, in maiden bloom.
From Latium and from all the Ausonian lands
Many had sought her; comelier far than all,
Turnus, for noble ancestors renowned; 70
Whom the queen sought with zealous love to make
Her son-in-law; but portents of the gods,
With various omens of great dread, opposed.
    Deeply secluded in the palace court
There stood a laurel tree with sacred crest, 75
Preserved for many a year with pious awe,
Found, it was said, when first Latinus built
His citadels, and consecrated them
To Phœbus; whence the inhabitants derived
Their name Laurentes. To its top—strange sight— 80
There flew a dense and sudden swarm of bees
With loud and humming noise across the air,
And, clinging each to each, hung from the boughs.
"A foreign hero comes," the seer exclaimed;
"A host from that same quarter as these bees, 85
And seeking the same place, where they will rule
Our topmost citadel."
              Then, as beside
Her sire the maid Lavinia, standing, feeds
The altars with the consecrated brands—
Dread omen,[6] her long tresses seemed to catch 90
The blaze, and all her robes with crackling flames
To kindle, through her regal hair, and crown
Splendid with jewels—then involved in smoke
And glare to spread the fire through all the house.
A terrible and wondrous sight it was deemed; 95
For she herself, they prophesied, would prove
Illustrious in her fame and in her fates,
While to the people it portended war.

Alarmed at prodigies like these, the king
Repairs to the oracle of his prophetic 100

Sire Faunus, and there consults the groves
That lie below the deep Albunea,
Which, greatest of the forest streams, resounds
With sacred fountain, darkly hid, and breathes
Mephitic fumes. To here the Italian tribes   105
And all the Œnotrian land responses seek
Amid their doubts; here, when the priest has brought
His offerings, and beneath the silent night
Reclined on woolly skins of sheep, has sought
For sleep, he many a wondrous phantasm sees   110
Flitting about, and many a voice he hears,
And talks with divine shapes, and converse holds
With Acheron, in the deep Avernian shades.
And here the sire Latinus, when he seeks
An answer, slays a hundred fleecy lambs,   115
And on their wool lies stretched. Suddenly, a voice
From the deep grove he hears: "O son, seek not
To wed your daughter to a Latian prince,
Nor trust in bridal chambers all prepared.
A foreigner comes, thy future son-in-law,   120
Whose blood shall lift our name up to the stars;
Whose progeny shall see beneath their feet
All lands subdued and governed, wheresoever
The ocean greets the risen or setting sun."
These answers of his sire, and warnings given   125
In the still night, Latinus does not hide;
But Rumor now flying far and wide around
Among the Ausonian cities bore the words,
When to the Tiber's grassy river-bank
The sons of Troy had moored their fleet.

                                       And now   130
Æneas, fair Iulus, and the chiefs
Under the branches of a tall tree stretched
Their limbs, arranged the banquet, and beneath
Their meals, on the grass, placed wheaten cakes
(Jove so disposed their thought), and on this base   135
Of Ceres' gifts, wild fruits were heaped. It chanced,
All else being eaten, here their scant supply

Forced them upon their slender biscuit store
To turn their appetites, and violate
With daring hand and hungry tooth the disks   140
Of fated bread, nor spare their ample squares.
"What! are we eating up our tables too?"[7]
Iulus cried, nor further led the jest.
That word dispelled their cares. His father caught
The meaning from the speaker's lips, amazed   145
At its divine significance, and mused
Awhile thereon; then suddenly exclaimed:—
"Hail, land for me predestined by the fates!
And you, O true Penates of our Troy,
Hail! Here our home, and here our country lies.   150
For now I do recall to mind, my sire
Anchises told this secret of the fates:
'When, O my son, driven upon unknown shores,
Your food exhausted, you are forced to eat
Your tables in your hunger, weary and worn,   155
Remember then to hope for a steadfast home,
And found your walls, and build a rampart round.'
This was that hunger; this remained, the last,
Ending our sufferings. Come then, and blithe
Of heart, soon as tomorrow's sun shall rise,   160
Let us find out by different ways what men
Inhabit here, and where their cities stand.
Now pour your cups to Jove, and call upon
Anchises, and replace the festal wine."

Thus having spoken, with a leafy branch   165
He wreathes his brows, the Genius of the place
Invokes, and Tellus, first of gods,—the Nymphs
And Rivers yet unknown; then Night, and all
Night's orient stars, Idæan Jove, and next
The Phrygian Mother, and his twin parents   170
In heaven and in the shades of Erebus.
Here the Omnipotent Father in the heights
Thrice thundered, and displayed a cloud that burned
With light and gold, and waved it in his hand

Before them. Suddenly the rumor spread   175
Among the Trojan bands that now the day
Had come when they should found their destined walls.
With emulation they renew the feast,
Rejoicing in the mighty omen given,
And set the bowls, and crown the wine with flowers.   180

Soon as the early morning lit the earth,
The city and the confines and the coast
They explore by different ways, discovering here
The waters of Numicius' spring, and here
The river Tiber, and the towns where dwelt   185
The hardy Latins. Then Æneas sends
A hundred envoys, chosen from all ranks,
To the king's city—bearing in their hands
Branches of Pallas' olive-tree, enwreathed
With fillets—charged with gifts and overtures   190
Of peace. Without delay they haste to do
Their errand with fleet steps; while he himself
Marks out a rude trench where a wall shall be,
And builds upon the spot, and girds about
His first seat on these shores, with palisade   195
And rampart, in the fashion of a camp.

And now, their journey over, the warriors see
The Latins' lofty houses and their towers,
And pass beneath the wall. Before the gates
Were boys and youths in the first flower of life,   200
Riding their steeds, or taming them to draw
The chariot on the dusty course; and some
Were bending the stout bow, or hurling spears,
Or challenging each other to the race
Or glove: when a mounted messenger   205
Appears, who to the aged king brings word
That men of mighty stature and strange garb
Approach. The king commands them to be called
Into his palace, and there takes his seat
On his ancestral throne.

An edifice　　　　　　　　　210
Of stately form and spacious size there stood,
Upon the city's summit, lifting up
A hundred columns, once the royal seat
Of Picus, shadowed round with solemn trees,
And the religion of ancestral times.　　　　215
Here, to receive the scepter and to raise
The first signs of their royal sway, was deemed
By kings an omen that betokened good.
This was their senate house; here sacred feasts
Were held, when, having sacrificed a ram,　　220
The fathers at the extended tables sat.
Here statues of their ancestors were ranged,[8]
Of ancient cedar carved; here Italus,
Father Sabinus, planter of the vine,
With crooked pruning-knife, and Saturn old,　　225
And Janus, double-faced—all stood within
The vestibule; and other kings of old,
Who, fighting for their country, suffered wounds.
And here, upon the sacred pillars hung
Armor and captive chariots, and the keen　　230
Curved battle-axe, and flowing helmet-crests,
And mighty bars of city gates, and spears
And shields, and beaks of ships, torn off.
Here too, his augur's wand held in his hand,
And armed with scanty garment of the seer,　　235
A shield upon his arm, Picus himself,
Tamer of horses, sat; whom Circe once,
Enamored, changed, with touch of golden wand
And charms of magic herbs, into a bird,
And sprinkled colors on his wings.
　　　　　　　　　　　Within　　240
This sacred place Latinus takes his seat
On his forefathers' throne, and summons in
The Trojans;[9] and they, having entered, thus
With tranquil look he speaks: "Speak, Dardan chiefs,
For you to us are not unknown—your race,　　245
Your city, and your voyage over the deep,—

What seek you here? What cause, what urgent need
Across such breadths of azure seas has borne
Your ships, and brought you to the Ausonian shores?
If by some error in your course, or driven   250
By tempests, such as sailors often endure
Upon the ocean, you have entered here
Our river banks, to settle in our ports,
Then do not shun our hospitality,
But know the Latins to be Saturn's race,   255
Not by constraint of bonds or laws kept just,
But in the fashion of the ancient god
Holding their faith and honor by free will.
And I indeed do recall a legend
To mind, obscured somewhat by lapse of years,   260
Told by Auruncans old, that from these lands
Came Dardanus, and the Idæan cities reached
Of Phrygia, and the Thracian Samos, now
Called Samothrace. He, leaving Corythus,*
Now in the starry courts of heaven is throned,   265
And adds another altar to the gods."

He spoke; and Ilioneus thus replied:—
"O king, the illustrious son of Faunus,
We come not to your shores by tempests driven,
Nor from our course direct has any star   270
Nor any coast misled us. We have all,
With purpose fixed, and of our own free will,
Come to your city, driven out from realms
The mightiest once the sun in all his course
Beheld. From Jove our origin; in Jove   275
Their ancestor the Dardan youth rejoice.
Our king himself, Trojan Æneas, born
Of that high race, has sent us to your gates.
How great a storm, poured out by ruthless Greeks
On the Idæan plains—by what fates driven,   280
Europe and Asia clashed, even he has heard

---

*Assumed by Cranch and others to be present-day Cortona; not localized by Vergil.

(If such there be) who in the extremest lands
Of earth, by circling ocean sundered far
From all his kind, or in the midmost heats
Of scorching suns, is shut from other zones.   285
Swept by that deluge over seas so vast,
Some small abode for our country's gods we ask,
Some inoffensive shore, and what stands free
To all, the waves and air. We shall not bring
Dishonor to your realm; nor shall your fame   290
Be lightly esteemed, nor for such favor done
Our grateful feelings ever be effaced.
Nor shall the Ausonians ever grieve that Troy
Was taken to their lap. By Æneas' fates
I swear, and by his strong right hand, in faith   295
Of friendship, and in arms alike approved—
Many a nation (nay, despise us not
That thus of our free will, with suppliant speech,
We come bearing these fillets in our hands)
Has sought to join us to itself; but fate   300
Divine commanded us to seek these lands
Of yours. Here Dardanus was born, and here
Apollo calls us back with urgent voice
To Tuscan Tiber and the sacred wave
Of the Numician fount. Gifts too we bring,   305
Small remnants of our former fortunes, snatched
From burning Troy. Out of this golden bowl
My sire Anchises poured the sacred wine.
And these were Priam's, when he sat and gave
The assembled people laws; this scepter his,   310
And this tiara; and these robes were wrought
By Trojan women."
                       While he spoke, the king
Sat motionless, his looks fixed on the ground,
And rolled his eyes in thought. Not embroidery
Of purple wrought, nor Priam's scepter moved   315
The monarch as the marriage of his child
Absorbs his mind, revolving in his breast
The oracle of Faunus: this is he,

Come from a foreign land, by fates foretold
To be his son-in-law, and called to rule   320
The realm with auspices that equaled his;
Whose future race for valorous deeds renowned,
Should by its prowess dominate the world.
At length he speaks with joy: "May the great gods
Speed their own augury and our design!   325
Trojan, we grant what you ask, and do not spurn
Your gifts. While I am king, you shall not want
A fertile soil, or wealth like that of Troy.
But let Æneas come himself, if such
Desire be his to ally himself with us;   330
Let him not shun our friendly countenance.
Part of our peaceful league will be to have touched
Your king's right hand. Now bear this message back
To him: I have a daughter, whom to unite
In marriage with a prince of our own race,   335
The fateful voices from my father's shrine
And many a warning sign from heaven forbid.
From foreign shores a son-in-law should come
(This fate, they say, for Latium is in store),
Who, mingling race with ours, shall lift our name   340
To starry heights. That this is he the fates
Require, I must believe; and if my mind
Foreshadows any truth, him I desire."

He spoke; and to each Trojan gives a steed
(Within his royal stalls three hundred stood,   345
With glossy skins); to every one in turn
A swift wing-footed courser overspread
With housings of embroidered purple cloth;
And golden chains are hung upon their breasts;
And, decked with gold, on golden bits they champ.   350
A chariot to the absent prince he gives,
Also a pair of harnessed steeds of blood
Ethereal, from their nostrils breathing flame,—
Born of that spurious race which Circe bred*

---

*A mixed breed of horses—mortal mixed with an immortal strain from the sun-god.

By stealth, without the knowledge of her sire. 355
With gifts and words like these, the sons of Troy
Upon their steeds return with peaceful news.

But lo, relentless Juno, journeying now
Back from Inachian Argos in her car
Borne through the fields of air, from distant heights 360
Looks down from Sicilian Pachynus,
And sees Æneas joyous, and his fleet.[10]
There at his walls he plans, and trusts the soil,
And leaves his ships. Pierced with sharp grief, she stood;
Then shook her head, and bitter words poured out:— 365
"Ah, hated race! Ah, Phrygian fates that cross
And baffle ours! And so they did not fall
On the Sigean plains,* nor captive met
The captive's doom, nor burned with burning Troy,
But found their way through battle and through flames. 370
My power, indeed, at length lies exhausted;
Or I have rested, satiate, from my hate!
And yet I dared to chase them through the deep,
These exiles from their land, opposing them
Over all the sea, the forces of the sky 375
And waves consumed in vain. Of what avail
To me the Syrtes, Scylla, what the vast
Charybdis? In the harbor they desired,
The Tiber hides them, careless of the sea
And me. Yet Mars was able to destroy† 380
The Lapithæ's gigantic race: the sire
Of gods himself yielded to Dian's wrath
The ancient Calydon.‡ What punishment
So great did Calydon or Lapithæ
Deserve? But I, the royal spouse of Jove, 385
Who, wretched, could endure to leave untried
No plan, attempting all, am overcome

---

*A reference to Troy. Sigeum was a cape near Troy.

†Having been provoked by Bacchus.

‡When Oeneus, king of Calydon, left Diana out of his sacrifices; the boar she sent to ravage his land was killed by Meleager.

By Æneas. But if my power's not enough,
I shall not pause to seek what aid I may.
And if I cannot bend the gods above,   390
Then Acheron I'll move. What though his course
Into his Latian realms I cannot bar,
And by unalterable fate he takes
Lavinia for his wife? Yet I may oppose
Delay thereto and hindrance; yes, destroy   395
The people of both kings. So at this price
Of lives let son-in-law and father form
Alliance. With the blood of Rutuli
And Trojans, you, O virgin, shall be dowered.
Bellona at your nuptials shall attend.   400
Not Hecuba* alone conceived and bore
The hymeneal torch, but Venus too
Shall see her son another Paris prove,
And a new firebrand light another Troy!"

  Having spoken, the dreadful deity   405
Flies earthward. From the infernal shadows forth
She summons dark Allecto from the cells
Of her dire sisters; in whose bosom burn
Fell war, and wrath, and treachery, and crimes,—
A monster, hated by her sire himself,   410
Pluto, and hated by her sister fiends;
Into so many direful shapes she turns,
From her dark head so many vipers sprout.
Whom Juno stimulates with words like these:—
"Grant me, O virgin daughter of the Night,   415
This service, your peculiar task, lest now
Our honor and our broken fame give way,
And Trojan craft succeed to circumvent
Latinus with this marriage, or obtain
Possession of the lands of Italy.   420
You can array in battle kindred souls
Of brothers, and embroil the peace of homes
In bitter hate; and in their households bring

---

*Wife of Priam; she dreamed she was pregnant with a torch before she gave birth to Paris.

Scourges and funeral torches. Unto you
A thousand names belong, a thousand ways   425
Of harm. Ransack your teeming bosom. Break
This formed alliance. Sow the seeds of strife;
And let the youthful warriors with one will
Demand and seize their weapons for the war!"

Forthwith, in fell Gorgonian venom steeped,[11]   430
Allecto seeks the realms and lofty halls
Of the Laurentian king, and lays her siege
Before Amata's silent chamber door;
Who, brooding over the coming of these guests
From Troy and Turnus' baffled nuptials, sits,   435
Burning with woman's rage and restless cares.
At her the goddess flings a serpent plucked
Out of her dark-blue hairs, and thrusts it through
The inmost heart and bosom of the queen
That, wrought to fury by the monster, she   440
May embroil the household. In the serpent glides
Unfelt, illusive, between her robe and breast,
With viperous breath; about her neck becomes
A golden collar, forms the fillet round
Her head, with drooping length, and binds her hair,   445
And slips around her limbs. So while the first
Contagion with its humid poison glides,
Encroaching on each sense, and wreathes her limbs
With fire—nor yet the flame is wholly felt
Through all her breast—gently, the mother's way,   450
She speaks, weeping upon her daughter's fate
And Phrygian nuptials: "Shall Lavinia then,
O father, be a Trojan exile's bride?
No pity for your child, nor for yourself,
Nor for her mother, from whose arms the first   455
North wind that blows will see this robber chief
Perfidious bear our maiden over the seas?
Is it not thus the Phrygian shepherd* makes

---

*A reference to Paris.

His way to Lacedæmon, and bears off
Ledæan Helen to the Trojan walls?   460
Where is your plighted faith? Where the regard
You had for us so long? And where the hand
Of friendship and of kindred blood, so often
To Turnus given? If for a son-in-law
Of foreign birth you seek, to share our rule,   465
And such your fixed intent, such the command
Urged by your sire, I hold that every land
Which, free, disowns our rule, is foreign land;
And that the gods so mean. And if the birth
Of Turnus and his house be sought and traced,   470
Inachus and Acrisius were his sires,
And they who dwelt in far Mycenæ's midst."

But when with words like these she tries in vain
To move Latinus, and the snake has crept
With raging venom deep into her heart,   475
And through her frame, then, wretched, goaded on
By vast phantasmal images, she raves
Delirious, up and down the city streets;
As when a top, whirling beneath the whip,
Spins through some empty court, lashed round by boys   480
Intent upon their play. In circling curves
It moves: the youthful groups look down amazed,
And at the flying box-wood stare, and lend
Their souls to every stroke. So swift, the queen
Flies through the city, and the brutal crowds.   485
Worse her lawless course: with fury wild
She feigns to worship Bacchus; to the woods
She flies, and hides her daughter in the shades
Of leafy mountains, so she may evade
This Trojan marriage, and delay the rites.   490
"Hail, Bacchus!" now she shrieks; "worthy alone
Are you of this fair virgin: she for you
Assumes the thyrsus, round you leads the dance,
And cherishes her sacred locks for you!"

The rumor flies and spreads. With one accord,   495
Fired by the fury's torch, the matrons all
Desert their homes and seek the new abodes,
And spread their necks and tresses to the winds.
And others fill the air with tremulous shrieks,
All clad in fawn-skins, bearing vine-wreathed spears.   500
The queen herself a burning pine-wood torch
Lifts in the midst, and sings the nuptial chant
For Turnus and her daughter, while she rolls
Her bloodshot eyes; then frowning suddenly:—
"Women of Latium, wheresoever you be,   505
If in your reverent hearts there yet remains
For sad Amata any loyal love,
If any pain for a wronged mother's rights,
Then loose the fillets from your hair: with me
Begin these orgies." So through woods and through   510
The desert haunts of beasts Allecto drives
The queen, beset and stung on every side
By goads of Bacchus.
           Then when she perceives
How keenly she had whetted these first stings
Of rage, and in confusion thrown the house   515
And counsel of the king, hence borne away
On dusky wings the somber goddess flies
To Turnus' city (built by Danaë,
It's said, who with her Argive court was wrecked
Upon this shore, and called in olden days   520
Ardea; which great name still lives, though all
Her glory has departed). Turnus there
At midnight in his palace chamber slept.
Allecto lays aside her threatening face
And shape infernal, changed to an aged crone;   525
Her grim face ploughed with wrinkles, her white hair
Bound with fillet and wreathed with olive leaves:
Changed into Calybe, a priestess old
Of Juno's temple, she appears before
The youthful warrior, and accosts him thus:—   530
"Dare you, O Turnus, see these toils of yours

Lavished in vain, your scepter pass away
To Dardan colonists? The king denies
To you your bride and dowry bought with blood,
And for his kingdom seeks a foreign heir.   535
Go now, and brave the dangers that can reap
No thanks, but only scorn! Go, and smite down
The Tuscan bands. Protect the Latin race
With peace. The omnipotent Saturnia gives
Command that I bear this message to you   540
In the still night. Rise then, and, light of heart,
Prepare to arm the youths, and bid them march
Forth from the gates; and slay the Phrygian chiefs
That sit on your fair river-banks, and burn
Their painted ships. Celestial powers command.   545
And let the Latin king, should he refuse
Your bride, nor keep his promise, know at length
By proof the might of Turnus roused to arms."
With scornful smile the youth made answer thus:—
"Think not the tidings have escaped my ears,   550
That to the Tiber's waves a fleet has come;
Nor feign such terrors: Juno forgets us not.
But you, good mother, dulled by mold of years,
Worn out in mind and body, your old age
Broods to no purpose over groundless cares,   555
Amid the warlike armaments of kings
Mocks your prophetic vision with false fears.
It is to you to tend the images and fanes:
Let men, whose province it is, make peace and war."

These words inflamed Allecto's soul with wrath.   560
While yet he spoke, a sudden trembling seized
His limbs. His eyes were fixed. So many snakes
Hissed from the Fury's head, so terrible
Her form appeared. Then, as he strove to rise
And speak, she thrusts him back, rolling her eyes   565
Of glaring flame; and, lifted from her hair,
Two serpents rear their necks. Her sounding lash
She cracks, and adds these words, with raving lips:—

"Behold me then——me, feeble and outworn
With mold of years—amid the wars of kings   570
Mocked by old age with false and groundless fears!
Look well on me: from my fell sisters' home
I am here—and war and death are in my hand!"

This said, against the warrior's breast she hurls
Her torch; with lurid glare it burns and smokes,   575
Fixed in his heart. A dreadful terror breaks
His sleep: great drops of sweat bathe all his limbs.
Wildly he calls for arms; for arms he seeks
About his chamber and through all the house,
Maddened with thirst for war, and rage insane.   580
As when beneath a bubbling cauldron's ribs
The flames of crackling twigs roar round the sides,
The water swells and leaps with fervid heat,
Till unrestrained it steams above the rim,
And the dense vapor rolls into the air.   585
So, the alliance broken, to his chiefs
He points the way to King Latinus' throne,
And bids them arm, protect the Italian land,
And thrust the invaders out; that he himself,
A match for Trojans and for Latins both,   590
Will come. This said, he calls upon the gods;
With rival zeal for war the troops are stirred;
These by their chieftain's youth and beauty moved,
Those by his ancestry or famous deeds.
While Turnus thus with daring courage fills   595
The Rutuli, upon her Stygian wings
Allecto moves against the Trojan camp.
With arts of new device, she then spots a place
Where beautiful Iulus by the shore
Was hunting the wild beasts with snares and steeds.   600
She cast a sudden madness on the hounds
And touched their nostrils with the well-known scent,
And fired them with the rage to chase a stag.
This the first cause of troubles proved, and lit

The flames of war within the peasants' hearts.

This stag was of a lovely form,[12] with large
Fair antlers; from its mother's udders snatched
And reared by Tyrrheus' children and their sire
Himself, the keeper of the royal herds,
And guardian of the fields that stretched around.   610
His daughter Silvia was used to deck
The creature's horns (accustomed to her sway)
With woven wreaths, and comb its hairy sides,
And wash it in the stream. Patient beneath
Her hand, familiar at the household meals,   615
It roamed the woods, and to the well-known door
Returned at night, however late the hour.
Far from its home, Iulus' rabid hounds
Give chase, as down the grateful stream it floats,
Or cools its heat upon the verdant bank.   620
Ascanius, kindled with the love of praise,
Aims an arrow from his bow, and the fates
Prompt his uncertain hand. With whizzing sound,
Through flank and bowels flies the shaft. The beast,
Wounded and bleeding, in the well-known stalls   625
Takes refuge, and as if imploring aid,
Fills all the house with piteous moans. And first
Silvia calls loud for help, and claps her hands,
To summon the rude peasants. Swift they come
(For hidden in the woods the Fury lurks).   630
One with a charred and sharpened brand is armed,
One with a knotty club; whatever they find,
Rage turns into a weapon. Tyrrheus leaves
The oaken log which, cleaving into four,
His driving wedges split, and calls his men,   635
And, breathing hard, snatches his rustic axe.

The Fury from her watching places finds
The hour most fit for mischief. Perched upon
The summit of the cottage roof, she sounds
The shepherd's call, and through her crooked horn   640

Pours her Tartarean voice. The woods around
Tremble with fear, and all the forest depths
Resound: far off, the lake of Trivia hears,
And the white waters of the sulphurous Nar,
And fountains of Velinus; while with awe   645
Pale mothers press their children to their breasts.

Then, at the signal of the dreadful horn,
On every side the untamed peasants snatch
Their arms, and rush together; and the youths
Of Troy all from their open camp pour forth   650
To help Ascanius. Battle lines are formed.
Now not with rustic contest of rude clubs
And sharpened stakes the war is waged, but fought
With two-edged steel; and far and wide around
Bristles a deadly crop of naked swords;   655
And brazen armor flashes in the sun,
And glimmers on the clouds: as when the sea
Begins to whiten in the rising wind,
Swells by degrees, and higher still and higher
Mounts from its lowest depths into the sky.   660

Here in the foremost ranks young Almo falls,
The eldest of the sons of Tyrrheus, pierced
By a whizzing arrow. In his throat the wound
Chokes his soft voice and slender life with blood.
Many a hero's corpse around there fell: 665
Even old Galæsus, striving to make peace;
Most just he was, and in Ausonian fields
Most wealthy once. Five flocks of sheep were his;
Five herds of cattle back from pasture came;
And with a hundred ploughs he turned his soil.   670

While yet with equal arms the war is waged,
The Fury, having done her promised task,
And with the opening battle steeped the field
Of war in blood and slaughter, leaves behind
Hesperia, and victorious turns her course   675

Through aether, and addresses Juno thus,
With haughty voice: "Behold, the work achieved
For you, in discord and disastrous war!
Now bid them join in friendly truce and league,
While with Ausonian blood the Trojans reek!   680
This also will I add; if such is your will,
With rumors I will rouse the neighboring towns,
And fill their souls with maddening thirst for war,
So they may flock from every side with aid.
I'll strew their fields with arms." Then Juno thus   685
Replied: "Enough of terrors and of frauds.
The causes of the war stand firmly fixed.
Now hand to hand they fight. The arms which first
By chance were given, are steeped in fresh blood now.
Such be the bridals, such the nuptial rites   690
That they shall celebrate, this wondrous son
Of Venus, and the Latin king. But you—
The Olympian Ruler wills no farther flight
Of yours through these ethereal regions. Hence!
If the future brings more tasks, I will guide   695
The affairs myself." Thus spoke Saturnia.
The fiend then spread her hissing serpent wings,
And left the skies, and sought the infernal shades.
   Midway in Italy there is a place
Beneath high mountains, famed in many lands,   700
The valley of Amsanctus, girt around
With shadowy woods. A torrent in the midst
With crooked course brawls over the sounding rocks.
Here frowns an awful cave, the breathing hole
Of Dis, a gulf that opens pestiferous jaws,   705
And yawns on Acheron abrupt. Down here
The Fury plunges, and relieves the heavens and earth
Of her detested presence.
                    Nonetheless
Meanwhile, Saturnia completes the war
Begun. The peasants from the battlefield   710
Into the city rush, and bear the dead;
Young Almo, and the gashed and bloody face

Of old Galæsus. They implore the gods,
And call the king to witness. Turnus comes,
And in the midst of the accusing crowd   715
Doubles their dread of slaughter and of flames;
Cries that the Trojans, mixing Phrygian blood
With theirs, are called to lord it—he thrust out.
Then they whose mothers, fired by Bacchus, leap
And dance through pathless woods (Amata's name   720
Is no slight spell), assemble from all sides,
Importunate for war. These all forthwith,
In spite of all omens and the fates divine,
Demand this dreadful war, and crowd around
The palace of the king. He, like a rock   725
That stands unmoved amid the sea, resists;
Like a sea-rock amid the loud uproar
Of barking waves around, the surging foam
And sea-weed slipping from its rugged sides.
But when no power avails to overcome   730
Blind counsels, and all moves at Juno's nod,
The royal father having often called
The gods to witness, and the empty winds;
"Alas," he cries, "we are broken by the fates,
And driven by the storm. O wretched men!   735
With your own sacrilegious blood, these deeds
Shall be atoned. For you, O Turnus, you,
The impious cause of war, dire punishment
Remains in store. Too late unto the gods
Your prayers and vows shall rise. For me, my rest   740
Is all prepared. My haven is at hand;
Robbed only of a calm and happy death."
He said no more, but shut himself within
His house, and left all guidance of the state.*

Hesperian Latium had a custom, long   745
Held sacred by the Albans, and by Rome,
The mistress of the world, adopted now,

---

*Latinus steps aside as the war begins.

Whenever they move to war: whether against
The Getæ they press on in battle grim,
Or the Arabs, or Hyrcanians, or pursue   750
Their way toward India and the morning star,
To win their standards back from Parthian hordes.
There are two gates of War, so called of old,
Sacred by long religious awe, and fear
Of Mars; shut with a hundred brazen bolts,   755
And iron bars of all-enduring strength.
Janus their keeper never deserts his post.
Here, when the sentence of the chiefs is war,
The consul, robed in state, in Gabine mode,
Unlocks the grating gates himself, and calls   760
To arms; the warriors all repeat the cry,
And brazen horns mingle with hoarse assent.
Even so they urged Latinus to proclaim
War against the Trojans, and the dreadful gates
Unbar. But from this touch he shrank averse,   765
And shunned the hated task, and hid himself
In darkness. Then the queen of gods, herself
Descending from the skies, pushed with her hand
The unwilling gates, and turned the hinges back,
And open burst the iron gates of war.   770

Now all Ausonia burns, that before slept
Calm and unmoved. Some take the field afoot;
Some, mounted on tall steeds, through clouds of dust
Spur by in furious haste. All seek for arms.
Others their bucklers and their javelins cleanse   775
With unctuous lard, and grind the battle-axe,
And take delight to see the standards spread,
And hear the trumpet's blare. Five large cities
Their anvils bring, and whet their steel anew,—
Atina, Ardea, and Tibur proud,   780
Crustumium, and Antemnæ turret-crowned.
Some forge strong helmets, and bend willow wands
For shields; while others hammer corselets out
Of brass, or silver greaves. To this must yield

All love and honor of the plough and scythe;   785
And even their fathers' swords are wrought anew.
And now the trumpet sounds, the password runs;
One snatches down his helmet from his walls;
Another harnesses his restive steeds,
And dons his shield and triple-twisted mail,   790
And girds his faithful sword upon his side.

Now, Muses, open wide your Helicon,
And wake the song—what kings were roused to war;[13]
Who led, who followed to the battlefield;
What heroes in those early days gave fame   795
To Italy, and with what arms is blazed.
For you, O goddesses, remember all,
And can recount. Feebly the breath of fame
From those far days comes whispering in our ears.

First to the war from Tyrrhene shores goes forth   800
Mezentius, fierce condemner of the gods,
His bands arrayed in arms. Next Lausus goes,
His son, for manly beauty unsurpassed
By all save Turnus; Lausus, who could tame
The mettled steed, and fell the forest beast,   805
Down from the city of Agylla leads
A thousand warriors in vain. Happier he
Had been beneath paternal rule more just,
Or had Mezentius never been his sire.

Fair Aventinus next, Alcides' son,   810
Drives over the field his car that won the palm,
And his victorious steeds. Upon his shield
He bears the emblem of his mighty sire,
A Hydra cinctured with a hundred snakes.
It was he the priestess Rhea in the woods   815
Of Aventine brought forth in secret birth,—
The woman mingling with the god; what time
The great Tirynthian conqueror touched the shores
Of Latium, Geryon being slain, and bathed

In Tyrrhene waters his Iberian herds.   820
For arms, his soldiers bear long pikes and spears
And tapering swords and Sabine darts; while he
Himself, on foot, clothed in a lion's skin
With grim and shaggy fur, the white teeth worn
About his head, strides through his royal halls   825
In the rough garb of Hercules his sire.
    Then two twin brothers come from Tibur's walls
(Named from Tiburtus, brother to these two),—
Catillus and bold Coras, Argive youths;
In the front ranks and through the thick-set spears   830
They sweep: as when from the high mountain-tops
Of Homole or snowy Othrys rush
Two cloud-born Centaurs with impetuous leaps;
And as they thunder down, the dense woods yield,
And the loud-crashing underwoods give way.   835

Nor did Præneste's founder fail to come,
Cæculus, held by every age to be
The kingly son of Vulcan, born among
The rural herds, and found amid the fire.
A band of rustics from around attend   840
His steps; they who in steep Præneste dwell,
Or Gabian Juno's fields, or on the banks
Of the cool Anio, or the spray-wet rocks
Of Hernic streams; and they whose pasturage
Fertile Anagnia yields, or Amasene.   845
Not all are armed; nor shields nor rattling cars
Are theirs: but some sling balls of lead, and some
Carry two spears; and tawny wolf-skin caps
They wear: the left foot naked on the ground,
And on the right a sandal of raw hide.   850

Messapus next, steed-tamer, Neptune's son,
Invincible by fire or steel, calls forth
His sluggish tribes and bands unused to war,
And draws his sword again. With him appear
Fescennian and Faliscan troops, and those   855

Who hold Soracte's steeps, and dwell amid
Flavinian fields, or on Ciminius' mount
And lake, and in Capena's woods. These all
Move on in equal ranks, and praise their king
With songs: as when a flock of snowy swans,   860
Winging their way through clouds, returning home
From seeking food, sonorous strains are heard
From their long throats; the river echoes back,
And far and wide the Asian marshes ring.
None would have thought that from a troop like theirs   865
Could cluster these battalions clad in brass;
But rather that some airy cloud of cranes
With clamors hoarse were flying from the sea.
Lo, Clausus, born of ancient Sabine blood,
Leads on a mighty host, himself a host;   870
From whom the Claudian family derived
Its name, diffused through Latium, since the state
Of Rome was shared with Sabines. Leagued with him
A mighty Amiternian cohort comes,
And they of ancient Cures: bands that hold   875
Eretum, and Mutusca's olive groves;
All those who in Nomentum's city dwell,
Or on Velinus' dewy fields; and they
From Tetrica's rough rocks, and from the sides
Of Mount Severus, and Casperia,   880
And Foruli, and from Himella's stream;
They who drink the Tiber, and Fabaris;
Whom frigid Nursia, and whom Horta sends;
And tribes from Latium; also those who dwell
Where Allia's ill-omened waves divide   885
Their lands. All these come thronging thick and fast
As rolling waves of Libyan seas, what time
The fierce Orion in the wintry floods
Has set, or as the dense and bearded crops
That burn in summer suns upon the plains   890
Of Hermus, or the yellow Lycian fields.
They march with ringing shields. Beneath their tread
The earth is startled.

Next Halesus comes,
Of Agamemnon's line, a foe to all
Of Trojan name. He to his chariot yokes   895
His steeds, and hurries on for Turnus' aid
A thousand men of aspects fierce and rough;
They who the fertile Massic soil upturn,
And plant with vines; and those who from their hills
The Auruncan fathers sent, and neighboring fields   900
Of Sidicina; those who Cales left;
And dwellers by Volturnus' shallow stream;
And rough Saticulan and Oscan bands:
These carry tapering darts, with pliant straps
Deftly adjoined; the left arm bears a shield;   905
Their swords are crooked, for close combat shaped.

Nor, Œbalus, shall you depart unsung,
Whom a Sebethian nymph to Telon bore,
It's said, when he the Teleboan isle
Caprea ruled, an aged king. His son   910
Disdained his father's land, and wide around
Extended his sway over Sarrastes' tribes,
And shores by Sarnus watered; they who hold
Batulum, Rufræ, and Celenna's fields;
And they on whom Abella's fruit-trees look.   915
These in Teutonic fashion hurl their spears,
With caps of cork-tree bark upon their heads,
And shine with brazen shields and brazen swords.

You too the mountain steeps of Nursæ sent
To battle, Ufens, fortunate and famed   920
In arms, born of the rugged Æquian race,
Who hunt through woods, and clothed in armor, till
The stubborn clod, and whose delight it is
To live by plunder and perpetual spoil.
    Then came a priest of the Marruvian race,—   925
A wreath of fertile olive decked his helm,—
Strong Umbro, sent by King Archippus; he
With hand and voice knew how to lull to sleep

The serpent tribe, the poison-breathing snakes,
And soothed their rage, and cured with skill their bite.   930
But not against the Dardan spear that pierced
His breast did all his medicines avail;
Nor did his sleepy incantations help
His wounds, nor herbs culled on the Marsian hills.
For you the Anguitian woods shall mourn; for you   935
The Fucine wave and all the liquid lakes.

Next Virbius came, Hippolytus' fair son,
Whom, famed for arms, his mother Aricia sent;
Reared in Egeria's grove, and marshy shores,
Where Dian's rich and easy altar stands.   •   940
For, as the legend goes, Hippolytus,
By his step-mother's artifices slain,
Dragged by his frightened steeds, to appease the wrath
Of his own father, to the upper air
And the ethereal stars came back once more,   945
Revived by Pæon's herbs and Dian's love.
Then the almighty father, angered that one
Of mortal mold should rise again to life,
Hurled the divine inventor of such art
Medicinal down with lightning to the gloom   950
Of Stygian shades. But tender Trivia hid
Hippolytus, and to the Egerian nymph
Confided him, to pass his humble life
Amid the lonely woods of Italy,
And change his name to Virbius. From there it comes,   955
That from Diana's temple and her groves
They drive away the horn-hoofed horses, since
They, frightened by the monsters of the sea,
Dashed on the shore the chariot and the youth.
But nonetheless, his son trains the mettled steeds   960
For the field, and drives them to the war.
     With noble form, overtopping by a head
The rest, comes Turnus, armed, among the first:
His lofty helmet crowned with triple crest
Bears a Chimæra breathing from its jaws   965

Ætnæan fire; more baleful rage the flames
The more the battle waxes hot and blood
Is poured. In glittering gold upon his shield—
A memorable theme—is wrought the form
Of Io,* now a heifer, overgrown   970
With bristly hair and with her horns erect,
And Argus watching her, and Inachus†
Pouring a river from his sculptured urn.

Then comes a cloud of followers on foot;
And over all the plain the bucklered hosts   975
Grow thick; the Argive youths, the Auruncan bands,
Rutulians, and Sicanian veterans,
And armed Sacranians, and Labici come,
With painted shields; all those who till your fields,
O Tiber, and Numicius' sacred shore,   980
Or drive the ploughshare through Rutulian hills,
And the Circæan promontory; those
Whose meadows Jupiter of Anxur guards,
Whose verdant groves Feronia consecrates,
Where spreads the gloomy marsh of Satura,   985
And the cool Ufens through the valleys seeks
Its winding course, and pours into the sea.

Last comes Camilla, of the Volscian race,
Leading a band of riders to the field
Clad in brazen armor, a warrior queen: 990
Her hands unused to ply Minerva's work
Of spindle and of household embroidery;
A virgin she, enured to toils of war,
Could outstrip the fleet winds in their course;
Could fly above the fields of grain, and leave   995
The stalks untouched, nor harm the tender ears;
Or skim the swelling billows of the sea,

---

*Girl beloved of Jupiter, transformed by Juno into a heifer and watched over by the hundred-eyed monster Argus.

†Io's father, a river-god.

Her rapid feet unwet. Forth from their homes
And fields the warrior youths and matrons crowd
In amazèd wonder to see her move;   1000
To see how royally the purple veils
Her polished shoulders, how with golden clasp
Her hair is bound, her Lycian quiver borne
And, tipped with steel, her pastoral myrtle spear.

BOOK 8

As soon as Turnus from Laurentum's tower[1]
Had raised aloft the signal for the war,
And the hoarse horns had blown; when he had roused
The mettled steeds, and urged the troops to arms;
Suddenly, with one accord, all Latium joins   5
Tumultuous, and the youths rage with fury.
Messapus, Ufens, and Mezentius too,
Condemner of the gods, lead on their hosts,
And levy troops, and strip the broad fields bare
Of laborers. Also Venulus is sent[2]   10
To Diomedes' city, seeking help,
And telling how the Trojans gain firm hold
In Latium with Æneas and his fleet
And household gods, demanding to be called
Their king by fate's decree, while many tribes   15
Flock to the Dardan hero, whose renown
Is spreading far and wide through all the land.
What in these plans he aims at, what event
Of war desires, should fortune favor him,
Appears more manifest to Diomed   20
Than to Prince Turnus, or the Latin king.

So pass affairs in Latium. These events
The Trojan hero sees, and fluctuates
On a great tide of anxious cares; now here,
Now there dividing his swift thoughts; his mind   25
Whirled to and fro, in everything unfixed;
As when within a vat with brazen rims
The tremulous light upon the water falls,
Caught from the sun, or from the radiant moon,
Glancing around on every place, and now   30
Darts upward, and the fretted ceiling strikes.

It was night: on all the weary life of earth,
On man, and birds, and flocks, deep sleep had fallen;
When on the river-bank Æneas throws
His limbs, beneath the cool and open sky,   35
His breast disturbed with gloomy thoughts of war,
As slowly over his frame his late rest steals.
Then, through the poplar leaves, the god who ruled
The spot, old Tiberinus,[3] from his calm
And pleasant riverbed was seen to rise.   40
A sea-green vapory robe veiled his figure,
And shadowy reeds were woven round his hair.
He with these words dispelled the hero's cares:——

"Son of a race divine, who now brings back
To us the Trojan city, from the midst   45
Of foes, and guards the eternal name
Of Pergamus; O long expected here
On the Laurentian soil and Latin fields!
Your home, your household gods are here assured.
Do not desist, nor fear the threats of war.   50
The anger of the gods has passed away.
Even now, lest to your mind these things should seem
Sleep's idle fancies, on the shore you'll find
A huge sow underneath the ilex-trees,
White, on the ground, with thirty sucking young   55
Of the same color, clustered round her teats.
Here shall your city be, your rest from toils.
From there, when the rounds of thirty years are full,
Ascanius shall found the illustrious city
Of Alba. No uncertain thing is this   60
I prophesy. Now in what way you may
Achieve victoriously what presses most,
I will briefly unfold. Upon these shores
The Arcadians, a race born from Pallas*
Followers of King Evander, chose a spot,   65
And built a city on a rising hill,

---

*Evander's grandfather, after whom Evander's son was named.

Called Pallanteum,* from their ancestor.
These with the Latin race wage ceaseless war.
Take them for friends, and make a league with them.
I, by my channel and my river-banks,   70
Will lead you on, that you may glide along
Against the opposing current with your oars.
Up then, O goddess born! and while the stars
Of early dawn are setting, offer prayers
To Juno; overcome her wrath and threats   75
With suppliant vows. To me, when victory smiles,
You shall give due honors. It is I whom you
Behold, laving the banks with swelling flood,
And flowing through the fertile harvest fields,—
Cerulean Tiber, river most beloved   80
By heaven. My spacious home is here; and here
The crown of lofty cities shall arise."

He spoke; and in the deepest riverbed
Sank down and hid: while from Æneas' eyes
Night and sleep vanished. Up he rose, and saw   85
The Orient splendor of the heavenly sun;
And scooped up water in his hollowed hands,
With due observance: then poured forth these words:—
     "O nymphs, Laurentian nymphs, from whom the streams
Are born; and you, O father Tiber, known   90
In these your sacred waters; O receive
Æneas, and at last guard him from perils.
In whatsoever fount your waters hold
Your presence, pitying this hard lot of ours,
From whatsoever spot you issue forth   95
In beauty, you with honors and with gifts
I will forever praise. O hornèd River,
You sovereign ruler of Hesperian waves,
Be near, and seal the promise you have given!"

---

*Town built by Evander on the Palatine Hill, one of seven hills that will become the site of the future city of Rome.

So saying, two ships with double tiers and oars   100
Well fitted he selects, and arms the crews.
But lo! a sudden marvel greets their eyes.
A sow, surrounded by her young, all white,
Stretched on the shore, is seen, among the trees.
Æneas to the altar takes them all,   105
A sacrifice, great Juno, even to you.

All through that night the Tiber calmed his flood,[4]
And, ebbing backward, stood with tranquil waves,
Smoothing its surface like a placid lake,
That without struggling oars the ships might glide.   110
So on their way they speed with joyous shouts.
Along the waters slip the well-tarred keels;
The waves gaze with wonder, and from afar
The woods, unused to such a sight, admire
Upon the stream the heroes' glittering shields   115
And painted vessels. Night and day, they ply
Their oars, pass the long bending river's curves;
And through green shades of overhanging trees
They pierce, along the tranquil waters borne.
The fiery sun had reached his noonday height,   120
When from afar they see a citadel,
And walls, and scattered houses here and there;
Which now Rome matches with the skies, but then
Evander's small and humble town. Then, swift,
They turn their prows, and near the city's walls.   125

By chance, upon that day, the Arcadian king*
Was offering solemn rites of sacrifice
To great Amphitryon's son† and to the gods,
Before the city, in a sacred grove:
Pallas, his son, with him, and all the youths   130
Of rank, and senators of humble state;
With fumes of incense, and with tepid blood

---

*Evander and his people emigrated to Pallanteum from Arcadia in Greece.
†A reference to Hercules.

Of sacrifice, the altars smoked. But when
They saw the tall ships through the shadowy trees
Approach with gliding pace and silent oars,   135
The sudden vision startles them: they rise
And leave the feast. Bold Pallas then forbids
That they should thus break off their solemn feast;
And snatching up a javelin, he flies
To meet the strangers. On a rising ground   140
He stands, and from a distance hails them thus:—
"Ho, warriors! What cause has brought you here
On untried ways? And where now do you head?
Your race? Your country? Do you bring peace or war?"
Æneas then, a peaceful olive-branch   145
Extending, thus made answer from his ship:—
"Trojans you see, with arms that war against
The Latins. Driven out by them, in war,
To Evander we have come. Deliver this,
And say to him, the chosen Dardan chiefs   150
Have come to ask a friendly league in arms."
Pallas stood amazed at so great a name.
"Whoever you may be, O come," he cries;
"And with my father speak; and be our guests
Beside our household gods." With cordial grasp   155
He took the hero's hand, and both advanced,
Leaving the river, and wended through the grove.

Then to the king Æneas speaks,[5] with words
Of friendly tone: "Best of the Grecian race,
Whom fortune bids me supplicate for aid,   160
With peaceful olive-branches fillet-wreathed:
I had no fears, indeed, because you were
Arcadian, and a leader of the Greeks,
And by your birth allied to Atreus' sons.
But my own conscious worth and oracles   165
Divine, our ancestors akin by blood,
And your wide fame, have moved me to ally
Myself with you, urged by the fates to come,
Yet of myself so willed. For Dardanus,

Founder and father of the Ilian state, 170
Son of Electra—so the Grecians say—
Came to the Trojan people: she was born
Of mighty Atlas, who sustains the orbs
Of heaven upon his shoulders. Mercury
Is your father, whom white Maia bore 175
On cold Cyllene's top. But Maia too,
If we may credit what we hear, was born
Of that same Atlas who supports the stars.
Thus from one blood the race of each divides.
With this reliance, no ambassadors 180
I have sent, nor tried you first with cunning arts.
I, I myself have risked my life, and come
With my petition to your royal court.
This Daunian race that wages war on you,
If they expel us, believe that they lack nothing, 185
But all Hesperia falls beneath their yoke,
And all the upper and the lower sea.
Then let us give and take in friendly faith.
Strong hearts we have for war, courageous souls,
And warriors tried in action."

                  Thus he spoke. 190
The king had long scanned well the speaker's face,
His eyes, and his whole form: then thus replied:—
"How joyfully do I receive and greet you,
Bravest of Trojans; and how I recall
Your sire Anchises' words, and tones, and face! 195
For I remember that when Priam came
Seeking his sister's realm, and Salamis,
He journeyed to Arcadia's frigid bounds.
My cheeks then bloomed with the first down of youth;
I gazed, admiring, on the Trojan chiefs; 200
On Priam gazed, Laomedon's great son;
But loftier than them all, Anchises stood.
My youthful heart was all aflame with zeal
To meet the hero, and to grasp his hand.
I approached him, and we met; and eagerly 205
To Pheneus I brought him. He to me,

When leaving, gave a wondrous quiver, filled
With Lycian arrows, and a cloak with gold
Inwoven, and a pair of golden reins,
Which now my Pallas keeps. So then, the hand   210
You seek, of friendly league, I give; and when
Tomorrow's sun shall rise, you shall depart
Gladdened with aid of warriors and supplies.
Meanwhile, since you have come here as friends,
Celebrate now with us these annual rites   215
Of ours, we are forbidden to defer,
And to our tables come as welcome guests."

This said, he bids the interrupted feast
Be served again, and cups replaced. Himself
He leads the heroes to their grassy seats: 220
And first, Æneas to a maple throne
Invites, overspread with shaggy lion's skin.
With rival zeal the attendants and the priest
Bring roasted flesh of bulls, and baskets heaped
With bread, and pour the wine. Æneas then,   225
And all the Trojans, feast upon the chine
And entrails of the sacrificial ox.

Their hunger now appeased, Evander speaks:—[6]
"These solemn forms, this customary feast,
This sacred altar, are on us imposed   230
By no vain superstition, ignorant
Of the ancient gods. O Trojan guest, these rites
We observe, because preserved from dire dangers,
Renewing thus the honors that are due.
First look upon that craggy pile, on stones   235
Suspended; scattered far and wide, the rocks
Are strewn; how lonely and deserted stands
That mountain fortress; with what wild ruin
The cliffs are dragged and toppled from above!
That was the cave hewn in a vast recess   240
Where dwelt the terrible half-human form
Of Cacus; where no sunbeams found their way;

And ever with fresh slaughter smoked the ground.
On the proud portals fixed hung heads of men,
Pallid and ghastly in their clotted gore.   245
This monster's sire was Vulcan; his the flames
And smoke that issued from his mouth. His boast
Was in his mighty bulk. But time at length
Brought long-wished aid and the advent of a god.
Alcides came, the great avenger, proud   250
From triple Geryon's slaughter and his spoils,
And hither drove his captured bulls, which filled
The river and the vale. But Cacus, fired
With fury, left untried no stratagem
Or crime; took from their stalls four comely bulls,   255
And four heifers, of beauty unsurpassed;
And, lest their hoof-prints should betray the theft,
He dragged them backwards, with the tracks reversed,
And hid them in his gloomy cave. No signs
The seeker found to lead him to the place.   260
Meanwhile, when now Amphitryon's son prepared
To move his full-fed herd, and to depart,
The cattle, as they left, began to low,
And filled the woods and hills with their complaints.
When, from the cave, one of the cows returned   265
The sound; and thus, though guarded close, betrayed
The hope of Cacus. Burning then with rage,
Alcides seized his arms and knotted club,
And gained the mountain's summit. Cacus then
For the first time was seen to shrink and quail,   270
With troubled eyes; and swifter than the wind
He fled to his cave. Fear to his feet gave wings.
Then, having entered his retreat, he broke
The chains, and dropped the enormous stone that hung
Suspended by his father's skill in iron,   275
And with the heavy mass his doorway blocked.
But lo! the enraged Tirynthian god* was there;
His eye searched all about through every part

_____
*A reference to Hercules.

To find an entrance, while he gnashed his teeth
With rage. Thrice round the Aventine he searched,   280
With burning wrath. Thrice he essayed the door
Of rock in vain, and thrice sat down to rest.
There stood a sharp crag on the cavern's ridge,
With steep-cut sides and towering height, the abode
Of fierce, ill-omened birds. This, as it hung   285
Above the river, bearing full against
Its sides, he shook, and loosed it from its base.
With sudden crash it falls, and the wide air
Resounds; the river-banks leap asunder;
Back rush the frightened waters: and the cave   290
Of Cacus stands revealed, with all its vast
And gloomy rooms. As though by some great shock
The earth should to its very center gape,
And all the infernal world and pallid realms
Hateful to gods disclosed, and from above   295
The drear abyss unbared, within whose deeps
The trembling ghosts shrink from the light let in;
So, caught amid the unexpected glare
Of sudden daylight, prisoned in his cave,
With strange and hideous voice the monster roars.   300
Alcides from above comes pressing on
With all his arms, and with huge stones and clubs
Assails him fast. But, wonderful to tell,
He, seeing no escape, pours from his throat
Great clouds of smoke, that nothing be discerned,   305
And from the bottom of the cave rolls up
A smoky night of mingled gloom and fire.
But this Alcides did not permit; enraged,
With headlong leap he plunges through the flames,
There where the smoke ascends in thickest waves,   310
And the huge cave with blackest vapor boils.
Here Cacus in the darkness breathing fires
In vain, he seizes, grasping like a knot
His limbs, and clinging, throttles him, until
His eyes start from their sockets, and his throat   315
Is drained of blood. Then open wide, the doors

Wrenched off, the gloomy den is seen, and shows
The stolen cattle and plunder he forswore.
Forth by the feet the hideous corpse is dragged.
The peasants gaze insatiate on the face   320
And dreadful eyes, and on the hairy breast,
And the fell throat with its extinguished fires.
Since then, we pay the hero honors due,
And joyfully observe this sacred day;
Potitius* first, and the Pinarian line,   325
The guardian of these rites of Hercules,
Built in the grove this altar, which we call
Our Greatest, and this name shall ever bear.
Wherefore, O warriors, wreathe your hair with leaves,
In honor of this deed; reach forth your cups;   330
Invoke the god, whose name both you and we
Revere, and willingly pour out the wine."
Thus having spoken, with the sacred leaves
Of double-tinted poplar he enwreathed
His hair, from which the hanging garlands drooped;   335
And in his right hand grasped the sacred cup.
Then joyfully the warriors pour the wine
Upon the table, and adore the gods.

Meanwhile the sinking sun brought evening near.
And now the priests, Potitius leading them,   340
Came clad in customary garb of skins,
And bearing torches, and prepare to lay
The grateful offerings of the evening feast,
And heap the altars with the loaded plates.
And round about the sacrificial fires   345
The Salians sing, their brows with poplar crowned;
One band of youths, another of old men;
The praises and the deeds of Hercules[7]
They chant: how as a baby he grasped and crushed
The serpents his step-mother Juno sent;   350
How he in war great cities overthrew,

---

*Priest of Hercules.

Troy, and Œchalia; how a thousand tasks
Of stern effort, by King Eurystheus'*
Command, and hostile Juno's, he achieved.
"You, O unconquered one, you did subdue   355
The cloud-born Centaur shapes, the double-formed,
Hylæus and Pholus; and the Cretan boar;
And the huge lion beneath the Nemean rocks.
Before you shuddering shrank the Stygian lake.
At your approach the keeper of the gates   360
Of Orcus trembled, crouching over his heaps
Of half-gnawed bones within his bloody den.
No dreadful shapes appalled you: not Typhœus
Himself, of towering height, and wielding arms.
Nor could the Hydra's swarm of serpent heads   365
Surprise you unprepared. Hail, you true son
Of Jove, who adds such glory to the gods!
Be with us, and your favoring presence deign!"
So with their hymns they sing and celebrate
The hero's deeds; and Cacus breathing fire,   370
And his grim cave, they add. The wood resounds
And the hills echo back the ringing notes.

And now their sacred rites performed, they all
Turn to the city. Burdened with old age
The king moves onward, keeping at his side   375
Æneas and his son, and cheers the way
With various discourse; while all around
The hero, admiring, turns his mobile eyes,
And, pleased, inquires, and hears the records told
Of each memorial of the men of old.   380
Evander then, Rome's earliest founder, spoke:—8
"These groves were once by native Fauns and Nymphs
Inhabited, and men who took their birth
From tough oak-trunks. No settled mode of life
They had, nor culture; nor knew how to yoke   385
Their steers, or heap up wealth, or use their stores

---

*Eurystheus was king of Mycenae; he ruled over Hercules' twelve labors.

With frugal hands; but the rough chase supplied
Their food, or boughs of trees. Then Saturn came
From high Olympus, fleeing before Jove,
An exile from the kingdoms he had lost.   390
This stubborn race dispersed through mountain wilds
He brought together, and to them gave laws;
And called the region Latium, since he had lurked
In safety on its shores. Beneath his reign
The golden age, so called, was seen. In peace   395
He ruled his people; till by gradual steps
There came a faded and degenerate age,
And love of war succeeded, and of gain.
Then came Ausonians and Sicanians;
And often the name Saturnia was changed.   400
Then kings succeeded, and the immense form
Of rugged Thybris, from whom came the name
Tiber; while that of Albula was lost.
Me, driven from my country to lands remote,
Chance and inevitable fate have placed   405
Upon these shores; the nymph Carmentis too,
My mother, urging me with warnings dread,
And great Apollo who first prompted me."

Then moving onward, he shows an altar
And gate, which now the name Carmental bears   410
In Rome; an old revered memorial
Of the prophetic nymph who first foretold
The future heroes of Æneas' line,
And noble Pallanteum; next, points out
The grove, which Romulus the Asylum named;   415
Then the Lupercal, cool beneath the rocks,
Named after Pan, by Arcadian custom;
And Argiletum's grove he shows, and tells
Of Argus' death, his guest; and calls the spot
To witness, he was guiltless of the deed.   420
Then on to the Tarpeian rock he leads
The way, and to the Capitol, now decked
With gold, then rough with bushes wild.

Even then the dark religion of the place
Haunted the timorous peasants with vague fears.   425
"Within this grove, upon this wooded hill,"
He said, "some deity his dwelling made;
But who or what, none knows. The Arcadians
Think they have seen great Jove himself, when often
With his right hand he shook his darkening shield,   430
And called his clouds around him. Those two towns
With ruined walls you see there, the relics old
And monuments of ancient days: this one
Was reared by Janus, that by Saturn built;
Saturnia and Janiculum their names."   435
With such discourse they approached the dwelling place
Of poor Evander: here and there his herds
Were lowing in the places where now stand
The Roman Forum and Carinæ's pride.
Reaching the house,—"Alcides once," he said,   440
"Fresh from his conquests, passed into these halls.
You also, O my guest, dare to despise
The pomp of wealth, and make your soul's desires
Worthy of such high deity; nor come
Disdaining our small means and humble state."   445
Saying this, beneath his narrow roof he led
The great Æneas, and upon a couch
Of leaves, overspread with Libyan bearskin,
He placed his guest. The night comes on apace,
And folds the earth around with dusky wings.   450

But Venus, her maternal love alarmed[9]
By the Laurentian threats and tumult wild,
To Vulcan, in their golden chamber, speaks,
And in her utterance breathes a love divine:—
"While Grecian kings were devastating Troy,   455
Whose falling towers were doomed by fate to flames,
I asked no help for those unhappy ones
From you, nor armor of your skill and power;
Nor you, dear husband, did I wish to employ
In fruitless labors, though I owed so much   460

To Priam's sons, and often wept to see
The cruel sufferings of Æneas. Now,
On the Rutulian shores, by Jove's command,
He plants his feet. Therefore I suppliant come,
And of your power divine, which I revere,   465
I ask for arms,—a mother for a son.
You to Nereus' daughter once did yield,
And you Tithonus' spouse with tears did move.
Behold, what tribes combine, what strong-barred gates
And ramparts frown against me, to destroy   470
My chosen ones!" So saying, her snow-white arms
She winds about her hesitating lord,
And fondles him with soft embrace. He soon
Melts in the well-known flame, and through his nerves
And limbs the penetrating passion thrills: 475
As when the fiery rifts of lightning run
With thunder-peals across the gleaming clouds.
She, conscious of her charms, perceives with joy
The spell her beauty and her wiles have wrought.
Enthralled by his undying love, the sire   480
Then speaks: "Why seek so far your argument?
Why should your faith in me, O queen divine,
Grow less? Had such been your desire, even Troy
I might have helped with arms; not mighty Jove
Nor fate forbidding her proud walls to stand;   485
And ten more years to Priam's life have given.
And now, if you prepare a war—your will
So fixed—whatever lies within my art,
Of labor or of skill, in molten gold
And silver, or in steel, through fire, and breath   490
Of winds, I promise you. Cease then by prayers
To put your strength in doubt." He spoke, and pressed
With fond embrace his spouse, and sank to sleep.

Then, when the night had passed her middle course,
And sleep given way to rest, what time the wife,   495
Compelled to labor at the meager loom
And distaff, to sustain her life, revives

The smoldering coals and ashes on her hearth,
And adds the night onto her daily toil;
And by the firelight sets her maids their tasks;   500
So she may keep a chaste bed for her spouse,
And rear her little ones: so at that hour
The potent fire-god, not less slack, awakes
From his soft couch, and plies his wonted work.

    Near Sicily and Æolian Lipari   505
An island rises steep, with smoking rocks.
Beneath, by huge Cyclopean forges scooped
And eaten out, the vast Ætnean caves
Thunder, and mighty anvil strokes are heard;
And all the caverns roar and hiss, with blasts   510
Of fiery steel, from panting furnaces.
This the abode of Vulcan, lending its name
To the surrounding soil. Here from on high
The fire-god lights. Below, the Cyclops toil
Over their forges; Brontes, Steropes,   515
And naked-limbed Pyracmon. In their hands
A thunderbolt, half polished, half unshaped
(Many of these the father sends from heaven
Upon the earth): three shafts they had added now,
Of hail, three of dark rainy cloud, three more   520
Of flashing-fire, and three of stormy wind.
Now with their work they mingled noise and fear,
And fierce terrific glare, and wrath, with wild
Pursuing flames. Elsewhere with urgent hands
They forge for Mars the car and flying wheels   525
With which he rouses men and towns to war.
Also the angry Pallas' arms are wrought;
The terrible ægis bright with serpent scales
And gold; the Gorgon worn upon her breast,
With twisted snakes and head lopped off whose eyes   530
Still turn and glare. "Away with all of this,"
He cries, "Ætnean Cyclops! Lay aside
These tasks begun, and here now turn your thoughts.
Arms for a valiant hero must be made.

Your strength, your swift hands, and your finest art   535
Are needed now. Hasten, then!" No more he said.
They all bend swiftly to their work, and share
Their tasks alike. The copper and the gold
Then flow in streams; and in the furnace melts
The deadly steel. A mighty shield they forge,   540
Proof in itself against all Latium's darts.
With orbèd plates on plates in sevenfold strength
They weld it. Some at the windy bellows work;
Some plunge the hissing copper in the trough.
The cavern groans with anvils. Up and down   545
With ringing blows and measured time they strike,
And turn the masses with the pincers' grip.

While amid the Æolian rocks the Lemnian sire
Thus speeds his work, the tender light of dawn
And songs of early birds beneath the roof   550
Waken Evander from his humble couch.
Up rises the old king, and dons his robe,
And binds the Tuscan sandals on his feet,
And girds about him his Arcadian sword.
From his left shoulder hangs a leopard's skin.   555
Two watchdogs from the threshold run before
Their master's steps. He, mindful of his words
And promise, seeks the chamber of his guest,
For private conference. Æneas too
Rose at an early hour. Pallas his son   560
Comes with the king, Achates with the chief.
They meet, join hands, and, sitting down, they talk
In unrestrained discourse. And first the king:—

"Great leader of the Trojans,[10] who being safe,
Troy never can be utterly overthrown;   565
Small is our strength proportioned to our name
To aid this war. The Tuscan river here
Hems us about. There, pressing round our walls,
Rutulian arms resound. But I intend
To make a league with you, of powerful tribes,   570

And armaments of wealthy kingdoms. Chance
Unlooked for shows a way of safety near.
By fate's requirement you have come to us.
Not far from here the ancient city stands,
Agylla, where the Lydian race, renowned   575
In war, once settled on the Etruscan hills.
At last, when it had flourished many years,
Mezentius with a proud and cruel sway
Held it. Why need I tell this tyrant's deeds
Of murder that no language can describe?   580
The gods requite such crimes on him and his!
A wretch, who bound the living to the dead—
Bound hands to hands, faces to faces chained—
And left them tortured in a loathed embrace
Of pest and blood, to die slow, cruel deaths.   585
But wearied out at last by these mad crimes,
The citizens rose up in arms against him
And all his house, and slew his friends, set fire to
His palace roof. He, fleeing from there, amid
The slaughter of the Rutuli, escaped,   590
And sought the friendly shelter and defense
Of Turnus. Wherefore all Etruria rose
Inflamed with righteous wrath, demanding war
Immediate, and the tyrant's punishment.
These hosts I give you; you their leader be.   595
For all along the shore their galleys crowd
With warlike cries, entreating to advance.
An aged soothsayer restrains their zeal
With fateful words: 'O brave Mæonians,
The flower and strength of old heroic times,   600
By righteous indignation against your foes
Impelled, and kindled by Mezentius' crimes;
No chief of Italy must lead this host.
Select a foreign leader.' Terrified
By such divine commands, the Etruscan troops   605
Encamp on yonder field. Tarchon himself
Has sent ambassadors, who offer me
The crown and scepter, and each royal badge,

If I will join their camp and be their king.
But envious old age with slow chilled blood   610
And strength worn down, too late for war's great toil,
Denies this rule to me. I would exhort
My son to take it, were it not that he,
Born of a Sabine mother and mixed race,
Drew from this land a portion of his blood.   615
You, favored by your years and foreign birth,
And whom the deities demand,—you take
This place, brave leader of the united hosts
Of Troy and Italy. I give, besides,
My Pallas, hope and solace of my age.   620
Under your master hand my boy shall learn
To endure the hard and heavy tasks of war;
And while still young, know you, and see your deeds.
Two hundred horsemen, choice Arcadian youths,
I send with him. Pallas himself will add   625
As many of his own."
                         Scarce had he spoken
(Æneas and Achates with fixed eyes
Sat musing gloomily on many things)
When from the clear sky Cytherea gave
A sign—a sudden flash, a sudden peal   630
Of thunder, and a shock that seemed to hurl
All things together. Through the aether rang
The Tyrrhene trumpets; up they looked: again
And yet again the fearful thunder crashed.
Then in the heavens serene, amid the clouds,   635
Arms are seen gleaming, and their clang is heard.
The others stand amazed. Æneas knew
The sound and promise that his mother gave.
"Seek not, my host," he says, "seek not to know
The event these prodigies portend: it is I   640
The heavens demand. This is the promised sign
My goddess mother gives, should war impend,
That she would aid me, bringing through the skies
Vulcanian arms. But ah, what carnage dire
Must fall upon Laurentum's wretched sons!   645

What penalties, O Turnus, must you pay!
What shields and helmets and brave forms will you,
O father Tiber, roll beneath your waves!
Now raise your battle cry, and break your leagues!"

He spoke, and from his throne rose up; and first   650
Stirs on the altars the Herculean fires
That smoldering lay, and, light of heart, draws near
The household gods adored the day before.
Due sacrifice they make of chosen sheep,
Evander and the Trojans all alike;   655
Then to his ships and to his friends returns.
From them he chooses those who best excel
In valorous deeds, to follow to the war;
The rest float down the river, and convey
Tidings to young Ascanius of his sire   660
And of his fortunes. Horses then are given
To those whose course is over the Tuscan fields.
A nobler steed is led forth for their chief,
Overspread with lion's skin and gilded claws.

Soon through the little town the rumor spreads   665
That to the shores of the Etrurian king
A band of horsemen rapidly advances.
Then matrons in their fear renew their vows.
Terror treads closer upon danger's steps,
And Mars's image towers a larger shape.   670
Evander, as his son prepares to go,
Grasping his hand, clings with a close embrace,
And, weeping unrelieving tears, thus speaks:—
    "Ah, would that Jove would only bring again[11]
To me my vanished years, as once I was,   675
When underneath Præneste's walls I fought
And conquered; when I burned whole piles of shields,
And with this hand sent Herilus to death;
To whom Feronia* his mother gave

*A rural deity.

Three lives, and weapons thrice in battle used!   680
Three deaths it took to slay him. Yet often
I slew him, and often despoiled of arms.
Then from your dear embrace I should not thus,
Dear child, be torn; nor had Mezentius ever,
Insulting over a neighbor chief, thus brought   685
Such deaths and devastations on our towns.
But you, O gods! and you, supremest Jove!
Pity, I pray, this king of Arcady,
And hear a father's prayers. If your decree—
If fate preserve my Pallas to me, safe,   690
And I shall live to meet him once again,
Then life I ask, whatever lot I endure.
But if perchance some dread disaster frowns,
Now, now release me from this cruel life,
While hope is vague, and cares hang in suspense,—   695
While still I clasp you to my heart, dear boy,
My latest and my sole delight—lest news
Too heavy to be borne assail my ears!"
    Such this last parting of the sire and son.
Then, faint and overpowered, they bear him home.   700

And now the riders through the open gates
Had passed; Æneas with the foremost goes,
And trusty Achates; then the other chiefs
Of Troy. Pallas himself rode in the midst,
Conspicuous with his cloak, and shield adorned   705
With painted emblems. Like the Morning Star,
By Venus more beloved than all the fires
Of heaven, when wet from Ocean's wave he lifts
His sacred light, and melts the shades away.
The timid mothers stand upon the walls,   710
And follow with their eyes the dusty cloud
And glittering squadrons. They through bushes scour,
The nearest way. Shouts ring. The line is formed.
Their galloping hoof-beats shake the crumbling plain.
    Near Cære's river cold a spacious grove   715
There is, to all around a sacred place

In the ancestral faith, enclosed about
By hills and gloomy firs. It is said that there
Silvanus, god of fields and flocks, received
Due sacrifice and festal rites among   720
The old Pelasgians, who first held the land.
Hard by, the Tuscan bands with Tarchon lay
Encamped secure; their legions might be seen
From the hilltop, far stretching over the fields.
Æneas and his warriors to this spot   725
Repair, and rest their limbs, and tend their steeds.

But Venus, the bright goddess, mid the clouds
Had now drawn near, bearing her gifts. Far off
She saw her son deep in a vale, alone
By the cold river, and appearing, spake: 730
"See, O my son, the promised work complete,
Wrought by my husband's skill; do not now fear
To challenge to the fight the haughty sons
Of Latium, or to confront fierce Turnus."
This saying, she approached, embraced her son,   735
And placed the radiant arms beneath an oak.
He, elated with such honors and such gifts,
Glances insatiate over every part;
Gazes in wonder, turning in his hands
The terrible helmet with its flaming crest,   740
The fateful sword of death, the corselet huge
Of bronzy bloody hue, as when a cloud
Burns in the sunbeams shining from afar;
Also the polished greaves of fine-wrought gold;
The spear; and then the shield, whose workmanship   745
No tongue can tell.
            The fire-god, not unskilled
In prophet-lore, and of the times to come,
Had wrought the Roman triumphs here, the events
Of Italy;[12] there all Ascanius' line
To come, and all the wars in order ranged.   750
Here lay the she-wolf in the cave of Mars,

And hanging round her udders the two babes*
Were playing, fearless, while she gave them suck,
Or bending back her neck, caressed by turns
And shaped them with her tongue. Nearby were seen 755
The walls of Rome; the Sabine women seized†
Amid the Circensian games, with lawless hands;
And the new war that suddenly rose, between
The men of Romulus and Tatius old,
With his rough Cures. Then, when war is over, 760
Before Jove's altars stood the armèd kings,
And held the sacred goblets, while with blood
Of slaughtered swine they join in friendly league.
Not far from this, Mettus was torn apart‡
By two chariots, four horses yoked to each 765
(Alban, you should have kept your promised faith);
And Tullus,§ who the traitor's bleeding flesh
Dragged through the thickets, till the briers dripped blood;
Also Porsenna,[13] threatening Rome with siege,
Commands that banished Tarquin be received. 770
The Æneadæ were rushing to their arms,
For liberty, while he, as with a threat,
Stood indignant, that Cocles dares destroy
The bridge, and Clœlia[14] with her broken chains
Has swum the river. On the upper part 775
The guard of the Tarpæan citadel,
Manlius,|| stood firm, and held the Capitol.
The royal house of Romulus was seen,
Rough with its new-thatched roof of bristling straw.
Here, flying through the gilded porticos, 780
A silver goose announced the Gauls were near:

---

*Romulus and Remus: twin boys born to Mars and Ilia, raised by a she-wolf on the shores of the Tiber.

†The rape of the Sabine women: Rome was overpopulated with men, so Romulus invited the women of a neighboring people, the Sabines, to see a show. When Romulus gave the order, the men of Rome surrounded the women and took them as wives.

‡The treaty with Rome was broken by Mettus; his punishment was to be torn in two opposite directions, which was suggestive of his actions.

§Also known as Hostilius; the third king of Rome.

||Held Capitol against the Gauls (387 B.C.).

They through the thickets had approached, and held
The citadel, by night and darkness screened:
Their garments and their hair were wrought in gold:
They shone in short striped cloaks: their milk-white necks   785
Were ringed with gold: each shook two Alpine spears,
And wore a long shield to protect his limbs.
Here were depicted dancing Salii,*
Naked Luperci, and the wool-tipped caps
Of flamens, and the shields that fell from heaven.   790
And through the streets in easy carriages
Chaste matrons a devout procession led.
Far off were seen the deep Tartarean realms
Of Dis; the penalties of crime; and you,
O Catiline,† upon a frowning cliff   795
Hanging in dread suspense, aghast with fear
Before the Furies: then, the pious souls
Apart, and Cato‡ giving laws to them.
Midway, a picture of the sea, in gold,
With foaming waves of silver, was inwrought;   800
Bright silvery dolphins through the waters swept
In circling course, and cut the frothy tide.
And in the middle of the sea appeared
The battle of Actium, and the brass-clad fleets;
And all Leucate§ you might see in arms,   805
And the waves blazing in the golden sheen.
And here Augustus Cæsar led to war
His people, and the fathers, and their gods.
He stands upon the lofty stern; two flames
Play round his brows; the star that led his sire   810
Shines over his head. Agrippa‖ marshals there
His hosts, impetuous, with propitious winds
And auspices; upon his brows

---

*Members of a Roman cult of Mars.

†Defeated by Cicero in 63 B.C.

‡The younger, of Utica; exemplum of stoic virtue.

§Southern point of Leucas, island west of Greece and near Actium; Vergil has conflated Leucas and Actium, site of Octavian's defeat of Antony and Cleopatra's naval forces in 31 B.C.

‖Foremost among Octavian's generals.

A golden naval crown with shining beaks.
There, with barbaric allies, and with arms   815
Of fashion multiform, comes Antony,
Victorious from the East and Indian shores;
Egypt, and forces of the Orient lands
He brings, and distant Bactra; and behind
Follows his course—O shame!—the Egyptian wife.*   820
Onward they come together, and the waves
Are tossed in foam beneath their long-drawn oars
And trident beaks: as though the Cyclades†
Uptorn were floating; or as mountains struck
Together; such a weight of tower-crowned ships   825
Was urged along. They hurl the blazing torch,
The flying steel propel; the watery fields
Redden with carnage of the fight begun.
The queen with ringing sistrum calls to arms,
Nor sees behind her yet the serpents twain.   830
The dog Anubis,‡ and all monstrous shapes
Of demigods, with weapons drawn oppose
Neptune, and Venus, and Minerva's power.
Mars cased in steel is raging in the midst;
The Furies fell are there; and Discord moves   835
Rejoicing, with her mantle rent. Behind
Bellona follows with her bloody scourge.
Actian Apollo from above beholds,
And bends his bow. Then, with that terror struck,
Egypt and India and Arabia all   840
Turn back and fly. The queen herself was seen
Loosening the ropes and hoisting sails to catch
The wind. Here had the fire-god shown how she,
Pale with the thought of coming death, was borne
Amid the slaughter on, with waves and winds;   845
While sorrowing, the Nile opened wide his breast
And ample robes, and called them to his arms,

---

*Cleopatra.

†Islands in the Aegean.

‡Egyptian deity with the head of a dog.

And hid the vanquished in his secret waves
Of sheltering blue. But Cæsar, borne along
In triple triumph[15] to the Roman walls,   850
Here to the gods of Italy devotes
Three hundred shrines. With games and joyous shouts
The streets are ringing; choirs of matrons throng
The temples; at the altars victims bleed.
He sits at Apollo's shining gateway,   855
Reviews the gifts of nations, and hangs up
The spoils upon the lofty temple gates.
The conquered tribes in long procession march,
With various tongues, and various garbs, and arms:
Uncinctured Africans and Nomads wild,   860
And Carians, and Gelonians armed with bows,
And Leleges. Euphrates'* waters flow
With gentler course. The far-off Morini
Are seen; the two-horned Rhine; the Dahæ fierce;
And the Araxes' stream that spurned his bridge.   865

Such things on Vulcan's shield, his mother's gift,
Æneas scanned in wonder; ignorant
Of all, yet with the imagery moved
To joy, upon his shoulders he lifts up
The fame and fates of his posterity.   870

---

*These four lines catalog rivers and peoples of the empire: the Euphrates is in Parthia; the Morini were a tribe in Gaul; the Rhine River is in Germany; the Dahae were Scythians; and the Araxes is a river in Armenia.

BOOK 9

WHILE these events in other places passed,[1]
Iris is sent by Juno from the skies
To valiant Turnus. He within a grove
By chance was sitting (once his ancestor's,
Pilumnus*), in a consecrated glen.   5
To whom, with rosy lips, Thaumantias† spoke:—
"Turnus, what none of all the gods would dare
To grant, if you should ask it, now, behold,
Revolving time brings of its own accord.
His city, fleet, and friends Æneas leaves,   10
And seeks Evander's kingdom and his court.
Nor is this yet enough: he penetrates
Cortona's farthest bounds; the Lydian bands
He arms, and peasants gathered from the fields.
Why do you linger? Now is the time to call   15
For chariots and for steeds.[2] No more delay!
But seize upon your foe's disordered camp."
She spoke, and toward the skies she spread her wings,
And, flying, traced her rainbow on the clouds.
The youth knew then the goddess, and his hands   20
Uplifted, and his voice thus followed her:—
"Iris, O glory of the sky, who sent
To me your radiant form, so swift impelled
Through clouds? Whence comes this sudden burst of light?
I see the heavens break open in the midst,   25
And stars go wandering in the firmament.
Such omens I obey, whoever you are
Who calls me now to arms." Then to the stream
He goes, and scoops the water with his hands,

---

*Father or grandfather of Daunus, father of Turnus.

†Also known as Iris; the rainbow.

229

Invokes the gods, and loads the air with vows. 30

And now his army moves across the plains,
Sumptuous with steeds and gold-embroidered robes
Messapus leads the van, and Tyrrheus' sons
Support the rear; and in the center rides
Their leader, Turnus, towering in his arms. 35
So with its seven peaceful channels swells
The deep and silent Ganges, or the Nile,
Back from the fields with fertilizing wave
Flowing, then shrinking to its usual course.
The Trojans now behold a sudden cloud 40
Of dust arise, and darken all the fields.
And first Caïcus from the mound in front,
Exclaims: "What is this black and rolling mass?
Quick,—bring your swords, your spears, and mount the walls!
Behold, the enemy!" Then with a shout 45
The Trojans enter, and bar up the gates,
And man the ramparts. Such was the command
Æneas, skilled in arms, departing, gave,
That should such chance occur, they must not dare
A battle in the open field, but keep 50
Within their camp and mounded walls, secure.
So though disposed by anger and by shame
To meet the foe in conflict, they obey
His wise commands, and making fast their gates,
Within their towers, well armed, they await the attack. 55

Turnus, who sped with flying pace before
His tardy troops, a chosen band with him
Of twenty horsemen, unforeseen approached.
On a white-spotted Thracian steed he rode;
His helmet is of gold, with flaming crest. 60
"And which of you, O youths," he cries, "with me
Will first attack the foe? Behold!" With that
He hurled a javelin through the air; and thus
Began the battle; then across the field
He gallops. With a shout his comrades join, 65
And follow him with fearful battle-cries;

And wonder at the Trojans' timid hearts,
Who will not take the field in open fight,
But cling to their encampment. Round the walls,
Now here, now there, the chieftain rides, and seeks   70
An entrance; like a wolf that raging prowls
About the folds, exposed to winds and rains
At midnight, while the bleating lambs lie safe
Beneath their mothers, and, enraged and fierce,
Snarls at the prey he cannot reach, impelled   75
By long, mad hunger that drains dry his throat.
So the Rutulian, gazing at the walls
And camp, his anger burns through all his limbs.
How find an entrance, how dislodge his foes
Entrenched behind their ramparts, forcing them   80
To fight on equal terms? The fleet that lay
Concealed beside the camp, girt round with banks
And channels, he determines to assail.[3]
To his exulting comrades then he calls
For fire, and grasps a flaming pine-wood torch.   85
Then to their work, by Turnus' presence urged,
They go, all armed with brands: they rob the hearths;
The smoking torches glare with pitchy flames,
And to the stars ascend the fiery sparks.

O Muses, say what god averted then   90
Such dreadful burning from the Trojan ships.
Though ancient the belief in this event,
The fame from it forever shall endure.

When upon Phrygian Ida Æneas first
His fleet was building, with intent to sail,   95
The Berecynthian mother of the gods,
It is said, thus made appeal to mighty Jove:—
"Grant now, my son, a boon your parent dear
Demands of thee, the ruler of the skies.
A grove of pines, cherished for many years,   100
Was mine, on Ida's summit, where to me
Offerings and sacred rites were paid; a place
Darkened by fir trees and by maple boughs.

These to the Dardan warrior in his need
I gladly gave, wherewith to build his fleet.   105
But now my heart is sad with anxious fears.
Do now dispel them: grant this to my prayers;
That by their voyage they may never be shaken,
Or overwhelmed by any stormy wind.
Let it avail that on our mount they grew."   110
To whom her son who rolls the heavenly orbs
Made answer: "But where do you call the fates,
O mother? What do you demand for these,
Your ships? Can they, built by hands of mortals,
Enjoy immortal rights? And shall Æneas,   115
Certain to win, pass through uncertain straits
Of danger? To what god was ever power
Like this allowed? But, rather, when their course
Is ended, and they reach the Ausonian ports,
What vessels shall escape the storms, and bear   120
The Trojan leader to the Italian shores,
Their mortal forms I then will change to shapes
Of sea-nymphs, cleaving with their breasts the waves
Like Doto, or like Galatea." Thus
He spoke, and sealed his promise by appeal   125
To his dread brother's Stygian streams of fire;
The torrents, and black gulfs of whirling pitch.
And as he nodded, all Olympus thrilled.

So now the promised day at length had come,
The destined time completed by the fates;   130
When the assault of Turnus on the ships
Warned the great mother to defend from flames
Their consecrated wood. And first a flash
Dazzled their eyes with unaccustomed light;
And from the east a great cloud streamed across   135
The heavens, and the Idæan bands appeared;
And through the air there rang an awful voice
That filled both armies: "Trojans, make no haste
To seize your weapons and defend your ships.
Turnus shall burn the seas before his hand   140

Can touch my sacred pines. Go forth, released
And free, as goddesses of ocean go!
It is the mother of the gods commands!"
Then all at once the vessels snap their cords,
And with their plunging beaks like dolphins dive   145
Beneath the waves; thence, wondrous prodigy,
As many virgin forms arise to view
And swim upon the surface of the sea,
As on the beach, before, stood brazen prows.

Amazement seized the Rutuli; and even   150
Messapus, with his rearing horses, quailed.
The Tiber, hoarsely sounding, checked his waves,
And backward from the deep retraced his course.
But Turnus fears not, confident and bold.
Yet more, he lifts their courage with his words[4]   155
And even chides. "These prodigies," he cries,
"Are intended for the Trojans; Jove himself
Snatches away their usual means of help.
They wait not for Rutulian fires and swords,
These ships of theirs. So now the seas for them   160
Are pathless, for their hopes of flight are gone.
One half of their success is lost to them:
The land is in our hands. The Italian tribes
Bring their armed thousands. They frighten me not,
These answers of the gods, whatever they be,   165
The Phrygians boast. Enough that it was given
To Venus and the Fates, that they should reach
The Ausonian shores. I also have my fate
Allotted, to destroy the accursed race,
Now that my bride is torn from me. That grief   170
Does not touch Atreus' sons alone, nor do Greeks
Alone appeal to arms for such a cause.
Yet to have perished once should be enough:
Enough to have committed once the offense
That should have made them loathe all womankind.   175
And these the men whose courage is sustained
By rampart interposed, and baffling trench,

Their slight partition between them and death.
And yet have they not seen their walls of Troy,
Though built by Neptune's hands, sink down in flames?   180
But you, O chosen warriors, which of you
Will rend their palisades, and dare with me
To invade their trembling camp? No armor wrought
By Vulcan nor a countless fleet I need
Against these Trojans. Let Etruria send   185
All her strong allies. They need not fear
The darkness, the Palladium's coward theft,
The keepers of the citadel struck down:
Nor that within the hollow of a horse
We hide. In open daylight we resolve   190
To ring their ramparts round about with fire.
Soon shall I make them think, that not with Greeks
And raw Pelasgian youths they have to deal,
Such as their Hector foiled for ten long years.
    And now, since the best portion of the day   195
Is passed, give the remaining hours to rest,
O warriors, well content that all succeeds.
Tomorrow morn stand ready for the battle."

Meanwhile the charge to place the sentinels
About the gates, and watchfires round the walls,   200
Is given to Messapus. He selects
Twice seven Rutulian men to guard the fort;
And following each there come a hundred youths
With purple crests and glittering with gold.
They shift their places, and relieve the guard;   205
And scattered over the field, their wine-cups drain.
The camp-fires blaze around; the sleepless night
Is given up to revelry and sport.

All this the Trojans from their ramparts see,
And man their walls; with fear they test their gates,   210
And bridge the space between outwork, walls, and tower,
And bring supplies of weapons for defense.
Mnestheus and brave Serestus urge the work.

To them, should adverse fortune so require,
Æneas had entrusted the command   215
Of all affairs. The entire band keeps watch
Along the walls, the common danger shares;
Each takes his turn, wherever defense they need.

Nisus was keeper of the gate,[5] the son
Of Hyrtacus, a valiant youth in war,   220
And swift with javelin and with flying arrows;
Sent by the huntress Ida to attend
Æneas. At his side Euryalus,
Than whom no youth more beautiful was seen
Among the Trojans, bearing Trojan arms: 225
As yet a beardless boy. These two were bound
In closest ties of love, and side by side
Had rushed together to the battlefield;
Now at the gate they held one equal post.
Then Nisus said: "Is it the gods who give   230
This ardor to our minds, Euryalus?
And must our strong desires be deemed divine?
Either to battle or some greater task
My soul is urging me, and will not rest.
You see what confidence possesses all   235
The Rutuli; their camp-fires here and there
Are feebly glimmering. Sunk in sleep and wine
They lie; and far and wide their posts are hushed.
Hear now the thought that rises in my mind.
Our leaders and our ranks with one accord   240
Ask for Æneas' presence, and that men
Be sent, who shall report to him the truth.
If now they promise what I ask for you,
(For me the glory of the deed is all
I seek), I think that I can find a way   245
Beneath that hill to Pallanteum's walls."
Amazement seized upon Euryalus,
Struck with the love of praise that fired his friend.
Then thus he answered: "Can you then refuse
To allow me in enterprise so great   250

To go with you? Shall I let you risk alone
Perils like these? It was not thus my sire
Opheltes, long enured to toils of war,
Taught me amid the Grecian terrors reared,
And sufferings of Troy; nor have I ever,   255
Following the great Æneas and his fates
Extreme, so borne myself, when in your sight.
Here in my breast there is a soul whose aim
Despises life, and deems its sacrifice
Small payment for that glory which you seek."   260

Nisus replied: "No, not to you, indeed,
Would I impute such thoughts. It were unjust.
So may great Jove, or whosoever looks
Upon our actions with impartial eyes,
Bring me in triumph back again to you.   265
But if,—for, in a crisis such as this,
You know full well there must be many a risk,—
If any adverse fortune or the gods
Should intervene, I would have you survive
Your friend: your years are worthier of life.   270
Let there be one to lay me in my grave,
Snatched from the battle, or by ransom won.
But if, as she is wont, Fortune forbids
This favor, let him to my absent corpse
Give funeral rites and fitting sepulcher.   275
Nor let me be the cause of bitter grief,
My boy, to a wretched mother, who alone,
Of many mothers, dared to go with you,
Nor cared to stay in great Acestes' home."
    But he replied: "In vain these useless knots   280
Of argument. My purpose does not yield.
Come, let us hasten!" And with that he wakes
The sentinels, who take their turn on guard.
Then both together go to seek the prince.

All other living creatures lay relaxed   285
In sleep, forgetting sufferings and cares.

But the chief leaders and the chosen youths
Of Troy were holding counsel on affairs
Of moment; how they should proceed, and who
The messenger should be to seek Æneas.   290
Within the camp they stood, holding their shields,
And leaning on their spears. Together then
Come Nisus and Euryalus, and ask
Admittance eagerly,—the matter grave,
Repaying the delay it would demand.   295
Iulus meets the excited youths, and bids
The elder speak. Then Nisus thus begins:—
"Hear with impartial minds, O Trojan chiefs,
And judge not by our years what we propose.
The Rutuli lie sunk in sleep and wine.   300
We have found a place fit for our secret plan,
Upon the double road beyond the gates
Lying nearest to the sea. Their smoking fires
Burn low. If you permit us now to use
This chance, we'll seek Æneas, and the walls   305
Of Pallanteum. Soon we shall return
With spoils, a mighty slaughter being wrought.
We cannot miss the way, for we have seen
While off hunting, the outskirts of the town
Gleam through the shady valleys, and we know   310
The river-shore entire." Aletes then,
Old and mature in thought, made answer thus:—
"O gods, in whose protecting presence Troy
Has ever been, not altogether doomed
To ruin is our Trojan race, while such   315
The valiant souls, the hearts assured you send!"
So saying, he threw his arms around their necks,
And grasped their hands, while tears streamed down his face.
"And what rewards, O warrior youths," he cried,
"What gifts for such brave deeds can we requite?   320
The gods and your own virtues will bestow
The best and fairest. But Æneas soon
Will give the rest; and young Ascanius too
Will never forget such high desert as yours."

"No, never," here Ascanius took the word;   325
"I whose sole hope is in my sire's return;
Nisus, by all our country's household gods,
The lares of Assaracus, the shrines
Of venerable Vesta, I appeal
To you; whatever my fortune and my hope,   330
I lay it in your faithful breasts. Bring back
My sire; then nothing can be sad to me.
Two fine-wrought silver goblets richly chased
With figures, which my father took as spoils,
When he subdued Arisba, I will give;   335
Also a pair of tripods, and of gold
Two weighty talents, and an antique cup,
Sidonian Dido's gift. And if we take
Italia, and the scepter of the realm,
And distribution make of spoils,—you have seen   340
The steed that Turnus rode, his armor bright
With gold; that steed, that shield, that flaming crest,
Nisus, I set apart for your reward.
Besides, twelve chosen female slaves my sire
Will give, twelve captives with their arms, and add   345
To these whatever lands Latinus owns.
But thou, O youth worthy of worship, you
Whose years are nearer mine, with my whole heart
I take you and embrace you through all change
Of fortune my companion. Without you   350
No glory will I seek in peace or war;
Such trust I place in you and in your words."
To this Euryalus made answer thus:—
"No coming day shall ever prove me averse
To daring deeds like this: I promise this,   355
Let Fortune smile or frown. But above all,
One boon I beg. I have a mother, born
Of Priam's ancient race, who came with me
To Italy. Troy could not hold her back,
Nor King Acestes' walls. I leave her now,   360
Without one farewell kiss, and knowing not
Of this my dangerous venture. By the night,

And by this hand I grasp, I could not bear
A mother's tears. But you, I beg, do you
Console her in her need, and care for her   365
Bereft of me. This hope let me indulge.
So shall I face more bravely every peril."
      The Dardan warriors all were moved to tears,
Iulus more than all: his heart was wrung
By such strong filial love. Then thus he spoke:—   370
"Be sure of all your brave attempt deserves.
Your mother shall be mine, and only lack
Creüsa's name. Nor slight our thanks to her
For such a son. Whatever befalls, I swear,
Here by this head, the oath my father swore,—   375
That if you do come back, and with success,
That which I promise you shall be bestowed
Alike upon your mother and your kin."
Weeping he spoke; and from his shoulder loosed
A gilded sword Lycaon's wondrous art   380
Had wrought and fitted in an ivory sheath.
To Nisus Mnestheus gives a lion's skin
With shaggy hair. Aletes makes exchange
Of helmets. Thus equipped, forthwith they go;
While to the gates the leaders, young and old,   385
Attend their steps with wishes and with prayers.
Iulus with a mind and manly thought
Beyond his years, gives many messages
Sent to his father, but in vain: the winds
Dispersed them all and gave them to the clouds.   390

They cross the trenches, and through shades of night
Pursue their way toward the hostile camp,
Fatal to many before their own fate came.
Scattered about they see their enemies
Stretched on the grass, overcome with sleep and wine.   395
Along the shore stood chariots with their poles
Upturned. Between the harness and the wheels
Lay men, and armor, mixed with jars of wine.
Then Nisus whispered: "Now, Euryalus,

The deed calls on us for a daring hand.   400
Here lies our way. You, lest some foe behind
Should strike, watch close, look well afar, while I
Lay waste, and open a wide path for thee."
    With voice suppressed he spoke. Then with his sword
Strikes at proud Rhamnes, stretched upon a pile   405
Of carpets, breathing heavily in sleep.
A prince he was, and Turnus' favorite seer.
But not with augury could he ward off
The fatal blow. Near him he slays three slaves
Who lay confusedly amid their arms;   410
The armor-bearer and the charioteer
Of Remus next, beneath his horse's feet;
He severs his head from his drooping neck;
His master's then he bears away, and leaves
The trunk that heaves and gurgles with its blood.   415
The earth is warm with black and bloody gore,
And all the couches drip. Then Lamyrus,
And Lamus, and the young Serranus fell—
The handsome youth, who long and heavily
Had played that night, and, overcome by wine   420
And sleep, was lying; happy had he then
Prolonged his play until the morning light.
Such carnage fell, as when a lion, mad
With hunger, spreads wild terror through the sheep
Amid the crowded fold, and bites and tears   425
With bloody jaws the tender flocks, all dumb
With fear. Nor less Euryalus, inflamed,
Deals death around amid the nameless crowd.
Fadus, Herbesus, Abaris, meet their fate,
Unconscious: Rhœtus too, who, wide awake,   430
Sees all, but trembling hides behind the bowls.
Then, as he rises, deep within his breast
The sword is plunged, and, steeped in death, withdrawn.
Out pours the crimson life-blood mixed with wine.
The other presses on, warm with his work   435
Of stealthy slaughter, toward Messapus' bands,
Where he observes the fires are burning low,

And tethered horses browsing in the grass.
Then briefly Nisus spoke: for he perceived
How their desire to kill was bearing them   440
Too far: "Let us desist. The dawn is near,
Unfriendly to our purpose. Deaths enough
Are dealt. A way is opened through our foes."
Full many a piece of solid silver wrought
They leave behind, and bowls, and armor bright,   445
And sumptuous carpets. Here, the trappings rich
Of Rhamnes, and his golden-studded belt,
Euryalus puts on; a gift once sent
By Cædicus to Remulus, when he
Made league with him through hospitable rites.   450
After his death, the Rutuli in war
Obtained it. These Euryalus now takes,
And round his shoulders binds the spoils, in vain:
Puts on Messapus' helmet rich with plumes;
Then from the camp to a safe place they go.   455

Meanwhile a mounted troop was moving on
From Latium's city, a detachment sent
From the main legion lingering on the plains,
Bearing a message to Prince Turnus. These,
Three hundred horsemen, Volscens at their head,   460
All armed with shields, were drawing nigh the camp.
When far off they spot the pair, who turned
Upon the left; for glimmering in the night
The helmet of Euryalus betrayed
The unknowing youth, and gleamed against the moon,   465
Not idly unobserved. "Stand!" Volscens shouts;
"What men are you? Why come you here in arms?
And where now are you going?" No reply
They made; but swiftly toward the woods they fled,
Trusting the friendly night. The horsemen hasten   470
To block their passage on the well-known paths,
And on both sides guard every avenue
Against escape. There was a forest dark,
Rough with wild bushes and black ilex trees

And tangled underbrush. At intervals   475
A pathway dimly seen ran through the wood.
The darkness and the heavy spoils he bore
Impede Euryalus, and in his fear
He now mistakes his way. Nisus flies on,
Not taking thought, and past his enemy   480
Had sped, and reached the groves that since were called
The Alban, then they were the lofty stalls
For King Latinus' herds. Soon as he stopped,
And backward looked, in vain, to find his friend,
"Euryalus!" he cries; "Ah, woe is me,   485
Where have I left you? How shall I retrace
The windings of the dark deceptive wood?"
Then back on his remembered steps he treads,
And, wandering through the silent bushes, hears
The tramp of horses, and the noise of men   490
Pursuing; in a little while, a shout;
And sees Euryalus, whom now, deceived
By darkness and the place, the entire brigade
Surrounds and seizes, with a sudden rush,
And drags him on, while struggling hard in vain.   495
What shall he do? With what force shall he dare
To rescue him? Rush in among their swords,
And so precipitate a glorious death?
Quick, brandishing a javelin, to the Moon
Above he lifts his eyes, while thus he prays:—   500
"O, goddess, you, the glory of the stars,
Latonian* guardian of the woods, be near,
And to my arm now give propitious aid!
If ever on your altars Hyrtacus
My sire laid gifts for me, if I myself   505
Have added anything brought from the chase,
Hung beneath your vaulted ceiling, or affixed
Upon your sacred pediment, direct
My weapon, that I may disperse this band!"

---

*Of the goddess Diana.

He spoke, and with the strength of all his frame   510
He hurled his steel. Swift through the dark it sped,
And pierced the back of Sulmo, and there snapped,
The broken javelin passing to his heart.
He falls, the warm blood rushes from his breast,
And his sides heave with long convulsive sobs.   515
On every side they look; when lo! again
Another spear drawn back, then whizzing flies;
And through both temples smitten, Tagus falls,
The glowing weapon buried in his brain.
Fierce Volscens rages, nor can he detect   520
The enemy, nor know on whom to turn.
"You then," he cries, "with your warm blood shall pay
For both!" And on Euryalus he turns
With naked sword. But Nisus, terrified,
Beside himself with fear, no longer hides   525
In darkness, nor can bear a pang like this.
"Me, me; it's I," he cries, "who did the deed!
On me direct your steel, O Rutuli!
The offense is mine alone. He did no harm,
He could not! Yonder sky and conscious stars   530
Bear witness that the words I speak are true.
He only loved too much his luckless friend!"
So Nisus spoke: too late; the sword was plunged
Deep in the white breast of Euryalus.
He writhes beneath his death-wound, and the blood   535
Flows over his shapely limbs. Upon his breast
His sinking head reclines. As when a plough
Cuts down a purple flowret of the field,
It languishes and dies; or beaten down
By rain the poppies bend their weary heads.   540
But Nisus rushes on his enemies.
Volscens alone among them all he seeks.
They, thronging close around him, thrust him back.
But nonetheless he presses on, and whirls
His flashing sword, till in the clamoring throat   545
Of the Rutulian chief he plunged the steel,
And, dying, dealt a death-blow to his foe.

Then on the lifeless body of his friend
He throws himself, pierced through with many a wound,
And there, at last, in placid death he slept.   550
    Ay, happy pair! If aught my verse can do,
No lapse of time shall ever dim your fame,
While on the Capitol's unshaken rock
The house Æneas founded shall remain,
And while the Roman father holds the state.   555

The Rutuli, victorious, seize the spoils,
And weeping bear their dead chief to the camp.
Here too was mourning over Rhamnes slain,
And young Serranus, and the rest, their first
And noblest, by one slaughter all dispatched.   560
They throng to see the dying and the dead,—
The place still warm with carnage, and the streams
Of blood. In turn they recognize the spoils;
The glittering helmet of Messapus know,
And trappings rich, recovered with such toil.   565

Now from Tithonus' saffron bed the Dawn
Arose, and shed fresh light upon the earth,
And pouring in his rays, the sun revealed
All hidden things; when Turnus stirs to arms
His warriors all, himself completely armed.   570
Each urges to the battle his mailed troops,
Whetting their rage with various reports.
But, on their lifted spears, ah, woeful sight!
The heads of Nisus and Euryalus
Are fixed, while shouting crowds follow behind.   575
The hardy sons of Troy confront their foes
Upon the left side of their walls; their right
Is bounded by the river. Here they guard
Their trenches broad, and stand with gloomy thoughts
Upon their lofty towers; and horror-struck   580
Behold those lifted heads that drip with gore,
Known but too well to their unhappy friends.

Rumor, meanwhile, the wingèd messenger,
Flies through the trembling camp, and reaches now
The mother of Euryalus. A chill   585
Curdles her blood. The shuttle and the web
Drop from her hands. Rending her hair she flies
With wild shrieks to the walls and foremost line,
Heedless of danger and of flying darts.
Her wailing fills the air.[6] "Euryalus,   590
Do I behold you thus!—you the delight
And solace of my old age, could you thus
Leave me alone,—ah, cruel!—and depart
On such a perilous mission, and no word
At parting to your wretched mother speak?   595
Ah, woe is me! On unknown earth you lie,
A prey to vultures and to Latian dogs;
Nor could your mother give you funeral rites,
Nor close your dying eyes, nor wash your wounds,
Nor cover you with the robe, which night and day   600
I wove with urgent haste, and with my loom
Lightened old age's lonely thoughts and cares.
Where shall I seek you now? Where find those limbs
Dissevered, and that lacerated corpse?
Is it this, my son, you bring now back to me?   605
Was it for this I followed you over land
And ocean? Pierce me through, O Rutuli!
If any filial pity you would show.
Me first! But you, great father of the gods,
In mercy thrust this hated life beneath   610
The shades of Tartarus; since otherwise
I cannot break the thread of cruel life!"

    Her sad lament wrings every soul; deep groans
Pass through the warrior's ranks. Their broken strength
Grows torpid for the battle. Thus while she   615
Adds grief to grief, Idæus and Actor come,
By Ilioneus and Ascanius sent
(Who weeps full out), and bear her to her home.

But now the dreadful trumpet's brazen blare

Is heard, and shouts resound.[7] The Volscians haste   620
To form their ranks beneath a roof of shields,
And fill the moats, and storm the ramparts. Some
Seek for an entrance, and to scale the walls,
Where thinly shows the opposing battle-line,
And where the armèd ring less densely gleams.   625
The Trojans with strong poles thrust back their foes,
And shower their weapons down of every kind,
Taught by long warfare to defend their walls.
Stones also they roll down of fearful weight
To break, if so they can, their sheltered ranks.   630
But underneath their iron roof their foes
Can well endure all hardships. Yet their strength
Suffices not; for where the serried mass
Most threatened, the Trojans rolled a huge rock,
Which fell, and dashed asunder far and wide   635
The Rutuli, and crushed their shielded roof.
No longer do the bold assailants dare
Contend in warfare blind, but bend their strength
To drive their foes with missiles from the walls.
Mezentius at another point comes on,   640
In aspect terrible, and brandishes
A blazing Tuscan pine, and fills the place
With fire and smoke. Messapus too is there,
Tamer of steeds, and of Neptunian race,
And batters down and tears the palisade,   645
And calls for ladders to ascend the walls.

You Muses, and your chief, Calliope!*
Inspire me now to sing what deeds of death
Were done that day by Turnus; what brave souls
Were sent to Orcus; and unfold with me   650
The war's vast outlines. For you, O goddesses,
Bear all in mind, and can rehearse them all.

---

*Muse of epic poetry.

Joined by high bridges to the walls, there stood
A lofty tower, which with their utmost strength
The Italians stormed,[8] and strove to overturn.   655
The Trojans made defense with stones, and down
Through hollow loopholes showers of javelins hurled.
Then Turnus, foremost, flung a blazing torch,
Which struck, and burning clung against the sides.
Blown by the wind, it seizes on the boards   660
And on the beams with its devouring flames.
Dismayed, the Trojans try in vain to fly;
Then as they backward crowd upon the part
Free from the fiery pest, with all its weight
The tower gives way, and falls; the mighty crash   665
Thunders through all the sky. Down to the earth,
The huge mass following, they fall, half dead,
And on each other's spears impaled, or pierced
By splintered beams. Helenor only escaped,
And Lycus; young Helenor, whom the slave   670
Licymnia to a Lydian king had borne
In secret love, and whom she had sent to Troy
With forbidden arms; he with naked sword
Was lightly armed, and with inglorious shield
Without device. He when he saw himself   675
Hemmed in by Turnus' hosts, the Latian lines
Opposing to the right and to the left—
As some wild beast, surrounded by a ring
Of hunters, rages against their spears, and bounds
Upon their points, and knows her doom is near—   680
So the youth rushes on his foes, prepared
To die, and where the spears are thickest leaps.
But Lycus, swifter far, flies through the hosts,
And gains the walls, and strives to grasp the ridge,
And reach some friendly hand. Turnus pursues,   685
As swift of foot, as with his threatening spear.
"Fool!" he exclaims, "and did you hope to escape
Our hands?" Then seizing him as there he hangs,
Tears down with him a huge piece of the wall.
As when Jove's eagle, swooping from above,   690

With crooked talons carries off a hare
Or snow-white swan; or as a raging wolf
Snatches away a lamb from out the fold,
Amid the piteous bleatings of its dam.
Shouts rise on every side. They charge amain,   695
They heap the trenches full with earth, and fling
Their blazing torches to the battlements.

    Then with a ponderous fragment from a cliff,
Ilioneus fells Lucetius, as he comes
Beneath the gate, a firebrand in his hand.   700
Liger strikes down Emathion; and, laid low
By Asilas, Corynæus falls; the one
Skilled in the javelin, and the other swift
With unsuspected arrow from afar.
Cæneus slays Ortygius, Turnus him: 705
Itys, and Clonius, and Dioxippus,
And Promolus, and Sagaris, all fell
By Turnus' hand, and Idas, as he stood
Upon the turret's height; and Capys slays
Privernus, by Themilla's spear first grazed.   710
He, thoughtless, threw aside his shield, and laid
His hand upon the wound: an arrow flew
And pierced his hand, and pinned it to his side,
And through the deadly wound his soul's breath ebbed.

    In splendid armor Arcens' son appeared;   715
An embroidered cloak, Iberian purple, decked
His noble form. He by his sire was sent
Into the war, and in his mother's grove
Was reared, beside Symæthus' stream, where stood
Palicus' easy altar, fat with gifts.   720
His spears now laid aside, Mezentius whirls
Thrice round his head his whizzing sling; the lead
Pierces the temples of the youth, who falls,
And on the sand lies stretched his lifeless form.

Then for the first time in the war, it is said,   725
Ascanius aimed his swift shaft at the foe,
Before this accustomed only to pursue
The wild beasts of the chase, and with his hand

Struck down the strong Numanus, whose surname
Was Remulus; who lately had espoused   730
The younger sister of Prince Turnus. He,
Swelling with new-blown pride of royalty,
Stalked in the foremost ranks, vociferous
With boast and taunt, and towering with huge frame,
Thus called aloud: "Are you not then ashamed,   735
Twice-captured Phrygians, to be shut once more
Within your ramparts, interposing walls
Between you and death? Lo, these are they who come
Claiming our brides in war! What god was it,
What madness brought you to the Italian shores?   740
No sons of Atreus shall you find in us;
No false, smooth-tongued Ulysses. From our birth
We are a hardy race. We plunge our babes
Into the river, soon as they are born,
And harden thus their frames to wintry cold.   745
Our boys are never weary of the chase.
They scour the woods. It is their sport to tame
Their steeds, and bend their bows, and wing their shafts.
Our youths, in labor patient, and enured
To humble fare, either subdue the earth   750
With harrows, or in battle shake the walls
Of towns. We pass our lives in handling steel:
We drive our oxen with inverted spears.
Age weakens not our strength; on our gray heads
We press the helmet; and it's our delight   755
To seize fresh spoils, and on our plunder live.
You in your embroidered vests of saffron hue
And glowing purple, indolently live;
Delighting in your dances, and your sleeves,
And caps, with lappets underneath your chins.   760
Yes, Phrygian women, indeed, not men!
Go to the summits of your Dindymus,
Where breathes the flute in your accustomed ear
Its two weak notes. The Berecynthian pipe
And timbrels call you. Throw your weapons down!   765
Leave arms to heroes of a sturdier stuff!"

This boaster's words, presaging evil thus,
Ascanius could not bear. Confronting him,
An arrow on his horsehair string he drew,
And stood awhile with arms extended wide,　　　　　770
And prayed to Jove: "All-powerful Jupiter,
Aid now my daring venture! To your shrines
Will I bring solemn offerings, and will place
Before your altars a young bull, snow-white,
With gilded horns, in size his mother's mate,　　　　775
And threatening head, and hoofs that paw the sand."

The Father heard, and from the sky serene
Thundered upon the left. The fatal bow
Twanged; and the dreadful arrow whistling flew,
And the Rutulian's hollow temples pierced.　　　　780
"Go, mock at valor with your haughty words.
This answer your twice-captured Phrygians send
Back to the Rutuli!" He said no more.
The Trojans second him with loud applause,
And to the stars, with shouts, extol his deed.　　　　785

Bright-haired Apollo from the ethereal heights
By chance was then surveying from above
The Ausonian troops and city; on a cloud
He sat, and thus addressed the victor youth:——
"Go on, increase in early valor, boy;　　　　790
Such is the pathway to the starry heights,
Descendant and progenitor of gods!
All wars that are ordained by fate shall end
In justice, when Assaracus' great line
Shall rule, nor Troy be able to contain　　　　795
Your growth." So saying, from the lofty sky,
Parting the breathing airs of heaven, he comes,
And seeks Ascanius, changed in features then
Into the likeness of old Butes' face,
Who once Anchises' armor-bearer was,　　　　800
And faithful guardian at the gate, but now
Companion to Ascanius. So stepped forth

Apollo, in all things resembling him;
In voice, in color, in his hoary locks,
And fiercely clanking armor. He then thus   805
Speaks to the ardent youth: "Son of Æneas,
Let it suffice, that you unharmed have slain
Numanus with your shaft. Apollo gives
This first praise unto you, and envies not
Feats that shall equal this. For what remains,   810
Restrain your hand from further deeds of war."
     So speaking, Apollo left his mortal shape,
Even as he spoke, and vanished in thin air.
The Dardan chiefs then knew the deity,
And knew his shafts divine, and as he fled   815
His rattling quiver heard. So by command
Of Phœbus, they restrain Ascanius now,
Who thirsts to join the battle. They themselves
Again renew the combat, and expose
Their lives to open perils of the war.   820
All round the battlements their clamor runs;
They bend their bows, and with their thongs they whirl
Their javelins: all the ground is strewn with darts.
Their shields and hollow helmets clash and ring.
The raging battle swells; as when a shower,   825
Borne from the west beneath the rainy Kids,
Lashes the ground, or, thick with hail, the clouds
Rush down upon the waves, when Jupiter
With fearful south winds whirls the watery storm,
And through the sky-wrack bursts the hollow clouds.   830
     Bitias and Pandarus, from Alcanor sprung
Of Ida (whom Iæra, sylvan nymph,
Reared in the sacred grove of Jupiter;
Tall youths who towered like their hills and firs),
Relying on their arms, open wide the gate   835
Entrusted by their leader to their charge,
And from the ramparts challenge the attack;
While they within stand at the right and left
Before the turrets, armed, their lofty heads
Flashing with plumes. So by some river's bank,   840

Whether the Po or pleasant Athesis,
Two breezy oaks lift up their unshorn heads,
And nod their lofty tops. The Rutuli,
Soon as they see an opened way, rush in.
Then Quercens and the fair Aquicolus,   845
And hasty Tmarus, and brave Hæmon, all
Either turned back, repulsed, with all their troops,
Or at the very gateway met their death.
Then fiercer grows the Trojans' hostile rage;
And now they gather thick, and hand to hand   850
Contend, and dare to press beyond the walls.

While Turnus, in another quarter, storms
With fury and confusion to his foes,
A message comes, that hot with havoc fresh,
The enemy had opened wide their gates.   855
Quitting his work begun, in towering wrath
He rushes to the Dardan gate, and seeks
Those haughty brothers. First, Antiphates,
Who foremost came, Sarpedon's bastard son,
Born of a Theban mother, he strikes down.   860
The cornel arrow cleaves the yielding air;
Beneath the breast the weapon pierces deep;
The life-blood spurts, and warms the buried steel.
Next Merops, Erymas, and Aphidnus fall;
Then Bitias, with his burning eyes, and soul   865
Aflame; not by a javelin: for no dart
Could ever have bereft that frame of life.
A ponderous phalaric spear it was
That whizzing flew, hurled like a thunderbolt;
That neither two bulls' hides, nor trusty mail   870
With double scales of gold, sustained the shock.
Down dropped his giant limbs. The shaken earth
Groaned, and his huge shield rattled as he fell.
So sometimes on Eubœan Baiæ's shore
There falls a rocky pile, whose mighty mass   875
Stood built into the sea; so toppling down
And dragging ruin in its fall, it lies

Dashed on the shallows, and the troubled sea
Is black with lifted sand. Steep Prochyta
Hears, trembling, and Inarime's hard bed   880
Piled on Typhoeus, by command of Jove.

Now Mars inspired the Latins with fresh strength
And courage, and more fiercely spurred them on;
While flight and terror on the Trojans' hearts
He threw. They crowd together from all sides,   885
Since now they see a timely chance is given
For battle, and the war-god fires their souls.
When Pandarus sees his brother's body stretched
Upon the earth, and how their fortune takes
An unexpected turn, with mighty strength   890
Pressing with shoulders broad against the gate,
He turns it on its hinges, and so leaves
Full many a comrade from the walls shut out
Amid the cruel fray; but others too,
As on they rush, he shuts in with himself:—   895
Infatuated man! who did not see
The prince of the Rutulians amid the troops
That entered, by his own rash hand shut in,—
Like a huge tiger amid a timorous flock.
For suddenly from his eyes a strange light flashed;   900
His terrible armor rang; his blood-red crest
Trembled upon his head; and from his shield
Came gleams of lightning. Then the Trojans knew
The hated countenance, the form immense,
And stood dismayed. But mighty Pandarus,   905
Burning with anger for his brother's death,
Leaps forth: "No palace of Amata this,
Your promised dower! No Ardea now holds
Turnus within his native walls! You see
Your enemies' camp, and you are powerless now   910
To leave from here." Then Turnus, undisturbed,
Smiling replied: "Begin, if there be any
Valor in your soul; and hand to hand
Meet me. You shall tell Priam you have found

Another Achilles here!" Then Pandarus   915
Hurled at him with his utmost strength a spear
Rough with its knots and bark. Upon the air
Its force was wasted. Juno intervened,
And turned aside the weapon, and it stuck
Fast in the gate. Then Turnus cried aloud:—   920
"Not so shall you escape this steel which now
My strong arm wields; nor is the hand so weak,
That grasps the weapon, or that deals the blow!"
So saying, with his lifted sword he towers,
And smiting down, through brow and temples cleaves   925
The youthful warrior's head and beardless cheeks,—
A hideous wound; and as he falls, the earth
Shakes with a jarring sound. Dying he lay,
With stiffening limbs, and armor dashed with blood
And brains; while down from either shoulder hung   930
His cloven head. Here, there flee
The Trojans in confusion and dismay.
And had the victor then thought to himself
To unbar the gates and let his followers in,
That day had been the last day of the war   935
And of the Trojan race. But fury now
And a wild thirst for slaughter drove him on
Against the opposing foe. First Phaleris,
And Gyges, whom he had wounded in the ham,
He overtakes, and snatching up their spears,   940
He stabs them in the back. Juno supplies
Courage and strength. Halys their comrade too
He slays, and Phegeus, smitten through his shield;
Alcander, Halius, and Noëmon next,
And Prytanis, who unaware of all,   945
Stood at the walls, and urged the battle on.
Lynceus too, advancing on him there,
And summoning his comrades, he assails
Upon the rampart with his glittering sword,
And closing on him with his utmost strength,   950
Struck off his head and helmet at one blow,
And scattered them afar. Then Amycus,

Slayer of savage beasts, than whom none knew
Better to tip with poison the sharp steel;
And Clytius, son of Æolus, he slew;   955
And Creteus, the Muses' faithful friend,
Lover of poesy and the chorded lyre,
Who framed sweet numbers to his strings, and sang
Forever of brave heroes, steeds, and wars.

Then hearing of the slaughter in their ranks,[9]   960
Mnestheus at length and brave Serestus meet,
And see their troops dispersed; the enemy
With the camp. And, "Where to," Mnestheus cries,
"Do you now take your flight? What battlements,
What other walls beyond, do you possess?   965
Shall one man, hemmed in here on every side
By your own ramparts, deal throughout your camp
Such work of death, unpunished, and send thus
So many chosen warriors to the shades?
O sluggish souls! no pity and no shame   970
For your unhappy country do you feel,
Nor for your gods, nor for the great Æneas?"
Fired by his words, they rally with new strength,
And stand in dense battalion. By degrees
Turnus retreats upon the side that joins   975
The river, and is bounded by its waves.
Shouting, the Trojans bear more fiercely down,
And mass their forces. So the hunters press
A raging lion with their darts and spears.
Dismayed, but glaring fiercely, he draws back;   980
His rage and courage both forbid to turn;
Nor can he spring upon them, though he would,
Powerless against the weapons and the men.
So Turnus, hesitating, backward moves,
With lingering steps, and boils with fruitless rage.   985
Even then, he twice attacked the enemy
Full in their center; twice along the walls
He chased them in confusion. But in haste,
Forth from the camp, the whole host now has joined

Against him single; nor does Juno dare   990
To give him strength enough; for Jupiter
Sends Iris down, bearing no soft commands,
Should Turnus not depart and leave the walls.
So neither with his shield nor strong right arm
Is the youth able to sustain such force;   995
So thick the storm of darts that hails around.
With blow on blow the helmet on his brows
Is ringing, and the solid brass is riven
By flying stones, his plumy crest struck off;
His bossy shield no longer can endure   1000
The shocks of battle; while the Trojans press
On with redoubled spears,—Mnestheus himself
A thunderbolt. Then, dripping from his limbs
Black sweat-drops run in streams; nor can he breathe.
Exhausted, panting, heaves his weary frame.   1005
Until at last with a great bound he leapt,
With all his armor on, into the stream.
The yellow flood received and bore him up
Upon its gentle waves, and washed away
The stains of slaughter from his limbs; and back,   1010
Rejoicing, to his friends returned the chief.

BOOK 10

$\mathcal{M}$EANWHILE the omnipotent Olympian doors[1]
Are opened, and the father of the gods
And sovereign of men holds a council
Within his starry courts, from where above
He sees the spreading lands, the Trojan camp,   5
And Latian tribes. The double-folding gates
Receive the gods; they sit; then Jove thus speaks:—

"Celestial Powers, why is your purpose thus
Turned backward, and why with these hostile minds
Do you contend? No token of assent   10
I gave, that Italy and the Trojan race
Should clash in war. Why this discordant strife
Against my decree? What fears persuaded these
Or those to draw the sword and rush to arms?
The lawful time will come for war—let none   15
Anticipate the day—when on the towers
Of Rome, fierce Carthage through the opened Alps
Shall bring destruction. Then, for war and spoils
Your hatred shall be free. But now hold off,
And willingly conclude our destined league."   20

Thus briefly Jupiter; but not so brief
The words of golden Venus, who replied:—
"O Father, O eternal power of men
And their affairs! for whom is there beside
That we can now implore? Do you not see   25
How these Rutulians insult; how, borne
Conspicuous on his steed amid the ranks,
Flushed with success, Turnus is rushing on?
Their guarded ramparts now protect no more

The Trojans; but within their very gates   30
And mounded walls the battle rages still;
And with their blood the trenches overflow.
Æneas, absent, knows nothing of this.
And will you never suffer that this siege
Be raised? Once more their enemies now threaten   35
Their rising Troy and with another host.
Once more against the Trojans comes the son
Of Tydeus, from Ætolian Arpi sent.
For me, I truly believe, new wounds
Are yet in store; and I, your offspring, still   40
Must await a contest with mortal arms.
If without your consent, against your decree
The Trojans come to Italy, for this
Let them atone, give them no aid; but if,
Obedient to so many answers given   45
From the celestial and infernal realms,
They came, how now can any one pervert
Your high commands or frame the fates anew?
Why call to mind the burning of their fleet
On the Sicilian shore?—the furious winds   50
Raised from Æolia by the king of storms?—
Or Iris, through the clouds dispatched to earth?
Now even the forces of the underworld
She moves—this region yet remained untried—
And, suddenly let loose on upper realms,   55
Allecto through the Italian cities raves.
I care no more for empire: this we hoped
While Fortune stood our friend. Let those prevail
Who you will have prevail. If upon earth
There be no spot your rigid spouse accords   60
Unto the Trojans, then, O Sire divine,
I do beg of you, by the smoking ruins
Of Troy demolished, let me send away
Ascanius safe; let my grandson survive.
Yes, let Æneas upon unknown seas   65
Be tossed, and follow whatsoever course
Fortune may grant; but give me power to shield

His son, and save him from the direful war.
Amathus, Paphos, and Cythera are mine,
And mine the mansion of Idalia.   70
Here let him pass his life, and lay aside,
Inglorious, his arms. Let Carthage rule
Ausonia with oppressive sway. From him
The Tyrian cities shall receive no check.
What profit had Æneas to have escaped   75
The pest of war, and through the Grecian flames
To have fled, and on the ocean and the land
Borne so many perils to the uttermost,
While Latium and a Pergamus revived
The Trojans seek? Better for them to have built   80
Upon their country's ashes, and the soil
Where Troy once was. Give back, O Sire, I beg,
To these unhappy ones their Simöis
And Xanthus, and again let them endure
The sufferings of Troy."
                Then, stung with rage,   85
The royal Juno spoke: "How is it that you
Force me to break my silence deep, and thus
Proclaim in words my secret sorrow? Who
Of mortals, or of gods, ever constrained
Æneas to pursue these wars, and face   90
The Latian monarch as an enemy?
Led by the fates he came to Italy;
Be it so; Cassandra's raving prophecies
Impelled him. Was it we who counseled him
To leave his camp, and to the winds commit   95
His life? or to a boy entrust his walls,
And the chief conduct of the war? or seek
A Tuscan league? or stir up tribes at peace?
What god, what unrelenting power of mine,
Compelled him to this fraud? What part in this   100
Had Juno, or had Iris, sent from heaven?
A great indignity it is, indeed,
That the Italians should surround with flames
Your new and rising Troy, and that their chief,

Turnus, should on his native land maintain   105
His own, whose ancestor was Pilumnus,
Whose mother was the nymph Venilia.
What is it for the Trojans to assail
The Latins with their firebrands, and subdue
The alien fields, and bear away their spoils?   110
Choose their wives' fathers, and our plighted brides
Tear from our breasts? Ask with their hands for peace,
Yet hang up arms upon their ships? Your power
May rescue Æneas from the Greeks and show
In place of a live man an empty cloud;   115
Or change his ships into so many nymphs.
Is it a crime for us to have helped somewhat
The Rutuli against him? Ignorant
And absent, as you say, Æneas is;—
Absent and ignorant then let him be.   120
You have your Paphos, your Idalium too,
And lofty seat, Cythera. Why then try
These rugged hearts, a city big with wars?
Do we attempt to overturn your loose
Unstable Phrygian state? Is it we or he   125
Who exposed the wretched Trojans to the Greeks?
Who was the cause that Europe rose in arms
With Asia, or who broke an ancient league
By a perfidious theft? Did I command,
When the Dardanian adulterer*   130
Did violence to Sparta? Or did I
Supply him weapons, and foment the war
By lust? You should have then had fear for those
Upon your side; but now too late you bring
Idle reproaches and unjust complaints."   135
So Juno pleaded; and the immortals all
Murmured their various sentences; as when
The rising breeze caught in the forest depths,
Muttering in smothered sighs and undertones,
Foretells to mariners the coming storm.   140

---

*Paris.

Then the Omnipotent Father, who rules over
The universe, begins. And while he speaks,
The lofty palace of the gods is hushed,
The fixed earth trembles, and the heights of air
Are silent; then the Zephyrs fold their wings,   145
And the great Ocean smoothes his placid waves.
"Hear then, and fix my words within your minds.
Since it is not permitted that a league
Between the Trojan and the Ausonian powers
Be made, and since your discord finds no end,   150
Whatever fortune falls today for each,
Whatever hope each one may build for himself,
Or Trojan, or Rutulian, he with me
Shall know no difference; whether through the fates
The Latians hold the Trojan camp besieged,   155
Or through Troy's fatal error, and mistake
Of doubtful warnings. Nor do I exempt
The Rutuli. To each his enterprise
Will bring its good or ill. Jove is the same
To all alike. The Fates will find their way."   160
By his Stygian brother's river-banks, the gulfs
And torrents of black pitch, he sealed his vow,
And bowed his head, and all Olympus shook.
Here ended speech. Then from his golden throne
Jove rose, and in the midst of all the gods   165
Attending, through the Olympian portals passed.

Meanwhile the Rutuli round all the gates
Pursue their havoc, and surround the walls
With flames; while in their ramparts close besieged,
The Trojans, hopeless of escape, are held.   170
Forlorn they stand upon their lofty towers,
In vain, and round the battlements oppose
Their thin ring of defense; in front are seen
Asius Imbrasides, Thymœtes, son
Of Hicetaon, the two Assaraci,   175
Castor, and aged Thymbris; and with these
Sarpedon's brothers both; and Clarus too,

And Themon, who from lofty Lycia came.
Lyrnessian Acmon, strong as Clytius
His sire, or as Mnestheus, his brother, comes,   180
Lifting a rock immense, a mountain mass,
His whole frame straining to its utmost strength.
With javelins some, and some with stones, essay
To make defense; or hurl their blazing brands,
Or fit the arrow to the string. And lo,   185
The youthful Dardan prince among them shines,
Venus' most precious charge, his comely head
Bare, like a gem that parts the yellow gold
Adorning neck or brow, or ivory cased
In boxwood or Orician terebinth.   190
On his white neck his flowing locks lie back,
Bound with a circle of soft gold. You too,
O Ismarus, the heroic tribes beheld
Aiming your darts, the steel with poison tipped;
You of a noble line of Lydia sprung,   195
Where through the fertile fields by labor tilled
Pactolus rolls along his golden sands.
And there was Mnestheus too, raised high in fame
Since he had beaten Turnus from the walls;
And Capys, from whom Capua since was named.   200

While these sustained the shocks of rugged war,[2]
Æneas in the middle of the night
Was ploughing through the waves. For having left
Evander, to the Etruscan camp he had gone,
And laid before the king his name and race,   205
What he desired of him, and what proposed;
Unfolds what force Mezentius to himself
Prepares to win, and Turnus' violent mood:
Warns him what confidence may be reposed
In man; and with his warnings mingles prayers.   210
Without delay Tarchon unites his force,
And strikes a league. The Lydians, disengaged
From fate's restraint, embark upon the fleet,
Placed by commandment of the gods beneath

A foreign leader. Then Æneas' ship   215
Leads on; the Phrygian lions yoked are carved
Below the prow, while Ida towers above,
An emblem dear to Trojan exiles. Here
The great Æneas sits, and in his mind
The various vicissitudes of war   220
Revolves. Beside him Pallas, sitting close,
Inquires about the stars and of their path
Amid the night; and of the sufferings
That he has borne on ocean and on land.

Now open Helicon,* O goddesses,   225
And aid my song to tell what bands meanwhile
Attend Æneas from the Tuscan coasts,
And man his ships, transported over the sea.

First, in the brazen Tigris, Massicus;[3]
A thousand warriors under his command,   230
Who Cosæ and the walls of Clusium left;
With bows, and arrows, and light quivers armed.
Grim Abas goes with him, his squadron all
With burnished weapons; and upon his stern
A gilded image of Apollo shone.   235
His native city Populonia
Had given to him six hundred warriors tried
In war; three hundred more from Ilva went,
An island rich and inexhaustible
In iron mines. Asilas came the third;   240
Interpreter of gods and men was he,
To whom the victims' fibers, and the stars,
The languages of birds, and fiery bolts
Of the presaging lightning, all were known.
A thousand men he leads in close array,   245
With bristling spears; all placed in his command
By Pisa, of Alphean origin,
Although a Tuscan city. Astur next,

---

*Mountain sacred to Apollo and the Muses.

A warrior of exceeding beauty, comes,
Confiding in his steed and motley arms.   250
Three hundred, with one purpose, follow him.
From Cære and from Minio's plains they come,
And Pyrgi, and Gravisca's sickly shores.
Nor can I pass you by, most brave in war,
Cinyras, leader of Ligurian troops.   255
Nor you, Cupavo, with your slender band;—
Your crest the plumage of a swan, the sign
Of your changed father's fate; love was the cause
Of evil fortune unto you and yours.
For, as they tell us, Cycnus, while in grief   260
For his belovèd Phaëton he sang
Among the poplar boughs, his sister's shade,
And with his music soothed his sorrowing love,
Brought on himself the semblance of old age,
A downy plumage; and so left the earth,   265
And singing, soared away among the stars.
His son, attended by his troops, impels
The mighty Centaur with his oars, whose form
Towers over the waves, and threatening holds a rock,
And with his long keel furrows the deep sea.   270

Next, with a cohort from his native shores,
Comes Ocnus, of prophetic Manto born,
And of the Tuscan River, who to you
Gave walls, O Mantua, and his mother's name,—
Mantua, a city rich in ancestors;   275
But not one lineage for all. Three lines
Are hers, and to each line four tribes. Of these
She is the chief city. From Tuscan blood
Her strength is drawn. From here Mezentius arms
Five hundred warriors sent against himself,   280
Whom Mincius, rising from his parent-lake
Benacus, veiled with sea-green reeds, conveyed
Down to the sea in ships of hostile pine.

Heavy Aulestes, rising to the stroke,
Lashing the billows with a hundred oars,   285
Comes, turning up the foam. The Triton huge
Conveys him, and with sounding conch affrights
The dark blue waves, and as he sails presents
A shaggy figure, human to the waist,
The rest a scaly monster of the sea.   290
Beneath his rough breast murmuring laps the surge.
    So many chosen chiefs, in thirty ships,
Sailed to help Troy, and with their brazen prows
Ploughed through the briny plains.
                                And now the day
From heaven had faded, and the tender moon   295
Was journeying in her nightly car midway
Through the Olympian sky. Æneas' cares
Allow his limbs no rest. He sits and guides
The helm himself and manages the sails.
When, in the middle of his course, behold,   300
A choir of those who once attended him:
Sea-nymphs benignant Cybele had dowered
With deity, and changed from ships to nymphs.
With even pace they swim and cleave the waves,
As many as the brazen ships that stood   305
Upon the shore. Far off they know their king,
And with their dancing motions circle him.
Cymodocea, skilled above the rest
In speech, her right hand lays upon the stern,
And with her left rows gently through the waves.   310
Him ignorant she then addresses thus:—
"Wake up, Æneas, offspring of the gods!
Awake, and give your full sails to the wind.
We are the pines of Ida's sacred top,
Your fleet, now Ocean nymphs. When sorely pressed   315
By the perfidious Rutulian prince
With sword and fire, we were constrained to break
Your cables, and upon the deep we came
In quest of you. The pitying Mother gave
These shapes to us, and made us goddesses,   320

Passing our days beneath the ocean's waves.
But now behind the trenches and the walls,
Thy boy Ascanius is shut in amid darts
And martial terrors of the Latin hosts.
Now the Arcadian cavalry have joined   325
The valiant Tuscans, and have reached the place
Appointed. Turnus with his troops resolves
To oppose their march, lest they should join the camp.
Rise then, and with the approaching dawn, array
Your men in arms, and take your unconquered shield,   330
The fire-god's gift, bordered with rims of gold.
Tomorrow's sun, unless my words seem vain,
Vast heaps of slaughtered Rutuli shall see."
She spoke; and with her right hand, not unskilled,
Impelled the lofty ship, which through the waves   335
Flew, swifter than an arrow that outstrips
The winds. The others speed along their course.
In unknowing wonder Æneas stands,
Yet with the favoring omen cheers his crew.
Then looking upward, in brief words he prays:—   340
"Idæan Cybele, Mother divine
Of gods, to whom your Dindymus is dear,
Your cities turret-crowned, your lions yoked
In pairs beneath your reins, be now to me
My leader in the battle; in due form   345
Confirm the issue of this augury
And help the Phrygians with propitious aid!"

Meanwhile night fled, and the broad day returned.
Then first his comrades he enjoins to note
The signal, and prepare their minds for war.   350
And now, while standing on the lofty stern,
The Trojans and their camp appear to view.
On his left arm he lifts his blazing shield;
When from their walls they raise a joyous shout.
New hope revives their martial rage; they hurl   355
Anew their darts: as when beneath dark clouds
Strymonian cranes a signal give, and cleave

The air with clamorous cries, and leave behind
The southern breezes with their joyous notes.
But the Rutulian prince and leaders all   360
Are struck with wonder, till on looking back
They see the fleet turned toward the shore, and all
The surface of the sea alive with ships.
Then burns Æneas' helmet and his crest;
His golden shield pours out great flashing flames.   365
As when at night a blood-red comet glares;
Or blazing Sirius bringing pest and drought
On stricken mortals, in his rising sheds
An ominous light, and saddens all the sky.

Yet Turnus his audacious confidence   370
Lessens not, resolved upon the shores to fling
His forces, and drive back the coming foe.
"What you desired is come," he cries; "to crush
The enemy in fair fight. Now Mars himself,
O warriors, is in your power. Each now   375
Has thought of his wife and of his home,
And calls to mind the great deeds of his sires.
Unchallenged let us meet them by the wave,
While in disorder they attempt to land
With slippery steps. Fortune assists the bold."   380
He spoke; and pondered whom he should lead on
Against the foe, to whom entrust the siege.

Meanwhile from his tall ships Æneas lands
His troops by bridges. Many watch the waves
Retreating, and leap upon the shallows;   385
While others trust to oars. Tarchon surveys
A portion of the strand where all is smooth,
And where the wavelets in unbroken curves
Lap on the quiet beach, then turns his prow,
And cries: "Now bend upon your sturdy oars,   390
My chosen band, and urge your vessels on!
Cleave with your beaks this hostile shore! Each keel
Shall plough its furrow; nor shall I refuse

To wreck my ship in such a port, if we
But gain the shore!" This said, the crews at once   395
Rise on their oars, and urge the foaming ships
Upon the Latian strand, until their beaks
Touch the dry land, with every ship unharmed;
All, Tarchon, save your own. For while she, dashed
Upon the shallows, on the fatal ridge   400
Hung, long suspended, in the laboring surge
She breaks asunder, and amid the waves
The crew are all exposed; the broken oars
And floating benches clog and stop their way;
While the receding tide drags back their feet.   405

No slow delay keeps Turnus back; but swift
He hurries his whole army to the shore,
And ranges them against the foe. The alarm
Is sounded. First against the rustic ranks
Æneas leads the attack; an omen this   410
Of coming slaughter amid the Latian hosts.
Theron is slain, a huge warrior, who Æneas
Sought of his own choice, and who with sword,
Through brazen shield, and corselet rough with gold,
Pierces his side. Then Lichas next he smites,   415
Who from his mother's womb was cut, and vowed
To Phœbus, since in infancy he escaped
The dangerous steel. A little farther on,
Huge Gyas, and the hardy Cisseus fall,
While they with clubs were striking down the troops.   420
The arms of Hercules availed them not;
Nor their own strength of hand; nor that they had
Melampus for their sire, Alcides' mate,
While earth supplied his toils. At Pharus too,
Full in his mouth, while clamoring boastful words,   425
He hurls a spear. You, Cydon, too, while sad
Following your Clytius, your new love, his cheeks
Tinged with the yellow down of youth, had fallen
Beneath the Trojan arm, a piteous sight,
Oblivious of the love you had for youths,   430

Had not a band of brothers, seven in all,
The sons of Phorcus, stood against the foe.
Each threw a dart; some glance from helm and shield,
While some, just grazing, Venus turns aside.
Æneas then to trusty Achates speaks:—   435
"Supply me now with javelins; for not one
Of those which on the Trojan fields once pierced
The bodies of the Greeks, this hand shall hurl
In vain against the Rutuli." With that,
He grasps and throws a mighty spear. It flies,   440
And through the brazen plates of Mæon's shield
It pierces, cleaving corselet through and breast.
To him Alcanor flies, with his right hand
Sustains his dying brother; but again
A spear is hurled, and passes through his arm,   445
And, reddened with his blood, flies on its course;
And from his shoulder hangs the lifeless arm.
Then from his brother's body Numitor
Plucks out the dart, and at Æneas aims
The weapon, but in vain; for, turned aside   450
From him, it grazes great Achates' thigh.
    Clausus of Cures, trusting in his youth,
Now comes, and with his sharp spear driven deep
Stabs Dryops beneath the chin, and through the throat,
While speaking, snatching, at one thrust, both voice   455
And life away; his forehead strikes the earth;
The blood flows from his mouth. Three Thracians too,
Of lofty Borean family, and three
Their father Idas sent from Ismara,
Their native land, he slays, with various fate.   460
Halesus, and Messapus with his steeds,
And the Auruncan cohorts, all come up.
Now on this side and now on that, they strive
To beat each other back. The battleground
Is on the very entrance of the land.   465
As in the sky's expanse, the warring winds
Are matched with equal force, and neither they,
Nor clouds, nor seas give way; on either side

Doubtful and long, all elements opposed;
So clash the Trojan and the Latian hosts;   470
Foot fixed to foot and man confronting man.

    But in another place, where, scattered wide,
A torrent had rolled down the rocks, and torn
The thickets from the banks, when Pallas saw
The Arcadians, unaccustomed to contend   475
On foot, flying before the Latian hosts—
For over the rugged soil they could not urge
Their horses—he, the sole expedient left
In this distress, inflames their warlike zeal,
Now with entreaties, now with bitter words.   480
"And where now do you flee, my men?" he cries;
"By your own selves, and all your gallant deeds,
By Evander's name, your chief, and by the fields
You have won, and by my rising hopes that now
Grow emulous to gain my father's praise,   485
Trust not in flight. We with our swords must cut
A passage through; there, where the densest mass
Opposes, there your country calls both you
And me your leader. No divinity
Presses against us. Mortal men ourselves,   490
We deal with none but mortal foes. We have
As many souls, as many hands, as theirs.
Behold! the mighty ocean hems us in.
Land too we lack for flight. Is it the sea,
Or Troy, to which our path shall be?" He said;   495
And dashed into the thickest of the foes.

First, Lagus, led by inauspicious fates,[4]
Confronts him, coming with a ponderous stone.
Whirling his lance, the youth transfixes him
Between the spine and ribs, and backward draws   500
His spear that in his body stuck. Meanwhile
Hisbo attempts to strike him from above,
But fails, against his hope. For as he comes
Rushing, unguardedly, and mad with rage
At his companion's death, upon his sword   505

Pallas receives him; in his swollen lungs
The steel is buried. Next on Sthenelus
He charges, and upon Anchemolus,
Of Rhœtus' ancient race, who dared to invade
His step-dame's bed. You also on the field   510
Twin-brothers, Thymber and Larides fell,
The sons of Daucus, so alike that often
The pleasing error in each form and face
Deceived your very parents and their kin.
But cruel marks of difference on both   515
Pallas affixed: for his Evandrian blade
Struck off your head, O Thymber; and from you
Was severed, O Larides, your right hand,
Whose dying fingers twitch, and clutch the steel.

The Arcadians now by this success inflamed,   520
And by their hero's gallant deeds, are armed
With mingled rage and shame against their foes.
Then Rhœteus, in his chariot flying by,
The spear of Pallas pierces, and gives space
To Ilus for a while to escape his death;   525
For against Ilus he had hurled his lance,
Which Rhœteus midway intercepts, as he,
Close pressed by Teuthras and by Tyres, flies.
Rolled from his chariot, dying, on the field
He falls. And as in summer, when the winds   530
Wished for, arise, the shepherd scatters fire
About the woods, the tracts that lie between
Kindle and spread, till all the extended fields
Blaze in one dreadful battle-line of flame;
He sitting, sees the fire's triumphant march;—   535
So the whole valor of your troops combines
In one, O Pallas, and assists your strength.
     But now Halesus, terrible in war,
Bears down against them, covered with his shield.
Ladon and Pheres and Demodocus   540
He slays, and with his flashing sword strikes off
The right hand of Strymonius, reaching out

To clutch his throat; then with a stone he smites
The brow of Thoas, scattering splintered bones
And bloody brains. His father in the woods   545
Had hid Halesus; his prophetic soul
Presaged his fate. Soon as the aged sire
His eyelids closed in death, the destinies
Laid on his son their hands, devoting him
To the Evandrian spear. Him Pallas seeks;   550
But first he offers up this prayer: "Grant now,
O father Tiber, to this steel I poise,
Successful flight through strong Halesus' breast.
So on your oak his arms and spoils shall hang."
The god gave ear; but while Halesus screened   555
His friend Imaon, luckless, he exposed
His breast defenseless to the Arcadian spear.

But Lausus, in himself a warlike host,
Does not allow that his troops should be dismayed
At the dire carnage dealt by this warrior.   560
First Abas, who confronts him, he strikes down,
The battle's knot and stay. Down fall the sons
Of Arcady, the Etruscan warriors fall;
And you, O Trojans, by the Greeks unscathed!
Their leaders and their forces matched, both hosts   565
Clash in the conflict. Those upon the rear
Press thick upon the front; nor does the throng
Leave room to use their weapons or their hands.
Here Pallas presses on, there Lausus comes
Against him; near alike they stand in age,   570
Distinguished both for beauty. But for them
Fortune had not ordained that they should see
Again their native land. Yet Heaven's great king
Did not allow them to meet in arms; their fates
Await them soon from a superior foe.   575

Meanwhile as Turnus in his rapid car
Cuts through the opposing ranks, his fair sister
Warns him to haste to Lausus' aid. When he

Saw his comrades, "It's time now to desist
From battle," he exclaimed: "for I alone   580
Must deal with Pallas; he is due to me
Alone. Would that his father might be here
To see us!" Saying this, at his command
His followers quit the field. But wondering much
At the Rutulians' retreat, and these imperious   585
Commands, Pallas in amazement looks
On Turnus, and with fiercesome glance aloof
Surveys his mighty frame from head to foot.
And moving forward, answers thus his words:—
"Either for winning spoils of triumph now,   590
Or for a glorious death, I shall be praised.
For either lot my father is prepared.
Away then with your threats!" Saying this, he stepped
Into the middle of the field. The blood
Ran icy cold within the Arcadians' hearts.   595
Down from his chariot Turnus leapt, prepared
To meet him face to face. As from his lair
On high, a lion when he sees a bull
Stand meditating battle in a field,
And flies to meet him, so comes Turnus on.   600
      As soon as Pallas trusted that his spear
Could reach his foe, he made the first advance;
So Fortune, though with strength ill-matched with his,
Might speed his daring hand; then to the heavens
Appealing, speaks: "Alcides, hear my prayer!   605
By my sire's hospitality, the boards
Where you, a stranger, did partake with him,
Aid, I beseech, my daring deed begun.
May Turnus' dying eyes behold me strip
His bloody armor from his limbs half dead,   610
And see me conqueror!" Alcides heard
The youth, and deep within his heart suppressed
A heavy groan, with unavailing tears.
Then with consoling words the Sire supreme
Addressed his son: "To every one his day   615
Stands fixed by fate. The term of mortal life

Is brief, and irretrievable to all.
But to extend the period of its fame
By noble actions, this is virtue's work.
Beneath Troy's lofty walls what sons of gods   620
Have fallen: for with them even Sarpedon fell,
My offspring; Turnus also by the fates
Is called, and nears the verge of life." He spoke;
And turned his eyes from the Rutulian fields.

But Pallas hurls a spear with strength immense,   625
And from his scabbard draws his gleaming sword.
The weapon on the shoulder's plating glanced,
And through the buckler's border forced its way,
And against the mighty frame of Turnus grazed.
But he, with aim deliberate poising long   630
A steel-tipped javelin, against Pallas hurled
The shaft, and cried: "See whether ours be not
The weapon that shall make the deeper wound!"
He spoke; and through the middle of the shield,
With quivering blow the pointed javelin pierced;   635
Through plates of steel and brass, through fold on fold
Of tough bull's hide, through barriers of wrought mail,
Till deep into his breast the weapon sinks.
The hot shaft from the wound he strives in vain
To draw; from the same passage gushes out   640
His life-blood and his life. Down on his wound
He falls; his armor clangs; with bloody mouth
He bites the hostile earth in pangs of death.
But Turnus, striding over him, exclaims:
"O men of Arcady, be sure to bear   645
These words of mine to Evander. In such plight
As he deserved, I send his Pallas back.
Whatever honor may be in a tomb,
Whatever solace lies in funeral rites,
I freely grant. His hospitality   650
Accorded to Æneas, no slight cost
Shall be to him." With that, he pressed the corpse[5]
With his left foot, and seized and tore away

The heavy belt (stamped with a tale of crime,
How in one nuptial night a band of youths   655
Were foully butchered, and their bridal beds
Drenched in their blood. Clonus Eurytides
Had wrought the story in a mass of gold).
Grasping this spoil, Turnus exults with joy.
Alas, how ignorant is man of fate;   660
Elated with success, how hard for him
To keep within his bounds! The time will come
When Turnus shall well wish that he had bought
At a dear price, that Pallas had been spared.
Then will he hate these spoils, and hate the day.   665
    But Pallas stretched upon his shield is borne
Away by a group of friends, with groans and tears.
O grief and glory of your sire, to whom
They bear you back! This first day to the war
Gave you, and snatches you away. Yet you   670
Did leave vast heaps of the Rutulians slain.

And now, not rumor, but more certain word[6]
Of this disaster to Æneas flies:
That on the narrow edge of dire ruin
His friends were driven; and the hour to help   675
The flying Trojans, urgent. With his sword
He mows his way amid the nearest ranks,
His angry blade forcing a passage wide,
Seeking for Turnus, who with pride exults
In his new victory. Before him now,   680
Pallas, Evander, and the memories
Of those first banquets where he sat a guest,
And the right hands he grasped, all fill his eyes.
Four youths he seizes, sons of Sulmo; four
Whom Ufens reared, an offering to the shade   685
Of Pallas, destined with their captive's blood
To drench the fires upon his funeral pile.

At Magus next he hurled his hostile spear;
Who deftly stoops; the whizzing javelin flies

Above his head. Embracing then his knees,   690
Magus thus pleads: "Ah, by your father's shade,
And by your hopes of young Iulus, spare
This life, for my sire's sake, and for my son's!
I have a stately palace, and within
Talents of graven silver buried lie;   695
And weight of wrought and unwrought gold I own.
It's not on me the Trojan victory turns;
Nor can one life make such a difference."
    To whom Æneas answered: "Keep your gold,
Your silver talents for your sons. All rules   700
Of ransom and of interchange in war
Were swept away by Turnus, when he took
The life of Pallas. So Anchises' shade,
And so Iulus deems." With that, he grasped
With his left hand his helmet, and bent back   705
His neck, and, as he begged for mercy, plunged
The weapon to the hilt into his breast.

A little farther on, Hæmonides,
The Priest of Phœbus and of Dian, stood;
His brows with fillets and with mitre bound;   710
In glistening armor and refulgent robes.
Æneas meets him, and across the plain
Pursues; and standing over him as he falls,
Devotes him to the gloomy shades of death.
Serestus gathers up and bears away   715
His arms, a trophy to the god of war.

Then Cæculus, of Vulcan's race derived,
And Umbro, coming from the Marsian hills,
Renew the fight. Raging against them moves
The Trojan chief. He with his blade smites off   720
Anxur's left hand, and shears his buckler's rim.
Some mighty spell or boast he had pronounced,
And thought that in his words a virtue lay.
Perhaps to heaven itself his soul was raised,

Hoping to gain gray hairs and length of years. 725

Next Tarquitus, whom Dryope the nymph
Had borne to sylvan Faunus, threw himself,
In gleaming armor, against the chief incensed;
Who hurls a spear, and makes of no avail
His breastplate and his heavy shield; then down 730
To earth he strikes him, pleading sore, while much
He wished to say. Then rolling over the corpse
Still warm, thus speaks in wrath: "You, dreaded foe,
Lie there! No mother dear shall lay your head
In earth. No tomb within your native land 735
Shall weigh upon your limbs. You shall be left
To birds of prey, or thrown into the waves,
Where hungry fish shall feast upon your wounds!"

Next Lucas and Antæus he pursues,
Turnus' chief leaders; the strong Numa then, 740
And Camers with the yellow locks, the son
Of noble Volscens, wealthiest in land
Of all the Ausonian nation, and who ruled
Silent Amyclæ. As Ægæon once,
Wielding, it's said, a hundred arms and hands, 745
And flashing flames from fifty mouths and breasts,
When against Jove's thunders, on so many shields
He clashed, and drew so many swords; even so
Victorious Æneas, when his blade
Grew warm, raged over all the field, yes, even 750
Against Niphæus with his four steeds, turned;
But when they saw him coming, from afar
In his dire wrath, in fear they turned and fled,
And rushing wildly overturned their chief,
And whirled along his chariot to the shore. 755

Two brothers, Lucagus and Liger, now
Come driving on, by two white horses drawn;
While Liger holds the reins, his brother swings
A naked sword. Æneas could not brook

This furious onset. With opposing spear   760
He bears against them, towering in his might.
Then Liger cries: "No steeds of Diomed,
Nor chariot of Achilles, you now see,
Nor Phrygian fields. Now, and upon this ground
Shall end the war, and your own life!" So flew   765
The loud and raving words from Liger's lips.
But not with words the hero answered him,
But hurls his javelin. Then as Lucagus
Bends over the lash, and with his sharp steel goads
His coursers, and, his left foot forward thrown,   770
Prepares for battle, through the lower rims
Of his bright shield the weapon pierces deep
To his left groin. Thrown down from his chariot,
He writhes upon the ground in pangs of death.
Then thus Æneas speaks, with bitter words:—   775
"No fault of speed in your swift horses' feet
Betrayed you, Lucagus: no shadows vain
Affrighted them, to turn and flee. Yourself,
You leave your own chariot, leaping to the ground!"
With that he seized the steeds. But slipping down   780
From the same car, his wretched brother stretched
His hands, unarmed, beseeching: "By you yourself,
And by the parents who begot such worth,
O Trojan hero, spare the life of one
Who begs for mercy!" But Æneas said,   785
As still he pleaded: "Not such were your words
A moment since. Die! Let not brother leave
A brother thus." Then deep within his breast,
The spirit's latent seat, he plunged his steel.

Such were the deaths the Dardan chieftain dealt,   790
While raging like a whirlwind or a flood
Around the fields; until at length the boy
Ascanius, and the warriors whom their foes
Besieged in vain, come issuing from their camp.

Jove of his own accord, meanwhile, addressed   795

His spouse:[7] "My sister and my consort dear,
It's Venus, as you said, who does sustain
The Trojan powers: your judgment did not err.
These heroes have no swift right hands for war,
No courage stern, nor patience to endure."   800
To whom, submissive, Juno thus replied:—
"My spouse, most radiantly fair, why thus
Torment one who is sick at heart, and dreads
Your stern commands? If what I once possessed
Were mine, as mine it should have been, the power   805
I had to move your love, you would not now,
Omnipotent, refuse me this request:
That I may rescue Turnus from the strife,
And to his father Daunus bring him safe.
Now he must perish, and his pious blood   810
Pour out to satisfy the Trojans' hate.
Yet, from our race he draws his lineage
(Pilumnus in the fourth degree his sire).
And often with liberal hands and many a gift
Has heaped your courts." To whom the Olympian king 815
Briefly replied: "If for this fated youth
Time and reprieve from present death be sought,
And it is your will that I should thus decree,
Then snatch him from impending fate by flight.
Thus far indulgence is allowed. But if   820
Beneath these prayers of yours there lurks some boon
Of deeper import, and you think to shift
And change the whole war, then an empty hope
Is yours." But Juno, weeping: "What if you
Should with your will grant what your words refuse, 825
And Turnus' life remain assured? Yet now,
A heavy doom awaits this guiltless one;
Or else I wander wide of truth. But O,
That I may rather be by groundless fears
Deceived; and you, who have the power, reverse 830
To better ends the course you have begun!"

Thus having spoken, from the lofty sky,

Wrapped in a cloud, she sped, driving a storm
Down through the air; and to the Trojan lines
And the Laurentian camp pursued her way.   835
Then from thin mist, a wondrous sight to see,
She shapes a phantom in Æneas' form,
Arrayed in Trojan arms, and counterfeits
His shield, and crest upon his head divine;
Gives empty words, and soulless sounding voice,   840
And imitated gait; even like the forms
That flit about, it's said, when death is passed,
Or such as cheat the senses in our sleep.
The airy image in the battle's front
Leaps with exultant step, and challenges   845
The warrior with his darts and taunting words.
Turnus comes pressing on, and from afar
He hurls a whizzing lance: the phantom turns
Its back. Then Turnus, thinking that his foe
Was yielding ground, with his retreating pace,   850
Swells with a vain and empty hope, and cries:—
"Æneas, where to now? Do not desert
Your promised nuptials! This right hand of mine
Shall give the land you have crossed the seas to seek!"
So shouting he pursues, with brandished sword,   855
Nor sees his dream of triumph fade in air.

By chance there was a vessel lying moored
Beside a rock, with steps and bridge prepared,
In which the King Osinius had been borne
From Clusium's shores. Here as if in fear   860
The image of Æneas flies, and seeks
A hiding-place. Turnus, as swift, pursues;
Passes all barriers, leaps across the bridge;
But scarce had reached the prow, when Juno breaks
The cable, and upon the ebbing tide   865
Hurries the ship away. The airy sprite
Then cares to hide no further, but is borne
Aloft, and mingles with a dusky cloud.
Meanwhile Æneas seeks his absent foe

For battle, sending many a hero down   870
To death; while Turnus over the sea is swept
Before the gale. Backward he looks, nor knows,
Thankless for safety, what the event may mean.
Then lifting both his hands to heaven, he cries:—
"Omnipotent Creator, did you judge   875
That I deserved such dire disgrace as this?
And does your will decree such punishment?
Where do I come from, and where then am I borne?
What flight is this, and what am I who flee?
Can I behold again the Latian walls   880
Or camp? What will that band of warriors say,
My followers in arms, and who I thus
Basely abandon to a cruel death?
Even now I see them scattered, and can hear
The groans of those who fall. What can I do?   885
What earth can now yawn deep enough for me?
Pity me, rather, O you stormy winds,
And drive this ship, most heartily I pray,
Upon the rocks and cliffs and sandy shoals,
Where neither the Rutulians nor my fame   890
Can follow me!" With words like these, his soul
Here, there, fluctuates and turns;
Whether, for such disgrace, to plunge his sword
Into his frenzied breast, or throw himself
Into the waves, and swimming seek the shores,   895
And against the Trojans take the field again.
Three times he attempted either course; and thrice
Did Juno, pitying him, restrain the youth.
So, onward he was borne, with favoring tide,
And reached at length his old paternal home.   900

But prompted now by Jove, with fiery zeal
Mezentius takes the field, and leads the attack
Against the exulting Trojans. Then at once
The Tuscan troops rush on him, him alone,
With all their hoarded hate, and, pressing close,   905
Assail the warrior with their showers of darts.

He, like a rock that juts into the sea,
Braving the fury of the winds and floods,
And all the threats of heaven, stands fixed and firm.
Hebrus the son of Dolichaon down   910
To earth he strikes; and with him Latagus,
And Palmus, as he flies; but Latagus
First with a huge stone smites upon the face;
Then Palmus, hamstrung, leaves upon the ground
To roll, and gives his armor to his son   915
Lausus, to wear, also his plumy crest.
Phrygian Evanthes too he overthrows;
And Mimas, Paris' mate, of equal years,
Son of Theano and of Amycus,
Born on the very night when Hecuba   920
Brought Paris forth, the firebrand of her dream.
He in his native city buried lies;
But Mimas on Laurentian shores, unknown.

    And, as from mountain heights pursued by hounds,
A wild boar whom the piny Vesulus   925
And the Laurentian marsh for many a year
Has sheltered, and the reedy thickets fed,
When caught amid the toils, he makes a stand,
Furious, with bristling back, while none may dare
Oppose, or venture near him, but with shouts   930
And javelins at a distance hem him in;
But he, unterrified, on every side
With a deliberate resistance turns,
Gnashing his tusks, and shaking from his back
The lances; so with those whom righteous wrath   935
Against Mezentius fires; not one who dares
To meet him in close combat; from afar
They send their clamorous cries and galling shafts.

From ancient Corythus had come a Greek,
Acron by name, who had left his marriage rites   940
Unconsummated, and had joined the war.
Far off Mezentius sees him plunging through
The ranks confused, decked gayly in the plumes

And crimson favors of his promised bride.
Then, as an unfed lion, here and there   945
Roaming about the lofty stalls, and driven
By maddening hunger, if by chance he spots
A timorous kid or stag with stately horns
Exults, with open jaws and mane erect,
And crouching, fastens on his prey, and laves   950
His cruel mouth in gore—so rushes on
Mezentius through his enemies' thick ranks.
Down falls the unhappy Acron to the ground,
And dying, spurns the dark earth with his heels,
And bathes his broken weapons with his blood.   955

The warrior now disdains to hurl his lance,
And slay Orodes as he flies, with wound
Unseen, but runs and meets him face to face
In close encounter; not in stratagem
Superior, but in arms. Then with his foot   960
Upon his fallen foe, and on his spear
Leaning, exclaims: "Behold, my men, here lies—
No despicable portion of the war—
The tall Orodes." With a shout, his friends
Repeat the exulting pæan. But the chief   965
Utters these dying words: "Whoever you are,
Not long shall you, victorious, exult
Over me, nor shall I now die unavenged.
A destiny like mine awaits you too;
And on these very fields shall you soon lie!"   970
      To whom Mezentius with a bitter smile:—
"Die then! But as for me, the sire of gods
And sovereign of men will see to that."
So saying, from his breast he drew the steel.
Then stern repose and iron-lidded sleep   975
Weighed down the eyes that closed in endless night.

Then Cædicus strikes off Alcathous' head;
Sacrator fells Hydaspes; Rapo's sword
Parthenius and the hardy Orses smites;

Clonius and Ericetes fall before 980
Messapus' steel; one from his restive steed
Thrown down, the other fighting foot to foot.
Against him the Lycian Agis had stepped forth;
But, in ancestral valor not untried,
Valerus overthrows him. Thronius next 985
Is slain by Salius, he by Nealces' hand,
Famed for his skill to wing the viewless shaft.

Stern Mars now held in equal poise the deaths
And bitter griefs on either side. Alike
The victors and the vanquished slew and fell. 990
Nor these, nor those know what it is to flee.
The gods above with pitying eyes behold
The fruitless rage of both, and grieve to see
Such woes for mortal men. Here Venus sees,
And there Saturnian Juno views the strife, 995
While through the hosts raves pale Tisiphone.

But, shaking his huge lance, Mezentius stalks,
Swelling with rage, across the field. So moves
Mighty Orion, when his footsteps come
Cleaving a passage through the ocean deep, 1000
His shoulders towering high above the waves;
Or, bearing in his hand an aged ash
From the high mountains, walks upon the earth,
And hides his head amid the misty clouds.
So comes Mezentius in his armor huge. 1005
Æneas in the long battalion sees
His foe, and goes to meet him.[8] Undismayed
He stands, firm in his large and massive frame,
And waits to meet his noble enemy.
Then measuring with his eyes what distance fits 1010
His javelin's force; "Now may this god of mine,"
He cries, "this right hand, and the spear I wield,
Aid me! Oh, Lausus, you yourself, I swear,
Clothed in this robber's spoils shall stand today,
A trophy of Æneas' fall!" He spoke, 1015

And hurled his whizzing spear. It flew and glanced
From off Æneas' shield, then pierced the side
Of the renowned Antores, him who was
Alcides' comrade, and from Argos came,
And joined Evander, settling in a town   1020
Of Italy. He, luckless, by a wound
Meant for another, falls, and looks to heaven,
Remembering his dear Argos as he dies.
Then sped Æneas' spear; through concave orb
Of triple brass, through quilted linen folds,   1025
Through woven work of three bulls'-hides, it pierced,
Even to the groin; but it had spent its force.
Then swiftly from his side Æneas drew
His sword, exulting in the Tyrrhene blood
Thus drawn, and pressed upon his baffled foe.   1030
But Lausus saw, and heaved a bitter groan
Of filial love, while tears rolled down his cheeks.

And here, O youth most worthy to be praised,
You, and the hard fate of your piteous death,
And your most noble deeds, I shall not pass   1035
In silence, if an act so great as yours
Shall be believed by any future age!

Encumbered, and disabled by his wound,
Mezentius now drew back with faltering steps,
Trailing the hostile spear that in his shield   1040
Still hung. Then forward rushed his son, amid
The armèd troops, beneath Æneas' sword
Just raised to strike, and, keeping him at bay
Awhile, sustained the shock. With ringing shouts
His friends support him, till the sire withdrew,   1045
Protected by the buckler of the son;
And from a distance with their darts repel
The foe. Beneath the cover of his shield,
Æneas in his wrath confronts the attack.
As when the clouds pour down a shower of hail,   1050
The swains and ploughmen hurry from the fields,

And in some safe retreat the traveler lurks,
Or beneath the river-banks, or in rocky clefts,
While pours the rain, that when the sun returns
They may pursue the labors of the day;   1055
So, overwhelmed by darts on every side,
Æneas bears against the storm of war,
Till it has spent its thunder. Chiding then,
And threatening, he to Lausus calls aloud:—
"Where then to death and ruin do you rush,   1060
Daring to aim at things beyond your strength?
Your filial love betrays your heedless soul."
But he, infatuated, nonetheless
Exults; and now the Dardan chieftain's wrath
Higher and fiercer swells; until the Fates   1065
Collect the last threads of young Lausus' life.[9]
For deep into his breast Æneas' blade
Is plunged, through buckler and through armor light,
And tunic woven by a mother's hands
With threads of delicate gold. His breast is bathed   1070
In blood. The sad soul left its mortal frame,
And through the air fled to the realm of Shades.
But when Anchises' son beheld his face
And dying looks, so very pale, he groaned
With pitying heart, and stretched his right hand forth,   1075
Touched by the picture of his filial love.
"What worthy recompense, lamented youth,"
He said, "what honors can Æneas now
Bestow on virtues such as yours? Your arms,
In which you did rejoice, retain them still.   1080
And to the tomb and ashes of your sires,
If any consolation that may be,
I give you back. This solace too you have,
In your unhappy death, that you have fallen
By great Æneas' hand." With that he chides   1085
His hesitating followers, and himself
Lifts up the youth, his smooth locks smeared with blood.

Meanwhile the father on the Tiber's shore

With water stanched his wounds; and eased his limbs,
Reclining in the shade against a tree.   1090
His brazen helmet hung upon a bough,
And on the grass his heavy armor lay.
His chosen youths around him stand, while he,
Panting, and faint, relieves his burdened neck,
His flowing beard spread out upon his breast.   1095
Ofttimes of Lausus he inquires, and often
Sends messengers to call him from the field,
Bearing commands from his afflicted sire.
But Lausus' weeping friends were bearing him
Away upon his shield, a lifeless corpse;   1100
Great was his soul, and great the wound that slew him.
His sire, foreboding sorrow, knew their groans
Far off. Then on his hoary head he heaped
The unsightly dust, and stretched his hands to heaven;
And clinging to the corpse, "My son!" he cried,   1105
"Could such delight in life be mine, that I
Could allow him whom I begot to stand
And take my place before the foeman's steel?
And, by these wounds of yours, am I, your sire
Preserved, thus living by your death? Alas!   1110
Bitter at length is exile now to me,
Wretched! Ay, now the wound is deeply driven!
It was I, my son, who stained your name with crime,
Expelled from scepter and paternal throne
For my detested deeds. As I deserved   1115
My country's vengeance and my subjects' hate,
I should have forfeited my guilty life
By every kind of death; and still I live—
Nor men, nor life I leave—yet leave I will."

        With that, the warrior on his crippled thigh   1120
Lifted himself, and though his grievous wound
Retards him, not depressed, he bids his steed
Be brought, his solace and his pride, on which
Victorious he had come from every war.
Then to the sorrowing beast he thus begins: 1125
        "Long, Rhœbus, have we lived, if ever it be long

With mortals. Either you shall bear away
Victoriously, today, Æneas' head
And bloody spoils, and so avenge with me
The death of Lausus; or, if we should fail,   1130
We both will fall together. For, I know,
Never, my own brave steed, will you ever deign
To obey a stranger, or a Trojan lord."
He, mounting then his steed, adjusts his limbs
Upon the accustomed seat, and fills his hands   1135
With javelins; and his brazen helmet gleams
Upon his head, rough with its hairy crest;
Then gallops to the middle of the field.
Deep shame, and mingled grief, and frantic rage,
And love by maddening furies driven, and sense   1140
Of conscious valor, boil within his breast.
Then to Æneas he called aloud three times.
Æneas knew him, and exulting, prayed:—
"So may great Jove, and so Apollo prompt
Your hand! Begin the fight!" No more he said,   1145
But bore against him with his threatening spear.
    But he: "Why do you seek, you barbarous man,
To terrify me, now my son is slain?
This was the only way you could prevail
Against me. But I have no fear of death,   1150
Nor heed I any of your gods. Stand back!
I come prepared to die, but first I bring
These gifts for you!" He spoke, and hurled a shaft,
And then another, and another still;
While in a circuit wide he wheeled about.   1155
The hero's golden shield sustains the shock.
Three times round Æneas, facing him, he rides
In circles to the left, his hand, the while,
Still hurling lances. Three times upon his shield
The Trojan hero bears about with him   1160
A frightful grove of javelins, sticking fast.
Till tired of dragging on such long delay,
And plucking out so many barbèd spears,
Hard pressed, contending in unequal fight,

Revolving many stratagems, at length,   1165
Forward he springs, and darts his weapon straight
Between the temples of the warlike steed.
Rearing, the horse beats with his hoofs the air;
Then falls upon his rider closely pressed
Beneath his shoulder's weight. Then ring the shouts   1170
Of Trojans and of Latians to the skies.
But swiftly Æneas leapt, and with his sword
Snatched from the sheath, stood over him, and spoke:—
"Where is the fierce Mezentius now, and all
The wild impetuous force that filled his soul?"   1175
To whom the Tuscan, when with eyes upraised
His breath returned, and his bewildered mind:—
"You bitter enemy, why do you taunt
And threaten me with death? It is no crime
For you to slay me. Not for this I came   1180
To battle; nor did he, my Lausus, make
Such truce with you for me. One boon alone
I ask, if to the vanquished any grace
Be given: that in the earth my corpse may lie.
I know my subjects' enmity and hate   1185
Surround me. Save my body from their rage,
And bury me beside my son." He spoke;
And knowing well his doom, gave to his throat
The sword. Then with his life his streaming blood
Rushed forth, and over all his armor, poured.   1190

BOOK 11

MEANWHILE the Morning from the Ocean rose.[1]
Æneas, though his wishes strongly urge
To give a time of burial for his friends;
And by the memory of their deaths his soul
Is overcast; yet, with the early dawn,   5
Pays to the gods the vows a victor owes.
A huge oak-tree, its boughs on every side
Lopped off, he plants upon a rising ground;
And on it hangs the shining arms, the spoils
Of King Mezentius—yours, O warrior-god,   10
The trophy. There he puts the crest that dripped
With blood, and here the hero's shattered spears,
And breastplate twelve times dented and pierced through.
The brazen shield upon the left he binds,
And from the neck the ivory-hilted sword   15
Suspends. Then, while the chiefs around him crowd,
He thus addresses his exulting friends
With words of cheer: "Warriors, our greatest work
Is done; all lingering fear be banished now.
The spoils, the first-fruits of our victory,   20
Worn by that haughty tyrant,—they are here!
Here, by my hands Mezentius is laid low.
Now to the king and to the Latian walls
Our way is free. Prepare your arms; with hope
And courage strong, anticipate the war,   25
Lest obstacles impede you unawares,
Or counsel born of fear, with motions slow
Delay you, when the deities give leave
To pull your standards up, and lead your youths
From camp. Meanwhile let us commit to earth   30
The unburied corpses of our friends; for such
Is the sole honor known in Acheron.

Go then, and with your last sad offerings grace
Those souls of noble worth who with their blood
Have won for us this country. First of all,   35
To Evander's mourning city let us send
Brave Pallas, whom a day of darkness snatched
Away from us, and plunged in bitter death."

Weeping he spoke, and to the threshold went,
Where, by the corpse of Pallas on his bier   40
Stretched out, the old Accœtes sat watching.
He it was who had been armor-bearer once
To Evander; now, with sadder auspices,
Attendant on his own dear foster-son.
Gathered around the trains of servants stood,   45
And Trojan crowds; while Trojan women came
Mourning, as they were wont, with tresses loose.

Soon as Æneas entered the high gates,
Beating their breasts they raise a long loud groan,
And the halls ring with grief. When he himself   50
Beheld the pillowed head and snow-white face
Of Pallas, and upon his fair smooth breast
The open wound the Ausonian spear had dealt,
He thus began with tears he could not check:—
"Ah dear lamented boy, did Fortune then,   55
Just when she came with smiles, begrudge me you,
Lest you should see the kingdom I should win,
And to your home return with victory crowned?
Not this the parting promise that I gave
Your sire, for you, when with his last embrace   60
He sent me forth against a mighty realm,
And, fearful, gave me warning I should meet
Fierce foes, and battles with a hardy race.
And he, deluded by an empty hope,
Perhaps even now is offering up his vows,   65
Heaping the altars with his gifts, while we,
With grief and unavailing funeral pomp,
Attend the lifeless youth, now owing nothing

To any powers above. Unhappy sire,
You will behold the cruel obsequies   70
Of your own son! Is this our homeward march?
Our looked-for triumph, our high confidence?
But you shall not, Evander, with disgraceful
Wounds behold your warrior beaten back;
Nor you, O father, wish a fearful death   75
For one so saved. Alas, how great a guard
Have you, Ausonia, you, Iulus, lost!"

Thus having wept, he bids them lift away
The mournful corpse, and sends a thousand men,
From the whole army chosen, to attend   80
These last funereal rites, and bear a part
In the parental tears; a solace small
For that huge grief, yet due the unhappy sire.
Others, no less alert, with twigs of oak
And arbute weave a soft and pliant bier,   85
And shade the lifted bed with leafy boughs.
High on this rustic couch they raise the youth;—
So lies a flower by a maiden's fingers plucked,
Some violet sweet, or languid hyacinth,
From which not yet the form nor bloom have gone,   90
Though mother earth no strength nor nurture yields.
Two robes Æneas then brought forth, all stiff
With gold and crimson broidery, which once
Sidonian Dido, pleased to ply her task,
With her own hands had wrought for him, and wove   95
The tissue through with slender threads of gold.
With one of these, last honor to his friend,
He clothes the youth, and with the other veils
His hair, which soon the funeral flames must burn.
And many a prize from the Laurentian war   100
He heaps, besides, commanding them to lead
In long array the booty they had won.
To these he adds the weapons and the steeds
Of which he had despoiled the enemy;
And those whose hands he had bound behind, to send   105

As victims to the hero's shade, condemned
To sprinkle the altar flames with their blood.
Also the leaders he commands to bear
The trunks of trees with hostile armor hung,
And to affix their enemies' names thereon.   110
Accœtes, wretched and worn out with age,
Is led, who beats his breast and tears his cheeks,
And throws his body prostrate on the earth.
The chariots of the hero then are led,
Dashed with Rutulian blood. His war-horse next,   115
Æthon, his trappings laid aside, moves on,
The big tears coursing down his sorrowing face.
And others bear the helmet and the spear;
For all the rest victorious Turnus held.
Then the sad phalanx comes, the Trojans all,   120
And Tuscans, and Arcadians, following on
With arms reversed. When all the train had passed
In long array, Æneas paused, and thus
With a deep groan resumed: "War's direful fates
Now call us hence to other tears than these.   125
Great Pallas, here I greet you but to leave!
Forever hail! forever fare thee well!"
He said no more, but to the camp returned.

And now from King Latinus' city came
Ambassadors, who bore the olive-branch,   130
And asked for grace; that he would render back
The bodies of their dead in battle slain,
Strewn over the fields, with leave to bury them;
That, with the vanquished and the dead, all strife
Must cease;² that those once called his hosts   135
And kin by promised union, he would spare.
Whom, as their prayer was not a thing to spurn,
Æneas with a courteous grace receives,
And adds these words: "What undeservèd chance,
O Latians, has involved you in such war,   140
That thus you have avoided us, your friends?
Is it for peace to those bereft of life,

And taken by the chance of war, you ask?
Nay, I would grant it too to those who live.
Nor, unless destiny had here decreed   145
My place and settlement, would I have come.
Nor with this nation do I wage a war.
Your king renounced all hospitality
With us, and trusted Turnus' arms. More just
It would have been for Turnus his own life   150
To risk. If it be his design to end
This war with his own hand, and to expel
The Trojans, then with me he should have fought.
And he would have survived, whom power divine
Or his own strong right hand had given to live.   155
Now go, and for your dead build funeral fires."

So spoke Æneas. They stood astonished,
And silent, and upon each other turned
Their faces and their eyes, with looks intent.

Then agèd Drances, who in enmity   160
And accusations always hostile stood
To youthful Turnus, thus begins to speak:—
"O Trojan hero, mighty in your fame,
And mightier still in arms, with what high praise
Shall I extol your name?—which most admire,   165
Your justice, or your great efforts in war?
We truly shall with grateful hearts bear back
This answer to our city; and if a way
By any chance should open, will unite
You to our king. Let Turnus for himself   170
Seek his alliances. But, we ourselves,
Well pleased, will build your fated city's walls,
And on our shoulders bear the stones of Troy."
He spoke, and all as one murmured assent.
A twelve days' truce is settled; and meanwhile   175
The Trojans and the Latins, freely mixed,
Roam through the forests on the hills, in peace.
Beneath the axe the rowan tree resounds;

The pines that skyward shoot are overturned;
Nor do they cease to cleave the trunks of oak   180
And fragrant cedar, and to carry off
The mountain-ash trees in their groaning carts.

Now flying rumor, harbinger of grief
So great, comes to Evander's ears, and fills
His court and city; rumor which just now   185
Reported Pallas in the Latian fields
Victorious. The Arcadians rush to the gates,
And, as the ancient custom was, snatch up
Their funeral torches. In a long array
The road is bright with flames, that far and wide   190
Make visible the fields. The Phrygian bands,
Advancing, join the mourning multitude.
The matrons, when they see them near the walls,
Rouse the sad city with their cries of grief.³
But nothing can restrain Evander then   195
From rushing through the middle of the throng.
The bier set down, the father prostrate falls
Upon the body of his son, with tears and groans
Close clinging to the corpse, until at length
The words, long stifled by his grief, escape:—   200
"Was this the promise, O my son, you gave,
That in no rash encounter you would try
The risks of raging war? I knew full well
How far the fresh delight and fame of arms,
And the first battle's glory, all too sweet,   205
Might carry you away. Ah, first fruits dire
Of youth! Ah, hard novitiate in a war
So near at hand! and vows and prayers unheard
By any of the deities! And you,
Most sacred consort, happy in your death,   210
Nor for this grief reserved! while I am left
Still lingering, and outlive my destined days,
To stay behind my son, a childless sire!
It was I who should have followed to the field
The allied arms of Troy and fallen before   215

The lances of the Rutuli. This life
I should have given, and me, not Pallas, now,
This funeral pomp had homeward brought! Not you,
O Trojans, and your friendly league, wherein
You pledged your hands, do I accuse. This blow   220
Of fortune was but due to my old age.
And if untimely death has called my son,
Some solace it is to know that leading on
The Trojans into Latium, he has fallen,
Thousands of Volscians having first been slain.   225
Nor other obsequies would I prepare
For you, O Pallas, than Æneas gives,
With the great Phrygians and the Tuscan chiefs,
And all their host. Proud trophies won by you
They bring, from those whom your right hand has slain.   230
You also would have been among them here,
Turnus, a mighty trunk decked with armor,
Had Pallas been of equal years and strength
With yours. But why must I, unhappy, keep
The Trojans from the war? Go, bear in mind   235
These words, and take this message to your king:—
That if I linger out a hated life,
Now that my Pallas is no more, the cause
Is your avenging hand, from which the life
Of Turnus to a father and a son   240
You see is due. This empty post awaits
You only, and the fortune of your arms.
I seek not further joy, nor should I seek,
In life; but wish to the shades below
To bear with me these tidings to my son."   245

Meanwhile the Morn to wretched mortals brought
The light benign, and the day's work and toil
Renewed. Æneas now, now Tarchon built
Along the winding shore the funeral piles.[4]
Each there brought the bodies of his friends,   250
According to the custom of his sires.
The mournful fires are lit beneath; the sky

Is hidden in the darkness and the smoke.
Three times round the blazing piles they go, all clad
In glittering armor; three times upon their steeds   255
Encompass the sad flames with doleful shrieks.
With tears the earth is wet, with tears their arms.
The blare of trumpets and the cries of men
Ascend to heaven. Some throw into the fire
The spoils they snatched away from Latians slain,—   260
Helmets and splendid swords, bridles and bits,
And glowing wheels; some throw their well-known gifts,
Their own shields, and their unsuccessful spears.
To Death they offer up a sacrifice
Of bulls and swine; they slay from all the fields   265
The sheep borne off, and cast into the flames.
Then all along the shore their burning friends
They view, and watch the half-charred funeral piles;
Nor can they tear themselves away, till night
Inverts the sky, studded with blazing stars.   270

Nor with less sorrow do the Latians too,
In other quarters, build unnumbered pyres.
And many corpses of their warriors fallen
They bury in the earth; and some they bear
To neighboring fields, some to the city send.   275
The rest, a vast promiscuous heap of slain
Uncounted and unmarked by separate rites
They burn. Then all around, the extended fields
Blaze with their frequent fires, in rival zeal.
The third day from the skies had driven the shades,   280
When sadly on the funeral hearths they heaped
The piles of ashes and the mingled bones,
And a warm mound of earth above them threw.
    But from Latinus' city and proud courts
Comes the chief clamor and long wail of woe.   285
Mothers, and mourning brides, and tender hearts
Of sorrowing sisters, and young children robbed
Of parents, execrate the direful war,
And Turnus' nuptials; and demand that he,

Turnus himself, shall with his sword decide   290
The contest, since for himself alone he claims
The kingdom and the crown of Italy.
All this the bitter Drances aggravates,
And vows that Turnus is the only one
Summoned and challenged to the combat now;   295
While differing voices all declare for him
Protected by the queen's overshadowing name,
And by his fame upheld, and trophies won.
        Amid the tumult and commotion, come,
To add new griefs, the sad ambassadors   300
From Diomed's great city, who report
These answers: "That they had accomplished nothing
By all their toil bestowed; that neither gifts,
Nor gold, nor supplications could avail.
That other armed alliance must be asked   305
By Latium; or that from the Trojan prince
Must peace be sought." At this the king himself
Sinks down, overpowered by his weight of grief.
The anger of the gods, the new-raised mounds
Before him, show that by a power divine   310
Æneas is borne on with fateful aim.
Therefore by his imperial decree
He summons his great council, and his peers,
Within the lofty courts. They come flocking,
And stream along the crowded avenues,   315
And fill the royal palace. In the midst,
Oldest in years and first in regal power,
With joyless brow Latinus takes his seat.
Here he commands the ambassadors, who late
From the Ætolian city had returned,   320
Their message to deliver, and relate
In order due each answer they had brought.
Then all in silence sat; when Venulus,
Commanded, speaks: "We have seen, O citizens,
The Argive camp, and Diomed himself;   325
The dangers of our weary road overpassed,
We touched that hand by which Troy's kingdom fell.

We found the chief, victorious, building there,
On the Apulian plains, Argyripa,
His city, from his native Argos named.   330
Admitted, and permission given to speak,
We first present our gifts; then tell our name
And country, and what foes made war on us;
And why to Arpi we had come. Then thus,
Our message heard, he courteously replied:—   335
  'O happy people, of Saturnian realms!
Ancient Ausonians! Say what fortune now
Disturbs your peace, provoking wars untried.
All those of us, who with the sword despoiled
The Ilian fields (I make no note of stress   340
Endured in battle beneath the walls of Troy,
Nor of the heroes in their Simois drowned);
We all have borne unutterable woes
In every place, and of our crimes have paid
The penalties,—a band whom even Priam   345
Would pity. Let Minerva's baleful star
Bear witness, and the rough Eubœan rocks,
And dire Caphereus. Ever since that war
Have we on various coasts been tossed and driven;
Here Menelaus, Atreus' son, exiled   350
As far away as Proteus' columns; there,
Ulysses the Ætnean Cyclops sees.
Why name the realms of Neoptolemus?
The home-gods of Idomeneus overthrown?
The Locri dwelling on the Libyan shores?   355
Mycenæ's chief himself who led the Greeks,
Stabbed by the hand of his unnatural spouse,
Upon his palace threshold,—Asia's lord
By an adulterous enemy waylaid?
Or need I tell how, envied by the gods,   360
I could not to my native land return,
And my belovèd wife again behold,
And lovely Calydon?* Even now portents

---

*City of Aetolia, famous for the mythological boar hunt of Meleager. See footnote to 7.383.

Of terrible aspect pursue my steps;
My lost companions, into birds transformed,   365
Have flown away into the fields of air,
Or wander by the streams (ah, for my friends
How hard a penalty!) and fill the rocks
With wailing voices. And indeed such fate
I might have well expected, since that time   370
When madly with my sword I dared to assail
Celestial beings, wounding Venus' hand.
No, indeed, urge me not to wars like this.
Not with the Trojans have I any feud,
Now Troy is overthrown; nor do I think   375
With joy upon their former sufferings.
The gifts which from your land you bring to me,
Transfer to Æneas. Against his bitter darts
We have stood, and hand to hand encountered him.
Trust one who has known how in his shield he towers,   380
With what a mighty whirl he throws his lance.
If two such men besides the Idæan land
Had borne, the Dardan would have first advanced
Upon the Inachian towns, and Greece have mourned
Her fates reversed. Whatever obstacle   385
Lay at Troy's stubborn walls, the Greeks' success
By Hector's and Æneas' hand was balked,
And to the tenth year of the siege delayed.
Both alike famed for courage and for arms,
This man is first in piety. In league   390
Join hands with him, by whatsoever means;
But of opposing him in arms, beware!'
     Such are the answers, gracious sire, we bring,
And such his counsel in this serious war."

     Scarce had the legates spoken, when there ran   395
Through the Ausonian crowd a noise confused
Of agitated voices; as when rocks
Obstruct a rapid stream, the flood confined
Murmurs with fretting waves against the banks.
Soon as their troubled minds and lips are stilled,   400

From his high throne the king, first praying, speaks:—
    "It had been better, and I well could wish,[5]
O Latins, that before now we had resolved
Our chief affairs of state concerning these;
And not convene a council when the foe   405
Sits at our walls. An inauspicious war,
O citizens, we wage, against a race
Of gods, and men unconquered, unfatigued
By battles, and who never drop the sword,
Though routed! Lay aside what hope you had   410
In the Ætolian arms. Each one must be
His own hope; but how small this is, you know.
For all the rest of our affairs, you see
And feel in what a ruin all is thrown.
No one do I accuse. What the best strength   415
Of valor could accomplish has been done.
With our whole kingdom's prowess we have fought.
Now then I will declare and briefly show
What thoughts are in my doubting mind. Give heed.
Hard by the Tuscan river is a tract   420
Of ancient land I own; that to the west
Extends beyond the old Sicanian bounds.
There the Auruncans and Rutulians sow,
And with their ploughshares till the stubborn hills,
And pasture on their rugged slopes. Let this   425
And the high mountain's piny tract be given
In friendship to the Trojans. Equal terms
Of amity and peace let us declare,
Inviting them as allies to our realm.
There let them settle and build their cities,   430
If such their wish. But if of other lands
They wish possession and can leave our soil,
Then twice ten vessels of Italian oak,
Or more, if they can fill them, let us build.
The wood is lying all along the stream.   435
The number and the fashion of their ships
Let them determine. We to them will give
Money, and men, and fitting naval stores.

And let a hundred Latian men of birth
Go as ambassadors, and in their hands   440
Carrying the boughs of peace, and bearing gifts
Of gold and ivory, and a chair of state,
And royal robe, the emblems of our sway.
Advise for all, and help our cause distressed."

    Then that same Drances, filled with bitter stings   445
And envy all askant, at Turnus' fame,—
Large in his means, but larger yet in tongue;
Frigid in war, yet deemed no trifling weight
In counsel, and in strife of faction strong;
Endowed on his mother's side with noble blood,   450
But of uncertain birth upon his sire's,—
He rises, and on Turnus heaps reproach,
And with his words thus aggravates his wrath:—

    "You seek out counsel, gracious sovereign,
In matters which are dark to none of us,   455
Nor needing our voices. All must own
They know what best concerns the public good,
But hesitate to speak. Let him allow
That liberty of speech, and moderate
His windy boast, whose ill-starred influence   460
And conduct sinister (no, let me speak,
Though he should threaten me with arms and death)
Have caused so many of our chiefs to fall,
That the whole city sits in grief; while he,
Tempting the Trojan camp, trusting to flight,   465
Defies the heavens with arms. One gift beside,
One more, O best of kings, add you to those
So largely to the Trojans sent. Nor you
Let any violent hand intimidate;
But give your daughter, as a father may,   470
To an illustrious son-in-law, and seal
A union not unworthy, and confirm
This peace by making a perpetual league.
But if such terror of this chief pervades
Our minds and hearts, then him let us beseech,   475
Him supplicate for grace, that to his king

And country he may yield this right of his.
Why, O you head and cause of all these woes
To Latium, why so often do you thrust
Into open danger these our citizens?   480
For us there is no safety in this war.
We all, O Turnus, turn to you for peace,
And for that sole inviolable pledge
Which peace demands. Behold, I come, the first;—
I, whom you judge your foe, nor shall I stop   485
To say it is not so; suppliant I beg
That you wilt spare your own. Lay by your wrath,
And, routed, quit the field. We deaths enough
Have seen, and desolation, and defeat
Upon our plains. But if the love of fame   490
So stirs your soul, and such heroic strength,
And if a royal palace for a dower
Be so much in your heart, then dare the foe
With a brave breast. It must be so, indeed,
That Turnus with a royal spouse may wed.   495
We, abject souls, unburied and unwept,
Must strew the fields. And now if strength be yours,
If of your country's Mars one spark be left,
Look in your foe's face, who does challenge you!"

Up flamed the rage of Turnus at these taunts,   500
And, with a groan, broke from his breast these words:—
    "Abundant flow of speech you always have,
Drances, whenever war for action calls.
You are our foremost, when the fathers meet
In council. But it's not the season now   505
To fill the court with words that fly from you
In such profusion, you being safe at home,
Here, where our ramparts keep the foe at bay,
And while the trenches are not filled with blood.
So with your eloquence still thunder on   510
As you are inclined. Accuse me too of fear,
Drances, since your right hand has slain such heaps
Of Trojans, and with trophies everywhere

You have decked the fields. You to the proof can't bring
That lively bravery of yours. Not far,   515
Indeed, have we to seek our enemies;
They lie around our walls on every side.
Come, let us march against them! What, so slow?
Your Mars, is it in your windy tongue alone,
Those feet so swift to fly, he shows himself?   520
I routed! who shall justly say, base wretch,
That word of me, of one who soon shall see
The swelling Tiber heave with Trojan blood,
And see Evander's house, and all his race
Stretched on the ground, and the Arcadians stripped   525
Of all their arms! Not thus did Bitias test
My strength, and bulky Pandarus, and those,
The thousands, whom I sent to Tartarus,
All in one day, though shut within their walls.
No safety in war! Go, fool, and preach such things   530
To the Dardan chief, and those who side with you.
Then cease not to disturb all hearts with fears.
Extol the strength of a twice-conquered race,
And King Latinus' power depress. Yes, even
The Myrmidonian chiefs fear Phrygian arms!   535
Yes, Diomed and Achilles! Backward flies
The Aufidus from the Adriatic Sea!
While this dissembler feigns himself afraid
Of me and of my menaces; and so
Inflames his accusations by this fear.   540
Be not disturbed; for such a life as yours
I scorn to take. Safe let it dwell with you.

"And now to you, and your great counsels, sire,
Let me return. If in our arms no hope
Of further fortune you do entertain,—   545
If we are so deserted, so undone
By one defeat, and no regression left,
Then let us stretch weak hands, and ask for peace.
Yet O, if in our souls there were a spark
Of our accustomed valor, he, I think,   550

Were happier than all others in his toils,
And great of soul, who, ere he saw such peace,
Fell once for all, and dying bit the ground.
But if we have resources, if still fresh
Our youthful warriors, and the Italian towns   555
And people still are left to give us aid;
If with much blood the Trojans earn their fame;
If they too have their funeral obsequies,
Since upon all alike the storm has raged;—
Why then inglorious do we faint, as yet   560
Scarce entered on the war? Why do we tremble
Before the trumpet sounds? The lapse of days,
The ever-changeful work of shifting time,
Have brought us better things. Fortune, who comes
To many with an alternating play,   565
Has placed us on a firmer basis now.
If from the Ætolian prince there comes no aid,
We have Messapus, and the auspicious seer
Tolumnius, and the chiefs so many tribes
Have sent. Nor shall the fame of the those be small, 570
The chosen warriors from Laurentian fields.
Camilla also, of the Volscian race
Renowned, is ours, leading her cavalry on,
Her troops that shine in brazen mail. And yet,
If me alone the Trojans now demand   575
For battle, and if such be your desire,
And I obstruct your common good so much,
Not hitherto has Victory shunned my hand
With such a hate, that I should now decline
Any adventurous task, for hope so high.   580
Undaunted I will meet this chief, although
Like great Achilles he appear, arrayed
Like him in armor wrought by Vulcan's hands.
To you, and to the king, my future sire,
I, Turnus, second to no veteran here   585
In valor, have devoted this my life.
Is it me alone Æneas challenges?
Be it so, I pray ! Nor let the angry gods

Decree that Drances suffer the penalty
By his death, or, if it be a chance   590
Of valor and of fame, win such renown."

While they, discussing their perplexed affairs,
Contended thus, Æneas, moving on
With camp and army, toward their city came,
When through the royal court a messenger   595
Bursts in, and fills the city with alarm:—
"That from the Tiber, ranged in battle line,
The Trojans and the Tuscans on the plains
Were marching down." Then all at once dismay
And bristling anger heave the excited crowd.   600
The youths with hurrying haste call out for arms;
While, muttering sad and low, the fathers mourn.
Dissenting voices clamor all around;
As flocks of birds, when in some lofty wood
They light, or by Padusa's fishy stream   605
Clatter hoarse swans about the echoing pools.
    Then Turnus, seizing the occasion, speaks:—
"Ay, citizens, convene your council now,
And, sitting, sound your praise of peace, while they
Are hastening on upon our realms in arms!"   610
He said no more, but from the lofty halls
He dashed away. "You, Volusus," he said,
"Command the Volscian and Rutulian bands.
Messapus, Coras, with your brother joined,
Pour down your armèd horsemen on the fields.   615
Let some secure the gateways of the town,
And let some man the towers. The rest, with me,
Attend, as I command." Then to the walls
They flock from all the town. The king himself
Forsakes the council, and his great designs   620
Defers, afflicted by the gloomy time.
He accuses himself much, that with free choice
Trojan Æneas had not been received
Within his city as his son-in-law.
    Trenches are dug before the gates, and rocks   625

And palisades heaved up. The raucous trumpet
Rings out its bloody signal for the war.
Matrons and boys cluster in different rings
Upon the walls. The last extremity
Calls upon every one. The queen herself   630
To Pallas' temple and high citadels
Is borne, attended by a matron train,
With offerings. At her side Lavinia stands,
Cause of these ills, her lovely eyes cast down.
The matrons follow, and fill the temple full   635
Of censer fumes, and pour forth doleful prayers.
"Tritonian Virgin, strong in arms!" they cry,
"Great arbitress of war, break, with your hand,
This Phrygian robber's lance, and hurl him down
Prone on the ground beneath our lofty gates!"   640

Armed for the battle, fired with martial zeal,
Turnus himself is there; upon his breast
A corselet of Rutulian garb he wears,
And rough with brazen scales; his thighs are cased
In gold; his temples bare as yet; his sword   645
Is girt upon his side. From the high tower,
Glittering in gold, he runs exulting down.
Even now in thought he leaps upon his foe.
As when a steed has broken from the reins,
And, free at last, he leaves his stall behind,   650
Ranging the open field, and either seeks
The pastures and the herds of grazing mares,
Or the accustomed river, on he flies
With crest erect, and loud and lusty neigh,
And on his neck and shoulders floats his mane.   655

Him, face to face, Camilla, leading on
Her band of Volscian riders, meets.[6] The queen
Leaps from her horse, beneath the very gates;
And the whole cohort follows, from their steeds
Dismounting; when she thus addresses him:—   660
"Turnus, if valor its own faith may trust,

I dare, and pledge myself, to meet alone
The Trojan troops and Tuscan cavalry.
Allow me now to make the first essay
Of danger; while on foot you stay behind,   665
To guard the city." At these words, the chief
Upon the terrible maiden fixed his eyes.
"O virgin, pride of Italy," he said,
"What thanks, what answer can I speak? But now,
Since that brave soul of yours surmounts all fears,   670
This labor share with me. Æneas now,
So rumor speaks, and so our scouts report,
Has rashly sent before a band of horse,
Light-armed, to scour the plains; while he himself
Down from the lonely mountain steeps descends   675
Upon the city. I an ambuscade
Shall plan within a winding forest path,
And the two openings of the road invest
With armèd men. You in close fight engage
The Tuscan cavalry. With you shall stay   680
The brave Messapus, and the Latian troops,
And the Tiburtine band. The leader's charge
Is yours." He with the same advice exhorts
Messapus and the leaders to their task;
Then marches on to meet the enemy.   685

Within a valley lies a winding gorge,
Well fitted for ambush and the stratagems
Of war. Upon either side slope down
Close screens of forest foliage dark and thick;
A narrow path between, through steep defiles   690
That open their wicked throats at either end.
Above, upon the heights, there lies a plain,
Hidden from view, with lurking places safe,
Whither from right or left the attack be made,
Or threatening rocks be toppled from the cliffs.   695
The youthful warrior to this well-known spot
Repairs, and takes possession of the place,
And in the dangerous forest lies in wait.

Meanwhile Diana in the upper realms
Addressed swift Opis, one of the virgin band   700
Of nymphs, companions in her sacred train.
"O virgin," she began in accents sad,
"Camilla is going to a cruel war,
And with our weapons arms herself, in vain;—
She, dear to me before all other maids.   705
Nor is it new, this love Diana bears
To her; no sudden fondness moves her soul.
When from his kingdom Metabus was driven,
By hatred of his proud abuse of power,
And from Privernum's ancient city fled,   710
Escaping through the thickest of the battle,
He bore away with him his infant child,
Companion of his exile, calling her
Camilla, from his wife Casmilla's name.
He, in his bosom bearing her, pressed on   715
Toward the mountains and the lonely woods.
The Volscians all around him hovered close,
And pressed upon him with their cruel darts,
When, midway in his flight, the Amasene
Before him rolled, and overflowed its banks,   720
Swollen with the rain. He then prepared to swim,
But the love he bore his child restrained his steps,
So great the fear his precious burden waked.
Every expedient in his thoughts he turned,
Till, sudden, this resolve with pain he formed.   725
A lance enormous in his powerful hand
The warrior bore, well seasoned, tough with knots;
To this he binds his child, and wraps her round
With bark of forest cork, and deftly ties
The infant round the middle of his spear.   730
Then with his huge right hand he poises it,
And thus to heaven he prays: 'Latonian maid,
Blest dweller in the woods, to you this sire
Devotes his child, a handmaid vowed to you.
Holding your weapon, suppliant, thus she takes   735
Through air her early flight, to shun the foe.

O goddess, I beseech, accept your own,
To the uncertain winds committed now!'
He spoke; and drawing back his bended arm,
He hurled the lance. The billows sounded on.   740
Across the rapid river the poor child
Camilla flew upon the whizzing spear.
But Metabus,—for near and nearer yet
A mighty band was pressing on his steps,—
Plunged in the river, and victorious plucked   745
His spear, and with it, Dian's gift, the maid,
Out from the grassy turf. But him no house
Nor city walls received. Nor would he have deigned
Such fare, so savage and untamed was he.
Amid the lonely mountains there, he led   750
A shepherd's life. There in the thickets rough
And dismal haunts of beasts, he reared his babe
With the wild milk of mares, and strained the teats
Into her tender lips. Soon as the child
Had printed her first footsteps on the ground,   755
He placed the javelin in her little hands,
And from her shoulder hung a bow and arrows.
Instead of gold to bind her hair, and robes
With trailing folds, a tiger's skin was hung
Upon her back and trailing from her head.   760
Even then her tender hand hurled childish darts,
And whirled the smooth-thonged sling about her head,
And a Strymonian crane or snowy swan
Struck down. And many a mother sought her hand
In marriage for her sons, in Tuscan towns.   765
But she, content with Dian alone, maintains
Her maiden purity, and ceaseless love
Of javelins and of spears. I wish this war
Had not so hurried her away, to attack
The Trojan troops; for she is dear to me,   770
And one of my companions might have been.
But since the bitter fates have so decreed,
Go, nymph, glide down the air, and seek the shores
Of Latium, where with gloomy auspices

The battle now begins. Take these weapons,   775
And from the quiver draw the avenging shaft.
Whoever shall wound the consecrated maid,
Or Trojan or Italian, he by this
Shall pay to me the forfeit of his life.
Then her lamented body will I bear   780
Wrapped in a hollow cloud, and in a tomb
Lay her, with her unconquered arms, to rest
Within her native land." She spoke; the nymph
Sped, sounding, through the yielding air; a cloud
Of wind and darkness compassed her about.   785

Meanwhile the Trojan troops, the Etruscan chiefs,
And all the cavalry, approach the walls,
In order ranged. The coursers leap and neigh
Along the field, and fight against the curb,
And wheel about. An iron field of spears   790
Bristles afar, and lifted weapons blaze.
Upon the other side, the Latians swift,
Messapus, Coras and his brother, come;
Also Camilla's wing: in hostile ranks
They threaten with their lances backward drawn,   795
And shake their javelins. On the warriors press,
And fierce and fiercer neigh the battle-steeds.

Advancing now within a javelin's throw,
Each army halted; then with sudden shouts
They cheer and spur their fiery horses on.   800
From all sides now the spears fly thick and fast
As showers of sleet, and darken all the sky.
With all their strength, with lance opposed to lance,
Tyrrhenus and Aconteus rush forward,
And clash together with resounding shock,   805
Steed against steed. Aconteus from his horse
Is hurled afar, like some swift thunderbolt,
Or as a ponderous weight shot by engine,
And yields his life to the air. Confusion then
Seizes the Latian troops, who turn about,   810

And throw their shields upon their backs, and flee,
Urging their horses to the city walls.
The Trojans follow, and Asilas leads.
And now they neared the gates; when with a shout
The Latians turn, and wheel their ductile steeds,   815
And charge in turn. The others give full rein
And fly. As when with an alternate tide
The rolling waves now rush upon the land,
And foaming, flood the rocks, and climb to touch
The farthest sands, now backward swiftly suck   820
The rolling stones, and ebbing leave the shore.
Twice the Rutulians are driven to their walls,
And twice they turn and face their foes repulsed.

    But when in the third battle-shock they met,
Both armies intermingled, man to man;   825
Then dying groans, corpses, and armor mixed,
Bodies of men, and horses half alive,
Rolling amid heaps of slain, and pools of blood,—
So fiercely raged the fight. Orsilochus
Against the steed of Remulus (he feared   830
To brave the rider) hurled a spear that pierced
Below the ear and clung. The furious steed,
Galled by the wound, rears high. His rider falls
And rolls upon the ground. Catillus fells
Iolas, and Herminius huge of limb,   835
And great in arms and courage; yellow locks
Graced his bare head; his shoulders too were bare,
Exposed to wounds, yet ever undismayed.
Bent down with pain, he writhes beneath the spear
Through his broad shoulders driven deep and fixed.   840
The black blood flows around on every side;
And deadly strokes they deal, still fighting on,
And rushing through their wounds to glorious death.

But through the thickest of the carnage borne,
The Amazon Camilla bounds along,   845
Armed with her quiver, and with one breast bare.
And now she showers her javelins thick and fast,

And now unwearied grasps her halberd strong.
Upon her shoulder rings her golden bow,
Diana's arms. Even if at any time 850
Repulsed, she yielded ground, she turns again,
And aims her flying arrows from her bow.
Around her rode the attendants of her choice,
Larina, Tulla, and, with brazen axe,
Tarpeia, virgins of Italian race, 855
All chosen by the sacred maid herself;
They were her trusty ministrants, alike
In peace and war;—like Thracian Amazons
Trampling the river-banks of Thermodon,
And fighting with their motley-metalled arms, 860
Either around Hippolyta,* or when
Penthesilea in her martial car
Returns from war, and with tumultuous yells
The female bands leap with their crescent shields.

Who first before your weapon, and who last, 865
Dread maiden, fell, stretched dying on the ground?
Eunæus first, the son of Clytius, dies.
His breast unshielded, by her long fir spear
Is pierced; and from his mouth flow rills of blood;
And on his wound he writhes, and bites the ground. 870
Then Liris, and then Pagasus: the one
Grasping his reins, as from his wounded horse
He falls; the other reaching helpless arms
To stay him falling. Both at once are slain.
Amastrus next, the son of Hippotas, 875
Is added to her victims. Pressing on,
She Tereas and Harpalycus pursues,
Demophoön and Chromis. Every shaft
Hurled from her hand brings down some Phrygian slain.
The hunter Ornytus in armor strange 880
Is seen afar on an Apulian steed,
Upon his shoulders broad a bullock's hide,
Upon his head a wolf's wide yawning jaws

---

*Queen of the Amazons.

And white teeth, in his hand a rustic lance.
Amid his troops he moves about, and towers   885
Above them all. Him meeting (no hard task,
His band being routed), with her darts she pierced;
And thus addressed with stern and hostile mien:—

    "And did you, Tuscan, think that in the woods
You were here hunting beasts? The day has come   890
That by a woman's arm refutes your boast.
Yet to the shades of your fathers this,
No trifling honor, you shall bear away:
That by Camilla's weapon you did fall."

    Orsilochus and Butes next she slew,   895
Two huge-limbed Trojans. Butes face to face
Upon his horse she pierces with her spear,
Where between helm and corselet gleamed his neck,
Above the buckler that his left arm held.
Around Orsilochus she wheels in flight   900
Delusive, then in narrower circle turns,
Pursuing the pursuer. Rising then,
With her strong battle-axe she cleaves him through,
With strokes redoubled, while he begs for life;
And from the wound the brains besmear his face.   905

    The son of Aunus of the Apennines
Next meets her, and stops short with sudden fear.
Of Ligurian race not the last was he,
While fate permitted crafty stratagem.
He, when he sees that he cannot evade   910
By flight the conflict, nor avoid the queen
Pressing close on him, thus resorts to guile:—
"What wondrous courage does a woman show,
When mounted on a faithful battle-steed!
Put by your means of flight, and hand to hand   915
Meet me on equal ground, and fight afoot.
Soon you shall know whose windy boasting first
Shall bring its punishment." He spoke: but she,
Burning with rage, delivers to a mate
Her steed, confronting him with equal arms,   920
Undaunted, and on foot, with naked sword,

And with unblazoned buckler. But the youth,
Thinking to conquer by a stratagem,
Turns his fleet steed and flies, with iron heel
Goading his sides, and swiftly borne away.   925
"Ah, false Ligurian!" said the maid; "in vain,
Elated with your pride, in vain you try
Your country's slippery wiles; nor shall your tricks
To guileful Aunus take you safely back."
Then all afire, with swiftly flying feet,   930
She soon outstrips his horse, and, face to face,
Seizing his reins, assails, and strikes him down.
Not with more ease, that consecrated bird,
The falcon, from a lofty rock, pursues
And overtakes a dove amid the clouds,   935
And clutches him, and tears with crooked claws,
And blood and feathers torn drop from the sky.

But not with unobserving eyes these things
The sire of gods and men on high beheld.
The Tuscan Tarchon he enflames with wrath,   940
And to the cruel battle goads him on.⁷
So, amid the carnage, and the falling ranks
Tarchon is borne along upon his steed,
And animates the army's flagging wings,
With varying words appealing to each man   945
By name, and rallying all their baffled strength.
"O Tuscans, whom no wrongs can spur to rage!
O tame and spiritless! What fear is this?
What cowardice? And does a woman drive
Your straggling ranks, and put them thus to flight?   950
Why do we bear these swords and spears in vain?
Not thus to Venus and her nightly wars
Are you so slow; nor when the bended pipes
Of Bacchus call the choirs to sumptuous feasts
And brimming bowls—your joy, your high desire.   955
While your sleek augur bids you to the rites,
And the fat victim calls to lofty groves."
    So saying, he spurs his steed into the midst,

Resolved to encounter death. On Venulus
He charges in fierce onset; from his horse   960
He grasps and tears his foe, and bears him off
Before him. Then a mighty shout is raised.
The Latins turn their eyes. But Tarchon fierce
Flies on, and bears the warrior and his arms.
Then from his lance he breaks the sharp steel head,   965
And searches for the parts exposed, to deal
A mortal wound. His struggling foe essays
To pluck away his right hand from his throat,
Opposing force to force. As when on high
A tawny eagle bears a serpent off,   970
And clings to it with gripping claws, the snake,
Wounded and writhing, twists its sinuous rings,
And rears its bristling scales and hissing mouth;
But nonetheless the bird with crooked beak
Strikes at the struggling reptile, and the air   975
Beats with her wings. So from the hostile ranks
Tarchon exulting bears away his prey.
Following his lead the Etruscans all rush on.

    Then round the swift Camilla Aruns rides,
Destined to death, his javelin in his hand;   980
With cautious skill he watches for his chance.
Wherever the maiden drives her furious course
Amid the troops, he follows silently,
Watching her steps. Where with victorious speed
She from the enemy returns, that way   985
He turns his reins unseen, and wheels about;
Tries all approaches, traverses her path
Through all its rounds, and shakes his threatening spear.

    By chance appeared upon the field, far off,
Chloreus, who once was priest of Cybele.   990
Distinguished in his Phrygian arms he shone,
And rode upon a foaming courser, decked
With cloth overspread with plumy scales of brass,
And clasped with gold, while he in rich attire
Of foreign purple, from his Lycian bow   995
Shot his Gortynian shafts. Upon his back

A golden quiver rattled; and his helmet
Was made of gold. He wore a saffron scarf;
The rustling linen folds were embroidered over,
And gathered in a yellow golden knot;   1000
And in barbaric sheaths his thighs were cased.
    Singling him out, the huntress blindly chased;
Whether she wished to affix the Trojan arms
Upon the temple gates, or show herself
In captive gold, she, rashly, through the ranks   1005
Pursues, struck with a woman's love of spoils.
Watching his time, Aruns his javelin takes,
And thus to heaven he prays: "Apollo, you,
Soracte's guardian, greatest of the gods
We worship! You for whom the pine-wood fire   1010
Is fed, and we your pious votaries walk
Over heaps of burning coals,——grant, mightiest sire,
That from our arms this stain we may erase.
Not spoils, nor trophies from a vanquished maid,
Nor booty do I seek. My other deeds   1015
Will bring me praise. If by my hand struck down
This direful pest shall fall, then willingly
Will I return inglorious to my home."
Apollo heard, and in his mind decreed
That half his suppliant's prayer should be fulfilled,   1020
And half dispersed in air. That he should slay
Camilla, as she hurried heedless by,
He granted.[8] But that he should see again
His native land, this part the god refused;
And in the stormy winds the prayer was lost.   1025
Then, as the whizzing javelin cleaved the air,
The Volscians turned their eyes upon their queen.
But she heard no whizzing sound of javelin
Along the air, nor heeded any, until
Beneath her naked breast the weapon pierced,   1030
And clung, deep driven, and drained her virgin blood.
In trembling haste the attendants in her train
Rush forward and sustain their falling queen.
But Aruns, smitten with mingled joy and fear,

Flies, nor will further trust his spear, nor dare   1035
To brave the virgin's darts. And as a wolf,
Who, having slain a shepherd or a steer,
Before pursuit begins, in conscious guilt
Flees to the mountains by some secret path,
And with his coward tail beneath him, hides   1040
Trembling amid the woods; so Aruns flies,
Disturbed, and yet well pleased at his escape,
And mingles with the troops. She, dying, strives
To pluck the weapon from her wound; but deep
Between her ribs the pointed steel is fixed.   1045
Bloodless and pale she sinks; her heavy eyes
Are closed; the rosy flush has left her face.
Then thus, expiring, she to Acca speaks,
One of her equals, who before all others
Was true to her, and one with whom her cares   1050
Were all divided: "Acca, sister dear,
Thus far I have striven; but this bitter wound
Has ended all; around me all grows dark.
Haste, bear to Turnus these my last commands.
Let him advance, and from the city drive   1055
The Trojans; now, farewell!" With that she loosed
Her grasp upon her reins, and sinking, fell.[9]
From her cold limbs and languid neck, the life
With gradual ebb, departs; her drooping head
Is bowed in death; the weapon leaves her hand;   1060
And with a groan the indignant spirit fled
Into the shades below. Then a great cry
Ascends, that strikes against the golden stars.
The combat deepens with Camilla's death.
And the whole Trojan force, the Tuscan chiefs,   1065
And all the Arcadian troops come rushing on.

But Opis, Dian's guardian nymph, had sat
Long on the mountains, and had watched afar
The battle, undismayed. Soon as she saw,
Amid the clamor of the furious bands,   1070
Camilla stricken down by bitter death,

She groaned; and from her breast escaped these words:—
"Ah, too, too cruel punishment, dear maid,
You have borne, for warring against the Trojan hosts!
Nor does it profit you, that lonely life 1075
Amid the woods, given to Dian's service;
Nor on your shoulder to have worn our shafts.
Yet not inglorious in your last hour
Your queen has left you; nor shall this your death
Be without a name among the nations. 1080
Nor the disgrace of dying unavenged
Shall you endure. For whosoever dealt
Your death-wound, he shall suffer death deserved."

Beneath the mountain stood a spacious tomb
Of mounded earth, where King Dercennus lay, 1085
One of Laurentum's ancient sovereigns.
A shady ilex covered it. Here first
The fair nymph from a rapid flight alights,
And watches Aruns from the lofty mound.
Soon as she saw him, swollen with pride and joy,— 1090
"Why stray so far away? Here bend your steps,"
She cried, "O doomed one, that you may receive
Camilla's due reward. Shall you, too, die
By Dian's shafts?" Then from her golden quiver
The Thracian nymph took out a wingèd arrow, 1095
And, angry, drew it to its fullest length,
And bent her bow until the curved tips met;
Her left hand touched the arrow's point; her right
Grasping the string drawn back upon her breast.
At the same instant Aruns hears the sound, 1100
And feels the steel deep buried in his heart.
Him, in his dying groans, his comrades leave,
Unwitnessed, in the dust of fields unknown,
While Opis to the Olympian sky is borne.

Their leader lost, Camilla's light-armed troop 1105
First flies; in wild disorder next the Rutuli,
And bold Atinas. Routed chiefs and bands
All turn their horses toward the city's walls.

All power is unavailing to resist
The Trojans pressing on, and dealing death.   1110
Their languid backs bear off their bows unbent.
Their galloping hoof-beats shake the crumbling ground.
Toward the walls black clouds of dust are rolled.
The matrons on the watch-towers beat their breasts;
The cries of women to the heavens ascend.   1115
Those who are first to pour through opened gates,
Are pressed behind by mingling hostile troops.
With no escape from miserable death;
But on their very threshold, beneath their walls,
And sheltering roofs, are pierced, and breathe their last.   1120
Some shut their doors, nor dare even to their friends
To open a passage, and receive them in,
Imploring. And a dire slaughter ensues
At every entrance where defenders stand
Against the assailing foe. Some are shut out,   1125
Full in their wretched parents' sight, and roll
Plunged in the trenches, with death close behind.
Some wildly dash and batter against the gates
And barricaded doors. Even matrons too,
Fired by the love they bore their land and homes,   1130
Rush to the conflict, as Camilla did;
And hurrying, from the ramparts throw their darts.
Or, imitating arms of steel, they fight
With stakes of hardened wood and pointed poles,
Eager to die the first before the walls.   1135

Meanwhile to Turnus, ambushed in the woods,
Acca has brought the news of dire defeat
And wild disorder: that the Volscian troops
Are routed and destroyed; Camilla fallen;
The enemy, pressing on with furious charge,   1140
Has won the day. Fear seizes on the town.
He, furious (such the stern decrees of Jove),
Deserts his ambuscade and forests rough.[10]
Scarce had he issued on the open fields,
When, having crossed the ridge, Æneas treads   1145

The plains, and passes through the gloomy wood.
So, both at rapid pace, with all their force
Move onward to the walls; nor far apart
They march. Far off Æneas saw the plains
Smoking with dust, and sees the Latian troops 1150
Across the plains. And Turnus also knew
Æneas, in his formidable arms,
And heard the trampling feet and snorting steeds.
Then would they two have engaged in battle,
Had not the red sun in the western waves 1155
Plunged his weary coursers, and day declined
In night. Within their camps before the town
They rest, with trench and rampart girded round.

BOOK 12

As soon as Turnus sees the Latin hosts,[1]
Broken by unsuccessful war, lose heart;
That now fulfilment of his promise made
Is claimed, and he marked out by every eye,
With towering soul implacable he burns;   5
As when a lion in the Libyan fields
Badly wounded, by the hunters, in the breast,
Prepares at last for battle, and delights
To shake the muscles of his shaggy neck;
Fearless, he snaps the invader's clinging shaft,   10
And roars with bloody jaws. So Turnus' wrath
More fiercely glows. Then with tumultuous words,
Thus to the king he speaks: "No obstacle
Shall Turnus prove; there is no reason why
These dastard Trojans should retract their word   15
Of challenge, or decline their compact made.
I take the field! Command the sacred rites,
O Sire, and seal the bond. Either my hand
Shall send this Dardan foe to Tartarus,
Asia's deserter (let the Latians sit,   20
And see), and with the sword I will refute
The common charge, or let him rule over us,
Vanquished, and take Lavinia for his wife."

Then tranquilly Latinus answered him:—[2]
"O youth of valiant soul, the more you show   25
Such fierce and overtopping hardihood,
The more it is just that I with anxious thought
Should consult your safety, and weigh with care
All risks. Your father Daunus' realms are yours;
Yours many a city captured by your hands.   30

322

My wealth and favor too would go with you.
Other unwedded maids in Latian lands
There are, nor of ignoble birth are they.
Allow me to impart these things
Without disguise, not pleasant to be said; listen   35
With an attentive mind. It was decreed
That to no former suitors I should wed
My daughter; this all gods and men announced.
But overpowered by my love for you,
And by your kindred blood, and by the tears   40
Of my afflicted wife, I broke all bonds,
Snatched from a son-in-law his promised bride,
And took up impious arms. You see what wars,
O Turnus, what disasters since that time
Pursue me; and what sufferings you above all   45
Endured. Vanquished twice in dire conflict,
We can hardly hold our hopes of Italy
Within the city. With our blood the waves
Of Tiber still flow warm. The spreading fields
Are whitened with our bones. Why thus so often   50
Should I be driven from my purpose? Why
Such mad infatuation change my mind?
If, Turnus slain, I am ready to invite
The Trojans as my allies, then why not
End these dissensions rather, with him still safe?   55
What will my kinsmen the Rutulians say,
And what the rest of Italy, if you,
Wooing my daughter, I betray to death?
(May Fortune countervail my words of fear!)
Regard the various chances of the war.   60
Pity your aged sire, whom mourning now,
His native Ardea divides far from you."

       But not at all is Turnus' violence moved
By words. He rather towers in greater wrath:
The medicine but aggravates the pain.   65
As soon as he could speak, he thus began:—
"Whatever care you entertain for me,
Most worthy king, lay it aside, I pray,

And allow me to purchase praise with death.
We too, O Sire, can with no feeble hand   70
Scatter our spears and darts. The blood will flow
From wounds we deal. No goddess mother there
Will help, in female semblance of a cloud
Screening the fugitive in empty shades."

But filled with terror at this new design   75
Of battle, weeping, and forecasting death,
The queen held fast her ardent son-in-law.
"Ah, by these tears, by whatsoever regard
You have for Amata, you, Turnus, now,
Are the sole hope and solace that remains   80
Unto my sad old age. On you depends
Latinus' power and glory; upon you
Our house declining rests. One thing I beg;—
Refrain from battle with the Trojan power.
Whatever calamity to you may come,   85
Amid this combat, Turnus, comes to me.
With you I will resign this hated life,
Nor, captive, will I see Æneas made
My son-in-law." Lavinia, her hot cheeks
Suffused with tears, attends her mother's voice.   90
A deep blush burns and courses through her face;
As if one stained the Indian ivory
With sanguine crimson, or as lilies white
Glowing in beds of roses; such the hues
That spread over the virgin's face. But he,   95
Fired with tumultuous love, fixes his looks
Upon the maid, and burns the more for arms.
Then briefly to Amata thus he speaks:—
"No, not with tears, O mother, not, I beg,
With such an omen follow me, as now   100
Forth to the strife of bitter war I go.
For Turnus has no power to stay his death.
Idmon, my herald, these words of mine
Bear no pleasing message to the Phrygian king.
When, borne upon her glowing car, the Morn   105

Reddens tomorrow's sky, let him not lead
The Trojans on against the Rutuli.
Let Trojans and Rutulians rest from arms.
By our own blood we'll end the war, and there
Upon that field Lavinia shall be won."   110

This said, into the palace he withdraws
With rapid steps, and for his horses calls,
Which Orithyia* to Pilumnus gave.
Proudly he sees them neigh before his face;
They were whiter than snow, fleeter than wind.   115
The busy grooms surround them; with their hands
They pat their chests, and comb their waving manes.
Then he girds his mail about his shoulders,
Scaly with gold and orichalcum pale;
And fits for use his buckler and his sword,   120
And ruddy crest; that sword the god of fire
Had wrought for his father Daunus, and had plunged
The glowing metal in the Stygian wave.
Then he grasps his tough spear that leaned against
A mighty column in the middle court,   125
Auruncan Actor's spoil, and brandishing
The quivering steel, exclaims: "Now, now, my spear,
That never yet did fail to obey my call,
The hour is now at hand. Great Actor once,
Now Turnus' right hand wields you. Grant that I   130
May fell him to the earth with this strong hand,
Tear the effeminate Phrygian's corselet off,
And soil with dust his locks with hot iron crisped,
And moist with myrrh!" Such fury drives him on;
Sparks flashing from his glowing face, and fire   135
Fierce gleaming from his eyes. As when a bull,
Bellowing with dreadful voice, prepares to fight,
And whets his wrath in goring against a tree,
With angry horns; in prelude to the fray
He butts the winds, and tosses up the sand.   140

---

*Wife of the north wind.

Meanwhile Æneas, formidably clad
In the arms his mother gave, his martial fire
And zeal awakes, rejoicing that the war
Should now be ended on the proffered terms.
Then he consoles his friends, and calms the fears   145
Of sad Iulus, and explains the fates.
He bids them bear decided answers then
To Latinus, and terms of peace prescribes.

Scarce had the Morning tinged the mountain-tops,
When from the Sea the horses of the sun   150
With lifted nostrils breathing light, arose.
Beneath the city walls the Rutuli
And Trojans, measuring out the field, prepared
The ground for combat. To their common gods
Their fires and turfy altars in the midst   155
They built; while some, in sacrificial robes,
And crowned with vervain, bring water and fire.
Forth come the Ausonian bands in armed array,
All crowding through the gates. On the other side
The Trojan and the Tuscan armies come   160
With various arms, and marshaled all in steel,
As though the grim battle had called them forth.
Their leaders too, proud in gold and crimson,
Go coursing over the field. Mnestheus is there,
Sprung from Assaracus, Asilas brave,   165
Messapus, the steed-tamer, Neptune's son.
And, at a given signal, each to his place
Withdraws; they fix their spears into the ground,
And rest their shields. Then, with eager haste,
The matrons and the common crowd, unarmed, pour,   170
And the old men with feeble limbs, and fill
The towers and roofs, and throng the lofty gates.

But Juno, from the summit of the mount[3]
Which now is called the Alban, but which then
Not name nor fame nor honor had, looked forth,
And viewed the plain beneath; and saw both hosts,   175

The Trojan and Laurentian, and the town
Of King Latinus. Turnus' sister then
She thus addressed, a goddess who presides
Over pools and murmuring streams; this honor Jove   180
Had given to her, for violated
Maidenhood: "O nymph, the glory of the streams,
Most dear unto my soul, you know that you
Before all Latian maids who shared the couch
Ungrateful of great Jove, I have preferred;   185
And freely gave thee a portion in the heavens.
Learn now your grief, Juturna, lest you should
Accuse me. As far as fortune and the fates
Allowed for Latium's good, I protected
Your city's walls and Turnus. Now I see   190
The youth contending with unequal fates.
The day and hostile power of destiny
Draw near. I cannot with these eyes behold
The combat or the league. You, if you dare
Do anything more promptly for your brother's aid,   195
Do it, for it becomes you. A better lot,
Perhaps, will yet attend this hapless race."

    Scarce had she spoken, when Juturna's eyes
Overflowed with tears. Three and four times she beat
Her lovely breast. "This is no time for tears,"   200
Saturnian Juno said; "Haste! snatch from death
Your brother, if for you there be a way;
Or stir the war anew, and break the league
Begun. I authorize the daring deed."
She, having thus exhorted, left the maid   205
Perplexed and tortured in her inmost soul.

Meanwhile the kings go forth. Latinus comes,
In majestic form, by four horses drawn.
Twelve golden rays his shining temples crown,
The emblem of his ancestor, the sun.   210
Turnus is borne by two white steeds, and holds
And brandishes two spears of broad-tipped steel.
Father Æneas, on the other side,

Advancing, moves, source of the Roman race,
Blazing with starry shield and arms divine;   215
Rome's other hope, Ascanius, at his side.
The priest, in raiment pure, then led along
The tender youngling of a bristly sow,
And a young sheep unshorn. The victims then
Are brought before the blazing altar-fires.   220
They then turn their eyes to the rising sun,
Sprinkle the sacrificial meal, and mark
The victims' foreheads with the sword, and pour
Libations on the altars from their bowls.

    Then pious Æneas, with his sword unsheathed,   225
Thus prays: "Be witness now to my vows,
O sun, and you, O Land, for whom I have borne
So many toils;—and you, Almighty Sire,
And your Saturnian spouse, more clement now,
O goddess, I beg you;—you too, great Mars,   230
Father, who turn all wars by your decree;—
And you, O Founts and Rivers I invoke;—
All Powers worshipped in the depths of air,
And all whose dwelling is the azure sea.
If victory falls to Ausonian Turnus,   235
Then to Evander's city, it is agreed,
We shall retire vanquished; Iulus leaves
These fields; nor shall the sons of Troy thenceforth
Renew the war, nor stir the lands to strife.
But if for us the victory should decide,   240
As I believe it will,—and may the gods
Confirm the hope,—not then shall I command
The Italians to obey the Trojan rule;
Nor do I aim at empire for myself:
On equal terms let both the nations then,   245
Unconquered, join and make eternal league.
Their gods and sacred rites I will decree;
And let the father of my bride retain
His promised kingdom and control of arms.
For me, my Trojans shall build up my walls,   250

And call the city by Lavinia's name."

Thus spoke Æneas; then Latinus raised
His eyes to heaven, and lifted his right hand:—
"By those same powers, Æneas, by the Earth,
And by the Seas, and by the Stars, I swear,   255
Latona's twins, and Janus, double-faced,
The Infernal gods, and pitiless Pluto's shrines;
Let the great Father hear, whose thunderbolts
Confirm our leagues; these altars here I touch,
And call their fires to witness, and the gods: 260
No day shall ever violate this peace,
Or break this league, upon Italia's side,
Whatever befalls; nor any power shall bend
My will, though it should drown the earth with waves,
And melt the heavens in fires of Tartarus.   265
Even as this scepter (as he spoke he held
A scepter in his hand) shall never bud
With twigs and leaves and shadowy boughs again,
Since, severed from its trunk amid the woods,
It missed its mother stem, and laid aside   270
Its foliage and its branches beneath the axe,
Of old a tree, now by the artists' hand
Cased in bright brass, to serve the Latin kings."
      Thus they with mutual vows confirmed their league,
In sight of all the chiefs. Then in due form   275
They slay the sacred victims over the flames,
And tear their entrails out while still alive;
And heap the altars with their loaded plates.

But to the Rutuli this combat had
Long seemed unequal, and their minds were tossed   280
With various fears, the more when they perceive
More nearly how ill-matched in strength it stood.
Their fears increased, when with a silent step,
Turnus advanced with downcast, suppliant looks,
And reverently before the altars bowed,   285
With haggard cheeks and youthful frame all pale.

Then, when Juturna saw such signs caught up
And spread, and saw the wavering spirits sink
Amid the crowd, she took Camertus' form
(He was of noble race and ancestors,   290
And from his father's valor had derived
A name of note, himself renowned in arms);
And in the midst of all the armèd troops,
Not ignorant of expedients, she appears,
And various rumors spreads. Then thus she speaks:—   295
"O you Rutulians, are you not ashamed
To expose one life for all of equal worth?
Are we not matched in numbers and in strength?
Lo! Trojans and Arcadians, all are here;
Etruria too arrays her fated bands   300
Against our Turnus; yet we scarce should find
A foe, though only each second man should fight.
Our chief shall be exalted to the gods,
Before whose altars he devotes his soul;
And in the mouths of men his fame shall live.   305
But we, who now sit idle on these fields,
Our country lost, must yield to our haughty lords."

By words like these the warriors were inflamed
Yet more and more; a murmur through the ranks
Went creeping: the Laurentian troops themselves,   310
And those same Latians who but lately hoped
Respite from war, and safety to the state,
Now turn to arms, and wish the league unmade,
And pity the hard lot fallen on Turnus.
To these a stronger spur Juturna adds,   315
And from the upper sky she gives a sign,
Than which no miracle more closely pressed
Disturbance on their minds, or so deceived.
For now they saw the tawny bird of Jove
Chasing a flock across the ruddy sky   320
Of clamoring water-fowl; then suddenly
Sweep to the waves, and in his cruel claws
Bear off a goodly swan. The Italians gaze

With minds intent; when, wonderful to see,
The birds all wheel about with noisy cries,   325
Darkening the air, a cloud of flying wings,
And chase their foe, till, conquered by their strength
And weight, the eagle in the river drops
His prey, and disappears amid the clouds.

With shouts the Rutuli greet this omen;   330
Their weapons they prepare to seize.[4] Then first,
Tolumnius the augur thus exclaims:—
"This, this is what I often sought, with prayers;
I see, and must accept the divine power.
Your leader I will be, unhappy men;   335
You, whom this wicked stranger like timid fowls
Dismays with war, and devastates your shores.
Now let him plan his flight, and set sail
On the deep. But you with one accord close up
Your ranks, and from this combat save your king,   340
Whom they would snatch away from you." He spoke,
And, running, hurled a javelin at his foes.
Straight through the air the whizzing cornel-shaft
Flies with unerring aim. Then all at once
A shout arose: the thickly serried crowd   345
Is stirred, and each tumultuous heart ablaze.
Full in the pathway of the flying spear
There stood nine brothers, all of beauty rare;
One faithful Tuscan wife had borne them all;
Arcadian Gylippus was their sire.   350
One, a fair youth, in shining arms, is pierced
Just where the clasping belt confines the waist;—
Pierced through the ribs, and his limbs are stretched
On the yellow sand. At this the brethren,
A fearless band, with rage and grief inflamed,   355
Some with drawn swords, and some with missile spears,
Rush blindly forth. Laurentum's troops oppose.
Trojans and Tuscans pour in thick array,
And the Arcadian bands with painted shields.
So, to decide the battle with the sword,   360

All burn alike. The altars they despoil.
The sky is dark with stormy showers of steel.
They carry off the sacred bowls and hearths.
Even Latinus flies, and bears away
His baffled gods, since broken lies the league.   365
Some rein their cars, or leap upon their steeds,
And draw their swords. Messapus, eager now
To break the truce, against Aulestes drives,
Mounted upon his horse; a Tuscan king
He was, and wore the badges of a king.   370
Retreating, amid the altars placed behind,
Upon his head and shoulders down he falls.
Hotly Messapus follows with his spear,
And, rising on his steed, with ponderous lance
Thrusts heavily, while he implores for life.   375
"He has it now," the chieftain said; "this life
A worthier victim to the gods is given."
The Italians flock, and strip his limbs while warm.
Then Corynæus from an altar grasps
A burning brand, and, meeting Ebusus   380
Coming to aim a blow, confronts him full,
And dashes the flames in his face, that catch
And singe his heavy beard with burning scent.
Then, following up the attack, with his left hand
He grasps the hair of his astounded foe;   385
And, pressing with his knee, he holds him fast
Down to the earth, and stabs him through the side.
Then Podalirius with his naked sword
Pursues the shepherd Alsus, pressing close,
As in the battle's front, amid the darts   390
He rushes on; but Alsus, drawing back
His axe, strikes through his forehead and his chin,
And cleaves him down, and with the spattered blood
His armor is smeared; then the rigid rest
And iron sleep of death press down his eyes,   395
That close forever in eternal night.

But good Æneas, with uncovered head,
Stretched his right hand unarmed, and called aloud:—

"Where do, my men, where do you go so fast?
What sudden discord is this? Restrain your rage!   400
The league is made, and all its rules arranged.
I only have a right to take the field.
Yield now to me; dismiss these fears of yours.
With my hand I shall make the treaty firm.
These sacred rites make Turnus due to me."   405
But while he still is speaking, lo! there flies
A whizzing arrow aimed at the hero;
None knew by whose strong hand it was impelled,—
What accident, what god, brought such a fame
To the Rutulian arms; the high renown   410
Of such a deed was hid; no one made boast
That against Æneas he had aimed the blow.
As soon as Turnus saw the Trojan chief
Retiring from the ranks, the leaders all
Thrown in commotion, with a sudden hope   415
He fires; he calls for horses and for arms,
Springs proudly to his chariot with a bound,
And takes the reins. Then, as he flies along,
He many a hero's form devotes to death,
Many half dead he rolls upon the plain,   420
Or with his chariot tramples down their ranks,
Or drives them flying with his gathered darts.
As when, impetuous, by cold Hebrus' waves
The bloody Mars comes clashing with his shield,
And, kindling war, lets loose his furious steeds;   425
Upon the plain they outstrip the southern winds
And western winds; their trampling feet are heard
In thunder on the farthest bounds of Thrace;
And round about, attendants of the god,
The gloomy faces throng, black Terror and Wrath   430
And Stratagem;—so through the battle's midst
Fierce Turnus drives his steeds that steam with sweat
And rides, insulting, over the wretched slain.
Scattering the bloody dew, their rapid hoofs
Beat up the gory sand. And now he slays   435
Sthenelus and Thamyris; these hand to hand;
And Pholus at a distance; Glaucus, too,

And Lades, both the sons of Imbrasus,
Bred by their sire in Lycia, and equipped
With equal skill in arms, whether to fight   440
In combat close or outstrip with steeds the wind.

Eumedes in another quarter comes,
Borne to the middle of the fray; the son
Of ancient Dolon he, renowned in arms:
He bore his grandsire's name, his father's soul   445
And strength (who once into the Grecian camp
Went as a spy, and as a guerdon sought
The chariot of Pelides. Tydeus' son
Bestowed on him a different recompense
For such presumptuous claim, no longer now   450
Aspiring to possess Achilles' steeds).
When Turnus beheld him afar upon
The open field, he through the distance sent
A flying dart; then stops his harnessed steeds,
And, leaping from his chariot, meets his foe,   455
Half dead and fallen; and pressing with his foot
The warrior's neck, wrests from his hand his sword,
And plunges in his throat the shining blade.
"Trojan, lie there, and measure our fields thus,"
He cries, "and that Hesperia sought in war.   460
Such their rewards who venture with the sword
To brave me; thus they build their city's walls!"
Hurling his lance, he sends Asbutes then
To bear him company; then Chloreas next,
Sybaris, Dares, and Thersilochus;   465
Thymœtes too, thrown from his plunging steed.
As when the blast of Thracian Boreas roars
Along the deep Ægæan, and pursues
The billows to the shore, the incumbent storm
Drives over the sky the flocks of flying clouds;   470
So, wheresoever Turnus cuts his path,
The troops give way, the routed squadrons fly.
Against his rushing car as on he drives,
The blowing wind shakes back his flying crest.

Phegeus could not bear him and pressing on,   475
Shouting in his rage, he in his course
Opposed, and grasping at his courser's reins
Twisted their foaming mouths. While dragged along
He hangs upon the pole, the chief's broad lance
Reaches him, unprotected, piercing through   480
His double-woven corselet, with a wound
Grazing his skin. But he with shield opposed,
And with drawn sword confronts his enemy:
When, dashing on its course, the whirling car
Overthrew him headlong, stretched upon the ground.   485
And Turnus, following fast, struck off his head
Between the corselet and the helmet's rim,
And left the headless body on the sand.

But while victorious Turnus in the field
Is dealing death, Æneas to the camp,   490
Bleeding, is led, Mnestheus attending him,
And true Achates and Ascanius near.
On his long spear he leans, with faltering steps,
And strives impatiently to pluck away
The broken shaft, and seeks the nearest aid;   495
That they should make incision with the sword,
Lay bare the wound about the hidden steel,
And send him back again into the field.
And now Iapis came to lend his aid,
Son of Iasius, more than all beloved   500
By Phœbus; for on him the god himself,
Struck with deep love, had offered to bestow
His arts, his gifts, his skill in augury,
His lyre, and flying shafts; but he preferred
(To lengthen out a dying father's life)   505
That he might know the powers of herbs and cures,
And ingloriously pursue silent arts.
Chafing with bitter wrath, Æneas stood,
And leaned upon his mighty spear, unmoved,
Amid the crowd, by all the warriors' grief   510
And tears of sad Iulus. Then approached

The old physician, with his robe tucked back,
After the manner of his craft; his hand
With many a medicine and potent herb,
Attempts relief, in trembling eagerness,   515
But all in vain; in vain the barbèd steel
Solicits, and with grip of pincers firm
Essays to move; no way will Fortune show.
Apollo, his great patron, lends no aid.
And more and more the horror in the fields   520
Increases, and the terror comes nearer.
The sky stands dense with dust; around them crowd
The horsemen of the foe; the darts rain thick
Upon the camp; and to the heavens ascend
The death-cries from the cruel battlefield.   525

The goddess-mother, Venus, troubled now[5]
That unmerited pain had touched her son,
On Cretan Ida gathers dittany,
With downy leaves and crimson blossoms crowned;
To the wild goats the plant is not unknown,   530
When pierced by flying darts. This Venus brought,
Veiled in a shadowy cloud; she steeps the herb
In water poured into a shining vase,
Healing ambrosial juices sprinkling in,
And fragrant panacea; and with this   535
The old Iapis, ignorant of its power,
Bathing the wound, all pain his body left
At once, and to the bottom of the gash
The blood was stanched; and following now his hand,
Without an effort out the arrow dropped,   540
And all Æneas' former strength returned.
"Quick, bring the hero's arms! Why stand and wait?"
Iapis cries, the first to rouse their souls
Against the foe: "This thing was never done
By human means, nor any master's art.   545
Nor has my hand, Æneas, saved you now.
Some greater power divine has wrought the cure,
And sends you back to achieve yet greater deeds."

He, eager for the combat, had encased
His legs in golden greaves on either side;   550
Impatient of delay, he shakes his lance.
When he had fitted to his side his shield,
His corselet to his back, he throws his arms
Around Ascanius' neck, and through his helm
With gentle kiss embracing him, thus speaks:—   555
"From me, my son, learn valor and the might
Of stern endurance; what your lot may be,
Let others teach. In battle my right hand
Shall save you, lead you on to great rewards.
Bear this in mind, when riper years quite soon   560
Shall come; and to your soul recalling often
The examples of your race, let then your sire,
And Hector, too, your uncle, spur you on."

Thus having spoken, he issued from the gates
With towering form, and shook his ponderous lance.   565
Antheus and Mnestheus too in dense array
Rush forth, and, crowding from the abandoned camp,
The troops go pouring out. The blinding dust
Fills all the plain; the trembling earth beneath
Rocks to the trampling tread of hurrying feet.   570
Turnus and the Ausonians from a hilltop
Saw their coming; a cold shudder
Ran through their ranks. Juturna first of all
Heard them, and knew the sound, and fled dismayed.
Æneas, scouring over the open plain,   575
Whirls his black squadrons on. As when beneath
The bursting skies, athwart amid ocean moves
A storm-cloud to the land; alas! what fears
Alarm the wretched peasants' shuddering hearts!
Ruin upon the trees, and far and wide   580
Destruction on the harvest fields will fall;
The winds fly on before, and to the shores
Bear the deep rumbling of the approaching storm.
So on the opposing ranks the Trojan chief
Leads his battalions all compact and dense   585

In serried files. Thymbrœus with his blade
Strikes down the heavy Osiris, Mnestheus slays
Archetius, and Achates Epulo,
And Gyas Ufens; even Tolumnius falls,
The augur, who was first to hurl his spear   590
Against his foes. A shout ascends to heaven;
And the Rutulians, in their turn repulsed,
Show all along the fields their dusty backs.
The fugitives Æneas scorns to slay;
Nor those who meet him armed, and face to face,   595
Will he pursue. He seeks Turnus alone,
And strives to track amid the darkening dust;
And him alone challenges to combat.

The warrior maid, Juturna, alarmed at this,
Overthrows Metiscus, Turnus' charioteer,   600
Between the reins; and from the beam he falls,
Left far behind. She mounts into his seat,
Guides with her hands the undulating reins,
And takes Metiscus' voice and look and arms.
As when through spacious courts of some rich lord   605
Flits a black swallow, round the lofty halls,
Picking a scanty meal, or seeking food
To feed her chirping young, through empty porch,
Round pool and pond her twittering notes are heard,—
So through the hostile ranks Juturna drives,   610
And round and round her rapid chariot flies.
Now here, now there, she displays her brother
In triumph, nor permits him to engage,
But shuns Æneas on his track. But he,
No less in winding mazes wheels about,   615
To intercept, or follows on his steps,
And shouts to him across the broken ranks.
As often as he his enemy descried,
And with the flying coursers tried his speed,
So often Juturna turned aside the car.   620
Alas! what can he do? On changing tides
He fluctuates in vain; conflicting plans

Disturb his mind. Messapus then by chance
Came swiftly riding, bearing in his hand
Two javelins tipped with steel, and one of these 625
He hurls with certain aim; Æneas stopped,
And covered by his shield, upon his knee
Dropped down; the flying javelin, nonetheless,
Struck off the plumy crest upon his helm.
Inflamed with wrath at such insidious arts, 630
When he perceived the chariot and the steeds
Still borne afar, he calls to witness then
Jove, and the altars of the broken league;
Into the thick of battle rushes on,
Terrible, with the auspicious aid of Mars, 635
Lets loose the reins of anger on his foes,
And deals fierce and undistinguished slaughter.

What god can now declare unto my verse
The dire events, what carnage vast ensued,
What deaths of chiefs? Whom Turnus now pursues, 640
And now the Trojan hero, over the fields?
Was it the will of Jupiter that thus
The nations whom eternal peace one day
Would join should clash in such a dire conflict?

Rutulian Sucro hurrying comes (here first 645
The Trojans in their full career were checked);
But as he came, Æneas in the side
Plunged his sword through the ribs, the speediest death.
Turnus on foot encountered Amycus,
Thrown from his horse; his brother too he met, 650
Diores; one with lance, and one with sword
He slays, and bears away their severed heads
Dripping with blood, suspended to his car.
Talos, and Tanais, and brave Cethegus
Æneas kills, all three at one assault. 655
The sad Onytes too, of Theban race,
And Peridia's son. Turnus strikes down
The brothers sent from Lycia, Phœbus' land;

Also Menœtes, an Arcadian youth,
In vain averse to war; his humble home   660
And craft had been on Lerna's fishy streams;
Unknown to him the great rewards of fame,
While on hired fields his father sowed his grain.
And as two fires let loose from different sides,
Through forests dry and crackling laurel twigs—   665
Or as from mountain-sides two foaming streams
Come roaring down, each flooding, its own way,
The open fields, with wide devastation—
So through the conflict rush the opposing chiefs.
They do not know what it is to yield; their breasts   670
Now boil with rage suppressed, now, bursting forth,
They sweep to battle with their utmost strength.
    One whirls a ponderous stone, and fells to earth
Murranus, boasting of his ancestors
And race descended from the Latin kings.   675
The wheels, beneath the harness and the yoke
Drag him along, beat down by trampling hoofs
Of steeds regardless of their master's fate.
The other encounters Hyllus, who in rage
Comes driving on; against his gilded brows   680
He hurls a spear, that brain and helmet pierced.
Nor could you, Creteus, bravest of the Greeks,
Save yourself from Turnus; nor did the gods
Protect Cupencus from Æneas' sword
That pierced his breast; nor did his brazen shield   685
Avail him at all. You too, O Æolus,
Beheld Laurentum's fields, upon the earth
Stretched at your length, you whom the Grecian hosts
Could not overthrow, nor he who overturned
Great Priam's realm, Achilles; here your life   690
Now touched its goal. Yours a lofty palace
Beneath Mount Ida, in Lyrnessus too;—
Here on Laurentian soil a sepulcher.
So all the Latian and the Dardan hosts
Are turned upon each other. Mnestheus now,   695
And brave Serestus, and Messapus come,

And strong Asilas, and the Tuscan bands,
And all Arcadia's wingèd cavalry.
Each for himself, all to their utmost strive;
No stop, no stay; one zeal inflames them all.   700

His fairest mother prompts Æneas now
To turn and march upon the city walls,
And frighten the Latins with a sudden blow.
For while he strove to follow Turnus' tracks,
Amid the various ranks, and here and there   705
Around him looked, he saw the town untouched
And tranquil amid the shocks of war. At once
His mind is kindled by a greater plan
Of battle. Round him then he calls his chiefs,
Mnestheus, Sergestus, and Serestus brave,   710
And takes his station on a rising ground.
The Trojan bands assemble, crowding close,
Nor do they lay aside their shields and spears.
He, in the midst, thus speaks: "Let no one thwart
The purpose I announce. Jove stands with us.   715
Nor, though the plan be sudden, let your wills
Be slow to aid. The cause of all the war,
This city, and Latinus' rule itself,
Unless they will consent to accept our yoke,
And, vanquished, yield, I will this day overturn,   720
And lay their turrets smoking on the ground.
Am I, forsooth, to wait till Turnus deigns
To accept the combat, and, though often vanquished,
Return to take the field? O citizens,
The source of this unhallowed war is here.   725
Bring torches! Reassert the league with flames!"

He spoke; and all, alive with equal zeal,
Move in a dense battalion to the walls.
Ladders and torches suddenly appear.
Some storm the gates, and kill the first they meet.   730
Others with showers of darts obscure the sky.
Æneas himself stretches his right hand,

Beneath the city's walls, amid the foremost,
Upbraids Latinus with accusing voice,
And calls the gods to witness, that again   735
He is forced to fight; that twice the Italians now
Become his foes; that twice they break the league.
Dissension stirs the trembling citizens.
Some to the Dardans would fling back the gates,
And open the town, and drag the king himself   740
To the ramparts; while others seize their arms
And hasten to defend the walls. As when
A shepherd in some secret pumice rock
Has tracked a swarm of bees, and filled the holes
With bitter smoke; alarmed, they run about   745
Here and there throughout their waxen camp,
With loud and angry buzzing; through their cells
Roll the black fumes, until with stifled noise
The cave within resounds, and clouds of smoke
Go pouring forth into the empty air.   750

    Such fortune on the exhausted Latians fell,
And shook their city to its base, with woe.
The queen, when she beholds the enemy
Approach the town, and sees the walls attacked,
And torches hurled upon the roofs,—no troops   755
Of the Rutulians near, nor Turnus' bands,—
Wretched, believes the youth in battle slain;
And, struck with sudden pangs of grief, cries out
That she had been the cause and guilty source
Of such disasters; and with raving words,   760
As one about to die, rends her purple robes
With her hands; and from a lofty beam
Ties fast the noose of her unsightly death.[6]
The unhappy Latian dames hear the tidings.
Lavinia tears her golden tresses, then, and   765
Roseate cheeks; and round her all her train
Runs wildly, and the palace far and wide
Rings with their shrieks; then all the city hears
The melancholy tidings spread about,
And deep dejection reigns. Rending his robes,   770

Latinus goes, bewildered at the fate
Thus fallen upon his queen and ruined town.
He heaps the dust upon his hoary head,
Upbraiding often himself, that of his own accord
He had not, before this, received   775
Trojan Æneas as his son-in-law.

Upon the plain's remotest bounds, meanwhile,
Turnus pursued a shred of straggling troops,
With slower pace, elated less and less
Now, with his coursers' speed; when to his ears,   780
Listening intently, borne upon the wind,
Came from the troubled city confusèd cries,
An unknown terror, and a mournful din.
"Alas! what grief is this within our walls?
What wild alarms arise from every street?"   785
So speaking, bewildered, he drew back his reins
And stopped. His sister then, who had assumed
Metiscus' form and face, his charioteer,
And guided still the chariot, steeds, and reins,
Thus, turning to him, spoke: "Let us pursue   790
The Trojans, Turnus, here, where victory still
Prepares the way; others there are, whose hands
Can well defend the city. Æneas there
Joins battle, and attacks the Italian hosts.
We too among the Trojans scatter death.   795
Nor shall you with less honor from the field
Withdraw, nor count less numbers of your slain."
Turnus replied: "Sister, long since I knew
Your presence, when by artifice you first
Did break the truce, and in this warfare join.   800
Now you in vain deceive me, though divine.
But say, who sent you down from Olympus
To undertake such toils? Was it to see
Your wretched brother's cruel death? For now
What can I do? What fortune brings to me   805
Promise of safety? I myself have seen
Murranus fall, none dearer now to me

Survives; calling aloud on me, he fell.
Great was the wound that slew so great a chief.
The hapless Ufens too has fallen, that he   810
Might not see or know this my dishonor.
His corpse, his armor, are the Trojans' spoils.
Shall I look on and see our homes destroyed,
The sole disaster lacking, in our loss,
Nor with this hand refute the bitter words   815
Of Drances? Shall I turn my back? This land,
Shall it see Turnus flying? Is it then
So hard a thing to die? O Powers beneath,
Aid me, since those above avert their eyes!
Free from that stain, I will descend to you,   820
An unpolluted soul, that never yet
Was unworthy of my illustrious line!"

Scarce had he said these words, when Saces comes,
Borne through his foes, upon a foaming steed,
And wounded by an arrow athwart the face.   825
He calls on Turnus with imploring words:—
"Our last and only safety rests with you,
Turnus; have pity now upon your own.
Æneas storms, an armèd thunderbolt,
And threatens to overturn the topmost towers   830
Of Italy, and bring destruction down.
Even now the brands are flying to the roofs.
On you the Latians turn their eyes; on you
They call. The king himself, Latinus, doubts
Whom he shall call his son-in-law, with whom   835
To make alliance. Besides all this, the queen,
Your own most steadfast friend, slain by herself
In wild despair, has left the light of life.
Messapus and Atinas, they alone
Before the gates sustain the battle's shock.   840
On every side the dense battalions stand,
A fearful harvest-field of naked swords,
While you are urging on your chariot wheels
Over a deserted plain." With dumb, fixed gaze,

Confused by shifting aspects of affairs, 845
Stood Turnus then. Within his heart boiled up
An overwhelming shame, rage mixed with grief,
Self-conscious valor, and love by fury racked.

As soon as the shadows fled from his brain,
And light was restored, back to the walls he turned 850
His blazing eyes, wild tumult in his soul.
When lo, the curling flames had seized the tower
Between the floors, and rolled into the sky;
The tower, which he himself, with jointed beams,
And wheels beneath, and bridges overhead, 855
Had built. "Now, sister, now the fates prevail.
Do not ask me to pause. Wherever Heaven may lead
And Fortune stern, let us pursue our course.
This combat with Æneas stands resolved;
Resolved, to bear whatever bitterness 860
There be in death; nor, sister, shall you see
Further disgrace for me. Yet first allow,
I pray, that I may give this fury vent."

He spoke; and, leaping down from his chariot,
Plunged through the hostile spears; he leaves behind 865
His grieving sister, and with rapid pace
Breaks through the middle ranks. And, as a rock
Comes crashing from a mountain-top, torn off
By storms, or washed away by swollen rains,
Or underslid by loosening lapse of years, 870
Down the steep cliff the awful mountain-mass
Falls bounding to the earth, and sweeps away
Woods, flocks, and men; so through the broken ranks
Goes Turnus, rushing to the city's walls,
Where tracts of earth are drenched in blood, and darts 875
Fly whistling through the air. Then with his hand
He makes a sign, and lifts aloud his voice:—
"Forbear, Rutulians! Latians, lower your spears!
Whatever fortune may befall, it's mine.
More just it is that I, instead of you, 880

Should expiate alone this broken league,
And so decide the battle with my sword."

Then all the troops drew back, and gave him place.
But hearing Turnus named, Æneas now
Forsakes the walls and towers, all hindrances   885
Puts by, from every enterprise breaks off;
With joy he exults, and dreadful with his arms
Comes thundering on; as great as Athos he,
As great as Eryx, or father Apennine
Himself, when with his waving oaks he roars,   890
And, joyous, lifts his snow-peaks to the skies.

Then the Rutulians, and the Trojan hosts,
And all the Italians turned their eyes to look,—
Those who were holding the high battlements,
And those who battered at the walls below,—   895
And laid their weapons from their shoulders down.
Amazed, Latinus sees two mighty chiefs,
Born in far distant quarters of the earth,
Met to decide the battle with the sword.
Then they, as soon as on the open plain   900
The lists were cleared, advance with rapid pace,
And hurl their javelins from afar, then clash
With din and shock of shields and ringing arms.
Earth groans. Fierce fall their sword-strokes, thick and fast
Redoubling. Chance and valor mix in one.   905
As in the spacious Sila, or on the heights
Of Mount Taburnus, when two hostile bulls
Rush to the conflict with opposing fronts;
The trembling keepers fly, and all the herd
Stands mute with fear; the heifers faintly low,   910
Uncertain which shall rule the pasture-ground,
And whom the herd shall follow; they, meanwhile,
With ponderous strength, close locked, deal many a wound
With horns that thrust and gore. Blood bathes their necks
And shoulders, while their bellowing fills the grove. 915
Even so Æneas and the Daunian chief

Clash with their shields, that all the air resounds.[7]
With equal balance Jove himself sustains
Two scales, and lays therein the fates of each,
To see which one the toilsome conflict dooms,   920
And on which side the weight of death inclines.
Here Turnus, thinking he is safe, leaps forth,
And rising to his height, with lifted sword
He strikes. Trojans and trembling Latins shout;
Both armies stand intent. The treacherous sword   925
Breaks short, and in the middle of his blow
Deserts its furious lord, unless by flight
He saves himself. Then, swifter than the wind,
He flies, soon as the unknown hilt he sees
Grasped in his hand disarmed. The rumor is,   930
That in his haste, when battle first began,
While mounting to his car with coursers yoked,
He left behind his father's sword of proof,
And in his hurry snatched Metiscus' blade,
That long had served him while the Trojans fled   935
And turned their backs. As soon as on arms divine
(By Vulcan wrought) the mortal blade was tried,
It snapped like brittle ice beneath the blow,
And on the yellow sand the splinters shone.
So Turnus in mad flight over all the plain   940
Wheels in uncertain orbits, here and there.
For on all sides the Trojans stood around
In dense array, and here a wide morass,
And there steep walls, a barrier interposed.

Nor less Æneas, though his wound retards,   945
So that at times his knees impede his course,
Follows and presses, step with step, behind
His trembling foe. As when a hound, who has tracked
A stag that is hemmed in by a river,
Or hedged by terror of the crimson plumes,   950
Baying, gives chase; the beast meanwhile dismayed
By the steep banks and by the hunter's snares,
Backward and forward flies, a thousand ways,

While the keen Umbrian dog follows him close
With open mouth, now nearly holds him fast,   955
Now snaps, as though he held, with chiding cry,
His prey escaping still his empty jaws;
Then shouts arise, the banks and lakes resound,
And all the sky is ringing with the noise;—
So Turnus flies, and as he flies, he chides   960
The Rutuli; each one by name he calls,
Demanding eagerly his well-known sword.
Æneas death declares and dire ruin,
Should any one approach; the trembling troops
He overawes with threats to raze their town;   965
And, wounded as he is, still presses on.
Five circuits they complete in their career,
And five retrace, now this way and now that;
For now no slight or trifling prize is sought:
It's Turnus' life and blood that is required.   970

It chanced a wild olive with bitter leaves,
Sacred to Faunus, had stood on this spot.
The wood of old by sailors was revered.
Here, when preserved from shipwreck, they were used
To affix their gifts to the Laurentian god,   975
And hang their votive robes. With reckless haste
The Trojans felled the consecrated trunk,
That they might fight upon a well-cleared field.
Here stood Æneas' spear; his arm had driven
The weapon hither, where in the impassive roots   980
It stuck. The Dardan hero stooped and tried
To wrench the steel away, and so pursue
The foe he could not overtake by speed.
Then, wild with terror, Turnus cries aloud:—
"O Faunus, pity me! And you, kind Earth,   985
Hold back the steel;—if ever I have held
Your honors sacred, by the sons of Troy
Profaned in war." Thus he invoked the god,
And not with fruitless prayers. For struggling long,
And wasting time upon the sluggish stump,   990

Æneas could not with his utmost strength
Relax the wood's firm grip. While striving still,
The Daunian nymph assumes Metiscus' form
Once more, and runs, and gives back to her brother
His sword. Venus, indignant to behold   995
The daring of the nymph, approaches now,
And tears the weapon from the root. The chiefs,
With towering strength, with arms and courage fresh,
This in his sword, that trusting in his spear,
Stand, breathless in the combat, front to front.   1000

Meanwhile the omnipotent Olympian king[8]
Speaks to Juno, looking from a yellow cloud
Upon the conflict: "O consort-queen,
When shall this end? What further still remains?
You yourself know, confessing that you know,   1005
Æneas for a hero is deified
And destined for the starry skies by fate.
What plan do you pursue? What hope is there,
That in the chilly clouds you still now linger?
Was it a seemly thing that one divine   1010
Should bear a mortal wound? Or that the blade,
Wrested from Turnus' hand, should be restored,
And to the conquered strength renewed be given?
(For without you, what were Juturna's power?)
Yield to our prayers, and desist now at length;   1015
Nor let such grief consume your silent heart,
Nor from your sweet lips let these gloomy cares
Encounter me so often. The end is near.
You have had power to harass the Trojans
By sea and land, kindle war unspeakable,   1020
Tarnish an honored house, and overcloud
Nuptial rites with grief. Further attempts than these
I now forbid." Thus Jupiter; and thus
Saturnia answered, with submissive looks:—
"I admit, great Jupiter, it was because   1025
I knew that will of yours, I have withdrawn,
Unwillingly, from Turnus and his lands.

Nor would you have seen me sitting thus apart,
Enduring all this shifting good and bad:
But armed with flames, and on the battle's edge   1030
Drawing the Trojans on to deadly war.
Juturna, I confess, I did persuade
To help her hapless brother; greater deeds
Than that approved, to hazard for his life,
But not to bend the bow or hurl the dart.   1035
I swear by Styx' relentless fountain-head,
The sole religious dread that binds the gods.
And now in truth I yield, and, hating, leave
This warfare. Yet one thing I do beseech
For Latium and your royal seed, no law   1040
Of destiny forbids; when peace is made
By this auspicious marriage,—be it so,—
And laws and leagues unite the hostile tribes,
Do not ask the Latins to change their ancient name;
Do not let them be called Trojans and Teucri,   1045
Nor change their speech or dress. Let Latium be.
Let Alban monarchs through the centuries reign;
Let Rome's posterity attain their might
Through virtue of Italia. Troy has fallen.
Then let it fall forever with its name."   1050
     Smiling, the Founder of events and men
Replied: "You are in truth the sister of Jove,
And Saturn's other seed, to roll such waves
Of wrath beneath your bosom! But come, now,
Subdue this fruitless anger. What you will,   1055
I grant; and, vanquished, willingly submit.
The Ausonians shall retain their ancient tongue
And customs; and their name shall be as now.
But, mingled with the mass, the Trojan race
Shall settle in their land. I will ordain   1060
Their customs and their sacred rites, and all
Shall be Latins, one common speech to all.
Hence, mingled with Ausonian blood, shall rise
A nation above men and gods in worth,
Nor matched by any race in serving you."   1065

Juno assents with glad and altered mind,
And leaves her cloudy dwelling in the sky.[9]

This done, the Sire revolves another plan;
How to withdraw Juturna from the aid
She gives her brother's arms. Two sister Pests   1070
There are, called Diræ, whom the unwholesome Night
At the same birth brought forth; with them too came
Tartarean Megæra; snaky coils
About their heads they bore, and wings of wind.
They at the throne of Jove appear, and stand   1075
Upon the threshold of the infernal king,
Sharpening the stings of fear in wretched souls,
Whenever the king of gods prepares disease
And death, or frights the guilty towns with war.
And one of these Jove from on high sends down   1080
To meet Juturna as an ominous sign.
Down in a whirlwind swift to earth she flies,
As when an arrow from a Parthian's bow,
Parthian or Cretan, shot through cloudy skies,
A deadly shaft with cruel poison tipped,   1085
Comes whistling and unseen across the shades;
So flew to earth the daughter of the Night.
      Soon as she beholds the Trojan army,
And Turnus' troops, she all of a sudden shrinks
To the small figure of that bird which sits   1090
At times by night on tombs or lonely towers,
And late and long amid the darkness hoots,
With ominous voice; so changed, in Turnus' sight,
Flies, screaming, back and forth, and beats her wings
Against his shield. Benumbed and chilled   1095
With fear, his limbs relax; his hair with horror stands;
His gasping voice is gone. But when far off
She knew the Fury's cries and whistling wings,
Wretched Juturna tears her loosened locks,
And tears her face, and beats her breast. "What help,   1100
O Turnus, can your sister bring you now?
I, wretched,—what is left for me to do?

Or by what art can I prolong your life?
How can I brave a portent such as this?
Now, now I quit the field. O evil birds,   1105
Do not add terrors to my fear; I know
The beating of your wings, your shrieks of death.
The proud command of Jove cannot deceive
This his return for stolen maidenhood!
Why did he give me an immortal life?   1110
Why take away the fatal law of death?
Surely I might have ended such griefs now,
And to the shades below accompany
My unhappy brother. I immortal? I?
What can be sweet to me of all I own,—   1115
What without you, my brother? Ah, what earth
Can open deep enough for me, and send
A goddess to the shades below!" She spoke;
And round her head a veil of watery blue
She wrapped, and, groaning, plunged into the stream.   1120

Æneas, brandishing his mighty lance,
Comes pressing on, and thus with angry words:—
"What new delay does Turnus plan? Why now
Draw back? It's not a running contest now,
But face to face, with sharp and cruel arms.   1125
Take to yourself all shapes; call to your aid
Whatever you can of valor or of skill;
Aim with your wings to reach the lofty stars,
Or hide yourself in the deep and hollow earth."
But Turnus shook his head: "Your violent words,   1130
Insulter, frighten me not. It is the gods,
And Jove, my enemy, who dismay me now."

He said no more; but, looking round, he sees
An ancient rock,[10] of size immense, that lay
Upon the plain, a landmark between the fields.   1135
Scarcely could twelve chosen men such as the earth
Produces now have borne it on their backs.
With hurried hand the hero grasped the stone,

And rising, ran to hurl it at his foe.
But as he runs, and lifts the ponderous weight, 1140
He does not know what he aims to do; his knees
Totter beneath him, and his blood runs cold.
The stone is hurled through empty air and rolls:
It neither clears the space nor deals the intended blow.
And as in dreams, when languid sleep at night 1145
Weighs down the eyelids, and in vain we strive
To run, with speed that equals our desire,
But yield, disabled, midway in our course;
The tongue and all the accustomed forces fail,
Neither voice nor words ensue;—even so it was 1150
With Turnus;—with whatever valorous strength
His soul aspired, the fiend denied success.
Conflicting thoughts roll hurrying through his breast.
He sees the Rutuli, he sees the town,
And stops in fear, and dreads the threatening steel; 1155
Nor does he know how to escape or how to attack
His enemy, nor anywhere beholds
His chariot or his sister-charioteer.

Thus as he hesitates, Æneas shakes
His fatal spear, and chooses just the spot 1160
To pierce, and hurls the lance with all his strength.
Never did stones from battering engine shot
So rend the air, or thunderbolt resound.
Like a black whirlwind flies the deadly steel, 1165
Through corselet's rim, through sevenfold plated shield,
With ringing stroke, and pierces through his thigh.
Down to the earth upon his bended knee
The mighty Turnus sinks. The Rutuli
Rise all together with a groan. Around
The hills and lofty woods roll back the noise. 1170
He, suppliant and humble, lifts his eyes,
And reaches forth his hand. "This I have deserved
Indeed, nor do I deprecate this blow.
Use now your fortune. If for a wretched sire
You have any regard (such once to you 1175

Your sire Anchises was), pity, I beg,
My father Daunus' venerable age;
And me, or if you would rather, send back,
Despoiled of life, my corpse unto my friends.
You have prevailed. The Ausonians have beheld   1180
A vanquished enemy stretch forth his hands.
Lavinia is your bride. Stretch not your hate
Beyond what you have done."

                                   Stern in his arms
Æneas stood, and rolled his eyes around,[11]
And his right hand repressed; and more and more   1185
Those words began to bend his wavering will;—
When, on the lofty shoulder of his foe
The unlucky belt appeared,—young Pallas' belt
Shone gleaming with its studs he knew so well;
Pallas, whom Turnus overpowered and slew,   1190
And now wore on his shoulders the hostile badge.
He, as his eyes drank in the hateful sight,
Those spoils, memorials of that cruel grief,
Inflamed with fury, terrible in wrath,
"And do you think," he cried, "to escape my hand,   1195
Clothed in the spoils you have snatched from my friend?
It's Pallas, Pallas slays you with this blow,
And takes his vengeance with your accursed blood!"
He spoke, and plunged his sword into his breast.[12]
Relaxed, the limbs lay cold, and, with a groan,   1200
Down to the Shades the soul, indignant, fled.[13]

Endnotes

1. (book 1, line 1) *I sing of arms and of the man:* The famous first words (*arma virumque cano*) introduce the reader to the two main subjects of the poem: man and war. As much a study of human interaction and psychology as of the political fallout from armed confrontation, the twelve books of the epic follow the two thematic threads introduced here. These two nouns also refer to Vergil's most important source: the two epics of Homer, one of which (the *Iliad*) focused on war, the other (the *Odyssey*) on the journey of a man.

2. (1.2–3) *from the coasts of Troy to Italy/And the Lavinian shores:* The geographic boundaries of the poem are set: it will move, broadly speaking, from Troy to Italy and the Lavinian shores. Lavinian refers to Latinus' daughter, Lavinia, who was betrothed to the Latin Turnus but will be married, ultimately, to the Trojan Aeneas. Lavinium was a great cult-center and the site of Aeneas' first settlement in Italy. By specifying that Italy is marked by Lavinian shores the reader is reminded that Troy, too, was more than just a geographic location. The Trojan War began over a similar love triangle when the Trojan Paris abducted the Greek Menelaus' wife, Helen.

3. (1.6) *cruel Juno's sleepless wrath:* Aeneas' antagonist, the goddess Juno, is introduced. Sister and wife of the king of the gods, Jupiter, Juno provides the complications of the plot of the poem. It is possible to see her as the protagonist of one of the themes of the poem, that associated with arms and the wrath of war, while Aeneas, marked as he is by piety, champions the second theme. Whether these forces are opposing or interdependent is one of the questions that surfaces repeatedly throughout the poem.

4. (1.9–10) *the Latin race,/The Alban sires, and walls of lofty Rome:* The triple result of Aeneas' journey is the founding of the Latin race; the succession of Alban leaders; the building of the city of Rome. Each is marked by a different city: Lavinium; Alba Longa, founded by Ascanius and the Trojans' second Italian home; and Rome, founded by Romulus and Remus. Bringing the gods to Latium also refers to the transfer of power from East to West that the poem constantly records and that underlies the imperial plan of the emperor Augustus. See the Introduction.

5. (1.11) *O Muse:* The invocation of the muse is expected at the start of ancient epic. It is striking here because it doesn't appear in the first line of the poem, as it did in Homer, thus asserting the presence of both an author and the higher authority of the muse.

6. (1.16) *Carthage:* With the introduction of Carthage, history enters the poem. The Punic Wars, fought from 264 to 146 B.C., established Rome's pre-eminence in the western Mediterranean. By setting the first third of the epic in Carthage, Vergil makes it clear that the poem will be as much about history as about literature. The setting also allows Vergil to shift the focus of the poem from the East to the Mediterranean basin: the entire poem—its action, as opposed to the flashbacks—takes place in the geographical space between Carthage and Rome. That Vergil identifies Carthage as Juno's favorite enables him to play out the antagonism between the god and the hero in a geographic and historic context.

7. (1.36–38) *The judgment given by Paris . . . snatched Ganymede:* The causes of Juno's anger are listed as three: (1) the Judgment of Paris, in which Paris chose Venus over Juno and Minerva as the most beautiful goddess and was rewarded with the offer of Helen, the most beautiful woman; (2) the hated Trojan race: because of the Judgment of Paris, Juno had supported the Greeks throughout the Trojan War and, as G. P. Goold points out, the Trojan race derives from Dardanus, offspring of Jupiter and Electra, Juno's rival; and (3) honors given Ganymede. Jupiter's infatuation with the boy Ganymede, which resulted in his being made wine steward of the gods, was yet another instance of Jupiter's marital infidelities.

8. (1.44) *Sicily:* Halfway, roughly speaking, between Rome and Carthage, Sicily provides a transitional space in the poem. Aeneas visits the island twice: first on his way from Troy, as detailed in book 3; it is here that his father dies. Aeneas will return to Sicily after he leaves Carthage at the end of book 4.

9. (1.49) *"Shall I who have begun, desist, overcome":* Stressing her isolation and powerlessness, Juno in her opening speech—the first words spoken in the poem—establishes her position as outsider and primary antagonist. Minerva had the power to destroy Ajax "the lesser" after he assaulted Cassandra in Minerva's temple on the last night of Troy; Juno, though sister and wife of Jupiter, wields no such power. The storm she persuades the king of winds, Aeolus, to stir up causes Aeneas to be blown off course and land in Carthage.

10. (1.187–188) *As when/Sedition rises:* The themes of man and war are broadened to include control and rage, as is indicated in this, the first simile of the poem. In addition, the statesman is introduced as being exemplary.

11. (1.201) *there is a place:* The description of Carthage is based at least in part on that, in the *Odyssey*, of Odysseus' landing at Ithaca as he returns home.

12. (1.228) *Æneas climbs upon a cliff:* Aeneas' ascent of the hill re-

minds one of Neptune's ascension from the deep and, later, Jupiter's view down from Olympus. Throughout the poem Vergil associates height with power and authority.

13. (1.293–294) *"O you/Who does rule over men and gods"*: Venus recounts Aeneas' troubles, contrasting him with Antenor, another Trojan, who arrived safely on Italian soil long before Aeneas and is said to have founded Patavium (Padua).

14. (1.333) *"Spare your fears, Cytherea . . ."*: Jupiter's account of Aeneas' legacy complements and fills out the opening lines of the poem as it details the progress of Roman history from Aeneas to Caesar, and it establishes an empire without end, while promising that the gates of war will be shut and "wicked Furor" chained inside.

15. (1.410–411) *To him then, in the middle of a wood,/Appeared his mother*: Aeneas' encounter with his mother is revealing both for her willingness to deceive him and for his naïveté. Nevertheless, she is able to inform him of significant elements of Dido's past, which makes her seem congenial to him and makes it clear to the reader that the two leaders are very similar characters—both exiles by circumstance—in comparable straits.

16. (1.480) *As much as a bull's hide could compass round*: The word Byrsa is etymologically related (falsely) to the Greek word for bull's hide. One story ran that Dido defined the area of her city by cutting the hide into thin strips, or one long concentric ribbon. The length of these pieces, when stretched out, encloses an area of substantial size.

17. (1.544–546) *Following their pathway . . . city and its towers*: Here Vergil begins his description of Carthage. The simile of the bees is taken from Vergil's earlier agricultural poem, the *Georgics*. Vergil often draws on his own earlier works, the *Eclogues* and the *Georgics*. As with his treatment of other poems, however, it is important to consider the change in context and to allow for the introduction of irony.

18. (1.581) *a temple to Juno*: The temple is notable for its wall paintings, or bas-reliefs, which portray scenes from the Trojan War and draw on stories from Homer and the later epic cycle, anonymous and fragmentary ancient Greek poems that round out the story of the heroic age. Given that it is a temple built for Juno, the pictures would, presumably, have depicted Greek victory. As W. R. Johnson points out, what we are given instead are stories of Trojan defeat, since we see the pictures through Aeneas' eyes. The *ekphrasis*, or narrative description of a visual work of art, functions as a hermeneutic tool, suggesting that readings of works of art—literary as well as visual—are dependent on who is doing the reading. The scenes also suggest that for every victory there is a defeat, a theme Vergil returns to frequently throughout the poem.

19. (1.642) *Dido the queen in all her loveliness*: Dido's introduction, in which she is likened to the goddess Diana accompanied by an entourage, is

based on the description of Nausikaa in the *Odyssey* and prepares the way for the description of Aeneas in book 4, where he is likened to Diana's brother, Apollo. The overtly imperial themes (see the Introduction) of the epic are often played off against issues of civil war, which, in turn, are often introduced by discussion of siblings, both mortal and divine.

20. (1.733) *"Trojans, dismiss your fears . . .":* Dido reassures Ilioneus, the Trojan spokesman, that her people both know of and support the Trojan cause. Aeneas and his companion Achates, who have been protected by a cloud, are finally revealed. Aeneas radiates godliness like Odysseus in the land of the Phaeacians.

21. (1.846) *The Grecian Helen's ornaments:* Gift-giving is an interesting thread to follow in the epic, as objects from Greeks and Trojans (and later Arcadians, Latins, etc.) are passed along, much like the transfer of power and myth that the poem relates. Here not only Helen but also her equally significant mother, Leda, are brought into the story.

22. (1.864) *"O son, who are my strength, my mighty power":* Venus, worried for her grandson, arranges to replace Ascanius with Cupid. This decision serves a double purpose: it both protects the Trojan Ascanius, the future of the Roman race, and settles Cupid squarely in Dido's lap, where he, together with the stories Aeneas tells, inflames Dido with love for the Trojan. It is to Venus' advantage for Dido to fall in love with Aeneas, since to the Romans erotic love is at least disabling and often destructive. Cupid would arguably look like Ascanius: he and Aeneas are stepbrothers; at this point Cupid and Ascanius would look roughly the same age.

23. (1.980) *Thus did the unlucky queen prolong the night:* The book ends with a banquet that reinforces allegiances between Tyrians (Dido's countrymen) and Trojans. The song sung by the bard Iopas emphasizes the origins of cosmology, thus making the end of book 1 echo the end of the first book of the *Iliad*. Dido asks to hear about the Trojan War, both the Greek and Trojan sides, and of the seven years that have passed since Troy fell.

BOOK 2

1. (book 2, lines 1–2) *when thus/Æneas from his lofty couch began:* Books 2 and 3 should be read as a unit. Together they constitute the story Aeneas tells Dido following the banquet on the first night in Carthage; the books cover the time from the last night in Troy to the landing in Carthage. Vergil marks the unity of the books in several ways: book 2 begins with the verb *conticuere* (they fell silent), and book 3 ends with a line beginning *conticuit* (he fell silent). The figure of the Greek spy, Sinon, who sets the deceit of the Trojan horse in motion in book 2, is matched by the figure of Achaemenides, a Greek left behind by Odysseus on Sicily and encountered by the Trojans at the end of book 3; in both instances the Trojans heed the Greeks, though with very

different results. Cassandra, whose prophecy is doomed to be ignored, likewise links the books, as she appears at the fall of Troy and is cited several other times on the journey from Troy to Carthage. Within the arc of these constants, however, Vergil strives to indicate change: Sinon's argument is very different from that of Achaemenides; Cassandra's dire figure as Troy falls is contrasted with her astute prophecies as the Trojans make their way toward Italy.

The books are also linked by the fact that they represent, to a large extent, Vergil's own *Iliad* and *Odyssey*, with book 2 telling the tale of Troy, and book 3 the odyssey of Aeneas. In each case, Vergil takes on Homer, doing him one better: where the *Iliad* recounts the ninth year of a ten-year war, book 2 of the *Aeneid* tells of the last night of that epic war, going beyond where the *Iliad* left off and telling the story from a Trojan, not a Greek, perspective. Images of violence pervade the book, both the literal violence of war at Troy and the authorial conflict between a poet and his predecessor. Book 3 of the *Aeneid* alludes to Odysseus' journey while also avoiding any place Odysseus stopped, with the exception of the cyclops' territory in Sicily—and there the looming, pathetic figure of Polyphemus, blind, hovers like the image of Homer himself: weak, impotent, failing in his efforts to dominate the story.

The two books are tightly interwoven within the setting at Carthage. Book 1 of the *Aeneid* ends at night, following the banquet; book 2 begins, also at night, with the Trojan horse story and the last fateful night at Troy. Book 3 heads out of the darkness, smoke, and fog of burning Troy toward the rising sun of Italy: "And now Aurora reddens in the east;/the stars had vanished; when, far off, we see/the dusky mountains and the long low shore/of Italy" (3.662–665). Book 4 begins with the dawn of the day following the banquet. Vergil's ability to weave the story within its frame seamlessly only complicates the questions of ironic juxtaposition that the narrative relies upon.

2. (2.3–4) *O queen, you do command me to renew/A grief unutterable:* Aeneas' emphasis on speech and silence is striking. He is about to introduce the key player in the final downfall of Troy, Sinon, who, through his clever use of words persuades the Trojans to admit the horse filled with Greeks into Troy. Aeneas himself, through the tale he will tell, plays a similar role in Carthage: through his speech he ingratiates himself and his men to Dido. Whether Aeneas is the Trojan horse of Carthage is a reasonable question to ask at this point.

3. (2.20) *a horse:* The story of the Trojan horse is not told in the *Iliad* (though it is recounted by Demodocus in book 8 of the *Odyssey*). As Aeneas explains here, the horse is proffered as an offering to the goddess Pallas Athena (Minerva) and constructed through Pallas' intervention. Filled with Greeks, the horse is the cause of the final fall of Troy.

4. (2.54) *With conflicting views:* Discussion of what to do with the horse—carry it inside the city, throw it into the ocean, burn it—culminates in the priest Laocoön's famous assertion: "I fear the Greeks, even when they

bring us gifts."

5. (2.81) *a young man tightly bound:* Laocoön's admonition is interrupted by the capture of Sinon. Pretending to be a renegade from the Greek army, Sinon begs for clemency in order to escape his fate as the sacrifice the Greeks need to make in order to calm the seas and return home safely (to match the sacrifice of Agamemnon's daughter Iphigenia, required at their departure; see 2.162). Priam, king of the Trojans, takes him in, asking only that he tell them the meaning of the horse. Sinon, forswearing the Greeks, explains that this horse is intended to atone for the stolen Palladium, the sacred image Odysseus and Diomedes took from Pallas' temple: "if by your hands this horse/Should mount into your city, Asia then,/Unchallenged, would advance to Pelops' walls [Mycenae, or Greece in general]/In mighty war, and our posterity/Experience these fates" (2.272–276).

6. (2.282) *Here another dire event . . . :* While sacrificing to Neptune, Laocoön and his two sons are killed by twin serpents that rise up out of the sea. This is interpreted as a sign that Laocoön's warnings were a sacrilege. The horse is brought into the city, despite clear indications that there is something hidden inside it.

7. (2.371) *the hour when first their sleep begins:* As Aeneas sleeps, a vision of Hector appears, the first of many such visions that will come to Aeneas. Hector is the key Trojan fighter in the *Iliad;* it is his encounter with the Greek Achilles, provoked by Hector's killing of the Greek Patroclus, that serves to end the Greek epic. The final confrontation of the *Aeneid* is based on this Iliadic scene, though Aeneas in this case is matched more clearly with Achilles than with Hector. Hector is one of fifty sons of Priam. In this scene he arrives to warn Aeneas of the Greek assault on Troy and to alert him to the fact that he has been chosen as leader of the Trojan band. He hands Aeneas the *penates,* household gods that will travel with the Trojans to Rome and serve as markers of cultural continuity, and urges him to leave.

8. (2.509) *Androgeus meets us . . . :* Androgeus, a Greek, mistakes the Trojans for allies. After he and his comrades are killed, Trojans don their uniforms and pretend to be Greeks. The emphasis here is on how easily dress and language can be manipulated to alter identity. This is important both for its link to Sinon earlier in the book, and for the discussion at the end of the epic about the importance of retaining Latin dress and language when the Trojans are victorious.

9. (2.620) *Priam's walls:* Priam's palace serves as the focus of the city: like its owner, when it falls, Troy has clearly fallen as well. As in the *Iliad* the palace represents even here a place of calm and memories of peaceful times—until Achilles' son, Pyrrhus (Neoptolemus), breaks through the door and kills first Polites, a son of Priam, and then Priam himself at the altar. The desecration of sacred bonds of family as well as sacred places is as clear as it is abhorrent. Behind this scene lie the events from the end of the *Iliad* in

which Priam appeals successfully to Achilles to return Hector's body for burial. Neoptolemus' own death will be told in book 3. Only a short time after Priam's successful appeal, all of these bonds are broken: Achilles' son kills Hector's brother, Priam's son, in front of his father.

10. (2.770–771) *So I alone / Remained:* The sight of Priam kindles Aeneas' memory of his family and he heads home. On the way he encounters Helen, "Tyndarus' daughter," the cause of the war. In a passage whose authenticity is questioned, he plots to kill her, recognizing that she is no threat, but angry that she should be able to return home unscathed. Venus stops Aeneas from harming Helen and shows how the fall of Troy is the will of the gods, not the result of human action. The behind-the-scenes look we are granted of the gods tearing down Troy offers a rare glimpse of the deities Neptune, Juno, Pallas, and even Jupiter all fighting to destroy the city.

11. (2.856) *when I reached my old paternal home . . . :* At home Aeneas succeeds in persuading his father to leave after a double sign occurs: a halo of fire plays around Ascanius' hair, followed by a crack of thunder on the auspicious left side. Aeneas lifts his father, who now agrees to leave Troy, on his shoulders—he was made lame, having been struck by lightning for boasting of his affair with Venus—and leads his son by the hand. The image of three generations burdening each other in different ways, while also helping—Anchises, for example, from his vantage point can see farther ahead and warns Aeneas of the approaching enemy—has become iconic. It did not originate with Vergil, however, having been used, for example, as propaganda by Sextus Pompey before the *Aeneid* was written. Here, though, it is adapted as an image of *pietas* and developed throughout the epic, echoed, for example, at the end of book 8, in Aeneas' shouldering of the shield on which the scenes of the future of Rome are portrayed.

12. (2.999) *I saw her not again:* The loss of Creüsa, Aeneas' first wife, is based on a scene Vergil wrote at the end of the fourth book of his *Georgics* recounting the story of Orpheus and Eurydice, an identification made all the stronger by the fact that Aeneas' wife was traditionally called Eurydice. There the singer Orpheus persuades the infernal powers to release his dead wife as long as he does not look back upon her as he leads her out of the underworld. Here Aeneas goes back into the flames and is unable to retrieve his wife. The ironic pairing of the two scenes questions the power of the hero versus that of the poet. Creüsa's being left in Troy parallels the identification of Italy as the Lavinian shores: throughout the poem land is associated with the feminine. Creüsa's prophecy is vague, suggesting that Aeneas will head west (Hesperian land) although it does specify the Tiber River as the endpoint of the journey.

13. (2.1079–1080) *And now / The star of morning:* With the rising morning star, Aeneas heads away from Troy, joining his comrades and still carrying his father on his shoulders.

BOOK 3

1. (book 3, line 1) *When by the mandate of the gods the power . . . :* Here begins the second half of the story Aeneas tells to Dido. With Troy fallen to the Greeks, Aeneas leads a small band of Trojans away, with only the prophecy of Creüsa to guide them: they are to head west. Clearly modeling his account on Homer's *Odyssey*, Vergil, as he does so often, overlays the literary antecedent with a political purpose: even as he has his hero head out to found his new home and so mimic, to a certain extent, the journey of Odysseus, he also maps out, in this journey, parameters of the future Roman Empire. The journey Aeneas describes, in short, is both exploratory and defining: he lays claim to future imperial rights as he has Aeneas make stops throughout the Mediterranean—even as he revises the *Odyssey* to focus on the Trojan, rather than the Greek, postwar journey. All of the events in the book should be read with this double purpose, one looking back toward Homer, the other looking forward toward the emperor Augustus.

2. (3.18) *Not far away there lies a peopled land . . . :* At Aeneas' first stop the horrors of war are continued in the graphic and metamorphic tale of Polydorus (Polydore in this translation). The youngest son of Priam and Hecuba, he was killed for gold by Polymnestor, king of Thrace, and transformed into a bush whose branches bleed as Aeneas tries to pick them for a sacrificial offering. This city was to be called Aeneades, as spelled in this edition. Polymnestor's greed prompts the narrator to ask: *Quid non mortalia pectora cogis / auri sacra fames* ("Cursèd thirst for gold, / What crimes do you not prompt in mortal breasts?" [3.70–71]), a question that hangs over the third book as a whole as well as over the memory of fallen Troy.

3. (3.92) *Amid the sea there lies a lovely isle:* Escaping from Polydorus, the Trojans sail to Delos, their second stop, where Apollo tells them they are to seek out their "ancient mother." Anchises interprets this oracle as referring to Crete, since that is where Teucer, the Trojan progenitor, was born.

4. (3.169) *And upon Crete and our forefathers call:* No sooner have they settled in Crete, the Trojan's third stop, and started to found the city of Pergamea but a plague strikes, nearly wiping them out. The *penates* appear to Aeneas in a dream and tell him that the ancient mother is not Crete but Hesperia, since that is where Dardanus was born. Anchises recalls that Cassandra had foretold this, but because of Apollo's curse on Cassandra, no one believed her. The significance of this identification is discussed in the Introduction; the fact that the Trojans have a homeland that is not only not Troy but, more to the point, pre-dates Troy is tremendously important for the overall purpose of the poem.

5. (3.270–271) *I landed on the shores/And islands of the Strophades:* Heading farther west, the Trojans make their fourth stop the Strophades, only to be attacked there by the Harpies, monsters that are part female, part bird of prey. Phineus, king of Thrace, who was struck blind by the gods for tormenting his children, had been tormented by the Harpies until he was freed from them by the Argonauts, who chased the Harpies to the Strophades. Celaeno warns that the Trojans, having eaten all the Harpies' livestock, will reach Italy, but not before they are forced to eat their plates, a prophecy that is fulfilled, in a sense, in book 7.

6. (3.355) *Thus having gained the unexpected coast:* Heading up the western shore of Greece, the Trojans sail past Ithaca, home and *telos* (goal) of Odysseus and the *Odyssey*. The fact that the Trojans pass Ithaca without stopping suggests that the *Aeneid* will not cover the same ground as the earlier epic; it will outstrip the earlier work. The Trojans then land at Actium, their fifth stop, where they "make Actium famed with Trojan games." As Vergil will show clearly in his description of the shield in book 8, the later battle at Actium (31 b.c.) between Octavian and his opponent, Mark Antony, is the decisive moment in Octavian's rise to power. By stopping at Actium, Aeneas lays claim to the land for the later emperor and predicts his victory there. At the time the *Aeneid* is being written, the emperor Augustus had instituted games at Actium, in celebration of his naval victory. Both of these are acknowledged by Aeneas' actions.

7. (3.376) *Here an incredible report we hear:* Leaving Actium, Aeneas stops at Buthrotum, where he finds a small-scale replica of Troy, inhabited by the Trojans Andromache, Hector's wife, and her new husband, Hector's brother, the prophet Helenus. Helenus fills out Aeneas' picture of what lies ahead by telling him to hug the southern shore of Italy, but not to land, and warns him of the straits between Italy and Sicily, telling him to avoid passing through them, ostensibly because of the dangers of Scylla and Charybdis, but also marking his differences from earlier wandering heroes like Odysseus and Jason, both of whom had passed through the straits. For both of these earlier heroes as well, the western edge of Italy marks the western limit of their journey, while for Aeneas, as we have seen, Carthage and Sicily are to be included. It is also significant that Helenus does not mention a stop at Carthage. Likewise, he mentions that Aeneas must travel to the underworld, but he omits the fact that he will see his father there.

8. (3.644) *our way to Italy:* Bidding farewell to his countrymen, Aeneas and his men cross the sea and come within sight of the Italian peninsula for the first time. They greet it with a triple cry of "Italy!" But as they approach, it seems to threaten war as well as peace. They see a temple to Pallas, and they worship Juno, covering their heads as Helenus had instructed.

9. (3.740) *At length the early dawn arose:* Here they meet Achaemenides, a Greek abandoned to the cyclops by Odysseus. Like Sinon, Achaemenides appeals to the Trojans who, again, show clemency. The only place where the *Odyssey* actually intersects with the *Aeneid*, this is also the least Odyssean of moments in book 3: while the details of Achaemenides'

story come directly from the *Odyssey*, the tone is entirely alien to it. Achaemenides represents Odysseus as a selfish, arrogant character, more in keeping with what the Trojans would have felt than the Greeks. Despite the similarity with the disastrous Sinon episode at the beginning of book 2, the result here is entirely different: having taken Achaemenides on board, the Trojans sail swiftly around Sicily, as Achaemenides points out landmarks along the way, thus helping them on their journey. The details here come not from Homer but from the Hellenistic poet Callimachus and suggest the influence of Hellenistic sources. The portrayal of Achaemenides as helpful rather than deceitful complicates the identification of Aeneas: is he, in Carthage, more like Sinon or Achaemenides? Will he be destructive to Dido or helpful?

10. (3.868–870) *Alpheus, Elis' river . . . Mingles with Arethusa's stream:* In a tale told in detail by Ovid, Arethusa was a Greek nymph who, attempting to escape the river-god Alpheus, was led underground to Sicily. Surfacing there, Arethusa was transformed into a spring, where she mingled with the waters of Alpheus, who had succeeded in following her there.

11. (3.882–883) *Then the port/Of Drepanum receives me:* The Trojans land at Drepanum, near Eryx, which is named for Aeneas' half-brother, slain by Hercules. The place was marked in Vergil's time by a temple to Venus Erycina. It is here that Aeneas' father dies unexpectedly; and from here that Aeneas and his men, as they start what they believe will be the last leg of their trip to Italy, are blown off course to Carthage.

BOOK 4

1. (book 4, line 1) *But pierced with grievous pangs long since, the queen . . . :* With book 4 we re-enter the *Aeneid*'s present. Back in Carthage, Aeneas' story is over, the night is through, and Dido is portrayed as having fallen in love with Aeneas, a condition likened through imagery to a wound. Throughout the book the identification of Dido as a wounded animal is strong, as is imagery of sacrifice. The question, however, remains: sacrifice to what? Is she sacrificed to Jupiter as a cost of the great cause of founding the Roman Empire, or is she sacrificed to Juno as a means of keeping her cause in play? Both are arguably true: the Roman Empire would not have been founded if Aeneas had stayed in Carthage, and had Dido not died tragically, Juno's cause would not have been promoted through the curse Dido levels against the Trojans.

In Latin, Dido's story begins with the adversative conjunction *at* ("but") that sets the tone for the book. Not only have we shifted from Aeneas' flashback to the action of the epic, but the perspective has shifted as well, from that of the narrator in book 1 and Aeneas in books 2 and 3 to Dido's perspective now in book 4. Throughout book 4 we are privy to Dido's thoughts and actions, and for the most part we view Aeneas from the outside.

This extends to Dido's death as well: we stay with Dido until her death, whereas Aeneas has already left.

2. (4.28) *I see the traces of my earlier flame:* Dido's husband, Sychaeus, was killed by her brother-in-law Pygmalion. She had sworn allegiance to Sychaeus and resists involvement with Aeneas as a result. Dido's sister, Anna, argues for forging a connection with Aeneas on the grounds that Dido needs the ally in this new land. It is an argument that Aeneas himself will make when he reaches Italy, and speaks to the importance of Carthage. Set against the history of the Punic Wars, in which the fate of the Western powers hovered precariously between Carthage and Rome, these arguments would have resonated strongly with Vergil's audience.

3. (4.91) *as a heedless deer:* The simile of the wounded deer offers insight into both Dido's and Aeneas' positions: the narrator suggests that Dido is a wounded animal—perhaps sacrificial—but Aeneas as well is presented as inept: he has wounded the deer unintentionally and unknowingly. If Dido is a sacrificial animal, perhaps it is fairest to see Aeneas as a sacrificial agent. Neither is fully in control.

4. (4.113) *Towers that were begun:* The association here between language and building is one that Vergil follows throughout the epic. When Dido is introduced in book 1, her strength as statesman is tacitly confirmed by the progress of her building program. This identification between effective rhetoric and architecture is expanded to suggest an alliance between speech and civilization: when the gods are shown to have power in book 1, it is through the careful use of speech. The association between speech and civilization—between speaking Latin well and being a good Roman—is one that Cicero articulates and that becomes the cornerstone of Roman republican thought. The emperor Augustus, though using it for different ends, adopts this identification between language and power; it is this identification that Vergil uses as the basis for the association here between building and speech and, in Dido's case, for love as the destroyer of both.

5. (4.119–120) *a subtle pest/Possessed the queen:* If Dido is a sacrificial animal, it is love that has caused the wound and the disease that permeates her body. Love as a disease is a trope that recurs frequently in Greco-Roman literature.

6. (4.138) *Then Venus answered:* Venus and Juno's agreement here that Dido and Aeneas will become involved is made from the goddesses' own vantage points. Juno, as goddess of marriage, believes that an alliance between Dido and Aeneas will keep Rome from being founded, while Venus, as the goddess of erotic love, has already suggested, starting in book 1, that she believes desire will destroy Dido.

7. (4.170) *Meanwhile Aurora from the ocean wakes:* The appearance of both Dido and Aeneas at the hunt is significant. Dido is likened to a hesitant bride, with echoes of the long epithalamium by Catullus (Carmen 64)

while Aeneas is compared to Apollo, thereby recalling Dido's initial entrance in book 1, where she was likened to Diana. The fact that Aeneas is not just Apollo but Apollo on Delos, his birthplace, complicates the image: on the one hand, it suggests that Aeneas, like Apollo, is home; on the other, it reminds us of the fact that, for Aeneas, Delos was determined to be a temporary home when he and his men landed there in book 3. Is he home, like Apollo in Delos, or is this a temporary home, like Aeneas in Delos?

8. (4.199) *The mountains steep, and pathless haunts of beasts:* The image of Ascanius hunting wild animals in the mountains outside Carthage is a rare carefree moment in the text, with resonances of the Homeric Hymn to Hermes, an ancient Greek poem that tells of the birth and exploits of the god Hermes (Roman Mercury).

9. (4.215–216) *Dido and the Trojan prince/Find refuge in the same cave:* Dido and Aeneas seek refuge in a cave during a storm that Juno causes while they're on the hunt. Dido, the text says, calls it marriage, "and beneath this name/Conceals her fault."

10. (4.227–228) *Then through the cities wide . . . flies Rumor forth:* The association of height with power is played out in two complementary images: on the one hand, there is the quasi-allegorical representation of Rumor, who is said to be the daughter of Tellus (Earth) and a monster who grows with the telling. Like a medieval personification allegory, the traits of the abstract concept are presented in concrete, physical terms. Rumor has as many eyes as tongues; she starts small and continues to grow as she moves. Rumor's power is undone by the opposite action: through Rumor, Dido's suitor Iarbas hears of Aeneas and complains to Jupiter, who then sends Mercury down from Olympus to warn Aeneas that he must not stay in Carthage. Mercury's downward journey is as graphic as Rumor's upward growth, as his flight is identified by the main landmark of Atlas' mountain, which he passes en route. In addition to establishing almost an Ariel and Caliban quality to the pair—Mercury flits by the stolid and frozen Atlas—this passage serves to counteract whatever power Rumor had acquired, asserts the strength of Olympus over the older gods, and introduces the figure of Atlas into the equation. Atlas, we will learn in book 8, was the source of the Trojan race and an ancestor shared with Evander, the Arcadian who will become an ally of Aeneas as a result of this blood relationship. He is the rock on which the whole enterprise is founded; significantly, he has no connection whatsoever with Carthage.

11. (4.335) *and cut the Libyan winds:* "I have intentionally omitted the line 'Materno veniens ab avo Cyllenia proles,' for three reasons: 1. It is superfluous; 2. It is awkward and out of place; 3. It belongs to a passage whose authenticity is suspected.—Tr. [translator's note]." The line can be translated as "The Cyllenian offspring coming from his maternal grandfather." There seems to be no justification for the translator's concern here: the line is not

suspect and, far from being "superfluous" it introduces the importance of genealogy to this scene.

12. (4.394) *At length Æneas she addresses thus:* The speeches between Dido and Aeneas are indicative of their mutual rhetorical prowess. Dido, accusing Aeneas of fleeing her (he is, after all, in exile), is told by Aeneas that he is not in flight but instead pursues Italy, though not of his own free will: *Italiam non sponte sequor* ("Not of my own accord/Do I seek Italia"). Italy, he claims, is his love and his country. Dido tells him to pursue Italy, but she will follow him, even after she is dead. The imagery here is evocative, as Cleopatra, depicted on the shield in book 8, is likewise shown to be a woman pursuing her man. Throughout book 4 Aeneas has been portrayed—by Iarbas, among others—increasingly as a decadent easterner, a description used in Augustan propaganda of Antony, as a result of his affiliation with Cleopatra. By suggesting a similarity between Dido and Aeneas and Cleopatra and Antony the narrator succeeds in enabling Aeneas to leave. Dido is not so lucky, but before her final downward spin into suicide she, too, wrests some power for the future through her curse against Aeneas.

13. (4.540) *What were your thoughts, O Dido, seeing this?:* Dido's downward spiral is actually an upward ascension: the narrator seemingly wrests himself away from Aeneas and, in addressing Dido directly, makes it clear that she, at this moment at least, is in a position of power. As she looks down on the Trojans from her tower, they are likened to ants. Dido holds the gaze of the text, while the Trojans merely scurry around in preparation for departure. This sense of power continues as she tricks her sister into building her funeral pyre and, before dying, levels a curse that will ensure a future for her people through enmity between Carthage and Rome: the curse both paves the way for the Punic Wars and establishes Carthage as Rome's greatest enemy.

14. (4.559–560) *Go, sister, speak to him,/This haughty enemy, with suppliant words:* Dido asserts that she is no sworn enemy to Aeneas and his people, having neither sworn allegiance with the Greeks as they set sail at Aulis, nor, more recently, troubled Aeneas' father's ghost.

15. (4.583–584) *As when the Alpine winds contend/Against an oak:* The simile that compares Aeneas to an unbending oak tree, with his roots in Tartarus and his branches in Olympus, aligns him with the unmoving Atlas earlier in the book and helps reorient our perception of him, especially when Mercury shows up not once but twice, urging him to leave at Jupiter's request, because a woman is *varium et mutabile* ("a fickle, changeful thing" [4.753]). The tree's leaves, however, do fall like tears.

16. (4.823) *O, may some avenger rise:* This and the five lines that follow detail Dido's curse, establishing a justification for the Punic Wars.

17. (4.879) *The flames were rolling:* Dido's funeral pyre is likened to the burning of Tyre. Aeneas has become the enemy, invading a foreign land and leaving it in ruins. From a fellow exile, an Apollo to Dido's Diana, Ae-

neas has been transformed into the enemy, a Greek to Dido's Trojan.

BOOK 5

1. (book 5, line 1) *Æneas with his fleet was sailing on:* The fifth book is pivotal. Opening off the coast of Carthage, it closes off the coast of Italy. The action in between takes place in Sicily, a transitional space in its own right. The bulk of the book focuses on games held in celebration of the anniversary of Anchises' death a year earlier in Sicily. In this Vergil is both looking back to the funeral games for Patroclus in the twenty-third book of the *Iliad* and forward to the lusus Troiae, equestrian drills instituted by Augustus. Other transitional themes emerge: as much mention is made of the Roman future as of the Trojan past; Anchises' funeral is balanced by the coming-of-age war exercises of Ascanius; the decision at the end of the book to leave the older Trojans on the island signals a shedding of the past in preparation for the advent of Romanness in the later books. If the entire *Aeneid* is about the movement from Troy to Rome and past to future, book 5 presents these themes in their most crystalline form.

The book opens with Aeneas looking back, in confusion, at Dido's funeral pyre in Carthage. Aeneas is spared the direct confrontation with Dido's death that the reader is forced to experience. Not unlike his arrival in Carthage, swaddled in a cloud, Aeneas' departure, wrapped in unknowingness, enables him to move on unimpeded.

2. (5.12) *When overhead there stood a dark gray cloud:* The storm they encounter—the cause of which here remains unexplained— parallels the one that swept them off course to Carthage in book 1. Here it blows them back to Sicily, where the Trojan Acestes spies them from a hilltop. Comparable to the greeting they will receive on the Italian peninsula, first from Latinus, then from Pallas and Evander, Acestes' welcome, like Dido's, suggests they have arrived somewhere established.

3. (5.57) *"Brave Dardans, race of lineage divine":* Realizing that a year has passed since Anchises' death, Aeneas announces that he will institute a series of competitions involving Trojans and Sicilians to celebrate his father's death. Consisting of four games plus an adumbration of future prowess, the men gather to participate in a boat race, a foot race, a boxing match, and an archery match; the young men then follow with an exhibition of their horsemanship. In each case the competition shows off qualities of the men in a limited play space with low stakes, as contrasted to the later high-stakes competitions of battle. Presented in a structure that is Iliadic, the particular details revealed are Roman. In each case, the competition involves the interaction of Trojan and Sicilian, the intervention of divine forces, and the identification of Aeneas as a just ruler.

4. (5.141–143) *four well-matched ships . . . Enter the lists:* The boat

race is based on the chariot race in *Iliad* 23, as Vergil indicates through the simile in 5.179–187. In this race the men are introduced in relation to the Roman families each will establish. Aeneas rewards the participants with gifts of varying worth.

5. (5.347) *a race-course ran:* The foot race focuses on the friendship between Nisus and Euryalus, and the strong bond evident there. Their willingness to sacrifice one for the other will be played out in a larger arena, with higher stakes, in book 9.

6. (5.434) *"And raise his arms, his hands with gauntlets bound":* In this boxing match, the Trojan contender, Dares, who "alone with Paris could contend," first cannot find an opponent. Acestes, the Sicilian host, finally convinces Entellus, the Sicilian trained by Aeneas' half-brother Eryx, to enter the competition. The ensuing fight illustrates two things: the interaction between Trojans and native Sicilians, and the rage of battle. Aeneas is noteworthy for his insistence on a fair match, which includes supplying both contenders with the same weight boxing gloves and stopping the fight before anyone gets killed. Dares is led away when Entellus, in the heat of the moment, attacks mercilessly, and each is awarded a prize. Entellus receives a bull, which he sacrifices with one blow to Eryx.

7. (5.576) *Then all who would contend in archery:* A dove is fastened to the top of a mast. Four men strive to shoot it off. The first strikes the mast, the second the rope the bird is attached by, thus freeing it. The third shoots the bird. The fourth, Acestes, sends his arrow into the air, where it bursts into flames. This is seen as an omen, because of which Acestes is named victor.

8. (5.641–642) *"Go now,/And tell Ascanius . . .":* The description of Ascanius' exhibition match likewise links the past and future, as the future Romans show up looking just like their Trojan fathers. Their weaving paths are likened first to the labyrinth in Crete, then to dolphins in the sea: first to the past the Trojans recently escaped, then to the future, where Octavian will identify dolphins as symbolic of his victory at Actium; it is for this reason that dolphins are shown cavorting on the shield. Vergil links this equestrian exhibition to the games revived and expanded by the emperor Augustus.

9. (5.708) *Here, changing Fortune showed an altered face:* Juno sends Iris, in disguise as the Trojan Beroë, to the tired and disgruntled older Trojan women who are away from the games and lamenting the never-ending journey toward Hesperia. She refers to Italy as *fugientem* ("an Italy that flees before" [5.743–744]), which is in keeping with its description, and that of so many goals, throughout the first half of the poem. Like Creüsa in Troy, Italy escapes the Trojans' grasp. Juno causes the women to set fire to the ships in an effort to remain in Sicily. This story is told elsewhere of the Trojan women, yet it usually is set in Italy proper; it is Vergil's innovation to place it in Sicily. The burning ships result in Aeneas' decision, with the help of the gods, to invite those too tired to travel on to Italy to remain behind in Sicily, where Ae-

neas lays out a proto-Roman town, leaves behind a leader who establishes law, etc. In this, Vergil draws on the notion that Sicily was the first province and follows Cicero's identification (in *Verrines* 2.2.1) of Sicily as the land that made the Romans realize the benefits of empire. Aeneas leaves behind some Trojans to coexist with Sicilians, thus setting up the model for future provinces.

10. (5.857) *A vision of Anchises' face:* Aeneas receives a prophecy from his father, telling him he must visit the underworld and see him there.

11. (5.928) *But Venus, full of cares and fears:* Venus appeals now to Neptune, to make sure her son and grandson will survive these latest trials. Neptune's response takes the reader back to the *Iliad*.

12. (5.1002) *O Palinurus!:* The book ends with the death of the helmsman Palinurus, who falls overboard, leaving Aeneas completely in charge. Throughout the book he has increasingly acquired greater leadership responsibilities. Here near the end of the Trojan sea journey, he becomes the sole helmsman.

BOOK 6

1. (book 6, line 1) *Weeping he spoke, then gave his fleet the reins:* Aeneas' journey to the underworld is a book often read in isolation, as it offers the most typological events in the epic. Yet book 6 is more deeply integrated into the poem as a whole than any of the others. Picking up on the transitional theme of book 5, where before our eyes Trojans are made Romans and Trojan virtues are understood in terms of their Roman legacy, book 6 spells out in vivid detail how history will unfold from Aeneas' sons down to Vergil's own time. The book is framed by two *ekphrases* (narrative descriptions of visual spectacles), which, like the *ekphrasis* on the temple walls in Carthage, guide us in looking at the narrative work we are engaged in reading. Between these two *ekphrases* lie a series of confrontations between Aeneas and characters from his past, including the helmsman Palinurus, who died on the trip from Sicily, and Dido herself, who appears in the company of her first husband. The book ends with an allusion to Homer's *Odyssey*, as Aeneas and his father leave the underworld through the gate of false dreams, derived from the dream of Penelope in book 19 of the *Odyssey*.

Not only is book 6 linked to the transitional themes of book 5; more strikingly, it should be read in conjunction with book 7. These two books, taken as a pair, bridge the divide between the two halves of the poem, and offer us two angles on very similar material. In book 6 we travel with Aeneas to the underworld, which Vergil asserts lies directly beneath the Italian peninsula; he enters it at Cumae. In this book he encounters a series of heroic figures, who present him with a pro-imperial view of the Roman mission. In 7, as we shall see, we encounter Italy on a different level, as Aeneas lands at present-day Ostia and travels up the Tiber to Latium. The two journeys are laid against one another and should be read as a diptych. Moreover, while book 6 is peopled with imperial males, book 7 is marked by the presence of women, starting with Caieta, Aeneas' nurse, who is buried on Italian soil, and moves through the stories of other females, including Circe, Amata, Lavinia, Juno, and Allecto, and ending with Camilla, the Volscian warrior who fights for the Latins. We are thus offered Italy, when we get there, from two different angles, although we are left to sort out the meaning on our own. The imperial message of book 6 is tempered by the indigenous message of book 7, even as the masculine voice that predominates in book 6 is matched by the feminine voice that prevails in book 7.

The journey to the underworld is preceded by a description of a temple to Apollo at Cumae built by Daedalus after his escape from the island of Crete. Like Aeneas, he journeyed west, landing, in most accounts, on Sicily. Vergil moves his landing to Italy to underscore the parallel between Daedalus and his hero. The temple has doors with bas-reliefs that tell the stories of Daedalus' exploits on Crete, from building the labyrinth to house the minotaur to Ariadne's escape with the help of Theseus. Vergil as narrator makes a point of saying that the one story Daedalus doesn't depict is that of the death of Icarus, who fell into the sea when he failed to heed his father's advice.

Aeneas' trip to the underworld depends on several first steps: he must talk to the Sibyl, prove that he is worthy of the trip by obtaining the golden bough and burying a recently lost comrade, and pass successfully by a series of monsters after crossing the River Styx in the company of the boatman Charon. These steps have become canonical to us. Dante draws heavily on each of these phases, but Vergil's sources are less clear. Aeneas lists his predecessors in this type of *catabasis*, or underworld journey—Orpheus, Pollux, Theseus, and Hercules—yet Vergil adds his own touches.

2. (6.56) *The Sibyl's answers:* The Cumaean Sibyl, one of ten female prophets in the ancient world, foretells both Aeneas' immediate tasks at hand—the descent, she says, is easy, the return hard—and also the longer-range jobs ahead. She refers to the battles for Italy as the war of a "new Troy." Apollo had offered to give the Cumaean Sibyl whatever she asked for; she requested longevity (to live as long as the number of grains of sand in her hand) but neglected to request youth or beauty.

3. (6.176) *There is a golden bough:* The golden bough is a talisman: it glitters unnaturally in the midst of the forest and rattles on its tree. The Sibyl tells Aeneas that he will either be able to pluck it right off, or no matter how hard he tries it will not yield. As Michael Putnam has argued, the answer is somewhere in the middle: the bough hesitates before yielding, suggesting that Aeneas is a hero, but perhaps not "the" hero.

4. (6.337–338) *before the very vestibule/Of opening Orcus:* The entrance to the underworld is marked in the narrative by allegorical descriptions

of abstract concepts and, sitting under a huge elm tree, shapes of monsters, including some of the exiled giants as well as other monstrous mythological figures, such as the Harpies.

5. (6.367) *By these dread rivers waits the ferryman:* Crossing the River Styx, in a boat steered by Charon, Aeneas then encounters the monsters Cerberus, who is calmed with a honeycake (which Dante will transmute into the mudcake of his *Inferno*) and Minos (who, in Dante's hands, will indicate the circle of hell an individual will inhabit by the number of times his tail wraps around him).

6. (6.544) *Not far from this the Fields of Mourning:* The purpose of Aeneas' journey to the underworld is to meet up with his recently deceased father, who is to give him guidance on his future in Italy. Before he locates his father, however, in the blessed groves, he passes through the Fields of Mourning and the region of the war heroes. He walks by but does not enter into Tartarus, where the Sibyl relates stories of those punished there. Turning right at a fork in the road, he enters the blessed groves, where he meets members of Teucer's line, which includes his father. His father points out to him the heroes of the future Roman race.

7. (6.550) *Here Phaedra and here Procris he now sees:* Starting here, Aeneas meets a series of mythological figures marked by love. *Phaedra* (6.550): King Minos' daughter and wife of Theseus, she was caused by Venus to fall in love with her stepson, Hippolytus. When he rejected her, she falsely accused him of loving her and caused his death. Overcome by remorse, she committed suicide. *Procris* (6.550): She doubted the fidelity of her husband, Cephalus, and followed him one day on a hunt. Hearing her rustling in a bush and believing she was an animal, he threw his javelin and killed her. *Eriphyle* (6.551): She sent her husband—Amphiaraüs, king of Argos—to fight and die in the battle of the seven against Thebes. Her son Alcmaeon killed her to avenge his father. *Evadne* (6.552): When her husband, Capaneus, one of the seven against Thebes, died in battle, she threw herself on his funeral pyre. *Pasiphaë* (6.553): King Minos' wife, she was caused by Neptune to love a bull. Daedalus built a cow costume for her so that she could mate with the bull. The offspring from this mating was the monstrous Minotaur. *Laodamia* (6.554): Her husband, Protesilaus, was destined to be the first Greek warrior to fall at Troy. She killed herself in order to follow him to the underworld. *Caenis* (6.554): Neptune transformed the nymph Caenis into a man, who took the name Caeneus. *Dido* (6.556): Most significant for Aeneas is Dido, whose depiction is based on that of Odysseus' encounter with Ajax in the underworld and the Argonauts' glimpse of Hercules at the grove of the Hesperides. Like Ajax, and in marked contrast to her role in book 4, Dido maintains a stony silence in the face of Aeneas' pleading.

8. (6.591–592) *by those frequented who in war/Were famous:* After leaving the Fields of Mourning, Aeneas and his guide encounter those

renowned in war. *Tydeus* (6.592): A Greek warrior in the seven against Thebes and father of Diomedes. *Parthenopaeus* (6.593): Son of Atalanta, he was one of the seven against Thebes. *Adrastus* (6.594): Leader of the attack of the seven against Thebes, he was destined to live, though the other six die. Ten years later, he led the six sons of the fallen warriors in another attack on Thebes and razed it to the ground. *Glaucus* (6.597): A Trojan warrior, he was the son of Hippolochus and commander of the Lycians. *Medon* (6.597): A Trojan warrior, he was a son of Antenor. *Thersilochus* (6.598): A Trojan warrior, he was another son of Antenor. *Polyphoetes* (6.599): Also known as Polyboetes, he was a Trojan priest of Ceres. *Idaeus* (6.600): A Trojan warrior, he was Priam's chariot driver. *Deiphobus* (6.612): Son of Priam and Hecuba, he married Helen after Paris' death.

9. (6.687–688) *No strength of man, or even of gods, avails/Against it:* Aeneas is not allowed to enter Tartarus, but he is told who lives there: *Tisiphone* (6.689): one of the avenging Furies along with Allecto and Megaera; *Rhadamanthus* (6.703): son of Jupiter, brother of Minos; he became a judge in Elysium, presiding over Tartarus, for his practice of justice in life; *Hydra* (6.715): a fifty-headed monster; *Titans* (6.720): the twelve children of Uranus and Gaia, who ruled before Jupiter overthrew them; *sons of Aloeus* (6.723): Otus and Ephialtes, the twin sons of the giant Aloeus; together they attempted to reach Jupiter by piling Mount Pelion on Mount Ossa and Ossa on Olympus, but were defeated; *Salmoneus* (6.726): brother of Sisyphus; when he fashioned himself the equal of Jupiter, Jupiter struck him with a thunderbolt; *Tityos* (6.739): a giant killed by Apollo and Diana for attempting to rape their mother, Latona; *Pirithoüs* (6.747): a son of Ixion's wife and friend of Theseus; together, the two attempted to carry Proserpina out of the underworld but were caught and chained to a rock; Hercules later managed to save Theseus but left Pirithoüs behind; *Ixion* (6.747): a mortal who dared to love Juno; when Jupiter discovered his deceit and made a phantom of his wife, Ixion mated with the phantom and fathered the centaurs, and Jupiter punished him by affixing him to a rack-like wheel; *the race of Lapithae* (6.748): a people ruled by Pirithoüs, at whose wedding they were attacked by centaurs, whom they defeated; *Theseus* (6.769): fabled king of Athens and hero of many exploits; the most famous was his trick to kill the Minotaur in the labyrinth of Crete and steal away with Minos' daughter, Ariadne, whom he later abandoned; *Phlegyas* (6.770): father of Ixion and ancestor of the Lapithae; he burned a temple of Apollo and was therefore punished in Tartarus.

10. (6.795–796) *they reach the pleasant realms/Of verdant green, the blessed groves of peace:* Finally, Aeneas and his guide reach the blessed groves, where Anchises, Aeneas's father, resides. Here they encounter *Teucer* (6.806): traditional ancestor of the Trojans; it is from his name that the Trojans are sometimes called Teucri; *Ilus* (6.808): a son of Tros and a founder of

Troy, which is sometimes called Ilium from his name; grandfather of Priam; *Assaracus* (6.808): a son of Tros and the grandfather of Anchises; *Dardanus* (6.808): son of Jupiter and Electra and ancestor of Priam; he became the mythological founder of Troy; as a result, the Trojans are often called Dardanians; *Musaeus* (6.830): a mythological Thracian poet.

11. (6.904) *"Know first, the heavens, the earth, the flowing sea . . ."*: This is Anchises' explanation of the fate of a ghost after death. First there is a long stage of purgation. Once the soul is fully purified, it enters Elysium for a period of a thousand years (or longer, if blessed), at which stage it is reborn into a new body after drinking from the waters of Lethe, which erase any memory of its former existence. The purgation souls endure is dictated by the life they have led.

12. (6.944–945) *"Hear now what fame henceforth shall attend/The Dardan race"*: Here are named future Roman heroes, heirs to Aeneas: *Silvius* (6.953): the son of Aeneas and Lavinia, king of Alba Longa, a city in Latium founded by Ascanius; *Procas* (6.958): king of Alba Longa some time after Silvius; father of Numitor and Amulius; *Capys* (6.959): king of Alba Longa; *Numitor* (6.959): king of Alba Longa, father of Ilia (also called Rhea Silvia) and grandfather of Romulus and Remus; *Silvius Aeneas* (6.960): a king of Alba Longa of whom little is known except that he was kept from his throne; *Romulus* (6.970): son of Ilia and Mars, eponymous founder of Rome; his uncle Amulius, who deposed Numitor in Alba Longa, ordered that Romulus and his twin brother, Remus, be drowned, but instead they were abandoned, suckled by a she-wolf, and reared by a farmer; grown up, the brothers defeated Amulius, restored Numitor at Alba Longa, and founded Rome on the Tiber (with this Vergil skillfully elides the competing foundation myth of the city, suggesting that Romulus and Remus founded Rome on the land originally scouted out by Aeneas generations before); *Caesar* (6.986): a Roman statesman, Julius Caesar (100–44 B.C.) ascended through the political ranks of the republic to become the most powerful man in Rome of his day; after defeating his rival, Pompey, he would have been crowned emperor had he not been assassinated; *Augustus Caesar* (6.990): (63 B.C.–A.D. 14; known as Octavian) the adopted son of Caesar, who defeated Sextus Pompey and Mark Antony in the wars that followed Caesar's death and so became the first emperor of Rome; *Tullus* (6.1019): Tullus Hostilius, third king of Rome after Romulus and Numa; he attacked and destroyed Alba Longa; *Ancus* (6.1021): Ancus Martius, fourth king of Rome; *Brutus* (6.1024): member of the Junian clan who expelled the Tarquin family of kings and established the Roman Republic in 510 B.C.; *Decii* (6.1034): a father and son, both named Publius Decius Mus; both sacrificed their lives in wars for Rome; *Drusus and his line* (6.1034): a powerful family of Roman aristocrats that bore many consuls and senators, and of which Augustus' wife Livia was a member; *Torquatus* (6.1035): Titus Manlius earned the name Torquatus, which refers to a kind of

necklace, by killing an enormous Celt in a war against the Gauls in 361 B.C.; *Camillus* (6.1036): Marcus Furius Camillus was a Roman dictator who defeated the Gauls after they had sacked Rome in 390 B.C.; *Cato* (6.1056): (234–149 B.C.) Marcus Porcius Cato, also called Cato the Elder; a Roman statesman and stern moralist, he advocated the absolute destruction of Carthage in the Punic Wars; *Cossus* (6.1057): Aulus Cornelius Cossus: Roman consul, in 428 B.C., he killed the Etruscan king Lars Tolumnius and dedicated his breastplate to Jupiter; *Gracchi* (6.1057): generally refers to two brothers, Tiberius Gracchus (tribune of the plebs in 133 B.C.) and Gaius Sempronius Gracchus (tribune of the plebs in 123 and 122 B.C.); both were killed for attempting constitutional reforms; *Scipios* (6.1058): two Roman statesmen-general, Scipio Africanus (c. 236–183 B.C.), who defeated Hannibal in 202, and his grandson through adoption, Scipio Aemilianus (c. 185–129 B.C.), who destroyed Carthage in 146; *Fabricius* (6.1059): Roman consul in 282 and 278 B.C.; the staunch opponent of Pyrrhus of Epirus; *Serranus* (6.1060): cognomen of Regulus, called to the consulship in 257 B.C. while sowing his fields, from which he gets his name (*serere* is Latin for "to sow"); *Fabii* (6.1061): Q. Fabius Maximus Cunctator, of the powerful Fabii clan; known as Cunctator ("Delayer") because of his delaying tactics that successfully wore down Hannibal's army; *Marcellus* (6.1074): (died 208 B.C.) Roman general against the Gauls in the Second Punic War; *his son* (6.1087): (c. 43–23 B.C.) a descendant of the earlier Marcellus, and nephew of Augustus, he was a likely successor to Augustus but died young.

  13. (6.1127) *Sleep has two gates:* The gates of true and false dreams derive from Penelope's dream in *Odyssey* 19. The fact that Aeneas leaves by the gate of false dreams suggests that much of what has just been revealed will be qualified in reality, and that Anchises' vision may be of little help to his son.

BOOK 7

  1. (book 7, line 1) *You also to our shores, Æneas' nurse:* The start of the second half of the poem, book 7 marks the new beginning in many ways. While tied closely to the preceding book, this book also marks the greatest change as it chronicles the shift from the sea journey, or Odyssean, part of the poem to that of asserting Trojan rights to the Italian land through Iliadic struggles. As mentioned above, the parallel with the *Iliad* is strong: not only are the Trojans invaders fighting for the land, the fight is initiated over a woman. Even as the Trojan Paris took Helen from the Greek Menelaus, so the Trojan Aeneas will take Lavinia from the Latin Turnus.

  The book opens with an epitaph to Aeneas' nurse, a Trojan woman who died and was buried on Italian soil. In addition to explaining the name of the town and creating a link to the last line of the preceding book, the mention of Caieta introduces a theme that will sound strongly through this book: that of the female voice and its association with the land of Italy. From the burial of Caieta through the evocation of the Fury Allecto, who is roused by Juno from the depths to start the war between the Trojans and the Latins, to, finally, the image of Camilla, with which the book ends, this book is notable for its focus on women.

2. (7.12) *They skirt the nearest shores to Circe's land:* Aeneas and his men sail up the coast of Italy from Cumae to the mouth of the Tiber at present-day Ostia. They pass by Circe's island without stopping, in contrast, most notably, to Odysseus, whose stop there had disastrous effects on his journey overall, but also in contrast, as we will learn, to the native Italian king, Picus, Latinus' father, whom Vergil asserts mated with Circe before being transformed into a woodpecker that haunts the Latian forests. Aeneas sails between the fates of these two men even as he avoids stopping at the island itself.

3. (7.31) *The sea was blushing in the morning's rays:* The description of the Tiber River pouring into the ocean is a rare lyric moment in the text, one that caught the attention of readers as different as Augustine, who draws on it in the *Confessions*; Dante, who alludes to it in the *Purgatorio*; and Shakespeare, who pays homage to it in *A Midsummer Night's Dream*.

4. (7.46) *Come now, O Erato:* Here is further indication that this is the beginning of the second half: a second invocation to the muse. In contrast to the opening of the poem, Vergil here evokes a specific muse, Erato, who is the muse of lyric and amorous poetry, appropriate to the love motif prevalent in book 7.

5. (7.57) *Latinus, now an aged king, was reigning:* Rooted first in the story of the exiled Saturn, Latinus, son of Picus, is father to Lavinia, his only child by Amata. Lavinia is engaged to Turnus, although Latinus has received a prophecy (7.84 ff.) telling him that the right match for his daughter will be with a foreign man.

6. (7.90) *Dread omen:* That Lavinia's hair and gown catch fire is throughout taken to signify both fame and war.

7. (7.142) *"What! are we eating up our tables too?":* Celaeno's prophecy that they will be so hungry that they will eat their plates before they land in Latium is shown to be an empty threat, as the Trojans eat the bread (their tables) on which they have piled their food, taco style.

8. (7.222) *Here statues of their ancestors were ranged:* Latinus' palace includes statues of native Italic gods and kings: *Italus* (7.223): an early Oenotrian king, commonly believed to be source of Italy's name; *Sabinus* (7.224): ancestor of the Sabines; *Saturn* (7.225): Jupiter's father; believed to have taken refuge in Italy when exiled from Olympus by his son; *Janus* (7.226): early king of Italy; welcomed Saturn in exile; lived on the Janiculum in Rome; *Picus* (7.236): son of Saturn and early king of Latium; *Circe* (7.237): daughter of the sun; sorceress who turns men into animals.

9. (7.241–243) *Latinus takes his seat . . . and summons in/The Trojans:* When Latinus meets Ilioneus and hears about the Trojans and, particularly, about Aeneas, he is persuaded that this is the man for Lavinia. This decision pleases neither Turnus nor Latinus' wife, Amata, whose fondness for Turnus is made clear from the start. Strikingly, Ilioneus' argument is more about connections than differences as he points out that the founder of the Trojans, Dardanus, comes from Italy. Aeneas is arguably as native as Turnus.

10. (7.362) *And sees Æneas joyous, and his fleet:* Juno oversees the arrival of the Trojans and, in a monologue that echoes her first speech of book I, vents her irritation with the ways of fate. In a line Freud made famous— "if I cannot bend the gods above,/Then Acheron I'll move" (7.390–391)— when he used it as the epigraph to *Interpretation of Dreams*, she decides to turn to the forces of the deep, since Olympus is clearly not of any use to her. She calls on the Fury Allecto.

11. (7.430) *Forthwith, in fell Gorgonian venom steeped:* Allecto first infects Lavinia's mother, Amata, then Turnus himself. She attacks Amata disguised as a snake, causing her first to spin like a top and then to run off to the wilds in a bacchic frenzy. To Turnus she appears in the likeness of a priestess, Calybe, who terrifies Turnus, although she is disparaged by him for her gender and age.

12. (7.606) *This stag was of a lovely form:* The real start of the war comes when the Latin Silvia's pet stag—an odd combination of wild and domestic deer—is wounded by an errant arrow from Ascanius' bow. Wars often begin over small events. Here, small as this event is, it resonates strongly with the metaphoric description of events at Carthage. There Aeneas the hunter wounded Dido the deer: here Aeneas' son wounds an actual deer belonging to a native. In many ways the second half of the epic represents an acting out of the potential of the first half.

13. (7.793) *what kings were roused to war:* The book ends with a catalog of the Latin heroes, many of whose histories are heard of only here. Some are related to mythological figures; more are shown to have affiliations with Roman towns of Vergil's day. The most important for the rest of the epic are four: Mezentius, whose cruel deeds against the Arcadians are described in book 8, and his son Lausus, who head the list, and Turnus and Camilla, who end it. Turnus' affiliations with the mythological Io suggest that his ancestral roots are deeper than we might have been led to believe. Camilla, as a female fighter coming last in the list, suggests a parallel, yet again, between these battles and those of the *Iliad* described on the walls at Carthage, where Penthesilea finished out the scenes. Moreover, the description of her flying over the wheat fields makes her sound semi-divine, a sort of Mercury figure. In many ways she comes, through the course of the poem, to embody the spirit of Italy; her death is linked not only with the death of Turnus but also with the transformation of Italy upon the arrival of the Trojans.

BOOK 8

1. (book 8, line 1) *As soon as Turnus from Laurentum's tower . . . :*
This book divides into two halves. The first tells of Aeneas' journey up the
Tiber from the Trojan camp near present-day Ostia to the site of Vergil's
Rome, where the potential ally Evander lives. The second describes the shield
that Venus presents to Aeneas; it depicts the history of Rome from Aeneas' to
Augustus' times. The two halves are closely connected: while visiting Evander,
Aeneas takes a tour of the city that echoes the order of events portrayed on
the shield. Moreover, Evander tells the aetiological tale of Cacus and Hercules, the monster of the Aventine subdued by the wandering hero; Cacus is
the son of Vulcan, the creator of the shield.

2. (8.10) *Also Venulus is sent:* Venulus, a Latin, is sent to Diomedes'
town for advice on how to defeat the Trojans. Diomedes had been one of Aeneas' main antagonists in the Trojan War; he preceded Aeneas to Italy.

3. (8.39) *old Tiberinus:* The river-god comes to Aeneas at night and
urges him to pursue an alliance with Evander, an Arcadian who lives on the
site of present-day Rome. Tiberinus tells Aeneas he will know the location of
their home when he sees a white sow with thirty piglets—which marks the location for the founding of Alba (which means "white") while also signifying
the thirty years before Ascanius will move from Lavinium to Alba Longa.

4. (8.107) *the Tiber calmed his flood:* Traveling up the Tiber, the current of which is magically stilled, Aeneas arrives at the bend in the river near
the Ara Maxima, where he finds Evander and other Arcadians celebrating the
anniversary of the victory of Hercules. Greeted first by Evander's son, Pallas,
Aeneas addresses Evander directly; he explains that their families are related
through Atlas, who is Evander's great-grandfather and Aeneas' ancestor via
Dardanus. Vergil places Dardanus' birth in Italy, following one version of the
myth, in which Dardanus' mortal father was the Italian Corythus. See the Introduction for the importance of this connection. Evander's son Pallas will
accompany Aeneas into battle and be killed by Turnus, an event that parallels
in many ways the death of Patroclus in the *Iliad*. It is the death of Pallas that
provokes the final scene of the epic, in which Aeneas kills Turnus over this action, even as Achilles kills Hector over the death of Patroclus.

5. (8.158) *Then to the king Æneas speaks:* Aeneas recounts for Evander their mutual kinship through Atlas. Evander responds with memories of
having met Aeneas' father, Anchises, in Arcadia.

6. (8.228) *Their hunger now appeased, Evander speaks:* The story of
Cacus and Hercules is interesting on several levels; not least is the role
granted violence in this story. While Cacus is clearly the monster—display-
ing the heads of victims on gateposts—his wrath is evenly matched by the
visiting Hercules who, when he discovers that his cows have been taken, goes
on a rampage around the Aventine Hill, eventually pulling the top off the

mountain and strangling Cacus until his eyes pop out. Vergil may be making a distinction between violence for violence's sake and violence toward a civilizing goal, but the line is very thin indeed. That this sort of story underlies the foundation of Rome is striking, even if it took place, as Vergil argues, "over there" on the Aventine.

7. (8.348) *The praises and the deeds of Hercules:* Here are listed the trials and successes of Hercules: *Troy and Oechalia* (8.352): two towns destroyed by Hercules; it is important to note that Troy had fallen at Hercules' hands before it was destroyed by the Greeks; *Hylaeus and Pholus* (8.357): centaurs killed in the battle with the Lapiths; *Cretan boar* (8.357): a boar or bull sent by Neptune; *huge lion beneath the Nemean rocks* (8.358): Hercules' first labor, explaining why he wears the lion skin; *Stygian lake* (8.359): a reference to Hercules' being required to capture the three-headed monster Cerberus and return him to the underworld; *Typhoeus* (8.363): one of the Giants who fought with the Titans against the Olympians; *Hydra* (8.365): Lernaean serpent with nine heads; it would grow two heads for every one lopped off.

8. (8.381) *Evander then, Rome's earliest founder, spoke:* Evander takes Aeneas on a tour of his city, which includes walking from the Ara Maxima by the Capitoline through the Forum and up to the Palatine Hill. Pallanteum is marked by its reverence for the gods, its natural beauty, and its humility, all of which are described with irony on the part of Vergil, who points out that cows grazed in the Forum and Evander's humble hut stood on the location where now the house of emperor Augustus (and temple to Apollo) was built. As the only place in the poem where Rome is described in detail, this pastoral view of the city is touching. Points of interest include: *Asylum* (8.415): In order to increase the population of his small city, Romulus opened a refuge for outcasts. *Lupercal* (8.416): This cave at the base of the Palatine was restored by Augustus. *Argiletum* (8.418): Here Argus, a guest of Evander, was killed, having plotted his overthrow. *Tarpeian rock* (8.421): Jupiter was thought to live at this outcropping on the southwest corner of the Capitolium. *Carinae* (8.439): This section of the Esquiline Hill was fashionable in Vergil's day.

9. (8.451) *But Venus, her maternal love alarmed:* Between the two sections of book 8 an interlude between Venus and Vulcan occurs. Striking for its insight into Venus' seductive character, this section also includes a memorable simile in which Vulcan, leaving Venus' side to start the cyclops working on Aeneas' shield, is likened to a woman getting up early to get the housework started. The role reversal between Vulcan and Venus helps in the transition from Vulcan as the father of violent Cacus to Vulcan the artisan, not unknowing of the future, who creates the shield.

10. (8.564) *"Great leader of the Trojans":* Evander's pledge of support to Aeneas' cause is based on his need to rid his people of the renegade Etruscan Mezentius, who had fled to Turnus for protection.

11. (8.674) *"Ah, would that Jove would only bring again . . .":* Evander

laments his own loss of youth and pledges to send his son to battle, though he fears he may not return.

12. (8.746–749) *The fire-god . . . Had wrought the Roman triumphs here, the events/Of Italy:* The shield, based most obviously on the shield of Achilles in the *Iliad*, differs in that on Aeneas' are portrayed specific historic events. In this it fits in with the parade of heroes in book 6 and the series of prophecies Aeneas has received since the last night at Troy. How the shield would have looked is a matter of great debate. Whether, as David West would have it in his essay reprinted in Stephen Harrison's *Oxford Readings in Vergil's "Aeneid,"* the battle of Actium was in the center or, as Alexander McKay has argued in his piece in Hans-Peter Stahl's *Vergil's "Aeneid,"* the temple of Actian Apollo on the Palatine Hill was the visual focus is hard to determine. The scenes move from Romulus and Remus up to the emperor Augustus; the stories are often focused on violence and resistance to that violence.

13. (8.769) *Porsenna:* He was an Etruscan king who reputedly led an army against Rome and besieged it in an effort to restore the Tarquin kings. It is said that a Roman named Gaius Mucius Scaevola went to Porsenna's camp to assassinate him but killed a royal official instead. Captured and threatened with torture, Mucius demonstrated his will by thrusting his hand into the fire. Impressed, Porsenna acquiesced and made peace.

14. (8.773–774) *Cocles . . . Cloelia:* Cocles (also known as Horatius) held the bridge against Porsenna. Cloelia, who was taken hostage by Porsenna, broke free and swam the Tiber. Her bravery incited Porsenna to free her and other captives.

15. (8.850) *triple triumph:* This is a reference to Augustus' procession in 29 B.C. upon his return to Rome celebrating his defeat of Dalmatia, the battle of Actium, and Alexandria. During the celebration, he closed the doors to the temple of Janus, thus symbolically ending war in the empire.

BOOK 9

1. (book 9, line 1) *While these events in other places passed:* After two books of preparation, the battle between the Latins and the Trojans finally begins in book 9. Compared to book 8, the ninth book lacks unity, yet thus it suggests the chaos and contingencies of actual battle. The heart of the book centers on the mission, raid, and deaths of Nisus and Euryalus, yet many other things happen along the way that both speak to the nature of war and prepare the epic for the final showdown in book 12. The book opens at the mouth of the Tiber, where Turnus is preparing for war in Aeneas' absence.

Visiting first Evander, then going farther up the coast to stir up more support for the Trojan cause, Aeneas is absent from the entire book. In fact, before the final encounters in book 12, we see him fighting only briefly, though intensely, in book 10, and he is also largely absent from the battles in book 11.

2. (9.15–16) *"Now is the time to call/For chariots and for steeds"*: Due to Aeneas' absence, and inspired by Juno, Turnus decides first to attack the Trojan camp. Aeneas had ordered his men to stay inside the walls if attack should occur; the result is a strange reversal, since the Trojans, hidden inside the walled city, play a role familiar to them from the *Iliad*.

3. (9.81–83) *The fleet . . . he determines to assail:* Turnus then attempts to burn Aeneas' ships. This action recalls that of Hector in *Iliad* 16, but with a different outcome. Here we learn that the ships that brought Aeneas from Troy are made from pines sacred to Cybele, the Magna Mater. Cybele is identified with Rhea, mother of Jupiter, and Vergil here includes a conversation between mother and son in which Jupiter promises to transform the ships into nymphs once they have reached their goal. Turnus, attempting to burn Aeneas' ships and so trap him in Italy, is confronted with the voice of the Magna Mater and left with a cluster of nymphs, who, in turn, swim up the coast to warn Aeneas of the impending battle.

4. (9.155) *he lifts their courage with his words:* Turnus' response sets the Iliadic tone. He likens himself to Menelaus and Lavinia to Helen.

5. (9.219) *Nisus was keeper of the gate:* The story of Nisus and Euryalus points back to book 5 and forward to book 11. These two Trojan warriors, who ran the footrace together, volunteer to sneak out of the stockade and retrieve Aeneas. In a scene eerily similar to the arrival of the Trojan horse, in which the Greeks are successful in part because the Trojans sleep heavily with too much wine, so Nisus and Euryalus, with Ascanius' blessing, sneak out of the Trojan stockade and make their way across the Latin camp, where most of the soldiers are sleeping. On their way out they slaughter many Latins and retrieve massive amounts of booty, fitting some of the armor to their bodies. They are spotted by a squadron, headed by Volscens, that has come to help Turnus and the Latins and, in the rout, become confused. Euryalus, weighed down by booty, becomes entangled in the brush; Nisus, calling for him (in words that recall Orpheus' lament for Eurydice and Aeneas' for Creüsa) heads back into the battle and, seeing Euryalus, sends two spears toward the heavens. The plan backfires. While the weapons do strike the Latins, they assume it was Euryalus who sent them, and they rush on him with their swords. Nisus claims his actions, but it is too late: Euryalus is killed; his death is described as a flower cut down in its prime, a simile both epic and lyric in source and effect, with echoes of Sappho and Catullus. It is a beautiful moment in the text, made more noteworthy by the narrator's address to the pair, in which he claims power to keep their story alive to the present day and beyond.

6. (9.590) *Her wailing fills the air:* The emotional thrust of the scene is increased by the impact of Euryalus' death on his mother. Nisus had tried to dissuade Euryalus from joining the raid on the grounds that he was too young. Having persuaded Nisus to let him go, Euryalus appeals to Ascanius to take care of his mother, one of a handful of Trojan women who decided to come to Italy rather than stay on Sicily. The death of Euryalus is thus all the more heart-rending, and Euryalus' mother's lament is painful to read, emphasizing, as it does, both the loss of a child and the loss of the homeland. Euryalus' mother is now far from home with no reason for being in this foreign land. As long as Euryalus was alive, there was some justification; with him dead, she is completely alone.

With Euryalus' mother's lament one of the themes of book 9 becomes apparent. On the one hand, much is made of gifts and booty: objects that speak to cultural transfer, willing or not. On the other, we have the laments of two women over the fate of those things sacred to them: Cybele with her nymphs from the sacred wood, Euryalus' mother over the loss of her son. The message is mixed in each case: the gifts Ascanius offers the two men on leaving is balanced by their death due to the booty they retrieve along the way. Cybele's ability to transform her sacred trees into nymphs, thus ensuring continuity in the new land of Italy, is balanced by the loss Euryalus' mother feels of both homeland and son. The price of founding Rome, the price of moving Troy west, is shown graphically and felt deeply through the course of this book.

7. (9.619–620) *But now the dreadful trumpet's brazen blare/Is heard, and shouts resound:* The battle picks up with discovery of the slaughter started by Nisus and Euryalus. Turnus first rages around the battlefield, killing wildly. Mezentius and Messapus are shown killing as well.

8. (9.654–655) *A lofty tower . . . The Italians stormed:* Strikingly, they push down the tower, much like the tower destroyed during the last night at Troy. Ascanius too gets involved, killing his first Latin, Numanus, who had taunted him and his men, calling them easterners (Phrygians) and contrasting their eastern decadence with the stoicism of the Latins. Apollo is shown on Olympus, backing Ascanius' decision to kill Numanus.

9. (9.960) *Then hearing of the slaughter in their ranks:* The battle rages outside the Trojan camp with deaths on both sides. Focusing increasingly on entrapping Turnus, the action ends with Turnus entering into the enemy camp, becoming trapped there, and eventually retreating, diving into the Tiber River to stay safe.

BOOK 10

1. (book 10, line 1) *Meanwhile the omnipotent Olympian doors:* The battle stage having been set by the previous book, the tenth book of the

Aeneid carries on with raging warfare while also setting in motion the events of the end of the poem. During the tenth book Evander's son Pallas will be killed by Turnus; in revenge, Aeneas, returned from his pursuit of allies, will cause the death of both Lausus and Mezentius, two key fighters on the Latin side.

The book begins with a divine council, in which Jupiter, Juno, and Venus debate the war. Among the striking elements of the discussion is Venus' clear concern over the fate of Ascanius (and surprising lack of concern for Aeneas). Aeneas has served his purpose: the Trojans have made it to Italy. What happens to him now is less important in the grand scheme of things than what will happen to Ascanius, who must survive long enough to produce heirs of his own. Also in this debate Juno makes it clear that while she has indeed been encouraging the Latins, Trojan failures are not her fault. The council ends with Jupiter declaring that he will remain neutral.

2. (10.201) *While these sustained the shocks of rugged war:* Aeneas' reentry is striking, since he comes by water. He thus appears at the battle not like a Trojan but like a Greek, and having been absent, he is most clearly identified with the Greek Achilles, whose return to the battle in *Iliad* 19 is equally marked. The identification of him with Achilles will become more and more pointed as the book develops. The arrival by sea is emphasized by the appearance of the transformed nymphs and the striking crash of Tarchon's ship, which recalls the ship race in book 5.

3. (10.229) *First, in the brazen Tigris, Massicus:* The catalog of Etruscans matches that of the Latins in book 7 and fills out the sense of the strength of the Trojan side. The Etruscans are identified by their hometowns, such as Cosa and Pisa. Ocnus is given special notice, since he is related to Manto, the eponymous hero of Vergil's hometown, Mantua.

4. (10.497) *First, Lagus, led by inauspicious fates:* Unlike Ascanius, Pallas appears to be used to fighting and starts right in. It is, however, when he attacks Lausus, Mezentius' son and so Pallas' counterpart on the Latin side, that Turnus becomes enraged, as Aeneas will over the death of Pallas. Turnus confronts Pallas and kills him. Before he dies, Pallas prays to Hercules, who tries to help, only to be told by Jupiter that every man must die. The address to Hercules is prompted by two things: the Arcadians' worship of Hercules for his destruction of Cacus told in book 8, and the association in *Odyssey* 11 between Hercules and a sword belt that shows battles so terrible that Odysseus says he hopes the goldsmith would never make another. Pallas' sword belt, like that of Hercules, is powerful in its reach: both foreshadow the rage that ends each epic.

5. (10.652) *With that, he pressed the corpse:* Turnus rips the sword belt off the dead Pallas. The scene depicted on the sword belt is the slaughter of the Danaids' husbands by their wives on their wedding night. This scene and its contemporary importance will figure strongly in the final scene of the

poem.

6. (10.672) *And now, not rumor, but more certain word:* The death of Pallas sets in motion the Iliadic events that follow. Even as the death of Patroclus causes Achilles to reenter the battle to avenge Patroclus' death by killing Hector, so Aeneas now for the first time enters the battle in an effort to avenge the death of Pallas. His rampage is wide-ranging but ends with the death of two key figures: Lausus and Mezentius. As we learn in book 8, Mezentius was a renegade Etruscan who had changed sides, being protected by Turnus against the Arcadians. He is the primary reason Evander agrees to lend his support to Aeneas, since a prophet has told them that only a foreigner can lead the attack. Mezentius represents the key death for Aeneas, then; it is the one that matters in his relationship with Evander, and, especially after the death of Pallas, whom he had sworn to protect, it becomes the one thing he can do to keep faith with the Arcadian.

7. (10.795–796) *Jove of his own accord, meanwhile, addressed/His spouse:* Juno and Jupiter confer, deciding to protect Turnus from the wrath of Aeneas, at least for now. Turnus is spirited away on a ship, fooled by a phantom Aeneas.

8. (10.1006–1007) *Æneas in the long battalion sees/His foe, and goes to meet him:* Aeneas' wounding and eventual killing of Mezentius—Aeneas wounds Mezentius' horse, which falls on top of him (10.1170)—is too little and too late for Pallas but remains a tremendously important event in the poem. In acquiring Evander as an ally, Aeneas agreed to two things: he would take on Mezentius, and he would protect Pallas. Failing the latter all he can do is accomplish the former. Moreover, Mezentius is the Cacus of his time; in killing him Aeneas becomes Herculean, instilling peace in a ravaged landscape. Yet, as with Hercules, the means to this end are as violent as the violence they are meant to stop.

9. (10.1065–1066) *the Fates/Collect the last threads of young Lausus' life:* Lausus is killed by Aeneas in large part because Pallas was killed: Pallas had attempted to kill him himself; Aeneas finishes that job while Lausus is trying to protect his father, Mezentius.

BOOK 11

1. (book 11, line 1) *Meanwhile the Morning from the Ocean rose:* The eleventh book is as much about parents and children in war as it is about war itself. It opens with the spoils of Mezentius, dedicated to Mars, and we are reminded of the death of both Mezentius and his son Lausus at the hands of Aeneas in the previous book. The image of the dead Mezentius looms over the book. Mezentius strikingly parallels Camilla as fighter and in death.

The book as a whole is divided into three sections: funerals, debate, and battle—the funeral of Pallas; the debate over the war, including the description of the truce and the reports about the embassy to Diomedes and Latinus' reply; and the story of Camilla. Pallas' funeral brings death into the pastoral Arcadian landscape, and the idyllic Arcadian countryside remembered from book 8 is shot through with grief and guilt over the death of its young heir. Aeneas' role as surrogate father colors his eulogy for the dead Pallas, which, in turn, complicates his relationship with Evander. The death of Mezentius is, as it were, offered up as a sacrifice to Evander, but it is not enough (nothing could be). The peace that Aeneas creates by killing Mezentius—a peace that parallels that accomplished by Hercules in killing Cacus—is shown against its cost. Evander and the Arcadians will never recover from the death of Pallas; whether their land is at war or not, their lives will never be at peace.

2. (11.134–135) *all strife/Must cease:* The speeches that follow begin with a request for a truce by the Latins to bury their dead. Both Aeneas and Drances respond with statements against war and in favor of a truce. The perversion of family and landscape emblematized by the death of Mezentius and Pallas is here summarized as part of the cost of war.

3. (11.193–194) *The matrons . . . Rouse the sad city with their cries of grief:* Pallas' funeral procession arrives at Pallanteum, where Evander asks Aeneas to avenge Pallas' death.

4. (11.248–249) *Æneas now, now Tarchon built/Along the winding shore the funeral piles:* Both sides bury their dead. The embassy sent to Diomedes returns with no help offered; although Diomedes fought against Aeneas in Troy he refuses to do so here. Aeneas, he says, is too great a warrior. Latinus proposes peace with the Trojans, which is supported by Drances against Turnus. Turnus responds, saying he is willing to take on Aeneas himself. Aeneas prepares for battle; Turnus arms himself, and when Camilla volunteers her services, Turnus plans an ambush on Aeneas.

5. (11.402) *"It had been better, and I well could wish . . .":* Latinus offers terms for a ceasefire: either offer the Trojans some land of their own or offer them boats so they can sail and settle elsewhere.

6. (11.656–657) *Him, face to face, Camilla, leading on/Her band of Volscian riders, meets:* The Volscian Camilla, introduced at the end of book 7, volunteers to help. The description of her time on the battlefield, her death, and her childhood takes up much of the remainder of the book. Her character is fascinating; introduced at the end of book 7, she is almost an allegory of Italy: a rustic figure forced into war. She is described as being raised by her father in the woods. When young, we are told, her father, being pursued, strapped her to a spear and threw her across a river, praying to Diana to watch over her. She was raised in the wilds and dedicated to Diana; she is thus nearly a personification of the rustic life that has been forced into war. Vergil makes it clear that this is not a situation unique to the Latins: they too had had their violence before, even as the Trojans had experienced times of peace and

beauty. But the juxtaposition of nature and war is violent wherever it occurs, and Camilla's story shows it at its worst.

7. (11.940–941) *The Tuscan Tarchon he enflames with wrath,/And to the cruel battle goads him on:* During Camilla's rampage, Jupiter intervenes and sends Tarchon to lead the Etruscan allies into battle. They capture the Latin Venulus.

8. (11.1021–1023) *That he should slay/Camilla, as she hurried heedless by,/He granted:* Camilla's death is strikingly similar to those of Nisus and Euryalus, as she too is delayed gathering booty and killed as a result. The parallelism—Camilla fighting for the Latins, Nisus and Euryalus for the Trojans—emphasizes the mutual losses of war that pervade the book.

9. (11.1056–1057) *With that she loosed/Her grasp upon her reins, and sinking, fell:* Camilla's connection with Turnus, first suggested at the end of book 7, is made explicit, and her role in the structure of the narrative is made more prominent. In many ways, Camilla picks up the thread of many of the themes associated with Dido and enables their transfer to the figure of Turnus. The issues that are first raised with Dido as Aeneas' first enemy, finally are played out through Camilla and Turnus; likewise, the curse of Dido can be seen to work its way through the narrative, indirectly, via these characters. While we may not see Carthage and the enmity between Carthage and Rome after Aeneas leaves, we see Aeneas fighting Dido's avatars up to the end of the poem. Camilla provides the transitional character between Dido and Turnus as she stands halfway between the two: as a female leader who gives in to rage she is like Dido; as a warrior weighed down and ultimately killed for booty she is like Turnus, whose display of Pallas' sword belt at the end provides the ultimate motivation for his death.

10. (11.1142–1143) *He, furious . . . Deserts his ambuscade and forests rough:* Camilla's death prompts Turnus to abandon his ambush of Aeneas.

BOOK 12

1. (book 12, line 1) *As soon as Turnus sees the Latin hosts:* The last book of the poem in many ways mirrors the opening book, though they approach themes and events from different angles. The last thirty lines of the poem in particular call up themes introduced at the beginning and cause us to circle—or spiral—back to the claims made in the opening thirty lines. For a long time people asserted that the ending was not as Vergil would have had it. While it is true that the poem remained unfinished at Vergil's death, it seems likely that what was unfinished was the stylistic rather than the structural or narrative level. There remain numerous incomplete or unpolished lines and a number of discrepancies that would perhaps have been made consistent with a little more editing. The ending of the poem, however unsettling we find it, should be read, nonetheless, as its conclusion and interpreted

as such.

Book 12 works steadily and relentlessly toward the final confrontation between Turnus and Aeneas on the mortal plane and the ultimate reconciliation between Juno and Jupiter on the divine one. Much of book 12 should be read against the backdrop of *Iliad* 22, in which Hector first taunts and then is pursued and finally killed by Achilles. The forward thrust of the book is stronger than in any other section of the poem, and one has the experience when reading it of feeling the inexorable drive of the fates at work. Nonetheless, within this forward momentum one is constantly thrown from side to side: Turnus begins the book being likened to a lion, not unlike his first description in book 7 as a proud and haughty prince. Yet, shortly after, he loses his confidence and weakens. By the time of the final encounter with Aeneas he has progressed from the subject of the sentence to the direct object, and from a noun to a series of participles—insubstantial action words. Vergil writes him out of the poem even as he makes Aeneas seem stronger and stronger. By the end, the encounter seems unfairly balanced—Turnus barely there, Aeneas huge and looming.

2. (12.24) *Then tranquilly Latinus answered him:* Latinus tries to persuade Turnus to refrain from fighting Aeneas.

3. (12.173) *But Juno, from the summit of the mount:* The gods agree that they should withdraw and let the mortals fight it out on their own, although Juno advises the immortal Juturna, Turnus' sister, to help her brother. Aeneas and Latinus swear oaths that look forward to a future beyond the war.

4. (12.331) *Their weapons they prepare to seize:* The Rutulians break the agreement about single combat, following an omen sent by Juturna. Aeneas is wounded and seems unable to fight.

5. (12.526) *The goddess-mother, Venus, troubled now:* Aeneas' mother intervenes and provides an herb—dittany—to speed the removal of the arrow from his leg, which enables him to return to battle. Aeneas pursues Turnus, as Achilles relentlessly pursued Hector. When he cannot get to Turnus, because of the intervention of Turnus' sister, Juturna, and the warrior Messapus, he strikes out at the enemy all around him. To a large extent we are back in the Troy of book 2, with Aeneas in slash-and-burn mode. This soon escalates into a general fracas, which is ended only after Aeneas, at Venus' suggestion, attacks the Latin capital.

6. (12.762–763) *and from a lofty beam / Ties fast the noose of her unsightly death:* Amata panics, hanging herself; and Turnus, after a moment of hesitation, hastens to the capital, where he orders his allies to leave the battle to himself and Aeneas.

7. (12.916–917) *Æneas and the Daunian chief / Clash with their shields, that all the air resounds:* In the first skirmish between the two, each loses his weapon—Aeneas' sticks in a tree, Turnus' (which is borrowed from his charioteer) shatters. Both have their weapons replaced, Aeneas by Venus

and Turnus by his sister, Juturna. Jupiter weighs their fates in the balance.

8. (12.1001) *Meanwhile the omnipotent Olympian king:* The action now moves to Olympus. Jupiter addresses Juno, asking her to stop the fighting. She agrees that the Trojans will win, but only on the condition that the conquered Latins can retain their language and their dress. They will not become Trojans: Troy has died, not in name only; it is Italian virtue that will enable Rome to be great. Jupiter agrees to this; for the importance of this compromise, see the Introduction.

9. (12.1066–1067) *Juno assents with glad and altered mind,/And leaves her cloudy dwelling in the sky:* The compromise, though, is more complete than even this would make it appear, for not only does Juno agree to these conditions and departs happily (*laetata*), but in the scene that follows, Jupiter reveals that he can wield *furor* if need be: his next and final act is to reach down by his throne and pick up a Fury, whom he throws down onto the battlefield. Juno has been in conversation with these forces of the deep, but Jupiter has studiously reigned from above; for him to acknowledge commerce with these darker forces is to suggest a degree of interdependence between husband and wife, *furor* and *pietas*, hitherto unrevealed. The acknowledgment of interdependence of opposed forces is what on some level enables the text and the war to conclude.

10. (12.1133–1134) *looking round, he sees/An ancient rock:* Turnus, in desperation, tries to hurl a boundary stone at Aeneas, but fails: while he can lift the stone, which "scarcely twelve chosen men such as the earth produces now have borne it on their backs," he cannot throw it any distance, and it falls short of hurting Aeneas. Turnus' state is likened to a nightmare as "in vain we strive/To run, with speed that equals our desire,/But yield, disabled, midway in our course;/The tongue and all the accustomed forces fail,/Neither voice nor words ensue" (12.1146–1150).

11. (12.1183–1184) *Stern in his arms/Æneas stood, and rolled his eyes around:* As Aeneas prepares to show clemency (he is said to be persuaded by Turnus' words) he sees the sword belt worn by Pallas and taken and displayed by Turnus. This sword belt functions on a series of levels. On the one hand, it reminds Aeneas of the death of his ally's son, the one he was sworn to protect. But on the other, it speaks to an even more contemporary concern, as it displays the story of the slaughter of the Danaids' husbands on their wedding night. This myth, described in brief in book 10, was used by Octavian as propaganda after the battle of Actium, in which he identifies with the brides, having built a series of statues of the Danaids and their father to be displayed in the portico of the temple to Actian Apollo on the Palatine Hill. For Vergil to depict the other side of the story—the bridegrooms, not the brides—on the sword belt is to suggest an identification between Aeneas and Octavian through the slaughtering brides. Turnus, suppliant, echoes the fate of the bridegrooms on the buckle, while Aeneas, victor, is like the brides. It remains

to be debated whether the ending should be read as supportive of Aeneas' (and Octavian's) actions or critical of them.

12. (12.1199) *He spoke, and plunged his sword into his breast:* Aeneas' sword is said to be buried (*condit*) into Turnus' chest. This is the same verb that occurs at the start of the poem, where it refers to the foundation of the city (*conderet*). The poem circles back to the start, but the angle of vision has changed. Founding a city involves sacrificing a victim: the story of Romulus and Remus, in which the weaker twin is murdered by the stronger for over-stepping a boundary, is not told by Vergil, though it is clearly present in the minds of his audience. In this action of sacrifice—the language is clearly sac-rificial—Turnus' becomes the first of a series of violent murders associated with the founding of a city. Through this Vergil harks back to the action taken at the end of Aeschylus' *Oresteia*, which argues that the city of Athens is founded on the Furies turned Eumenides, or nurturing forces. There is no such transformation here; the forces Juno represents throughout the poem re-main violent to the end. Yet they have moved from being shown as external to the process of foundation to being revealed as essential. Juno is happy be-cause her forces have been acknowledged—not tamed, but acknowledged. The foundation of Rome on the death of Turnus, replicated in the death of Remus and countless others, suggests that *pietas* and *furor* are arguably not opposed but interdependent.

13. (12.1201) *Down to the Shades the soul, indignant, fled:* The final line of the poem repeats the line used of Camilla's death. If Camilla provides not only a transition between Dido and Turnus but also represents that es-sential Italian force—Italia personified—it is fitting that she have the last word, that it be that life force that flees to the shades below. As we have seen in book 7, feminine forces are often associated with the land of Italy, and it is to these darker forces that Juno turns once the Trojans have landed in Italy. These are the forces that are recognized at the end of the poem; Dido's curse, translated into Italian terms, surfaces at the very end.

It is clear from the start of book 12, if not the start of the second half of the poem, that Aeneas will kill Turnus. That is, it is possible to argue that the fact that Aeneas kills Turnus because of the sight of the sword belt makes him more like the rash Aeneas of book 2, facing Helen, than like the increas-ingly controlled Aeneas we see through the rest of the book. If this is so, it is conceivable to suggest that the poem ends here because not only Turnus dies, but Aeneas dies as well—that is, the hero, the Trojan Aeneas, dies when he kills Turnus. Notice that in the parade of heroes in book 6 the list begins not with Aeneas but with his sons: the past ends with the death of Turnus. Juno has won not only because Aeneas demonstrates rage but also because that rage prevents him from continuing on as hero: he is not the model of *pietas* he aims to be. Yet he is a part of the story, of the past of Rome, and he has become an agent of the violent force that will continue to underlie and fuel the imperial drive.

Inspired by the *Aeneid*

"[Dante is] the central man of all the world."
—JOHN RUSKIN

Vergil's *Aeneid* is often thought of as Dante's point of departure for his *Divine Comedy*. Begun in 1308 and completed shortly before Dante's death in 1321, *The Divine Comedy* comprises three parts: the *Inferno*, the *Purgatorio*, and the *Paradiso*. Each consists of thirty-three cantos, which, along with an introductory canto attached to the *Inferno*, makes for a total of 100 cantos. The epic is composed in *terza rima*, another resonance of the number three—Dante's Christian allegory reflects the Holy Trinity in its structure all the way down to the individual lines. *The Divine Comedy* chronicles a man's journey through the depths of Hell, his pilgrimage along the summit of Purgatory, and his ascent to Heaven, where he sees and is embraced by the light of God. As it happens, this man is Dante himself. If it was brazen in Dante's day to write himself into his own poem, it was modest indeed to cast Vergil as his chaperone. In the introductory canto, Vergil speaks to Dante: "Thou follow me, and I will be thy guide,/And lead thee hence through the eternal place."

Just as Dante the character is led by Vergil through the first two realms of *The Divine Comedy*, Dante the poet took Vergil's lead as laid out in the latter's epic of Rome. "Few readers of Virgil's *Aeneid*," write Italian studies scholars Peter and Julia Conaway Bondanella,

> would ever know the Latin epic better than Dante, who absorbed many of the lessons he might have learned from a direct reading of Homer through an indirect encounter with Homer in Virgil's poem. In celebrating the birth of the city of Rome, destined to rule the classical world by Virgil's lifetime, the Latin poet could not have predicted that his

imperial capital would eventually become the capital of Christianity, or that the Latin race would be fully Christianized. The link of medieval Rome to both the Roman Republic and Empire, on the one hand, and to the rise of Christianity, on the other, was never far from Dante's mind when he considered what Rome meant to his own times. Virgil's Latin epic became the single most important work in the formation of the ideas that would eventually produce *The Divine Comedy*.

But while Vergil was commissioned by the emperor Augustus Caesar to write the *Aeneid*, it appears that Dante may have felt compelled by a higher purpose. Whereas Vergil's lofty verses were meant to connect the heroics of antiquity to the perceived nobility of Augustus' administration, Dante wanted to bring the grace of God to every Italian. He achieved this by composing his epic not in Latin, but in the common vernacular. As fourteenth-century Italian writer Giovanni Boccaccio said, Dante did this

> in order to be of the most general use to his fellow-citizens and to other Italians. For he knew that if he wrote in Latin metre, as previous poets had done, he would have been useful only to the learned, while by writing in the vernacular he would accomplish something that had never been done before, without preventing his being understood by men of letters. While showing the beauty of our idiom and his own excellent art therein, he gave both delight and understanding of himself to the unlearned, who formerly had been neglected by every one (translated by James Robinson Smith).

A hallmark of world literature, *The Divine Comedy* is great partly because of its accessibility. As T. S. Eliot said, "The language of Dante is the perfection of a common language."

The Divine Comedy takes place in the year 1300, from Good Friday through Easter Sunday. In a master stroke, Dante marries the classical convention of traveling through the underworld (à la Orpheus) with the Christian view that also regards Purgatory and Heaven as legitimate spiritual realms. Vergil had sent Aeneas only into Hades and back out again: "Through shadows, through the lonely night they went,/Through the blank halls and empty realms of Dis" (6.331–332). At the summit of Purgatory, Vergil tells Dante that, as a man, he can reveal no more. At this point, Beatrice, Dante's real-life love—whom he celebrated in his poem *La Vita Nuova* (*The New Life*; 1293) and who for Dante was the embodiment of grace—becomes the docent of Paradise. Dante not only looked upon his poetic forebear as a guiding light, but in the end, he went beyond him, exploring realms that in Vergil's universe didn't exist.

Dido and Aeneas, by Henry Purcell

The English early-Baroque composer Henry Purcell is often remembered for his sole opera—the short (it runs just under an hour), incomplete, and uncommonly gorgeous *Dido and Aeneas*. England's oldest opera, it premiered at a girls' school in Chelsea in 1689. The action occurs in three acts with two scenes apiece, along with several dance numbers (it was commissioned by Josiah Priest, a dance professor). The work's pervasive recitative is punctuated by arias that feature a ground bass—a brief, melodic bass line that repeats below melodies in the upper registers. This feature allowed Purcell to give Dido and Aeneas interesting, playful, and often surprising vocal harmonies. The accompanying strings convey emotional depths beyond those implied by the drama inherent in the plight of the Trojan refugees, the clash of royal temperaments, and other aspects of the ancient epic. Drawn from the fourth book of Vergil's *Aeneid*, Nahum Tate's libretto focuses on the love story of the opera's eponymous characters and jettisons what remains of Aeneas' fated quest. Tate's verses, which capitalize on the natural rhythms of English speech, quickly became a standard of the Baroque era. His book replaces the Roman gods with a sorceress and witches, a device reminiscent of his play *Brutus of Alba; or, The Enchanted Lovers* (1678).

The opera is extraordinary in its portrayal of the grief-stricken Dido's response when Aeneas announces he will leave. The following is from the opera's famous aria "When I Am Laid in Earth," sung by Dido:

> DIDO   By all that's good, no more!
> All that's good you have forswore.

> To your promis'd empire fly
> And let forsaken Dido die.

AENEAS In spite of Jove's command, I'll stay.
Offend the gods, and Love obey.

DIDO No, faithless man, thy course pursue;
I'm now resolv'd as well as you.
No repentance shall reclaim
The injur'd Dido's slighted flame.
For 'tis enough, whate'er you now decree,
That you had once a thought of leaving me.

The tragic finale, in which the Queen of Carthage dies, remains one of the genre's most moving break-up scenes. Though Dido's suicide is of explicitly epic proportions—and atypical among pre-nineteenth-century operas, in which a *deus ex machina* invariably swoops in to rescue imperiled heroes and heroines—Dido's anguish when Aeneas spurns her for his "promis'd empire" is universal. *Dido and Aeneas* is today regarded as a seminal contribution to English dramatic music, especially for its sharp characterizations, and Purcell's innovations in vocal harmonies were later a key influence on Handel's career.

Comments & Questions

In this section, we aim to provide the reader with an array of perspectives on the text, as well as questions that challenge those perspectives. The commentary has been culled from literary criticism of later generations and appreciations written throughout the work's history. Following the commentary, a series of questions seeks to filter Vergil's Aeneid through a variety of points of view and bring about a richer understanding of this enduring work.

Comments

JOSEPH ADDISON

The most perfect in their several kinds, are perhaps *Homer, Virgil,* and *Ovid.* The first strikes the Imagination wonderfully with what is Great, the second with what is Beautiful, and the last with what is Strange. Reading the *Iliad* is like travelling through a Country uninhabited, where the Fancy is entertained with a thousand Savage Prospects of vast Desarts, wide uncultivated Marshes, huge Forests, mis-shapen Rocks and Precipices. On the contrary, the *Æneid* is like a well ordered Garden, where it is impossible to find out any Part unadorned, or to cast our Eyes upon a single Spot, that does not produce some beautiful Plant or Flower. But when we are in the *Metamorphoses,* we are walking on enchanted Ground, and see nothing but Scenes of Magick lying round us.

 Homer is in his Province, when he is describing a Battel or a Multitude, a Heroe or a God. *Virgil* is never better pleased, than when he is in his *Elysium,* or copying out an entertaining Picture. *Homer's* Epithets generally mark out what is Great, *Virgil's* what is Agreeable. Nothing can be more Magnificent than the Figure *Jupiter* makes in the first *Iliad,* no more Charming than that of Venus in the first *Æneid.*

—from the Spectator (June 28, 1712)

Robert Burns

I own I am disappointed in the Æneid. Faultless correctness may please, and does highly please the lettered Critic; but to that aweful character I have not the most distant pretentions. I don't know whether I do not hazard my pretentions to be a Critic of any kind, when I say that I think Virgil, in many instances, a *servile* Copier of Homer. If I had the Odyssey by me, I could parallel many passages where Virgil has evidently copied, but by no means improved Homer.

— from a letter to Mrs. Francis Dunlop (May 4, 1788)

William Blake

What is it sets Homer, Virgil & Milton in so high a rank of Art? Why is the Bible more Entertaining & Instructive than any other book? Is it not because they are addressed to the Imagination, which is Spiritual Sensation, & but mediately to the Understanding or Reason?

— from a letter to the Reverend John Trusler (August 23, 1799)

Georg Wilhelm Friedrich Hegel

Whole nations have hardly been able to produce any poetical works except such rhetorical ones. The Latin language, for example, even in Cicero, sounds naive and innocent enough. But in the case of the Roman poets, Virgil and Horace, for example, we feel at once that the art is something artificial, deliberately manufactured; we are aware of a prosaic subject-matter, with external decoration added, and we find a poet who, deficient in original genius, tries to find in the sphere of linguistic skill and rhetorical effects a substitute for what he lacks in real forcefulness and effectiveness of invention and achievement.

— as translated by T. M. Knox, from *Aesthetics: Lectures on Fine Art* (1835)

Andrew Lang

Doubtless it was the "Æneid," his artificial and unfinished epic, that won Virgil the favour of the Middle Ages. To the Middle Ages, which knew not Greek, and knew not Homer, Virgil was the representative of the heroic and eternally interesting past. But to us who know Homer, Virgil's epic is indeed "like moonlight unto sunlight," is a beautiful empty world, where no real life stirs, a world that shines with a silver lustre not its own, but borrowed from "the sun of Greece."

Homer sang of what he knew, of spears and ships, of heroic chiefs and beggar men, of hunts and sieges, of mountains where the lion roamed, and of fairy isles where a goddess walked alone. He lived on the marches of the land of fable, when half the Mediterranean was a sea unsailed, when even Italy was as dimly descried as the City of the Sun in Elizabeth's reign. Of all that he knew he sang, but Virgil could only follow and imitate, with a pale antiquarian interest, the things that were alive for Homer. What could Virgil care for a tussle between two stout men-at-arms, for the clash of contending war-chariots, driven each on each, like wave against wave in the sea? All that tide had passed over, all the story of the "Æneid" is mere borrowed antiquity, like the Middle Ages of Sir Walter Scott; but the borrower had none of Scott's joy in the noise and motion of war, none of the Homeric "delight in battle."

Virgil, in writing the "Æneid," executed an imperial commission, and an ungrateful commission; it is the sublime of hack-work, and the legend may be true which declares that, on his death-bed, he wished his poem burned. He could only be himself here and there, as in that earliest picture of romantic love, as some have called the story of "Dido," not remembering, perhaps, that even here Virgil had before his mind a Greek model, that he was thinking of Apollonius Rhodius, and of Jason and Medea.

—from *Letters on Literature* (1889)

George Santayana

The distinction of poet—the dignity and humanity of his thought—can be measured by nothing, perhaps, so well as by the diameter of the world in which he lives; if he is supreme, his vision, like Dante's, always stretches to the stars. And Virgil, a supreme poet sometimes unjustly belittled, shows us the same thing in another form; his landscape is the Roman universe, his theme the sacred springs of Roman greatness in piety, constancy, and law. He has not written a line in forgetfulness that he was a Roman; he loves country life and its labours because he sees in it the origin and bulwark of civic greatness; he honours tradition because it gives perspective and momentum to the history that ensues; he invokes the gods, because they are symbols of the physical and moral forces by which Rome struggled to dominion.

—from *Interpretations of Poetry and Religion* (1900)

RONALD KNOX

Virgil—he has the gift, has he not, of summing up in a phrase used at random the aspiration and the tragedy of minds he could never have understood; that is the real poetic genius.

    —*Let Dons Delight* (1939)

T. S. ELIOT

Our classic, the classic of all Europe, is Virgil.

    —from "What Is a Classic?" (1944)

JORGE LUIS BORGES

Virgil is brought in because, for me, he stands for poetry. Chesterton, who was a very witty and a very wise man, said of someone who had been accused of imitating Virgil that a debt to Virgil is like a debt to nature. It is not a case of plagiarism. Virgil is here for all times. If we take a line from Virgil we might as well say that we took a line from the moon or the sky or the trees.

    —from *Borges on Writing* (1973)

JOSEPH BRODSKY

With few exceptions, American poetry is essentially Virgilian, which is to say contemplative. That is, if you take four Roman poets of the Augustan period, Propertius, Ovid, Virgil, and Horace, as the standard representatives of the four known humors (Propertius' choleric intensity, Ovid's sanguine couplings, Virgil's phlegmatic musings, Horace's melancholic equipoise), then American poetry—indeed, poetry in English in general—strikes you as being by and large of Virgilian or Horatian denomination.

    —from *On Grief and Reason: Essays* (1995)

Questions

1. Is the *Aeneid* relevant? Can the poem teach us anything about our-selves, about our political and military doings? Is it a guide—either to what we should do, or as a kind of cautionary tale of what we should not do? Should we see it as a tale not of what *has* happened, but of what *happens* in the course of empire building?

2. Is an epic poem about the making of America possible? If not, why not? Who would be the hero? Would he or she be an historical person-age or a mythical being? What, briefly, would be the plot?

3. How do you feel about Vergil's female characters, human and di-vine? Do certain traits recur in them? Did Vergil have a theory of fe-male psychology? Was he a misogynist, or the reverse, or basically just?

4. For all it costs to build an empire, does Vergil show us that in the case of Rome, at least, the gains outweigh the losses?

For Further Reading

CRITICAL STUDIES

Anderson, William S. *The Art of the* Aeneid. Englewood Cliffs, NJ: Prentice-Hall, 1969.

Barchiesi, Alessandro. *La Traccia del modello: Effetti omerici nella narrazione virgiliana*. Pisa: Giardini, 1984.

Commager, Henry Steele, ed. *Virgil: A Collection of Critical Essays*. Englewood Cliffs, NJ: Prentice-Hall, 1966.

Foley, John Miles, ed. *A Companion to Ancient Epic*. Oxford: Blackwell, 2005.

Hardie, Philip, ed. *Virgil: Critical Assessments of Classical Authors*. London: Routledge, 1999.

Harrison, S. J. *Oxford Readings in Vergil's* Aeneid. Oxford and New York: Oxford University Press, 1990.

Heinze, Richard. *Virgil's Epic Technique*. Translated by Hazel and David Harvey and Fred Robertson. Berkeley: University of California Press, 1993.

Horsfall, Nicholas. *A Companion to the Study of Virgil*. Leiden: Brill, 1995.

Johnson, W. R. *Darkness Visible: A Study of Vergil's* Aeneid. Berkeley: University of California Press, 1976.

Lyne, R.O.A.M. *Further Voices in Virgil's* Aeneid. Oxford: Clarendon Press, 1987.

Martindale, Charles, ed. *The Cambridge Companion to Virgil*. Cambridge and New York: Cambridge University Press, 1997.

Pöschl, Viktor. *The Art of Vergil: Image and Symbol in the* Aeneid. Translated by Gerda Seligson. Ann Arbor: University of Michigan Press, 1962.

Putnam, Michael C. J. *The Poetry of the* Aeneid. Cambridge, MA: Harvard University Press, 1965.

——. *Virgil's* Aeneid: *Interpretation and Influence*. Chapel Hill: University of North Carolina Press, 1995.

——. *Virgil's Epic Designs*. New Haven, CT: Yale University Press, 1998.

Syed, Yasmin. *Vergil's* Aeneid *and the Roman Self: Subject and Nation in Literary*

Discourse. Ann Arbor: University of Michigan Press, 2005.

Thomas, Richard F. *Reading Virgil and His Texts: Studies in Intertextuality.* Ann Arbor: University of Michigan Press, 1999.

Williams, Gordon. *Technique and Ideas in the* Aeneid. New Haven, CT: Yale University Press, 1983.

HISTORICAL AND LITERARY CONTEXTS

Conte, Gian Biagio. *The Rhetoric of Imitation.* Ithaca, NY: Cornell University Press, 1986.

Farrell, Joseph. *Latin Language and Latin Culture: From Ancient to Modern Times.* Cambridge and New York: Cambridge University Press, 2001.

Feeney, D. C. *The Gods in Epic: Poets and Critics of the Classical Tradition.* New York: Oxford University Press, 1991.

—. *Literature and Religion at Rome: Cultures, Contexts, and Beliefs.* New York: Cambridge University Press, 1998.

Gurval, Robert Alan. *Actium and Augustus: The Politics and Emotions of Civil War.* Ann Arbor: University of Michigan Press, 1995.

Hadas, Moses. *Sextus Pompey.* New York: Columbia University Press, 1930.

Hardie, Philip. *The Epic Successors of Virgil: A Study in the Dynamics of a Tradition.* Cambridge: Cambridge University Press, 1993.

Hinds, Stephen. *Allusion and Intertext: Dynamics of Appropriation in Roman Poetry.* New York: Cambridge University Press, 1998.

Keith, A. M. *Engendering Rome: Women in Latin Epic.* Cambridge and New York: Cambridge University Press, 2000.

Powell, Anton, and Kathryn Welch. *Sextus Pompeius.* London: Duckworth and the Classical Press of Wales, 2002.

Quint, David. *Epic and Empire.* Princeton, NJ: Princeton University Press, 1993.

Roberts, Deborah H., Francis M. Dunn, and Don Fowler, eds. *Classical Closure: Reading the End in Greek and Latin Literature.* Princeton, NJ: Princeton University Press, 1997.

Selden, Daniel. "Vergil and the Satanic Cogito." *Literary Imagination* 8.3 (2006), pp. 345–386.

Spence, Sarah. *Poets and Critics Read Vergil.* New Haven, CT: Yale University Press, 2001.

Stahl, Hans-Peter, ed. *Vergil's* Aeneid: *Augustan Epic and Political Context.* London: Duckworth and the Classical Press of Wales, 1998.

TEACHING TOOLS

Anderson, William S., and Lorina N. Quartarone, ed. *Approaches to Teaching Vergil's* Aeneid. New York: Modern Language Association of America, 2002.

Perkell, Christine. *Reading Vergil's* Aeneid: *An Interpretive Guide.* Norman: University of Oklahoma Press, 1999.

SELECTED CONTEMPORARY TRANSLATIONS

The Aeneid. Translated by Robert Fagles. New York: Viking, 2006.

Virgil: Eclogues, Georgics, Aeneid Books 1-6. Revised edition. Translated by H. R. Fairclough; revised by G. P. Goold. Loeb Classical Library. Cambridge, MA: Harvard University Press, 1999; and *Virgil: Aeneid Books 7-12, Appendix Vergiliana.* Revised edition. Translated by H. R. Fairclough; revised by G. P. Goold. Loeb Classical Library. Cambridge, MA: Harvard University Press, 2000.

The Aeneid: Virgil. Translated by Robert Fitzgerald. New York: Random House, 1983.

Aeneid/Virgil. Translated by Stanley Lombardo. Indianapolis, IN: Hackett, 2005.

The Aeneid of Virgil. Translated by Allen Mandelbaum. Berkeley: University of California Press, 1971.

The Aeneid. Translated by David West. New York: Penguin, 2003.